FIELDS OF FIRE

captures the fury of combat more authentically than any novel since *All Quiet on the Western Front* and *The Naked and the Dead*. It tells the agonizing story of brave soldiers engaged in jungle warfare—the nightmare of war as men fight for their lives against an invisible enemy in one of America's bloodiest, costliest conflicts. It has taken a full generation for a war novel as powerful and important as this to be written.

"More vividly than any writer before him, James Webb has captured the suicidal, inescapable, debasing character of combat in Vietnam . . . A book to be read, marked, learned and inwardly digested."

—*John Barkham Reviews*

"A novel of such fullness and impact, one is tempted to compare it with Norman Mailer's *The Naked and the Dead.*"

—*Portland Oregonian*

"The recent outpouring of eyewitness books about Vietnam presents at least a glimpse of the absurd hell it must have been. To the list of important, insightful works can now be added this novel by a former Marine captain."

—*Publishers Weekly*

FIELDS OF FIRE

A NOVEL

BY JAMES WEBB

BANTAM BOOKS

TORONTO · NEW YORK · LONDON

FIELDS OF FIRE

*A Bantam Book / published by arrangement with
Prentice-Hall, Inc.*

PRINTING HISTORY
Bantam edition / August 1979

For the 100,000 Marines who
became casualties in Vietnam.
And for the others who
became casualties upon their return.

ACKNOWLEDGMENTS

A special thanks to three old pros, Ted Purdy, Oliver Swan and Oscar Collier; to three patient ladies, Barb, Amy and Pat; and to one hell of a friend (and not a bad squad leader, either), Tom Martin. In addition, I would like to reaffirm my undying pride in having been a part of that anomalous insanity embodied in the word Marine. While no unit such as is pictured in this work ever existed, and while all the characters involved are wholly fictional, the fuel of this fiction was, of course, actual experience.

Author's note: As many of the words and terms used by Americans fighting in Vietnam were unique to that place and time, I have appended a "glossary of unusual terms" at the end of this book.

CONTENTS

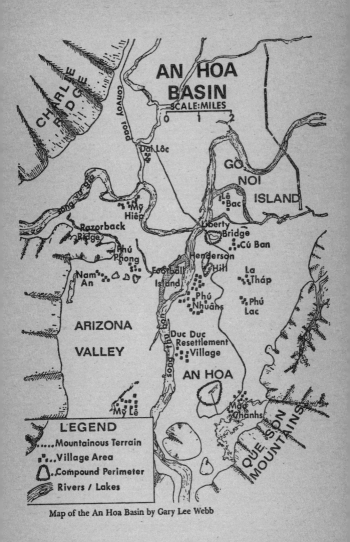

Map of the An Hoa Basin by Gary Lee Webb

PROLOGUE

"And who are the young men we are asking to go into action against such solid odds? You've met them. You know. They are the best we have. But they are not McNamara's sons, or Bundy's. I doubt they're yours. And they know they're at the end of the pipeline. That no one cares. They know."

—an anonymous general to correspondent
Arthur Hadley

Hodges sat against a wet, grassy paddy dike and lazily stirred a can of Beef and Potatoes with a dirty plastic spoon. Raindrops popped and sizzled as they pelted the tiny stove in front of him, which he had made by punching holes in another C-ration tin. His eyes were sunken, his face gaunt and bearded. He dragged mechanically on a muddy cigarette, mindless of the stream of water that was pouring off his helmet down the back of his neck. There was no way to avoid the rain. His body was crinkly from it and he didn't care anymore.

Snake approached and sat on the dike, at Hodges' shoulder. He took off his glasses and absently wiped mud off one lense, using his skivvy shirt. He put them back on without examining the wiped lense.

Across the paddy to their front, in the mist of a rain-drenched treeline, a group of dark-clothed figures hastened into a stone pagoda. The tank's turret followed the shadowed apparitions, its long 90-millimeter gun tube pointing toward the trees like an ominous finger. The turret halted and the tube exploded and in one quick moment a White Phosphorus shell erupted inside the pagoda, having been shot expertly through the door. Thick white smoke rushed from every opening of the pagoda, and mixed with the low rain-mist.

Snake nodded, lighting a cigarette. "Get some, tank. Half a dozen crispy critters in there, now."

Hodges grunted. "Fucking tank."

"Ahhh, Lieutenant." Snake continued to stare absently at the shrouded treeline. "More gooners than I ever seen. We could really be in the hurt locker tonight."

"That's what I mean. Fucking tank."

Snake shifted his gaze to the treadless tank that had anchored them in such an indefensible position. It sat like a wounded mastodon in the middle of the exposed paddy. The company was digging a perimeter around it, to protect it. "Senator's pissed off again."

"Is that all?" Hodges tested the juice from the Beef and Potatoes. "The man needs a baby-sitter. Do they have baby-sitters in the dorm at Harvard?"

"Kersey came down and told me to put a team in the treeline. The one on the other side. I sent Senator. You shoulda heard him bitch and moan."

"I hope you tied a string to his arm, so he won't get lost."

"Kersey told me to move my holes farther out, too."

"Out where?"

Snake grimaced. "In the middle of that paddy. He's a hopeless case, Kersey. I ain't gonna do it, Lieutenant. Enough is enough."

Hodges grunted again, with a sort of apathetic irony. "Old Kersey would like that. Then when you get blown away out there he can get another Silver Star."

"You want me to do it?"

"Nah. Go back and dig in behind the dike and eat your chow. If scumbag comes back, tell him to deal with me."

Snake allowed himself a small, appreciative smile. "I already told him that. Thanks, Lieutenant." The turret moved slowly again, and the gun exploded. To the north, out of their vision, there were other sounds of another unit fighting furiously. Hodges began eating his Beef and Potatoes, holding the can by the half-opened lid. He ate slowly, impervious to the other fighting.

Snake measured Hodges from his perch atop the dike. "Senator been talking to you, Lieutenant?"

"Senator?" The 90-millimeter gun exploded again. Hodges grinned wryly. "No. I don't speak Harvard."

"He ain't said anything about when you were mede-vacked and we lost Baby Cakes out on Go Noi?"

"Nope. Why? Was it his fault again?"

"No. No, sir. It wasn't his fault. But it wasn't our fault, either. You know how it is in the bush, Lieutenant. Sometimes things go *dinky dau*. You know that. But that Senator. He's got some weird ideas. He's been sulking every since the Bridge, but he's been worse lately. Five months you and him been with the platoon. You'd think the man would get some bush sense in five months." Hodges continued to eat, apparently uninterested. "Miss your woman, huh?"

Hodges grinned, suddenly awake. "Yeah, I do. Gonna marry me a Jap. Figure that one out, will you? I think we've all gone *dinky dau,* Snake. Senator's flipped out, you extended your goddamn tour, and I'm marrying me a Jap."

Snake stood up. The tank fired again. Far to the north an artillery mission dug into wet earth. "Well, I better go dig me a deep hole. We're gonna be sucking wind tonight. I never seen so many gooks." Snake turned to walk away, then called to Hodges. "Don't let that tank sneak off, Lieutenant."

Hodges shook his head. "Goddamn tank. Goddamn Kersey. Goddamn Senator. You better dig a *neck*-deep hole."

PART I | THE BEST WE HAVE

1.

SNAKE

FEBRUARY 1968   There he went again. Smack-man came
unfocused in the middle of a word, the unformed syllable
a dribble of bubbly spit along his chin, and leaned forward, that sudden rush of ecstacy so slow and deep it put
him out. His knees bent just a little and he stood there
motionless, styled out in a violet suit and turquoise, high-
heeled shoes. He had the Wave and his hair was so perfectly frozen into place that he seemed a mimic sculpture
of himself, standing there all still with skag.

Snake peeped into the doorway one more time, still
saw no one, and took a deep breath: I owe it to myself.
He grabbed a sink with one hand and unloaded with a
furious kick, perfectly aimed. Smack-man's head bounced
up like a football on a short string, stopping abruptly when
his neck ended. Then he slumped onto the floor, out cold,
breathing raggedly through a mashed, gushing nose.

Nothing to it. Never knew what hit him.

Snake quickly sorted through Smack-man, careful to re-
place each item as he found it. Two ten's were stuffed
inside one pocket. Whatta you know. Smack-man must be
a bag man. Smack-man should be ashamed. Snake pocketed the money, laughing to himself: for the good of society, and little kids on dope.

He stood, pushing his glasses back up his nose, and
scratched his head, studying his kill. Well, I gotta go tell
Mister Baum. What a bummer.

And in twenty minutes he was on the street again, walking briskly toward nowhere under winter's lingering chill.
His shoulders were raised underneath the gray sweatshirt,
guarding hopelessly against the wind. His head was tilted
to the side and back. A sneer sat tightly on his face.

What the hell. You gotta believe in yourself. It was the right thing to do.

A gust of wind swooped down from the amber mist of sky and chased him, rattling trash. Next to him the door of an abandoned rowhouse swung open and banged. The boards over its windows clapped against the building. His eyes scanned the building quickly and his narrow shoulders raised against the biting wind again, but otherwise there was no reaction from him.

Gotta be cool, man. Can't let no empty building spook you.

An old car clanked past him, spewing clouds of oil, and he eyed it also, not breaking his sauntering stride. Driving too slow. Looking for something. Hope it ain't me.

He was small, with a mop of brittle hair. The hair flopped along his neck, bending with any hint of wind. His face was narrow and anonymous but for the crooked memory of a broken nose and the clear eyes. The eyes were active and intense.

He left the sidewalk, turning inside a rusted fence, and walked up to a rowhouse stairway. He climbed the outside steps, pondering each one as if searching for an excuse not to ascend it, and did a mull-dance on the landing, finally being chased inside by another gust of wind.

Hell with it. Need a beer anyway.

The black stench of air clung to him as he climbed the inside stairs. Sadie stuck her head out on the second landing and he jammed a ten-dollar bill inside her stained cotton robe. The bill never stopped moving. Sadie extracted it with a lightning stroke and ogled it as if it were an emerald. Her wild gray hair came full into the hallway and she called to Snake. He was three steps up from her landing now.

"What you been up to, bad old Snake?"

"Trouble. You know that." He stopped on the stairs for one moment and gave her his ten-dollar sermon. "Now, go buy that dog of yours some diapers. Or a box of kitty litter. I'm tired of seeing his shit inside the door down there."

She slammed the door on him. He laughed, continuing up the stairs. Old bitch.

Inside his own door, a vision on the bed. He blinked once at the greater light and focused. It was his mother, in her bathrobe. She dangled imaginatively on the bed's edge, her chubby legs crossed, neither of them quite touching the floor. Her arms were up behind her head, pushing her hair over the top so that it fell down around her face. She looked as if she were carefully attempting to re-create a picture from some long-forgotten men's magazine. She watched the door with expectant eyes and dropped her hands in disappointment when she saw Snake. He shook his head slightly, then pulled out a cigarette and leaned against the doorway.

"Uh huh. What are you doing? Paying bills?"

She smoothed a wrinkle on the bed, studying it for a moment, not looking at him. Then she gave her hair a flip. She had bleached it artificial gold again, and she smiled her sugar smile and her sad, remembering voice came across the room on a puffy little cloud, floating lazily to his ears.

"You're home early, Ronnie."

"You noticed that."

She was naked underneath the robe. She leaned forward on the bed, finding the floor with her dangling feet, and the robe fell loosely away, revealing her. Snake shrugged resignedly. Something's going on. Again. He walked to the refrigerator and searched for a beer but they were gone. There had been two six-packs that morning.

"Old Bones out on a job?" She nodded, watching him from beside the bed.

"You sure he's working?" She laughed a little. He did, too. The old man's antics were legendary and unpredictable.

"Man came for him in a truck this morning and he left with his painting clothes on, carrying a sackload of beer." She shrugged, then looked at Snake with an insightful stare. "From the beer I'd say he's working. If it was hard stuff . . ." She made a funny face and shrugged again. "I think he's working."

There was nothing else to drink in the refrigerator. "Any coffee?"

"Instant."

He put some water on. She eyed him closely, walking from the bed into the kitchen. "Why are you home so early? Did you get fired again?"

He spooned the instant into the cup. "Yup."

She grinned, half-amused and half-curious, her eyes lingering on his wiry body. "Was it another fight? How can you stand to fight so much? You're so blind without your glasses! Was it *another* fight?"

He checked the water. Hot enough. He poured it into the cup. "Yup. Sort of."

She sat down and leaned over the table, admiring him. "How can a man be fired for 'sort of' being in a fight?"

He joined her at the table and sipped his coffee. Perfect. Then he lit another cigarette. "Well. It all started when I had to clean the women's room." She nodded eagerly, already knowing that he would make it into a great story. She had always told him that he shouldn't fight but she cloyed him with attention when he did. She had always admonished him to be civil but at times like this he was John Wayne, straight out of Dodge City. He casually sipped his coffee.

"I put the sign out in front of the door, you know, so nobody will walk into the room when I'm cleaning it. Then I wait until all the girls are out of there, asking each one when she leaves if there's anybody else still in there. I don't want to get into *that* kind of trouble, moral turpitude is a bust, you know that. Finally I go in and clean the toilets and the sinks, and I'm starting to mop the floor when this nigger dude stumbles in. Got a Jones on, I can tell the minute he walks into the room. He's just shot up, too. Don't know where the hell he got off, maybe right there in the movie room. Don't know if he could cook up without being caught but I guess it's as good as any other place. Nobody ever gave a damn when a match was lit that I ever saw. Maybe he was snorting. Who knows. He looked too out of it to be snorting. He was out on his goddamn feet. You know he's out of it if he walks into the wrong bathroom. Moral turpitude and all."

She reached over and took one of his cigarettes, ogling him as if he were telling a bedtime story. Really grooving on it. "Yeah. O.K. So what did you do?"

"Take it easy. Don't steal my lines, all right? The dude walks into the bathroom, taking a couple steps and then stopping, nodding out right on his feet, leaning all the way forward at the waist, all the way out. Then he wakes up real quick and goes 'whoooeeee, whooooooeee,' like that, and then falls asleep again, there on his feet. I don't know how the hell he made it to the bathroom. Well. I watch him do that a couple times. He smiles when he wakes up like everything's O.K. I try to check his fingers to see if he's got the poison but I can't tell, and he's pretty strong when he wakes up. Figure he's just got a strong shot in him.

"He's dressed pretty good. That don't always mean anything, I mean, why the hell would he be in a movie in the afternoon if he's worth a shit, it's a lousy movie anyway. But you never can tell."

He flipped his cigarette into the cluttered sink and slowly lit another, enjoying her eagerness. "Didn't know what to think, to tell you the truth. Coulda been anybody. But I watched him dropping off like that, and checked those clothes out, and I figured it was worth a shot." She nodded quickly to him, smiling, enraptured by his logic. Snake laughed ironically. "It was like the Lord his-self delivered him to me. Here we are in the girls' room, with a sign out front that says 'CLOSED,' ain't nobody coming in, ain't nobody there to say what happened, this dude is so far gone he could take a picture of me and still not remember me. Well. Just had to make me a play."

She was still smiling. She leaned forward in anticipation. "So you punched his lights out."

He laughed a little. "Well, I thought about it. You *know* John Wayne woulda dropped him with a poke between the eyes. But I figured the motherfucker would break my hand. Nigger heads are like that, you know? So the next time he gave a whooooee I kicked him right between the eyes. *Pow!*" He checked her face out. She was ecstatic. It was the high point of her day. "Kept my toe pointed so I wouldn't put my foot between his eyes. Don't need no murder rap from a junkie dead inside a toilet. Popped his nose like a light bulb. He had twenty bucks and four bags on him. Took the bucks. Left the bags."

She stared at him curiously. "So how'd you get fired?"

He squinted, sipping coffee. The coffee was almost gone. "Well, I had to report it. Everybody knew it was me inside the girls' room. Found Mister Baum and told him a dude got pushy with me when I tried to make him leave the girls' bathroom. Told him the dude looked a little drunk and started shoving me, so I poked him in the face."

She squinted back. "Sounds like a pretty good story to me."

"I thought so, too. But you know them hebes. Always worrying about getting sued. He tells me, 'Snake, you can't just go round hitting people when you work in a place like this.' I says, 'Mister Baum, you know I never started a fight in my whole life, but I just can't let people push me round, no matter where I work. What kind of a man lets people push him round?' And he says 'Snake, I think you done a good job for us but I gotta can you.' And he fires me and gives me full pay for the week. Plus I got the nigger's twenty bucks. Not bad, huh?"

She nodded approvingly: not bad. "What happened to the nigger?"

Snake stacked the coffee cup in the sink. "Who cares?" His face showed a moment of sparkle. "If he's got a hair on his ass he'll sue Mister Baum."

She leaned back in her chair, laughing. Not a bad story. Then she smiled and he could tell she was remembering again. She shook her head a little. "You're so bad, Ronnie. And so young to be so bad. Doesn't anybody scare you? Don't you *like* anybody?"

He did not answer. The question was rhetorical. He stifled the retort that once was commonplace, that she was not one to be lecturing anyway. She continued, though, in a rare moment when the emotion of the memory overwhelmed the reality of the present. "And you were stupid to quit school. You always did so well."

Again he did not answer. She's talking about history, he mused. Don't do no good to talk about it. Won't change it. And it was nothing but a hassle, anyway. Rules rules rules.

She gave him an acquiescent smile and floated those pillowed, remembering words again. "Well, I guess you'll be out job-hunting tomorrow morning, huh?"

"I don't know. I'm getting sick of it."

She shrugged, avoiding his eyes. She had already said too much. Or perhaps it would have been one of the rare days when her memories mounted until they drove him back into the street. Who knows. There was a measured clomping on the stairs then, and the door burst open. No knock.

A reddened face peered expectantly into the room as if it were his personal possession. The red face was meaty, heavy-bearded, framed by thinning black hair. The nose was mashed and grainy and the eyes seemed dull, unfocused. The man had huge hands and a belly that hung over his belt.

Snake understood immediately. He felt humiliated, but mostly he was embarrassed at being in the way. She's going to do it, he thought, starting for the door, there's no way I can ever stop that. Her life, anyway. She wants it and I got no right to get pissed. But he looked at the animal that had just entered his home for the purpose of smothering his mother underneath his rolls of fat and muscle, stroking that most special part of her insides, and his neck crawled with a rage that did not delude him as to its depth.

He knew that he could kill this fat man whose only pertinent fault was that he wanted to fill Snake's mother with the one thing she desired more than anything else. He could kill him and laugh for weeks about it. For one pulsing, heated flash he seriously considered using his knife. Then he became embarrassed at his own rage. I got no right, he decided. Don't do no good, anyway. It's what she wants. Hell with it.

Fat Man looked dully at his mother, seemingly too unfocused to understand. Maybe he's jealous, Snake mused. That's a laugh. He decided that he must leave the apartment, get out of their way. Fat Man was still standing in the door, half in and half out, trying to figure the whole thing out. Snake reminded himself that he would have to laugh about Fat Man once he escaped the apartment. *Christ,* is the bastard dumb. Where does she find 'em? But I bet he has a big one.

He turned to his mother and said, for the benefit of Fat Man, "Well, I'm cutting out, Mom. Catch you later."

She looked at him and he knew she could read the rage in him and she seemed burnt-out behind the eyes, as if she were fighting with a part of herself that she did not really care for but could not overcome. She touched his arm lightly, trying to hold him a reassuring moment, and said with that sad voice, "You don't know about love, Ronnie. What love does to people. You're too young to know about love."

He smiled thinly, conscious of Fat Man, who had heard his words and finally stepped inside the door. "Yeah. That must be it." He reached the door. "Later."

"When will you be home?" Just the tiniest effort, like a last particle of hope. He glanced at Fat Man staring dully at him and gave him a tight grimace of a smile, knowing his hate was futile, and accepting that.

"I don't know."

Then Fat Man, whose frayed nerve-wires had finally managed to pulse enough electricity to turn a dim light on in the back of his bruised brain, peered dimly at Snake and spoke with a mashed, gravelly voice. "Nice to meet ya." He spoke slowly, and smiled a half-witted grin.

Now how can anybody hate a dude as dim as that, thought Snake. He probably has to have somebody figure out traffic lights for him so he can cross the street. But Snake still clung to the warm emotion that the thought of cutting Fat Man's balls off gave him.

"Yeah." He slammed the door.

Concrete wasteland, beaten by the years and by neglect into crumbling uselessness. Unpainted fences and gates and little brown squares of yard, cold reminders of more vibrant days. Grass choked out by trash and bottles. Piles of garbage and broken appliances on the sidewalks. Clumps of people gathered in age groups like schools of fish. Women watching him pass with bored but cautious eyes.

He walked onto a wider, more active street. Cars flowed more thickly, constant streams of unstopping, terrified transients. Old business buildings, dying, scarred with signs. Old signs, rain-washed and year worn, marked candy stores and delicatessens and car clinics and pharmacies. New ones advertised porno shops and liquor stores and bars and grills and pawnshops. Boards over windows. Lighthouse For The Blind, Interdenominational Church, and purveyor of free coffee. Come back to the seed of civilization to save us from what we've become.

Zombie people, regurgitated by the gluttonous monster. Hostile young, running and hunting in wild packs, like the dogs that owned the alleyways. Dudes and chicks, brightly dressed, looking for action. Stolid, broken groups outside liquor stores. Addicts in their twos and threes, many younger than Snake, scratching and sniffing, searching for the bag man.

Snake walked quickly, saturated by it, his face hard with its challenging smirk. He was restless, afraid that some hit man would Just Know that fifty dollars bulged inside his wallet. His eyes constantly swept the sidewalks and the doorways as he walked.

He kicked a page of newspaper that the wind whipped past him and as it rose he caught it in his hand. It was yesterday's front page and there was a large picture of a man swaddled in bandages being hurried down a rubbled road on a stretcher. The men who hauled the stretcher seemed somber and determined. Above the picture the headlines read "Marines Retake Citadel at Hue."

Snake stopped walking and stared almost enviously at the picture. There's some mean motorscooters for you. Uh huh. Well, I'm gonna get me some of that. Bring me home a medal. No more mopping up other people's pee. That's right.

An old man swaddled in dirty wool noticed that Snake had stopped moving, and approached him cautiously. Snake caught the movement, threw the newspaper away, and put his shoulder into the man as he strode past him.

"Fuck yourself, you old fart."

He found Zimmerman's Candy Store, more recently Diamond Jim's Entertainment, now boarded up and gutted by human vultures. On the other side was Mack's.

Gonna taste Mack's needle one more time before I blow.

Two years earlier, when he was christened Snake, he had gone to Mack, who provided him an inerasable baptism. It began at his wrist and curled up his forearm, an angry black flecked with bits of deadly chartreuse wrinkles and a crimson mouth. Snake wore his symbol proudly, much as the rich flaunt jewelry. It was a display of his tastes and beliefs, a symbol that spoke for him. He loved his full forearm of Snake. He wanted another one.

Mack was burning a huge orange spider onto the shoulder of a sailor. The sailor had his jumper off and was studying a rivulet of blood that was trickling down the back of his arm from the needle. The sailor nonchalantly gripped a towel, soaking up the blood as it leaked down from the spider. Mack stopped now and then, wiping blood delicately from the area he was cutting, careful not to erase the template outline. Snake watched briefly and nodded to the sailor. Good choice. Boss tattoo. Orange. Truly heavy color for a spider.

The designs were on the walls, hundreds of them. Snake studied them, searching for the one that would announce him to the world. At last he found it. Lost in the middle of a hundred designs on the center wall at one moment, it jumped out at him and filled his senses at the next.

There was a skull perched atop crossed daggers. Around the daggers twined two snakes, their heads staring fiercely at the skull. Above the skull, in wide letters, was U S M C. Underneath the daggers it read *Death Before Dishonor*. He stared at it. All the right colors. Black and orange-red and a green that matched the other snake on his left arm. Oh, heavy. There it is.

Mack gauzed up the sailor and he pulled his jumper on and paid Mack. He came from behind the counter and nodded affably to Snake, his brother in ink, and departed. Snake pointed to his choice and moved behind the counter. Mack nodded curtly and found the proper template in a drawer.

He took Snake's arm and shaved and washed it, spraying the forearm with a soap solution kept inside a Windex bottle. Then he wiped the arm down with a towel wet from other brandings. Snake nodded approvingly. Very sanitary.

The preliminaries thus completed, Mack pressed the template onto Snake's forearm, marking the outline of the New Him in black powder, and cut the gun on. Snake watched the gun move slowly along the outline, blue spark jumping from the tip into him, cutting snakes and daggers and words into his skin. He gritted and bled a little and dug it. Deep burn. Boss tattoo.

Mack worked carefully, expertly, his baggy eyes protruding from his face. He was covered with his own choices, arms and neck and chest saturated with four decades of brandings. A man who put himself into his work. Finally he spoke, with slow, bored words, his eyes still intent on Snake's forearm. "You in the Marines?"

Snake watched the skull being shaded in. "Nope. Not yet."

The skull was finished. Green wrinkles brightened the snakes. Mack cocked his head. "Ain't this kind of ass-backwards? None of my business. I'll put general stars on yer shoulders if you want. But most guys wait till they been in awhile. Like that swab was just in here. Gave him a goddamn anchor two, three weeks ago."

Snake shrugged. "What the hell. When I make up my mind I make up my mind. Know what I mean? Felt like getting it today."

Mack colored the words. "What if they don't take you?"

Snake laughed, watching the needle. Here comes *Dishonor.* "You shitting me, Mack? I walk. I talk. I'm crazy as hell. They'll take me." He considered it for another moment. "If they don't I'll come back and you can put a rose over the whole thing and put 'Mom' under it. All right?"

Mack grinned slowly. "Yeah, you're crazy enough. They'll take you."

The tattoo was finished. Mack gauzed and taped it. In two days the tape could be removed and the snakes and skull and daggers and words would be forever Snake. He pushed down his sleeve and paid Mack and walked into the street once again.

He walked for an hour, bored and freezing. He passed a famous restaurant, one of those places that yet survived in the wasteland as a gathering place for the neat and elite. He stopped and stared through the large plate-glass window that bordered the sidewalk, gazing at the Beautiful People in their stylish clothes, languishing over their just-right meals. He became seized with scorn. He banged on the window and most of them looked curiously back at him and he mashed his face against the pane in a grotesque gargoyle stare and flipped two birds at them. Fuck you. All of you. Then he laughed hilariously for one short moment and scrunched his shoulders and continued on his undirected journey.

On the street it was black and cold and he walked hurriedly, shivering. Concrete walls hovered close to him, filled with predatory animals, creatures of the night. He was their prey. He fondled his knife tentatively and walked closer to the street, on the very edge of the sidewalk. He passed a few bored streetwalkers and a half-dozen bars. Dim melancholy lights and jukebox music and brackish odors surrounded him near every bar, inviting him to stop and die a zombie death.

Three blocks. Four. A car braked hard and pulled over next to him. He walked more quickly, not acknowledging the car's arrival. It crawled along beside him. A window rolled down. He glanced and saw a heavy-lidded face peering at him with stupored, hating eyes.

"Cocksuckin' dicklickin' mohfucka."

He looked behind him and ahead of him on the street. No cops. Yuh-oh. Bad news. There were four hating figures in the car. The heavy-lidded face mumbled at him again.

"Hey. Cocksuckin' dicklickin' mohfucka."

He jogged along the sidewalk and became enveloped by new brackish minglings. To his right was the No-Name Bar and Grill. He ducked inside, shaking his head.

What the hell. I was hungry anyway.

He bought two hamburgers and a cup of coffee at the No-Name, eating quickly at the counter. On one wall there was a jukebox. Its music cut through the barriers of Snake's subconscious. *All the people going places*, the singer moaned. *Smiling with electric faces. What they find the glow erases. What they lose the glow replaces*. Behind him a middle-aged couple was dancing. There was no dance area. They groped each other tightly, the dance an excuse to discover carnal parts of each other. The couple turned and a chair fell over. Someone swore at them. Someone else chided loudly, "It must be love."

The dancers did not hear. They were off in stupefied Nirvana, riding on each other's flesh. The chair was up-righted and the jukebox once again pervaded. *You can live without direction. And you don't have to be perfection. And life is love—in a neon rainbow*.

Snake ordered another coffee and drank it slowly, listening to the jukebox. He did not like the No-Name but there was no better place to go. He sat alone at the counter, watching people absently. They were all the same to him: dead. They'd merely forgotten to stop breathing.

Finally he could no longer stand it. He paid the tab and left a ten-dollar tip, rationalizing that it was Smack-man's

money anyway, and grooving on the rise he provoked
from the apathetic bartender. Then he walked quickly,
half-jogging through the streets. It was late and bitter cold.
The air attacked him and he shivered nakedly in his crispness. He reminded himself that he must get a coat. Then
he remembered that he would not need one. In a few
short days he would be gone.

There was a recruiting station at the wasteland's edge. It
fed on creatures from the run-down rowhouses. They were
vital sustenance.

The next morning Snake awoke early and walked to
the recruiting station. He wore his father's coat. His father
had not returned from his paint job of the day before.
Old Bones, mused Snake, snatching the jacket, is in bed
with about five bottles somewhere.

At the recruiting complex he contemplated the signs
that advertised each service. Each sign promised to fill some
void in his experience. "Tradition." "See the world." "Fly
with us." He was not impressed. He had already chosen
the Marines for one reason: everybody talked about how
bad they were. And I'm ba-a-ad, he laughed to himself.
We belong.

The complex had not yet opened. He sat on the steps
near the Marine Corps office, huddled inside his father's
coat, watching the wind whip trash along the sidewalk. By
the time the first recruiter came he was raw from the
wind.

Snake checked the recruiter out, grooving on the bright
blue trousers underneath the green overcoat, digging the
shaved head and face reeking with discipline. He chuckled
to himself. Only a Marine would dare to look like that
around here. He *must* be a bad-ass dude.

He stood when the recruiter reached the steps and began
to follow him through the door. Only then did the Marine
seem to realize that Snake had been waiting for him. He
turned and gave Snake a devouring glance.

"Need something?"

Snake nodded, anxious to get inside the building. He
was freezing. "Yup. Wanna enlist, man." He followed the
man inside, tapping his forearm. "Already got my tattoo."

The Marine suppressed a grin. "That was your *first* mistake."

Then down there in the knee-deep sand, inside the sweat-box that was boot camp, underneath the roofs of endless gray tin buildings and the canopy of sultry southern sky, something happened. He found a way to win.

It was nothing as magical as discovering some secret part that had lain dormant, but rather that his energies had finally found their outlet. He had always fought, and now it was right to fight. He had never been coddled, and now it was weakness to have been coddled.

And there was that hard core, the nucleus of ferocity which sustained him, and which no one else could dent. He could not be broken. He sensed the difference after three days. He came with no false prides, no sensitivities that a drill instructor's words could damage.

The trivialities of boot camp rolled off him. At worst, they were more of the same. He was beaten, but did not flinch. He sensed from the start that if he stuck it out, he won. When a drill instructor began to punish him he would stare impassively through the man, as if he felt nothing. Beat on me, Sergeant. Wear your goddamn arm out. It ain't any different. You can't squash me, and if you can't squash me, you lose. More, sir. Harder, sir. Faster, sir. I love it, sir.

It created a mystique about him. His ability to endure, that iron shell from which all other traits derived, was also a magnet that drew the other recruits to him. In the dark of the squad bay after lights out, during field problems, on the bivouacs, his calm assessment of each threat and crisis, his reasoned suggestions without regard to pain, caused him to be the man they sought for guidance.

And he loved it. To merely endure, to accept the pain that others feared and dreaded, was the ticket to a dignity that had eluded him all his life. And to fight, to grant his natural ferocity its whims, now brought him accolades instead of trouble.

He would take on anyone, do anything to perpetuate that respect from the others. Early during training the recruits learned pugil sticks. They fell out onto the athletic field and formed a circle around their drill instructor, who paced inside the circle, an angry demigod, holding what looked to be a broom with a sandbag on each end.

"This here," he chanted, "is a pugil stick. What you do

is try to kill each other with it. Now." He looked slowly around the circle, staring coolly into each quivering face. "I need me a couple bad-ass hogs. Who's the meanest hog in this here platoon?"

A tight-muscled Gargantua stepped out. Snake had already nicknamed him Statue Body. "The Private is, sir."

The drill instructor nodded once, then looked around the circle again. "Don't anybody else think he's a bad-ass? C'mon, girls. We can't let him play with hisself, can we?"

Nobody moved. Statue Body was standing cool inside the circle, looking like John Wayne. Snake checked him out, and finally shrugged. What the hell. The bastard can't kill me.

He stepped into the circle. "Sir," he announced, playing the DI's word games, "the Private is the meanest motherfucker you got."

He stood motionless inside the circle. The DI peered down at him, hands on hips, unspeaking. Then his head went back and he laughed uproariously. The platoon had been silent but when the drill instructor laughed, everyone laughed: God had spoken.

The drill instructor became enraged and screamed at the circle, pivoting to froth at them all. "*Shut* up." They were immediately silent. He paced the circle, just in front of the recruits. "You goddamn girls. You cowards. That little shit is the only one of you that had the balls to come out here and fight. You should be laughing at yourselves, you dippy *pukes!*"

He returned to Snake. There was a sparkle of warmth in his expression. Some day, Snake mused, standing at a rigid attention, he's gonna like the hell outa me. It's the tattoo. Every day he dumps on me for not rating it, but he digs it. Pretty good move to get it.

He tossed Snake a pugil stick. "O.K., Private. Let's see how bad you really are."

A football helmet and a groin protector were passed down and Snake donned them, then picked up the pugil stick. It was heavier than he had expected. He held it tentatively, took a secret deep breath, and moved over to Statue Body.

Statue Body was grinning widely, waiting for Snake to come into range. He carried the stick lightly and bounced on his toes like a fighter. What the hell, thought Snake. He moved in after the man and started to swing.

Pow. Next thing he knew he was on the turf. His head spun as if he was one toke over. He shook it, clearing the buzzing circles, and stood again. Statue Body grinned like a taunting Muhammad Ali. Snake moved after him again and Statue Body took one step to the side and popped him up the side of the head. Pow. Down again. Everyone was screaming.

The DI stood over him. "Get up, you little turd." He booted Snake lightly in the ass. "I thought you said you were tough."

Up again. Pow. Down again. Up again, dizzily, wobbly. Pow. The DI stepped back in and started to take the pugil stick out of his hands and he looked coldly at the Sergeant with steady blue invincible eyes. "Sir. The Private ain't finished yet."

The DI spoke quietly, privately to him. "He's killing you, boy."

"Give me a break. I'm wearing him down."

The DI checked the area quickly for officers. "O.K., Private. You got two minutes."

Up again, swing and miss. Pow. Down again. Up again. Pow. Statue Body seemed embarrassed now. The circle of recruits was silent. Up again and swing, Statue Body let it go by as if he were parrying a weak jab. Pow. Snake was back on the turf, trying to find his head. It was scrambled at his knees.

Statue Body was uneasy. He turned to the DI. It wasn't fun anymore. "Sir. The Private——"

Snake moved as quickly as a pouncing cat, holding the stick near one end like a baseball bat. He aimed for the back of Statue Body's head. *Pow*. Statue Body dropped like a stunned elephant. The platoon cheered wildly.

Statue Body was on his knees, still stunned. He started to get up. Snake knew that if he made it up Statue Body would kill him. Pow. He dropped him again. Take that, motherfucker. Statue Body bowled over, rolling like an egg. Balloop. Balloop.

Snake pounced again and stood in front of him, determined not to let him up. He peered into Statue Body's face with the same grin that Statue Body had used earlier.

The DI finally stepped it, stopping it. He raised Snake's

hand to the cheers of the circle of recruits. Champion. As the platoon yelled the DI whispered to Snake.

"You little shit. You are *mean*."

2.

ROBERT E. LEE HODGES, JR.

I

FEBRUARY 1969 There was a footlocker in a shed at home that his parents never opened. It was green, and had sat in the corner of the shed for as long as he could remember, under a gray footlocker that held some of his mother's old clothes. There was no indication on its outsides as to where or for what purpose it was acquired. It simply sat in anonymity under the larger gray one, year after year, its outsides slowly gathering rust and its insides taking on the musty odor of items left untended in humid places.

If his mother and father had ever sat down and discussed it, they would probably have agreed in rather few words to get rid of the footlocker. But for them to discuss it, it would have become necessary for one of them to broach the subject to the other. And they both tacitly realized that, if one were to mention it, the other would have cause for some sort of hurt and questioning.

If his mother were to mention it, his father would have immediate grounds to feel hurt: she would have been thinking about Him, the other man in her life. What, he could wonder, reveling in the hurt, made you think of Him again after all these years? And if his father mentioned it, his mother could feel righteous indignation that, even after all the years and the assurances and the solid base of their relationship, he couldn't cope. He would be showing the insecurity he felt in their life together, trying to drive the Other Man and all his traces completely from her life.

So the footlocker sat, year in and year out, gathering

rust and mildew in the shed. And only he had the temerity to open it and experience its contents.

He went to it on the last day before he left for Vietnam. He was alone in the small tar-paper house that he had grown up in, and had spent his morning sorting in boredom through his childhood things. He then sat in the small front room and attempted yesterday's newspaper, but could not concentrate on it. Finally he paced before the front window, wondering if his mother would return early from her shopping trip to Salt Lick, and, satisfied that she would not, he left the house and waded through dead grass and patches of horseweed to the shed.

It was a personal thing for him, something he would have considered sharing only with his mother, although he never had. He had discovered the contents of the locker when he was twelve, and they had always been a very special secret.

He slid the heavy door of the shed, stirring dust and spiderwebs, and entered it, pulling on a frayed cord that lit a bare light bulb. The footlocker sat in a far corner, guarded by cobwebs, unbothered and unmoved since the last time he had explored its contents.

He removed the gray footlocker, sitting on it, and sprang the weak padlock on the green one with a twist of his powerful hand. Then he flipped the latch and pulled the top open, turning his face at first from the odor.

There before him, in the musty browns and yellows which seem to accrue in all things with age, lay the remains of his real father.

Not the physical remains. Those had been lowered into a hole in the side of some European hill on a cold winter morning four months before he was born. The trunk held other, emotional remains. Two brown army uniforms of World War II vintage, replete with corporal stripes and a single ribbon he had earned before going overseas. A stack of newspaper clippings about the goings-on in the European theater during the late fall and early winter of 1944. A larger stack of letters to his mother, written in a rather bold but undeveloped scrawl. A brown scrapbook, half-full of pictures of his father and mother, singly and together. And a manila envelope containing the letter which informed his mother that his father had been killed, and three medals, including the Purple Heart.

He did not know the story those things in the footlocker, and about them. It was enough for him them, and was able to experience them.

He thumbed the scrapbook, rediscovering had forgotten, wondering again what it would like to have known him. Hello, Father. Real father sad and inglorious shrine. How unfortunate to have so much in the hills of another country and to then relegated to a forgotten footlocker in the corner of an other man's shed. How sad to have sacrificed your life for your country, to have faced the bullet on the fields of fire only to have your memory purged as a part of a jealous lover's insecurity. A jealous lover of your woman. And how sad to have carried the infantry rifle, only to have your tale hidden in a shed, while the ones who fought the war from behind a typewriter tell their stories for the thousandth time, over a beer at the American Legion.

Bob Hodges smiled then, fingering a picture of his father in an ill-fitting uniform, wearing a defiant solemn bold glare copied from some Rebel ancestor, his cap cocked to the side of his head. You were only a kid, Father. I'm older now than you were when you died. But you were a warrior, all right. So am I. Did you thrill to the drum, loving the march as I do? Did you inhale the smoke from the gunpowder as the weapons fired in training, wondering at the moment when the training would be real? Did you feel a kinship with the woods beneath your feet, and the heft of the rifle as you patrolled?

Hodges shook his head in wonderment at the picture. I'll just bet you did. It is your blood that yielded me this certainty, these things. And will I, in the end, meet your fate, Father? I'm not afraid. I don't want to, but I'm not afraid. You and all the others taught me that. Man's noblest moment is the one spent on the fields of fire. I believe that.

My war is not as simple as yours was, Father. People seem to question their obligation to serve on other than their own terms. But enough of that. I fight because we have always fought. It doesn't matter who.

He did not look a warrior. He was rawboned and rough-edged and quiet. He emanated a stringy, acquiescent

...ed to accept hard living and
... smiled but he was fond of
...with people with the bedrock
...What were all those men doing
...that automatic digger, Bobby?
...they was digging a hole.
...and unquestioning and gray, an
...se they carried pain comfortably.
...r's hands. They shot out almost em-
...pencil-thin wrists, thick and calloused
...were his most noticeable feature and
...em inside his pockets. He felt they
accentuated his ...ness.

He returned from the shed and finished sorting out his clothes and souvenirs. He placed his clothes in two piles, leaving the larger one for his stepbrothers and packing away a few items that were special to him. He similarly sorted his souvenirs, saving old baseballs and magazines, faded classroom notes, one scrapbook. Then he placed the more important items inside a gray footlocker next to his bed, and locked it.

The ordeal done, he opened a newly purchased suitcase, extracted his dress-green uniform, and donned it. For a long time he stood before the mirror in the hallway, fixing the knot in his tie just so, checking the alignment of his shooting badges, standing at attention and adjusting his cap. Then he smiled tentatively, saluted himself, and walked out the door.

She was waiting. He would be just in time for lunch.

He walked down the dirt road that scarred the ridgeline and turned onto the narrow strip of gray that hugged the draw. On the gray road there were occasional boxes of frame or tar-paper homes that sat too close to the road. Two cars and a truck passed. The drivers waved to him, and he waved back, feeling self-conscious yet mildly important in his uniform.

A rusted Chevrolet clanged up from behind him and screeched to a halt. Two older men leaned over to him from the car and smiled half-tauntingly. The nearer of the two spat out the window and called to him.

"Way-ull. Kiss my ass. Didn't know whether to salute ya or burp ya. A real live Looey."

Bob Hodges grinned self-consciously, slapping dust off

of his uniform. "You can do whatever you damn well like, long as you call me 'sir.' "

The other man laughed amusedly and leaned across the car seat. "You do real good over there, y'hear? We proud of you, boy."

"Thanks, Mister Tidwell. I'll surely try."

He reached the railroad tracks and left the road and followed the tracks for a quarter-mile, scanning the low ridges and the rock-strewn farms where the herders and the proud came so long ago. Jackson's people fought those rocks. Here they struggled still. Those sole places where a man still could walk where great-great-great-grandfather walked, still sleep where he died. Not because they were the first and seized it. Because it was the last and no one wanted it.

He took a dirt road that scratched a hump in the tracks and walked along it, through a stream of chilled winter dust. When the spring rains came the dust would be floods of ankle-deep mud. He walked two bends in the narrow road and stopped, facing her house.

On the old gray wood of the front porch there was a new antiqued white rocker. A gleaming aluminum television antenna jutted incongruously above the tar-paper shack. Her first television set. He had bought the television and the rocker for her with his advance pay.

He had been visiting her forever. At least it seemed that way. It was the best of his early days, when he would slick his hair down wet and brush it hard with his mother's brush, and button all the buttons on his shirt and spend his Sundays there. He would leave the house and walk the same roads and the tracks, throwing rocks at the barking dogs that seemed so big then, walking past the scattered houses and their gardens, thicks of green dotted with red and yellow.

He stood in his new green uniform and stared at the house and it became an aromatic memory. Days with lilacs and roses and the apple tree's explosions, the huge garden in the back that he would dig for her each spring. The heavy haunt of honeysuckle and the thickets where blackberries offered up sweets along the well path. And in the back, the outhouse he would lime for her each Sunday, and the chicken pen that once rattled truculently with the pecks of angry hens and the love-cry of a rooster.

Most of it was gone. The garden was a small one he would dig for her each Easter when he was home from school. She was too old for even chickens. The pen was a museum. The roses were wild, huge bushes of them. The honeysuckle owned the outhouse, and blackberries covered the well path.

In the bleak rainwinter air he stood on the road and remembered those early days, the summers when he would cross the damp, steamy yard of high grass and horseweed, fighting his way through the humid thickness, tucking his shirt in just so as he approached the porch. And in the summer she would be waiting for him on the porch, thick and gray on her old faded wood rocker, filling it with age and heaviness. When she saw him she would rock forward, slowly finding the porch floor with her feet, and then stand heavily there on the porch, looking at him with a mix of love and agony, and reach an arm toward him. Then she would call warmly, still not smiling, "Come on up here, boy. Come on in the house. Grandma's cooked you up a nice lunch, just special for you."

He would climb the porch steps, each Sunday feeling the wood grow older and softer, and look at the floor while she briefly hugged him. Then they would walk slowly, she behind him, into the darkness of her house.

They would eat a quiet lunch, just the two of them there in the dimness of the house, he struggling to remember proper manners and she serving him like an honored guest. The lunch would be rich with her own things, a part of herself: greens from her garden, chicken from her pen, homemade peanut candy.

He would sit small at the table, trying to be the man she was remembering through him, trying to ease the pain of her memories and make her present days more bearable. And lunch would soften her as water melts the stiffness of a sponge.

After lunch he would do chores for her: hoe weeds in her garden; lime the outhouse, maybe; mend a fence, perhaps. And then they would talk. She would always ask him. He would come in from choring and she would have the dishes cleaned and she would stare a moment and then ask him, each Sunday as if it were the first time. "You got time to visit? I know your mama's got lots of things for you to do." She would never mention his stepfather or his half brothers and half sister. They did not exist to her. He was the only product of her son and his mother, the only Hodges left, last of his father's family.

Since he was the last it had become perhaps the most important thing in her waning life that he should know of those who went before him. All the campfire stories and the front-porch chronicles, of the wilderness days and the Hodges who had fought and fallen, had dwindled down to him and her. And these tales, these forgotten pieces of history, would be passed to him or die. All the pain and misery and minor successes and major sacrifices would be learned by him or forgotten by the entire world. She was intent, compulsive: she would not let them be for nothing.

So she taught him all the Ghosts, over the years of Sundays, inside the shadows of her kitchen. And this is what he learned, under the patient drone of a suffering voice grown old and dry.

They took Abednego, he was a Hodges same as you, Scotch and Irish, mean as a curly-haired old dog, and he went to Buford's regiment. He was a private there, in Woodson's company, they say. He was a mountaineer already and this was only the Revolution, but you see we always been out here, since the first days when we took the wilderness, all the low blue mountains from Cherokee and Saponi and Tutelo. Those were some fights, what I mean, when it was just a man and his family against them Indians.

But they took Abednego and he was a private and when Buford fought the British over at Greenspring, Abednego was took a prisoner and they marched him and some others off to Richmond and kept them there. But finally they traded for some Redcoat prisoners so he was let go and he come on home. Then after the war they give him some land out in the mountains but then they took it back with something called a mortgage. You never could keep a Hodges out of debt, you know that. And when they got him with this mortgage they asked him if he didn't want one of them soldier's pensions but Abednego he didn't want to burden the government with no pension, said he didn't fight for no pension. So they put him in the debtor's prison for two years. And him a man of sixty-eight by then.

Then Isham, that was his son, he was in the militia for that War of 1812, but after it was finished he moved on over into Tennessee. Said they done killed off all the British in Virginia, and maybe there was a few left over in Tennessee. He married him a half-Cherokee gal named Polly Long and they had themselves a brood of kids.

One of them was Welcome, your great-great-grandaddy. He was the fifth man down. When they were hardly teenagers, him and his brother Mibau went up into Kentucky. They say Mibau killed a man down in Tennessee for trying to smooch his sister, and Isham sent Welcome with Mibau up into Kentucky because Mibau was hardly more than a boy and hadn't never been away from kinpeople. Well, they settled in the ridges here and they took up with some local gals. Welcome, he married a Hargrove, as I recall. Had more childrens than they could rightly count.

Then that terrible war come and old Welcome didn't hardly have him a boy left, time it was over. He lost three of 'em just in Pickett's Charge. You know, up to Gettysburg. Oh, he had him some fighting mean boys, ain't no doubt. They come down from the ridges, they were in the Ninth Kentucky, they wore just some old rags and called it a uniform. But they were fighting mean.

When the others finally come back they told old Welcome of it. They talked about a dusty, summer heat, and all of them sweating. Fifteen thousand of them in the field! I can hardly picture it, boy. They said that the dust come up from the ground like wind, blowing from their feet up to their eyes, straight inside their noses. And they walked inside it, couldn't even wipe it or keep from breathing it or even see beyond it. And they said you couldn't hear a thing but people stomping and swearing and horses snorting from the dust, like all fifteen thousand of them were so choked from fear and dust that they couldn't laugh or cry or even talk to the man right next to them.

Oh, but it was glory in them fields! Fields of fire, boy! They walked right into that cannon, all those Yankee guns and the guns ripped at them, all the smoke and fire and cannister and case shot, and they never lost a step! The ones who made it back to Welcome said whole rows of men were felled—whole rows, boy!—and they kept up their walking, stepping over and around mounds of men and horses lying there in that field like they'd stopped to take a nap or set them up a camp.

But then the whole row with those Hodges boys was ripped up and three of Welcome's fighting boys dropped down in that field. The ones that made it back said those Hodges never even got to fire their guns, that they'd walked a mile in all that heat and dust and they'd almost made it up to them damn Yankee cannons, but then the cannons beat them to it. They faced the cannons, though! Died on a day of glory!

And the ones who made it back had to fight up to the Yankee guns and then battle there with them Yankee cannoneers, hand to hand. Can you picture it, boy? But they got beat. There were too many Yankees. So they had to come on back across that wide dusty dead-man field of fire with them Yankee cannonballs achasing them, all the way back to the starting place.

Then General Lee himself come out to meet them. They all said he was crying, riding on his white horse from group to group, that white beard of his just soaked with tears. Told them he was sorry. Told them they were God's bravest creatures, that they'd earned a glory spot in heaven. Told them it was himself who lost the battle. That's the kind of man our General Lee was, son. That's why you and your daddy both were named for General Lee. He was a man of honor and he cried the day three Hodges died on the glory field.

And then Alec, Welcome's youngest. They come to get him when he had the fever and he left his sickbed, strapped over a horse. He told them he wasn't afraid. They left Alec hid underneath a low bush along the road to Corinth when the retreat began, sicking up into Shiloh's fresh spring grass, too weak to take another step. But Alec, he was hard. He made it all the way to the prisoner camp at Alton and the records said he didn't die until he caught the smallpox. Alec was a right fine boy. We're stretching it some, but we'll say he died on the fields of glory, too . . .

It was a continuum, a litany. Pride. Courage. Fear. An inherited right to violence. And the pride accumulated, even as the reasons themselves grew more amorphous.

Grandpa, who breathed the gas for Pershing, who almost died not for the honor of Old Glory, but for this vestige of lost hope he called the South. Who advised persistently that one had to leave it to understand and truly love it, that one had to sit in isolation and yearn for it, and that once one experienced the yearn he understood it more and loved it with a proper awe. And she (grandma) accepting vicariously the truthfulness of grandpa, who left the South for those two years and embraced it upon returning, but never ceased to ruminate on the glory of the two years he spent believing he was defending it by killing off Germans in France.

And she having to voice Grandpa's insistence for him because he had died short months after learning of his own son's death, giving up (Bob Hodges was to later surmise) under the crushing realization that, somehow, losing a son to the Germans in France was his own payback for having helped do away with a legion of Germans there in his youth. And, both times, the landscape of the South escaped unmarked, while its cemeteries burgeoned.

And finally his father. He was like his father. Hard and stubborn, Grandma would say fondly. And he looked like him, she would recall, smoothing down his topknot and remembering. She filled him with all his father's boyhood exploits, trying to make a dead man come alive in his son's mind. And, she would remind him, he died in glory. He fought with them across the whole of France, to save them Frenchmen from the Germans. And it was the Battle of the Bulge—you go read about it, boy. You find you some books in the library and look it up. We'll talk about it next Sunday. Your daddy died right there in the front lines, a combat soldier, staring cold into them Nazi eyes, knee-deep in the snow at the Battle of the Bulge.

In a town in France he could not pronounce, much less spell. With a vague, propagandized knowledge of who Hitler was, but without ever having heard of Munich or Chamberlain. After having joined the army with the rest of his contemporaries as if the whole backlands had been challenged to a pickup softball game.

Oh, but he faced them Germans. He had a nerve of steel, your daddy. And he could shoot. Once I seen him drop a squirrel that just peeked one eye around a tree trunk. Your daddy shot him right in the eye. And he was only twelve. Oh, you got to be proud of your daddy. He died standing up and fighting back.

After fifteen years of it, it was ingrained. It was the fight that mattered, not the cause. It was the endurance that was important, the will to face certain loss, unknown dangers, unpredictable fates. And if one did it long enough and hard enough, he might happen upon a rewarding nugget. But, in any event, he was *serving,* offering himself on the altar of his culture.

A litany, an inheritance of coursing, unreasoned pride. It pulsed through his own dark veins. That one continuous linking that had bound father to son from the first wild resolute angry beaten Celt who tromped into the hills rather than bend a knee to Rome two thousand years ago, who would hold out in an icy marsh by standing for days with only his head above water, and who would chew the bark off a tree, fill his belly with wood rather than surrender from starvation and admit defeat to an advancing civilization.

That same emotion passing with the blood: a fierce resoluteness that found itself always in a pitch against death, that somehow, over the centuries, came to accept the fight as birthright, even as some kind of proof of life. Even there on the ridges, two thousand years and a continent removed, transplaced from mountains to mountains as if it were as natural for them to live in rural poverty as it was for a bird to nest in a tree. Glorying in the fight like unmuzzled sentry dogs, bred to it, for the benefit of the ravishers who owned and determined the reasons.

It became a religion to him. He believed in God but most of all he believed in his father and the other Ghosts. God was all the way in heaven, but the Ghosts were with him everywhere he walked. He could cross a field and come up with a handful of arrowheads. He would go to bed and know he slept above Shawnee bones.

And he could scoop out history in a spadeful of mud. Through his childhood summers and later on his off days and vacations he and his friends would dig around the creek beds where the Yankees and Rebels had alternately made their camps. He would bring back a metal button or a spent bullet or an old spoon or a belt buckle and he would keep it in his bedroom for a week or month, contemplating unremembered agonies and glories that had left the item buried in the creek's mud. Then he would take it into Salt Lick or Hillsville and sell it to a gunsmith or an antique dealer for enough money to buy a soda, or a ticket to the movies.

And the movies. They were their own communion. If John Wayne wasn't God then he was at least a prophet. Hodges and a half-dozen friends would walk the five miles into Hillsville on Saturday afternoons and sit in awe through *The Sands of Iwo Jima, The Bridges at Toko-Ri, The Guns of Navarone, Anzio, The Battle of the Bulge,* and dozens of others. It was all there on the screen. Standing up and fighting back.

Then, after the movies, they would stand shyly at the outer fringe of the gathered farmers who had come to spend their Saturdays in the courthouse square. The men would sit in gaggles, chewing slowly on cuds of tobacco or rolling their own cigarettes, talking of their wars and scratching fading scars. There were monuments in the square: a stolid Confederate soldier peering south toward Tennessee, one of the few in a Kentucky town. A large stone marker commemorating those who served in World War I. A similar one for those who went to World War II. Hodges used to stare at the new stone marker: there was an asterisk by his father's name: *Robert E. Lee Hodges.

If there had been no Vietnam, he would have had to invent one. He often wondered if that hadn't been what old Mibau had done: finding an issue of honor in the warless mountains of Tennessee, because if there had not been an issue involving honor, then there would have been no honor. Killing a man in defense of his sister's purity and having to flee to Kentucky, so that, for the rest of his life, he could feel vindicated by his very isolation.

But there was Vietnam, and so there would be honor. It was the fight, not the cause that mattered. He would have his place in the town square and his name on a large stone monument. Perhaps he would have a scar somewhere to scratch as he chewed a tobacco cud on Saturday while young boys watched in awe. And he would be one with the Ghosts.

He had done well in Marine officer training. He was

quiet, but his shyness masked an unrelenting stubbornness, and when he spoke his words were spare, but authoritative. He had spent his life preparing for the Marines, although he had never comprehended that until he viewed some of the others. He knew the woods and he could shoot and he did not mind hot weather. He did not quit on the long runs or the terrible conditioning hikes because endurance involved pride and pride was honor and he was nothing if he did not retain his honor. And he knew tactics. Tactics were personal to him, much as the achings of a sick man would be to a doctor's son.

Bob Hodges stood in the chilled winterdust of the road, preparing to say good-bye to his grandmother, and could not avoid remarking to himself that this moment was completing a lifetime of preparations. There was no thought in his life that spanned beyond what he was about to do in Vietnam. He would fight his war, force his body through the lightless conduit, and worry about what was on the other side when he returned. He was not anxious to save Vietnam from itself and he did not relish facing North Vietnamese guns for a year, but he reasoned that, after all, a man cannot choose his country's enemy. Had Grandpa really hated the Hun in 1917, until told he should? And besides, Vietnam was something to be done with, a duty. Not for Vietnam. For honor (and a whisper saying, "for the South"). And mostly for the bench seat in the town square.

He walked into the house and greeted his grandmother with a big squeeze and a warm kiss. She fussed over his uniform, obviously proud, her old eyes filled with memories. She had fried him more chicken than he could possibly eat, and had made him an apple pie. She waited on him, doted over him as never before. She would not even allow him to help her clear the dishes.

Slowly, he realized she was afraid. He had not expected it. When the outside shadows deepened and he finally rose to leave she moved slowly to him and gave him an aching, too-long hug. Her eyes were wet. He hadn't noticed it until then.

"Sometimes I wish I'd never told you those stories, Bobby. I just wanted you to remember your daddy. Now, you be careful. Hodges never had a lick of luck at this."

Ghosts and glory. It stunned him to hear her say it. He hugged her back. "Now, don't you worry, Grandma. I'm coming back, if that's what you mean."

"Don't take no chances. That's what I *mean*." She gathered herself. "We're proud of you boy. All of us."

All of us. He did not know how she meant the statement, but it scared him. He suddenly felt pulled along, out of control. Afraid. The reality of what he was about to do shook him for the first time, as if all the years of considering it had somehow made the prospect of actually doing it a novel one. He managed a smile and kissed her, the old-skin of her cheek like a brush of velvet. Then he joined his ghosts in the cold black night. Every dead rock mocked him as he trudged along the railroad tracks to home.

II

It did not seem right that he be transported in such style to the desolation that awaited him. He watched a first-run movie as the jet streaked west and he mentally screwed each stylish stewardess a dozen times, as did the other two hundred khaki-clad fellow prisoners on the flight. He ate TV-dinner meals and slept. It was his first jet ride.

They stopped at Hawaii for an hour and he marveled at the Polynesian and Oriental mixes of people at the airport. They stopped again at Wake Island in the dead of night and he remembered Deveraux and the other madly brave Marines who had taken on a world of Japanese to defend that tiny crumb of island in the middle of nothing. He sent postcards of the island to his mother and grandmother and a girl he had dated in college.

They arrived in Okinawa, at the huge airstrip of Kadena Air Force Base, and were whisked away in shuttle buses to the Marine transient facility at Camp Hansen. He sat silently on the bus, chuckling occasionally at the humorous remarks of some of his friends from Basic School, absorbing the packed streets and the closely built stores and steambaths and bars, the swarms of smallish golden people. That's it, he thought amazed. Golden. They are the color of gold.

He was given a room in a transient BOQ, which he shared with two friends from Basic School. They were all told that it would be a week before they would process into Vietnam. In spite of his growing fears, it had frustrated him. He felt uneasy walking around the camp in the presence of hundreds of red-booted dirty long-haired deep-tanned men who were finally free of Vietnam and were on the way home. They stared at him derisively. They kidded him that he would be sorry.

He took to drinking, along with his other friends. It seemed that the only proper way to deal with his transitory state was to be so alcoholically obliterated that he could not recognize it. The Officers' Club bar opened at ten in the morning, and for the first two days he and his friends had been waiting on their stools. Once inebriated, they would shoot pool in the game room, or take taxi tours in the nearby villages.

He tried a steambath once. He paid his two dollars and walked the stark hall to the designated room. The walls were painted government green, compliments of a bucket of stolen paint. The girl was stocky, and dressed in high-waisted cotton underwear. She seemed bored. She worked on his muscles like a mechanic tuning a car: perfunctorily, without interest. She offered him a hand job and he hurriedly declined.

He and two friends went to one of the many bars. It was dark and close inside, smelling of musted alcohol and people sweating. The girls marched over to their table and one of them sat on his lap and dug her rump meaningfully into his crotch and he screamed in agony: for all her practice, she had sat on him wrong. When he howled she marched away in a huff. He left the bar, feeling embarrassed and naive.

By his third day on Okinawa, Hodges took to staying in his BOQ room for hours, pensively studying his Combat Leader's Notebook. He put off drunkenness until a more decent hour: after lunch.

One thing about the Officers' Club manager, mused Hodges through his drunkenness, the son of a bitch may be skating Nam, but he sure as hell knows how to hire some nice-looking women.

Their costumes were kind of stupid, really. Full dresses, bobby socks and tennis shoes. But they were cute. Somehow innocent after the terrors in the village. He liked the way they walked. They seemed conscious of every step they were taking, every muscle movement, as they went about their tasks.

She put his plate down in front of him. He thought he felt her breast against his shoulder. Vague, velvet pressing. Hard to tell. She smiled self-consciously and he squinted, focusing on her name tag. Yup. Same as a minute ago. Mitsuko.

"Hey, thanks, Mitsoooko."

"MITS-ko." It was the third time she had corrected him.

"Whatever. Hey. Did anybody ever tell you you're nice-looking?"

"Oh, yes."

"That's what I thought."

She smiled patiently, as if she were waiting for the next predictable line. He noticed then how young she was. He had been watching her for three days, sitting at tables under her care, throwing inane comments at her along with the others. Like pennies in a well, he mused. How many half-drunk officers have made a pass at her today? Hey. That's a damn good line.

"How many Marines have bothered you today?"

"Oh, no date Marines!" She smiled shyly, almost innocently.

"Well, that's not what I meant." He shook his head, laughing at himself in frustration. *Great* line, Hodges. You went and called the girl a whore. "Do you like to dance?"

She smiled tentatively, too unsure of her English to interpret his question at face value. She cocked her head, waiting for a punch line. He decided he liked the way she looked. Her small-boned, oval face, with its turban of black hair, looked regal. Well, cute, anyway.

"*No,* I just mean dance. You know——" Hodges bounced in his chair—"dance."

"It's awright." She walked away, over to the next table to take an order.

He lit a cigarette, stumped. Why the hell her, anyway? Half the waitresses seemed eager to date Marines. He tapped his ashes into the ashtray. She's too young. Can't be more than eighteen. But *damn* it. She walked by, carrying two platters.

"Hey, Mitsooko. Dance with me tonight, O.K.?"

"MITS-ko. No can do, bobaloo."

Another penny in the well. But she left him with a taste of pretty smile. She passed him again on the way back to the kitchen. "Your food is cold. You better eat!"

Unsolicited comment. Motherly. Major score. He ate slowly, and finally was the only one left at any of her tables. She seemed aware of him as she cleared the other places, much as a cat remains intent while seemingly ignoring a possible attacker. He lit another cigarette, watching her. Finally she came to his table.

"You finished?"

"Dance with me. Tonight." She pondered him, frustrated and innocent. She looked around for help. "Come on, Mit-sko, *please*. I go to Vietnam in a couple days." The line failed: everybody in the room went to Vietnam in a couple days. "Don't you like me?"

"I'm engaged." Her response was obviously rehearsed. "Okinawa boy."

"Whooppee-doo."

"What?" She smiled quizzically.

"American word for 'so what?' Come on." He rose to his feet, his face eager. "Let's go dancing, all right?" He grasped her shoulder. "You'll *love* it."

She seemed embarrassed. She glanced around to see if anyone else was watching. She turned to walk away. "No-o-o-o."

"I won't bother you anymore."

"What?"

"Go dancing tonight and I won't bother you anymore. Not tomorrow. Not the next day. Not ever. O.K.?"

She smiled humorously, then shrugged. "O.K."

Well, whatta you know, mused Hodges. The perfect line. Promise to leave 'em the hell alone and they'll do anything, even go out with you.

He waited for her in front of the club, smoking cigarettes and pondering his days of drunkenness. What the hell has all this got to do with Vietnam? He decided that it was a Marine Corps plot to make everyone frustrated enough that they would *want* to get into Vietnam. Must be it. And damn it, it sure as hell works.

Gliding shadow on the sidewalk. She had shed the absurd bobby socks and was dressed in Western clothes, a skirt and blouse. The first thing he noticed as she approached was her legs. They were well shaped, slim, an apparent rarity among Okinawan women. Hodges grinned, dismounting the fence he had been sitting on. Digit.

She walked up to him, obviously uneasy. She did not smile or even look at him as he called a taxi and opened the door for her. She moved to the other side of the seat. He scooted over next to her. Her perplexity was fresh and innocent. He was not terribly experienced in such matters, but she was making him look like a regular cavalier.

Hodges called to the taxi driver. "Koza." He remembered a dance hall from a few days before.

The taxi left the Camp gate, and wound down a crowded road, through the lighted, sign-drunk village. Kin village, mused Hodges, was nothing but a gate ghetto. He tried a few questions about sights on the streets, Japanese signs, pawnshops, steambaths, all the Conqueror's amenities. He found her incredibly shy. She attempted gamely to answer, but it was convoluted and intense, a mix of Japanese and English and American slang. He caught something about how Camp Hansen had once been "a tousan' farms," but could not decipher the rest.

They left the city and struggled southward down small hills, fighting a myriad of winding curves, and soon were driving along the beach road, which ran at the edge of the long, thin island. He watched the white sand in the gloomy light. She pointed to the silent surf from the taxi's dark.

"Good swim. Officer beach. No Okinawan."

It wasn't any louder or dirtier or cruder than it had been two nights before. It only seemed that way. Hodges ushered her in past scores of groping couples, Okinawan girls and American men, to a table in back of a large, packed dance floor. An Oriental band imitated the Rolling Stones, too loudly and obnoxiously, on an elevated stage.

She had tightened up the moment she had realized where Hodges was taking her. She insisted on moving all the way to the rear of the room, to a virtually hidden table. Hodges bought them each a soft drink. The music was beginning to sober him up. He studied her under the flashes of a strobe light. Her eyes were low and she was so refreshing. He felt a deep, protective affection for her, and began to comprehend his mistake in taking her to the club. He sensed that, somehow, he had insulted her.

The band relented from its wailing fuzztones and played a slow song. He put his hand on her shoulder. "Dance."

She stared at the couples on the floor. "No."

"Come on. That's what we came for."

They moved slowly along the edge of the dance floor, not really a part of it. He felt comfortable in her arms. She was deceptively curved underneath the loose clothes she wore, and strong. He felt like smothering her to him, poring over her body as some of the other dancers were doing, but he thought that it might make her cry. She was deeply upset. He chided himself. Way to go, Casanova. You really scored.

The song ended and he felt alone, adrift with her in a world that was hostile to them both. He put an arm around her and pulled her to him, she not resisting, and kissed her. She merely allowed herself to be kissed, not responding. Then she demanded that they leave.

They caught another taxi back to Camp Hansen. He was depressingly sober now, sobriety assuring him of the true distance between him and her, but also convincing him of his deep attraction to her. As they pulled away from the nightclub he smiled apologetically across the seat to her.

"Terrible, O.K.? Sorry."

He watched her in the taxi's dark, she looking straight ahead out at the narrow road, and he felt the ache of losing her. He kissed her again but still she did not respond one way or the other. She merely allowed herself to be kissed.

She had a long conversation with the driver. Her face became lit and she appeared amazed, incredulous. She translated bits and pieces to Hodges in apparent politeness, lest he feel excluded. A murder. Boy killed two shop-keepers with an ax. American boy. No. Okinawan mother, American father. No father.

Hodges mentally shrugged it off. He could not understand their excitement. She noticed that he seemed unmoved and touched his knee, intense. He shrugged to her, smiling ironically. "One murder?"

"No no no. You no understand. Okinawan never kill. This is terrible!"

"Must have been the American in him." It was supposed to be a joke. She withdrew her hand and ignored him, continuing to converse with the driver.

The taxi turned off the beach road and groaned up the short steep hill and entered the island road. In a few moments they were driving through Kin village again. They rode along the lighted street, the sign-drunk buildings depressing him now. Mitsuko spouted another command to the driver and he nodded once and pulled over to the Camp gate.

She smiled with effort, warm yet distant. "Taxi take me home. I pay. Good night."

Her face was only inches from his and he stared beyond the careful smile into eyes that were confused and innocent, and somehow hurt. What a bummer, mused Hodges. How the hell can I understand? Three days and it's Vietnam. How the hell can I *try* to understand? It can't be like this.

He touched her shoulder. "I can't leave you here." He gestured out into the streets. "Too many crazy Marines. Let me take you home."

She said nothing but her unchanged expression told him no. They sat close, staring at each other, each waiting for the other to capitulate. The driver stared courteously out the front window. Marines passing by the car on the way in from liberty elbowed each other and smiled at the figures in the car.

The nudging Marines finally tipped the scales. Mitsuko turned to the driver and spoke a low command and he nodded once again and drove off into the village. They bounced a few blocks and turned onto a dirt road, following it behind the street. The car stopped beside a stairway which led to a group of second-floor apartments that fronted on the street.

Hodges checked the fare and started to pay the driver. She protested again. "*No.* You take taxi back."

He ignored her, paying the driver. The taxi departed. He turned to her, smiling uncertainly. "I'll walk back. It isn't far." They stood under the stairs, looking at each other's image in the dark. Finally she gave him a small, confused smile and turned away. She began to walk up the stairs.

"Sorry. Good-bye."

He followed quickly, astounding himself with uncharacteristic boldness. He took her shoulder and stopped her and she turned around, angry, somehow insulted, but he needed her too much to worry about her insult. He pulled her to him, first gently and then tightly, kissing her and pushing her into the guardrail. Finally she responded, ever so slightly, not even wanting to.

He squeezed her and spoke soft words that she did not understand and then kissed her again, less clumsily than before. She kissed him back, a portion of her innocence crumbling with great remorse, admitting his attractiveness. Then she stared at him with a curious, examining look.

He held her and discovered that his eyes were wet. *"Please."*

She did not invite him. Nor did she ask him to leave. She merely turned and walked slowly up the stairs. He watched the golden legs ascend the steps and felt insane, controlled by their measured motion. He followed her. She unlocked the door and left it open, still not looking back for him.

He entered her apartment, closing the door and walking through the kitchen after her. She stood in the other room, facing away from him, still not acknowledging his presence. He placed both hands on her waist, standing behind her, holding it as carefully as fragile china.

He did not ask and she did not answer. Neither of them needed to. When she reached up and turned out the light they both understood. She stood with her back to him and pulled a long pin out of her hair and it fell straight and black and silky down her back. He gathered it in his hands and pressed it into his face and it was soft and clean and he kissed it, holding it that way. Then he gently pulled on it, turning her around, and lifted her face, her eyes still looking down, not meeting his, and he kissed her.

He held her that way for a long time, careful not to force himself on her, wondering at the fullness of her mouth, trying to understand that part of him that was exclaiming that this was perhaps the most beautiful moment of his life. He experienced the firmness of her back and hips and then the surprising fullness of her breasts. He marveled at the shyness of her response after she had finally committed herself so completely to him.

Then she slowly broke away from him, still not saying a word, and left the room. He stood awkwardly for a moment, watching after her. The hard white of a streetlight flashed on her as she re-entered the room but it was soft and gold and black where it touched her. She did not return to him, though, did not even look at him. Instead she knelt on the floor of her little room and folded down the *guton* that was her bed.

He noticed that he had begun to tremble. He dropped his clothes where he stood and joined her on the *futon*, losing his fears and loneliness in the solace of her warmth. Still she was shy, almost passive, but she was mercurial warm when he entered her and she spoke for the first time then, a sharp groan and a lovely word that he did not understand because it was a Japanese word. But he needed no translation.

Then it was over and they still held each other, almost as if both were in shock at their intimacy. He took her hair and wrapped it behind his neck, enveloping them inside the soft black cocoon that her hair made. She laughed softly, her face still fresh and innocent and bright, and he felt that he was somehow experiencing an emotion that had eluded him before, that was not supposed to be a part of him. Not there. Not then. But he felt it and he remarked to himself that he would do almost anything to preserve it.

He noticed it then, on the *futon*. She saw that he was staring at it and stood quickly, donning a happy-coat, making such a simple thing as that a poem. Then she gathered the sheet and carried it out of the room.

He held his head, laying back on the *futon*. Oh, wow. I didn't know there was such a thing any more, not on Okinawa. She re-entered the room and went into the kitchen, where she put on a pot of tea. He watched her movements, stunned. Her hair was down around her shoulders, framing her oval face. She was ignoring him again.

A *virgin!* All the way to Okinawa to learn the ways of sultry, sloe-eyed Oriental women, and he'd happened on a virgin! It explained a lot of things to him. He walked up behind her and put his hands on her shoulders. She stared into the teapot as it steamed, taking no apparent notice of his hands.

"Mitsuko. This was your first time."

She turned around and faced him. She seemed embarrassed, compromised. She nodded.

He shrugged helplessly. "Mine, too."

He walked loose and powerful on his way back to Camp Hansen, taking long strides in the middle of the street, avoiding shadowed pockets of buildings where Americans skulked with gutting knives, waiting to split a man's belly for the dollars in his wallet. He reached the camp gate and listened to the bar tales of the others coming in from liberty, all the cruel clichés about Oriental women. He thought of the groin-grinding bar girls of two days before, and for the first time understood the sad part of Mitsuko's stare that kept accusing.

Streetlight's hard light on the far wall, soft breasts pressed against his middle. How could she have such breasts beneath the unrevealing cloth of waitress uniforms? American songs on the radio. Japanese radio. Armed Forces Network. *Don't ask why. Don't ask how. Don't ask forever. Love me now.** Love breaks over green tea that he loaded down with sugar. "Teach me to write your name, Bobby. I show you mine in Japanese." And in the daytime, he still drinking at the club and she ignoring him, lest she be marked as a participant in the festival of lust. "I love you, Mitsuko. No, really. Really, I do." "Go back to sleep. Three days you go Vietnam."

He lay on his back in the large, stark room, his head against his seabag, smoking a cigarette. He had tried to sleep but the ceiling lights were brutally bright, and besides he was too keyed up. In an hour, at midnight, the room full of solemn, shaved-headed men would depart for Vietnam.

An aviator Captain and a First Sergeant sat across from him, conversing easily. The Captain carried a new guitar.

---

*From the song "Until It's Time For You to Go," by Buffy Sainte-Marie, © Copyright 1965, 1973 by Gypsy Boy Music, Inc. All rights reserved. Used by permission.

He was going back for the second time. He was telling the First Sergeant about how he got his Distinguished Flying Cross. He spoke of Vietnam with a studied familiarity that for some reason irritated Hodges. The First Sergeant was drunk. He was returning from emergency leave, after burying his wife. Foreign names rolled off his tongue like syrupy spit. Quang Tri Phu Bai Da Nang Hue . . . They both talked too loud and with too much certainty, as if they were competing for the admiration of the ninety-odd boots who sat miserably around them. Hodges thought about asking them to shut up, then tried to block them out.

He had spent three hours in her apartment, from the time she was off work until he had to leave to catch the bus for Kadena Air Force Base with the others. It had been their fourth night together.

Mit-sooo-ko. He had decided not to shower. It seemed like such a final act to wash her off him. He could smell her on his hands and in his hair. He loved smelling her and he knew that the odor would soon vanish in the muck of what awaited him. He wondered if he would ever see her again, if he would ever make it back to Okinawa. He hoped deeply that he would, and that somehow it would be soon.

But first there was Vietnam.

PART II | THE END OF THE PIPELINE

3.

Hodges began processing in Da Nang. At Division headquarters, he and several other new Lieutenants were
granted a quick audience with the Assistant Division Commander, then briefed by a string of Colonels regarding
the Division's area of operations. One of the Colonels
produced a detailed map, on which he had carefully placed
a mass of dots, one for each enemy contact in a certain
place. The map was loaded with dots. In some places they
were speckles, like polka dots, and in others they gathered to make large red smears.

The red dots reminded Hodges of blood, and their collective presence was like a slap that awakened him to the
reality of the bush. They were only dots, but each one, according to the Colonel, represented someone killed or
wounded. The Twenty-Fifth Marines area of operations,
where Hodges was headed, was a large red smear.

The first night he lay on a mildewed cot inside a tent
at the Motor Transport battalion's compound, which
housed Division transients. On a far ridge, all night long,
a .50-caliber machine gun expended ammunition in deep
burps. Shadows from distant flares lit one side of the wall,
on and off, and Hodges felt vulnerable, naked in his ignorance. He didn't have the slightest idea why the .50-cal
kept firing while the compound where he slept was not
even on alert. It irritated him. He was finally in Vietnam,
but he wasn't a part of it.

The following morning he and two others took a convoy
from Da Nang to the combat base at An Hoa. It was a
journey into darkness and primitivity, as little by little the
comparatively lush surroundings of Da Nang fell by the
wayside. Strings of American bases and well-kept villages
gave way to wide, ruptured fields, saturated with little
ponds, permanent bomb craters from the years of war.
The multitude of gravestones and pagodas beginning just
outside Da Nang bore chips and divots from a hundred

thousand bullets. Hodges could make out old fighting holes along many of the ridges, where units had dug into their night perimeters months and years before. He felt young, even more naive, a stranger to an ongoing game that did not demand or even need his presence.

At Liberty Bridge, the Vu Gia and Thu Bon rivers joined, isolating the An Hoa Basin from the rest of civilized Vietnam. The convoy crossed the river on a pull barge, one truck at a time. There was no bridge at Liberty Bridge. The old bridge had been blown by the VC years before, and the new bridge was not yet completed. On the far side of the rivers, after they passed a combat base that sat on a large J-shaped hill, was land as chewed and devastated as the pictures Hodges had seen of Verdun. Whole treelines were torn out by bombs. All along the road were tatters of villages that had been ripped apart by the years of fighting. Fields were porous with bomb and mortar craters. The scattered hootches that served as homes for the villagers were no more than straw thatch, often patched with C-ration cardboard, appended to large earthen mounds where the families that remained hid from the battles.

The convoy road ended at An Hoa. There was nothing beyond the combat base but the mountains, across the river, which stretched all the way to Laos. The enemy owned the mountains. Hodges quickly comprehended the isolation, studying the wasted terrain on all sides of the narrow convoy road. It was as if the convoy had passed through a distance-warp when it barged across the river, and had ended up a million miles from Da Nang.

An Hoa, for all its red dust and oven heat, seemed an oasis. He watched the base as the convoy approached, attempting to distinguish its structure. None was apparent. An outpost appeared, surrounded by reams of concertina and barbed wire, then another. The tents of the larger base were packed onto one red hill, then fell into a draw and continued on another bald ridge. Hodges remembered that it was a futile effort to attempt to find order, that An Hoa was merely another legacy passed on from French times, turned into an American base because there had already been an airstrip capable of use.

There's barbed wire, he finally decided, surveying a wounded countryside swollen with anger. That'll do for starters.

More processing in An Hoa. Regiment to battalion to company. He dragged his Valpac from place to place, receiving instructions about how to be a Good Lieutenant. His stateside utilities became completely soaked from his sweat. Finally the company supply clerk brought him to the supply tent, where he stored his Valpac and was issued jungle utilities and boots, a flak jacket, a helmet, and the full ration of combat gear. His new boots were embarrassingly unscuffed. His flak jacket was too bright a shade of green, undulled by the dust of the Basin, which penetrated every type of weave known to man. But, finally, he could begin to blend in.

That night the base was mortared and he shared a small bunker with four other men and a few fleeting rats. He heard the mortars fall in random bursts across the base and could not fight back a feeling about how neat it was. By God, he pondered, leaning like an unconcerned old-timer against the bunker wall, it's finally happening to *me*.

The next day, as he was walking to an indoctrination class with another new Lieutenant, the base was rocketed. He sprinted to a dry ditch and dove in, feeling like a true combat veteran. One rocket landed perhaps fifty meters away, directly on top of a tent, and he began composing in his own mind how he would put that into a letter to someone. But then he climbed out of the ditch and almost stepped on the severed hand of a man who had been inside the tent. It lay on the road, in perfect condition, having been blown more than a hundred feet by the rocket's explosion. The man's wedding ring was in perfect place. Someone from near the tent shouted that the First Sergeant was dead.

And it wasn't fun anymore.

On his second night in An Hoa he was awakened by a company clerk who told him that the company was in contact, and asked him if he wanted to watch. It was past midnight. He couldn't quite understand the man's meaning. Do I want to *watch*, he pondered over and over, gathering his flak jacket and helmet and weapon. Do I want to watch. Why? Is it on TV?

But he dutifully followed the man and joined several clerks from the company office on top of a large sandbag bunker. They pointed north, across the river, and he followed their fingers as his eyes searched into the hell that was known as the Arizona Valley.

And he sat, feeling slightly obscene, as if he were a peeping tom to someone's private doings, and watched his company dying across the river. Red and green tracers interlaced and careened into the black night air. Mortars and B-40 rocket-propelled grenades flashed and impacted, spewing dirt with whumps that he could hear from the three-mile distance he was watching. Illumination flares dangled like tiny streetlights in the distance.

He was washed with a mix of helplessness and fear that overrode any emotion he had ever experienced, and continued to stare, an armchair spectator to the sport of dying. And tomorrow, he said over and over as he watched, tomorrow that will be my very own Vietnam.

4.

Ogre was bleeding right outside the hole. Lying there, inching through the dust, grinning for a fat man's ass.

Not supposed to be grinning.

I'll bet that mother's stoned again, fretted Snake. Then he doubted himself. Been out on the listening post for five hours, now. Wouldn't smoke on no LP. Not out here. Not even Ogre. Then he double-doubted himself. Maybe Ogre would. Crazy fucker. He peered across an eternity of dust that began abruptly at the edge of his fighting hole. Ogre was fifteen feet away. Ogre peered back, the ugly square face grinning, yes grinning, behind the droopy moustache.

"Hey-y-y-y, Snake. You seen Baby Cakes?"

Came from the bomb crater. That's close, mused Snake. But they won't get any closer. Too late for them. We got 'em stopped.

An illumination flare popped in front of him and floated down on its parachute, brightening the distant treeline. It swung lazily, a phosphorescent pendulum. Snake peeped the crater in the flare's dim light. Fifty feet away, maybe. The flare flickered once, twice, and was out. Another grenade exploded in front of the hole. Ogre screamed again. He was maybe two feet closer.

"Snake. Heyyyy, man. Where's Baby Cakes?"

Machine gun from the treeline again. The rounds ripped through the perimeter like a daisy chain of cherry bombs. Got to find Phony. Snake bolted to the next hole, a quick crabwalk.

"Phony!"

Phony grinned earnestly, chewing C-rat gum, as if he were expecting some insane or at least irresponsible request from Snake, and grooving on it. "What's Ogre doing, man?"

Snake shrugged impatiently, his eyes on the crater. "Looking for Baby Cakes. Listen. See that crater?" Phony nodded. "There's four, maybe five gooks in it. We been keeping 'em down but we can't put any rounds out now. Might hit the LP. Christ knows where they are, with Ogre back here. Chuck a couple in the crater, OK?" Phony nodded again, still grinning, but concentratedly now. "And don't throw too hard. LP's *somewhere* on the other side. Hear?" Phony nodded yet again, apparently unconcerned. He was the only member of the squad with the accuracy to pull it off.

Another illumination round popped behind the treeline and Phony raised his head six inches out of his hole and peeped the crater. He gestured to Snake, popping his gun crazily. No sweat. He prepared two grenades. Snake crawled quickly back to his own hole. AK-47 bullets followed him. They raised dust near Ogre, too. But they were fired from the treeline, two hundred yards away, and most of them went high, into the center of the perimeter. Ogre screamed again. He was another foot closer.

"Where's Baby Cakes?"

Phony arched a grenade expertly, like a free throw. *Boom.* It was harvest time, the ground was brick hard, and shrapnel saturated the crater. There was a frantic, sibilant chattering inside it. *Boom.* The second grenade impacted, and the crater was suddenly silent. Snake smiled grimly. What the hell did they expect, snooping up so close? They're in the hurt locker now.

"Hey-y-y-y, Snake!"

Ogre. The flare went out and it was dark again, not even a moon. That's why we're in trouble, Snake remem-

bered. Beware the no-moon night. He paused for a
moment and then jumped out of his hole and stood nakedly in the black, pulling Ogre by the arms. Ogre screamed.
It hurt.

"Shut up."

Another group of enemy opened up from just across
a narrow, scraggly field, behind a paddy dike. The sound
of bullets was terrifying but the rounds went high again.
Snake pulled hard. In the next hole Cannonball fired his
grenade launcher steadily, a smooth rhythm of blooper
balls exploding near the dike. On the other side, Cat Man's
team laid down a steady base of small arms fire. No
sweat. Snake jumped back into his fighting hole and rolled
Ogre over the top of him.

"Where you hit?"

Ogre grinned confidingly. "I'm O.K., man. Yeah." He
looked around, the ugly face relaxed. "Now. Where's
Baby Cakes?"

Ogre's trouser legs were soaked. Snake ripped one of
them apart. Long gashes, deep, pulsing holes covered
Ogre's thighs. Snake screamed up the hill, toward the
command post. "Corpsman up!"

Doc Rabbit was already in Cat Man's hole. He crawled
heavily to Snake. Pop. Another illum flare burst. Doc
climbed into the hole with Snake and started to dress
Ogre's legs. Ogre continued the amused, chiding grin.
"Hey-y-y, Doc. I'm O.K. Go take care of Vitelli, man.
He is *all* fucked up."

Baby Cakes sprinted the fifteen meters from Cat Man's
hole, holding his helmet on his head with one hand, staying very low. He was a thick-necked, powerful shadow
that belly-slid up to Ogre when more rounds went off. He
drawled out abruptly: "What you want, Ogre?"

Ogre warmed to Baby Cakes. He seemed to be enjoying
the mystery he had provoked. "Baby Cakes. There you
are, man! Vitelli wants you, man. He just keeps saying, 'Go
get Baby Cakes,' you know every five seconds. 'Go get
Baby Cakes, go get Baby Cakes.' So finally I said, 'All right,
motherfucker, I'll *go* get Baby Cakes.' Hey. Vitelli is *all*
fucked up, man. So is Homicide. Hey, Doc. I'm O.K. You
go help Vitelli and Homicide, man. They are *all* fucked
up."

Artillery on the treeline. Crr*runch*. Crr*runch*. Round

after round. A battery, six cannons, unloading on the tree-line, from distant places like An Hoa and the Bridge and Hill 65. They all crouched, watching tautly, silently. Get some, artillery.

The low drone of a propeller-driven airplane emanated from the direction of Da Nang, so far west and north that it was from another world. Snake listened carefully. Will it be Spooky or Basketball? He hoped it would be Spooky. We need the gatling guns, he decided again. Don't need no Basketball flares.

Baby Cakes stared out into the dark at where the LP was. Snake scrutinized him. Don't do nothing stupid, Baby Cakes. Friends are friends, but . . . Baby Cakes took off at a dead run, out into the black. The near paddy dike erupted with AK-47s again. Baby Cakes hit the dirt. One hole down, Cat Man's team poured a steady stream of red into the dike. Further away, second platoon's lines were firing, too.

Ogre put his head up lazily when he heard the rounds go off. He had a shot of morphine in him now. "Where's Baby Cakes?"

Snake pushed his head back to the dirt and held it. "Shut up."

In the treeline there was a steady thunk of mortars igniting inside their tubes. Snake got tight inside his hole. Where's Baby Cakes? Near paddy dike opened up again. Must be ten gooks firing now, he decided. Cannonball retaliated with the grenade launcher. ThunkBoom. ThunkBoom. The blooper balls exploded flatly and the firing grew less intense.

The mortars that began in the treeline landed, walking their way quickly through the middle of the perimeter. Someone at the command post just up the hill from Snake screamed. Two people. Maybe more. When the mortars stopped Cat Man's people put more rounds on the paddy dike.

The plane arrived. It was a Basketball. Figures, thought Snake ironically. Just what we need with Baby Cakes out there. The droning monster dropped out huge flares that lit the perimeter like a stadium. Then Basketball shifted its orbit and a flight of Phantom jets streaked into the far treeline, dropping bombs and napalm.

The big machine gun in the treeline turned onto the

Phantoms. Huge balls of tracers reached toward the jets as they approached the treeline. Snake laughed to himself, almost enjoying the thought of a "wing-wipe" being shot at. Shoot at them awhile, you gook bastards. And I hope you run outa ammo.

More screams from the command post. Maybe three. Snake saw him move then, a hesitation in a fighting hole who thought once, twice, about it, then bolted across the scarred hill in a half-lope toward the command post. A torrent of tracers flew from the dike and they nailed him in the middle of a stride. He fell forward, landing on the back of his head and one shoulder, crumpling like a dropped deer. Snake shook his head knowledgeably. Who'd you think you were, Superman?

It's Marston, Snake noted. Only a new dude would do that. Not even here long enough to be named yet. Marston rolled once in the deadly bright of Basketball and looked bleakly to Snake, imploring him. Finally he grunted painfully.

"Snake. Snake."

Snake peered at Marston, sizing up his wound. Marston was just up the hill from him, twenty feet away. "Where you hit, Marston?"

Marson held the middle of his flak jacket. "In here. Ohhh *shit* it hurts."

Snake looked for Doc. Doc was gone, over with Pierson's squad. He crawled out of his hole then, and scooted up to Marston. Powder of the hill poured through his fingers as he pushed it. More rounds now, all around them: they were lighted targets. B-40 rocket boomed. Another.

"Marston, you're an ass."

"CP's *all* fucked up, man. Can't you hear 'em?"

"Fat lot of help *you* are. Now you're gonna get *my* ass blown away."

Marston was hit in the lung. He gurgled. "I'm sorry, Snake."

Snake was still five feet away. He stopped crawling and listened expertly to Marston's gurgles. "Roll onto the side that hurts."

Marston tried, and screamed. *"Ohhhh! JesusChristMy-God!"*

Snake crawled back toward his hole. In the far treeline

a new series of artillery rounds succeeded the departed Phantom jets. Marston called to him as he moved down the hill. "Don't leave me up here, Snake!" Marston tried to crawl and screamed again. Snake reached his fighting hole, grabbed a poncho, and crawled back to Marston. Marston was whimpering.

"Marston, you're a goddamned girl. Shut up. You did this to yourself." Snake laid the poncho out beside Marston, then grabbed his legs and flipped him lifeguard-style onto the poncho. Marston screamed. More AK bullets sprayed the hill.

"Shut up or I'll leave you here."

"It *hurts*."

"It's s'posed to hurt."

Snake dragged Marston down the hill. Marston screamed each time Snake jerked the poncho. Snake reached his hole again and called for Doc. No Doc. He screamed again. Still no Doc. He despaired of Doc and pulled the lone battle dressing off his own helmet, hating Marston for leaving his up the hill. He reached in and felt the hole. Marston screamed as if in torture when Snake's fingers slid along the slick wet inside of it.

The hole gurgled like a stopped-up drain. Snake put the inside of the plastic battle-dressing cover over the hole, and pulled the dressing supertight over that. Marston had given over to weak groans, too exhausted to scream any longer.

"Now. Lay on it till Doc gets here."

"Ohhh. It hurts too much."

"Don't give me any of your shit, Marston. You wanna die? Lay on it." He looked spitefully at Marston, then grinned encouragingly. "You tough, Marston? Hold on to it, then. You gonna be O.K."

The Basketball flares twinkled and died, one by one, like huge candles spending their wicks. It became quiet but for sniper rounds. In the far distance, maybe a mile away, a speaker droned. Some gook promising Australia vacations to anyone who surrendered. Something like that. No one listened. The company's 60-millimeter mortar section fired a perfunctory mission in the speaker's direction, nine or ten casually aimed rounds, as if to acknowledge its absurdity. No effect. Speaker continued. Sounds funny, thought Snake. Stupid gooks.

Baby Cakes. He was a shadow to the front of them, silhouetted by a low illumination flare from another part of the perimeter. He carried Vitelli over his shoulder, butt up in the air. The near paddy dike opened up again, quite suddenly, and Baby Cakes fell hard to the ground.

Snake's whole squad returned fire anxiously. Baby Cakes struggled up, still carrying Vitelli, and pointed his M-16 absently at the near dike, shooting a few rounds with one arm. He called to the lines.

"Marine coming in!"

Snake stared admiringly at the muscled figure that labored into the lines. You crazy bastard, Baby Cakes. With balls like that, how can you *walk?*

Baby Cakes dumped Vitelli next to Cat Man's hole. "Doc! Doc!" He turned to Snake, shouting frantically. "Goddamn it, where's *Doc?*"

Doc Rabbit trundled over, done with Pierson's squad for the moment. Rabbit was having a busy night. He was almost out of battle dressings.

He squatted over Vitelli. Vitelli was unconscious. He had a shrapnel hole clear through his chest, up high where the arteries were, and about five pieces in his face and head. Doc wiped his forehead and spoke somberly. "Nothing I can do, except call him an Emergency. Can't shoot him up with morphine, not when he's already out. Might kill him."

Baby Cakes was on his knees, looking pleadingly at Rabbit. "Doc. Doc. Do *some*thing, man!"

Snake noticed the blood welling up around Baby Cakes' neck. "You hit, Baby Cakes?"

"Got me just a minute ago."

Rabbit stripped off the flak jacket. There was a gouge out of Baby Cakes' upper back, a deep trough where the bullet dug. Priority medevac, mused Snake, categorizing. Rabbit laid Baby Cakes down on his stomach and shot him up. Baby Cakes continued to resist.

"Don't worry 'bout me, Doc. Help Vitelli, man."

Snake crawled over to Baby Cakes when Rabbit was finished. "Where's Homicide and Bagger? They O.K.?"

Baby Cakes grinned as if he were remembering a joke. The morphine was hitting him good. "Ah, they're O.K. Homicide has a ding up the side of his head. They caught about five grenades out there before Phony cooled that crater. But Bagger's O.K. Don't let him bullshit you."

"Where are they?"

Baby Cakes smiled again. Feeling no pain, Snake noted. "Oh. Yeah. They're in an old fighting hole somebody dug out there by the near dike. Radio's torn to shit. That's how Bagger came out O.K. He was wearing the radio."

"But they're O.K.?"

"Huh? Oh. Yeah. They said tell you they'll be in at first light." Baby Cakes drifted smilingly into the land of Nod. "Yeah. They're laying chilly out there. Wouldn't come back with me. Skating mothers . . ."

Quiet again. In the distance the loudspeaker droned occasionally. No one listened. Spooky had at last arrived and he circled, pouring down a steady stream of tracers at anything that dared to shoot or move, like a distant fire hose spraying narrow wavy streams of iridescent red water. Spooky's angry gatling guns had a way of calming things.

Snake sat down at the edge of his fighting hole, his feet inside it, and took a long swig from his canteen. He scratched a new mosquito bite, then another. He swore and took the squeezebottle of insect repellent from the band around his helmet and spread new bugjuice over his arms and face. It tingled as it ate its way into his pores.

He checked his watch. Four o'clock. No wonder I'm so goddamned tired. But they only got an hour before they have to make their *didi*. He grinned tiredly, watching Spooky work out on the treeline. They may be gone already.

Marston moaned again. Gotta get his ass outa here. Most ricky-tick. He leaned over and cuffed Marston gently up the side of the head. "Hold on, Marston. You gotta be tough. And when you get back I'm gonna name you Stupid. That's right."

He walked slowly to the platoon command post. A mortar had hit it dead center. Doc Anderson was dead. He lay in an unceremonial sprawl where the mortar blast left him, one arm reaching, the forearm blown away. Beyond the doc there was a sagging, rended poncho hootch that was supported by only two sticks. Next to the hootch the platoon commander lay somberly, peering, mumbling to the sky. One leg was gone. There was a battle dressing on one arm. The Lieutenant did not acknowledge Snake's greeting. He peered into the night, stroking his belly with both hands.

And Flaky had disappeared. That figures, mused Snake. That's the luckiest, flakiest puke I ever knew. Only Kerlovic was functioning. He lay on one side, swaddled in battle dressings, both trouser legs ripped all the way to his crotch. Both legs were wrapped, as was one arm. A large dressing covered one side of his head. He was talking on the radio.

Snake sat down next to him, waiting for him to finish. Kerlovic had been platoon guide until two days before, when the platoon sergeant was wounded and he took over for him. He had ten months in Vietnam, the only one in the platoon with more time than Snake. Snake looked at him, almost envious. And now he's going back to the World.

"How you feeling?"

Kerlovic managed a pained, sly grin. "Won't be able to use either leg till they discharge my young ass. How's the lines?"

"Number Ten, man. My squad's half gone. Think I got seven medevacs. Vitelli's dead. Don't tell Baby Cakes. Got another dude—that new dude, Marston—he's gonna die if we don't get him out most ricky-tick. Got a sucking chest."

"Wow, man. What a bust. Well, we got medevacs in the air. For emergencies, anyway. Priorities gotta wait till first light."

"You an emergency?"

Kerlovic tapped the battle dressing that wrapped his head and managed another pained, conspiratorial grin. "Head wound. What do you think?"

Snake shrugged, indulging him. "You owe it to yourself. Ain't nobody else gonna give a shit." The Lieutenant droned on into the black, ten feet away from them. "Hey. What's with Corky?"

"He's gone a little *dinky-dau,* man. Lost his leg pretty high up. I tied it off for him. He's O.K., but he keeps on asking me if his dick is all right! What can I say, man? I told him, 'Lieutenant, if it was all right when you got here, it's all right now. You didn't lose none of it tonight.' He keeps bugging me, says it don't feel right, would I check it out. Told him to check it himself. I'm sick

enough with all these goddamn holes in me. Look at me.
What if it's gone? You know what that would look like?
What if his balls are gone? I'd barf. How could I tell him
that?"

Snake nodded, commiserating. "You ain't in any shape
for that." He walked over to the Lieutenant and sat down
next to him, scratching a mosquito bite. "Hey, Lieutenant. Looks like you'll be skying out on us, huh?"

The Lieutenant looked up, focusing through sweet veils
of morphine. "Yeah. It's my leg. Won't be back." He
gazed uneasily toward the treeline. "If I get out. Won't be
back, though." He seemed to forget Snake for one floating
moment, caressing his middle tentatively, dreamily. He
reached his pubic hair and froze again. "Snake. Is my
dick all right?" He stared at Snake through his needled
peace. "Tell me the truth. Is it?"

" 'Course it is. Unless you're hung halfway to your
knees."

"It doesn't feel right." He clasped Snake's calf. "Check
it out. Would you?"

Snake stared unemotionally at him for a moment, then
shrugged. "All right, Lieutenant." He pulled the trousers
open and down. The oozing stump plopped out, joining a
pool where other parts of the Lieutenant had soaked into
the dry dust. His groin was slippery and dark with blood.
Snake noticed the penis intact, but could not tell about
the balls. "Dick's fine, Lieutenant." He found a canteen
and washed the middle parts. "So's your balls."

He eased the trousers back over the stump. The Lieutenant grimaced. "You're good as ever up there, sir. Couple
months you'll be out there busting cherries with the
best of 'em. Think about us sitting out here in the bush.
O.K.?"

The Lieutenant was no longer listening. His face was
almost ecstatic with relief. "Thank God. Thank the fucking
Lord."

Snake sat back down next to Kerlovic. Both shook their
heads. "Where's Flaky? He's s'posed to be on the net, not
you."

Kerlovic shrugged, accustomed to such vanishings. "He
beat feet when the first mortar round landed down the hill.
I ain't seen him since." Kerlovic stared mysteriously at
Snake. "Flaky just *knows,* man. I never seen anything like

it. He's so gaddamn flaky I feel like killing him, doing him myself. But he sure as hell knows, don't he?"

Snake nodded absently, scanning the blackened, bushy hillside. Finally he shouted. "Fairchild, get your ass up here or I'm gonna *do* you. I shit you not."

Kerlovic eyed Snake tentatively. "You better watch it, man. That's one sneaky little dude. He just might do *you*."

"Nah. He don't have the balls. And I do. And he knows it."

Flaky appeared, rising from the dust as if a phoenix. He had found an old fighting hole in the middle of the perimeter, left months or years ago by some other warring unit, and had tucked himself in for the duration.

Snake called to him in a harsh mimic. "You can come out now, Flaky. The Boogey Man is gone."

He walked slowly to them, not the least bit embarrassed at his cowardice, so accustomed to self-deprecation that it was his natural state. It was his key to survival. Flaky had cultivated his unreliability, honed it until he became a nonentity during crisis, able to cringe by himself in the nearest ditch.

The too-large trouser legs scraped baggily as he approached. Mildly frightened eyes surveyed the wreckage of the command post. The voice came high-pitched and patronizing. "Jesus. That was some real shit. You know?"

Kerlovic tightened one of his battle dressings. "Yeah. I know. How the fuck do *you* know?"

Snake spoke commandingly. "Flaky."

Ingratiating response: Flaky was indeed afraid of Snake. "Yeah, Snake?"

"Go take a casualty count. Emergencies and priorities. Hurry up."

There were still sniper rounds, occasional bursts from the treeline. Flaky stared for another moment at Snake, almost daring to be sullen. Snake reached over and picked up the dead corpsman's medical kit, then threw it into Flaky's gut. "And give that to Doc Rabbit. He needs some more morphine sticks."

Snake and Kerlovic sat motionless for three minutes. Snake was dreaming of the cigarette he would light at dawn. There was a chatter on the radio, and Kerlovic put the handset lazily to his ear. "This is three. Go, six." He listened. "Roger that. Thank you much." He looked over to Snake, grinning expectantly. "Bird's on the way, man. Emergencies to the zone." He shook his head, staring up into the black. "Christ, I can't believe I'm out of this shit-hole."

"You ain't. Yet." Snake surveyed the darkness. Spooky had gone home. "Tell six we need some headquarters people to carry medevacs to the zone. I got five men left, not counting two out on the LP. And three holes."

Sawgrass swished along the hill. Flaky was crawling back to the command post. He appeared deeply shaken. Snake shook his head in wonderment when he saw the bugeyes and the tight circle of mouth reappear. How does that dude keep making it?

"Jesus. Four dead. Two in Pierson's squad. Two in yours—Vitelli and that new dude, what's his—"

"C'mon Flaky, knock it off. I can do without it. Now, who we got for emergencies?"

"Doc says six in the platoon, counting Lieutenant and Kerlovic. And three priorities." Flaky's eyes bulged nervously. "Jesus. That's half of us gone, just tonight."

"Any routines?"

"Couple nonevacs." Flaky looked suspiciously at Snake, sizing him up. Far to the east a helicopter popped toward them. Another. "I got me a little piece of shrap-metal. Uh-huh. Got me a tee-tee Heart tonight."

Four men from the company command post jogged cautiously toward the lines. Kerlovic hailed them and pointed them toward where the wounded were lying. Snake walked up to Flaky. "Let me see."

Flaky held his upper arm tentatively toward Snake. There was a tiny cut on it. Snake guffawed. "How many times did you poke yourself with your C-rat opener to come up with *that*?"

Flaky blanched in the dark. "Don't know what you mean."

"Like hell you don't. Gonna call in your own Zulu, too. Ain't ya?"

Flaky defended himself meekly. " 'Course. I'm radio-man. I gotta call in casualties." He paused, studying Snake with practiced, apologetic deference. "Doc says it's O.K. Rabbit says it's a Heart."

"Yeah, but we know, don't we?" Snake shrugged, dismissing Flaky. There were more important things to worry about. "Hurry up and get two more so they'll send your young ass home, Fairchild. I'm sick of looking at you."

Flaky would never get shell shock: this way was easier.

Up the hill, in the center of the perimeter, a strobe light flashed, beckoning the medevac helicopters. The choppers circled widely, still very high, lightless to avoid gunfire. Two faceless headquarters people came and picked up Kerlovic. Snake hurried to him, grasping his hand tightly. "You lucky prick."

Kerlovic handed the radio handset to Snake. "Yeah, yeah. I *feel* lucky. Hey. Take care of yourself, Snakeman."

The helicopter spiraled down toward them as if it were caught in a tight, giant whirlpool, and then hovered above the strobe light. As it settled into the landing zone its shuddering rotors beat the dead night air and the perimeter was swept by angry turbulence. Snake turned his head away and down, protecting his eyes, and heard the scattered cracks of AK rifles. He looked up toward the treeline just in time to catch the sparkling flash of mortar tubes firing.

Gunships washed every inch of the treeline then, miniguns fanning through the trees, saturating it with spurts of luminescent tracers. But the mortar rounds were already in the air. Snake lay flat and heard the rounds impact behind him. BoomBoom. BoomBoom. BoomBoom. They landed on the far side of the hill, overshooting the zone.

Only two tubes firing. AK rifles instead of the big gun. Snake grunted knowledgeably in the helicopter's gale. The gooners have skyed out. That's just their rear.

Dust and poncho liners whipped through the air in the helicopter's wind. It shuddered out of the zone and disappeared into the black. The eerie, postmedevac silence hung like an extra burden on the ones left in the perimeter. Alone again.

Another hour leaked slowly from the night, like the last stale air from a punctured tire. The other medevacs were carried to the landing zone, those two extremes, the nonemergency and the dead. Snake sat dreaming of his cigarette, and finally could not resist. He lit it under a helmet and cupped it as he smoked, enjoying the smoky pain after hours of abstinence as much as a connoisseur enjoys a good cigar.

Ogre was carried past him, on the way to the LZ. Baby Cakes walked next to Ogre, refusing to be helped or carried. Snake grinned affectionately, waving to them. That, he remarked to himself, is one tough mother. Ain't anybody can outlast Baby Cakes. Ogre was talking with his high-pitched, languid words about eating pussy. Baby Cakes nodded drowsily, smiling to Ogre, mumbling a bit uncertainly. There it is, man. Uh huh. Gonna get some, too. Yeah.

There was a quick whoosh from outside the lines and a Green Star Cluster burst above them, casting the perimeter in a sickly haze for five quick seconds. The listening post was coming in. Homicide and Bagger crept toward the lines, exhausted, weighted down with poncho-liner blankets and a broken radio, in addition to their combat gear.

Then a sudden, echoing *boom* shook the predawn air. Snake sprinted to his fighting hole, meeting Homicide and Bagger as they reached the lines. Both were smirking vindictively. Homicide had a long, oozing slice along the side of his head. Hours of ooze had soaked the left side of his flak jacket. Nonetheless, he grinned comfortably.

Snake searched outside the lines. "What the hell was *that?*"

Homicide's black eyes flashed. "Them mohfuckas in that crater like to blow my ass away las' night. Jis' hadda kill 'em one more time, man." He scowled fiercely. "They's four of 'em in that crater. They *all* fucked up." He remembered. "How's Vitelli?"

"KIA."

Down the perimeter there were mutterings, lazy clunks of metal, silhouettes of tired figures in the bluing sky. First platoon was mounting out to check the treeline for kills and weapons. Bagger moved up beside Homicide, a stark contrast to him, short and meaty-thick, sandy hair almost to his eyes as he tossed his helmet to the ground. He spoke in a deep, syrupy Georgia drawl.

"God*damn!* Did they hit him again on the way in? We saw 'em open up on Cakes. Where's Baby Cakes?"

They stared silently at him. "Oh, no. *Him?*" Bagger stared down at his helmet, muttering. "I gotta get out of here."

Snake shook his head, in no mood to baby-sit. "Wrong. You gotta start thinking about what kind of team leader you're gonna make."

Bagger frowned morosely. "Come on, man. I ain't any team leader. I ain't anybody's boss. Besides, I only been here six weeks."

"You're the only one left in your team."

Bagger mulled it. "Well, can't get around that, can I? But I'm telling you right now I'll fuck it up."

"I already know that."

Snake collected his own gear and took it to the command post. What do you know, he thought, not altogether unpleasurably. And I'm platoon commander. For a little while. I can do it. Seven months of this and I can do it as good as any boot Lieutenant. Better.

At the command post Flaky was now dutifully manning the radio net. He looked up to Snake. "Six says we getting a new Actual today. Brand new Looey who just got into the rear."

"Groovy." Snake took his letter-writing gear from his pack, and opened the tablet. He wrote quickly in a tightly lettered scrawl.

"What you doing, Snake?"

"Writing a letter."

"That didn't take long."

"Didn't have much to say."

He found a can of C-ration fruit cocktail and opened it, eating hungrily. The sun was peeping over brown, rended earth, over fields scarred like an acned face, pocked and ripped by years of bombs and mortars. In another hour the sun would be so angry that it would not let them eat. He shed his flak jacket, pulled out a heat tablet from his low trouser pocket, and cooked up some cocoa in his canteen cup.

Flaky switched on his transistor. It was six o'clock. The radio blared out with a cheerful, optimistic voice that was sitting behind a microphone in the Other World of Da Nang.

"Goo-o-o-o-od *morning*, Vietnam!"

Snake lit a cigarette, stirring cocoa. First platoon was

halfway to the treeline. "Fu-u-u-uck him. What does he know about it?"

"About what?"

"Vietnam."

5.

Major Otto, the battalion executive officer, sat behind his field desk and examined Hodges' record book. He was young for a Major, in his early thirties. He seemed pleasant enough to Hodges, who had expected a hatchet-faced, ravening warrior after hearing of the Major's background. Otto had been a company commander during his first tour, and was highly decorated. His right forearm was gashed with a six-inch, purple trough left by a bone-shattering machine-gun bullet. And yet he had the inquisitive, sensitive demeanor of a brooding scholar.

He smiled casually to Hodges. "So. You think you're ready?"

Hodges stood at a loose parade rest in the musty heat of the tent. He was scheduled to attend three more days of regimental indoctrination school, but he had not found it helpful, and he had learned to hate the dust-filled boredom of An Hoa.

"Yes, sir. I'm ready."

"Think so? Good. They need you out there. Lost another Lieutenant last night." The Major watched him closely.

"Yes, sir. I heard."

"Yeah. Good old Dying Delta. They like to call themselves Deadly Delta. Hah." Otto chuckled. He had a beaten tone in his voice, as if he had seen the ritual so many times that it had lost its meaning. "Deadly Dying Delta."

Hodges watched him, dripping with sweat in the dark heat. Outside, a jeep rumbled past, leaving a wave of red dirt that seeped underneath the tent flap like creeping fog. In the distance, an artillery battery fired a mission toward the Arizona territory. The Major swiped at a fly, then lit a cigarette. As an afterthought, he offered one to Hodges.

"No, thank you, sir."

Major Otto sighed. "You'll learn." He dragged deeply on the cigarette, frankly studying Hodges. "Yeah. Dying Delta. You're not ready, Lieutenant. The only reason I'm telling you is I don't want you to panic when you get there and find out. Nothing in your entire goddamned life will have prepared you for the bush. Not a damn thing."

"Yes, sir."

"Do you know what I mean?"

"No sir."

"Jesus Christ." The Major dragged again on his cigarette. "Deadly Delta. Yeah. They really caught the shit last night."

"I watched it." It was almost embarrassing to admit it. He still felt uncomfortable about the irony of sitting on a bunker and watching someone else's war.

Otto leaned forward, absently rubbing the purple gash along his forearm. "Well, what kind of a person do you think goes through that shit day in and day out, Lieutenant? Because that's what it is. Shit. And that's the way you take it. Every stinking day. Something piddly-ass or something heavy. This isn't World War Two, where we can pull you out to Australia and a parade after a month of fighting. Nope. And it isn't 1965. When we first came into Vietnam we would send a company out on a two-day operation, then bring the men back for hot chow and liberty. Yeah. That's right. Liberty, Lieutenant. In Da Nang. Then we started week-long operations. Then it was a month. Now, well, we just leave 'em out there all the time. It's more convenient."

The Major offered Hodges a small, challenging smile. "They go wild, Lieutenant. And there's nothing you can do about it. You'll go wild, too. Wild as hell. You spend a month in the bush and you're not a Marine anymore. Hell. You're not even a goddamn person. There's no tents, no barbed wire, no hot food, no jeeps or trucks, no clean clothes. Nothing. You're an animal. It gets so that it's natural to squat when you take a shit. You get ringworm and hookworm and gooksores. You roll around in your own filth. You forget how bad you smell. Dead people, guts in the goddamn dirt, miserable civilians, it all gets sort of boring. You cry when your friends are killed, but a new friend comes in on the helicopter a few days later, and the dead friend becomes enshrined, a martyr to friendship. You teach the new friend about him, and you all remember him. It's very romantic."

"It doesn't sound very romantic."

"That's after a month. Or two. But Lieutenant. When you do it for *six*, or *nine*, or even longer, by Christ, you'll never shake it. The bush gets in your blood and you hate anyone who hasn't fermented in his own stench for months, or stood inside a dirt hole all night, waiting to kill a man who's trying to kill him first."

Major Otto scrutinized Hodges. "Oh, yeah. I've done a lot of thinking about it. That's something a grunt isn't supposed to do." He chuckled again, a sort of dry bark. "But what else can a man do in An Hoa? Oh. And An Hoa. It becomes an oasis. You like An Hoa, Lieutenant?"

"I hate it."

"You'll like it when you get back to it from the bush, I guarantee. So. What kind of person can take it, for months on end?"

Hodges felt uneasy. He had expected the Major to wave the flag and talk about Iwo Jima, then send him aboard the resupply helicopter with fire in his heart.

"Someone who is very dedicated, sir. Either that or someone who is very crazy."

"Well, there you are. That's it in a nutshell. You just hit the nail on the goddamn head."

Hodges continued to stand at a loose parade rest, watching Otto light another cigarette off the end of the one he was smoking. Otto again extended the cigarette pack to him. "You sure?"

"No, thank you, sir." Hodges stared solemnly at the Major. What does he want, he mused again and again.

"You see this?" Otto held out his arm. The bone was unnaturally curved, and the discolored scar shone like the vestige of a bad burn. "I got this a few miles from here. I thanked the fucking Lord the day I was hit, that this was all there was." Otto chuckled whimsically. "A few miles and a few years. Can you believe it? Here I am, back where I got my ticket home the first time, and the only thing that's changed is the people who are getting hit."

"Sir, I—"

"You're going to get hit, Lieutenant. You might as

well face it. You've got better than an eighty percent chance of getting hit. Did you know that?"

"I've heard a lot of figures. But I didn't know that. No, sir."

"How does that make you feel? Knowing you're going to get hit, I mean?"

Hodges felt the Major was taunting him. "I think I can handle it, Major. I've waited a long time to do this."

"Well, you won't have to wait much longer." Otto seemed to catch himself. "I'm supposed to be telling you to do a good job, to be a good Marine. Well, I want you to do a good job, and I know you will. And in a couple months, come back and see me, Lieutenant. We could talk, then. I'd like to know what you think about it. I don't mean the wild part. You can handle that. I mean the rest." Major Otto closed Hodges' record book, dismissing him. "Don't go out there thinking I was giving you a red-ass. I wasn't. I just look at you and say, 'that used to be me. But it isn't anymore.' "

Hodges made his way toward the Logistics Operations Center, where he would embark for the bush on a resupply helicopter. His conversation with Major Otto had left him feeling unsettled, and strangely jaded. I used to be Otto, Hodges mused, wondering at what the Major had left unsaid. No, he used to be me. But he isn't anymore. And in a month I won't be, either.

The helicopter rotor whipped red dirt into him like a thousand tiny darts, and he trundled clumsily up the rear door. He struggled under the weight of the gear he carried: flak jacket, helmet, pack, poncho, poncho liner blanket, four canteens of An Hoa water, an M-16 rifle, two bandoleers of ammunition, a LAAW rocket (carrying the disposable bazooka-like weapon more for effect than anticipated use), and the sundry odds and ends such as a towel and toothbrush that he had stuffed into his pack.

In five short minutes he was peering down at a mass of sawgrass and unpatterned lean-tos made of ponchos. Bronzed Marines in various stages of undress lay prostrate over their belongings, saving them from the rotorwash. A few poncho liners and pieces of C-ration cardboard whipped into the air from the helicopter's gale. Hodges

ran down the tailgate and into the weeds with a half-
dozen other new arrivals and stood lost in the middle of a
hundred scattered, apathetic figures who returned to cleaning weapons and writing letters as soon as the helicopter
departed.

Ho hum, joked Hodges to himself, vainly trying to dis-
cern order in the perimeter, wondering where the company
commander's hootch was. Another boot Lieutenant.

6.

The bomb crater was old and deep, as natural to the field
as would be a tree or dike. The shards of earth once set
loose from far into the earth had melted back into their
origins, two years of rain and sunbake having mended the
gaping wound, leaving only its memory in the deep pock
of a scar. A thin carpet of yellowed sawgrass continued
from the field down one side of it, as if an entranceway.
Hodges stood in the brittle grass at the crater's edge,
sweating freely from a skyful of sun, and peered down at
the first dead person he had ever seen.

Four, actually. The corpses leaned against the crater's
walls, two together here, the other two in individual death,
flat against the earth like bended reeds. There was a foot
gone on one of them, a blackened, gaping imperfection
with the beginnings of a tourniquet over it, the second
corpse dead underneath the foot. A head blown apart over
there, as if someone had killed the man again, in afterthought. Homicide had, earlier that morning. Weapons
and cartridge belts and parts of uniforms were gone,
spoils and souvenirs. All that remained were bodies.

Hodges looked closely at them. They were short-haired
and thin. Their skin was already beginning to singe with
rot. The killing wounds were black from the sun and their
edges were deep brown, the color of copper. Some jokester had placed a cigarette between the lips of one dead
enemy, no doubt for pictures. Another body held a similarly placed can of C-ration spaghetti in its lifeless fingers.

The flies had found them and they swarmed patiently around the wounds, looking for egg nests. In two days there would be great stenches. And maggots.

Flaky elbowed Hodges. There was a note of importance in his voice. "We got more over here, Lieutenant." As if he were offering up merchandise that was to be commented on instead of bought, and as if the comments themselves would be payment for his last night's travail, that Hodges dared to miss.

"Right over here."

Hodges followed the jaunting figure to a nearby dike. Behind the paddy dike, and in the narrow field beyond, there were five more dead men, similarly stripped of souvenirable parts, also surrounded by mobs of swarming flies.

"You all must have really been in the shit last night." There was a note in Hodges' voice that was almost envy: that every man on that barren piece of scarred earth, save him and the ones he brought with him on the resupply helicopter, had faced such a brutal test and had prevailed. And his only feat had been to sit on a bunker four miles away, in the regimental rear of An Hoa, and watch the tracers and the mortars land.

"There it is, Lieutenant. Been like this for ten days now. I'm the only one left from the CP. Me and Rabbit." Flaky was shrewdly sizing Hodges up. "Yup. I been radioman for three months. Already had me three lieutenants."

Hodges nodded absently. He had been hearing such stories since Basic School. Flaky still eyed him as he viewed the dead men, staring secretly at the set of his mouth and eyebrows, the squint of his eyes, the way he stood, looking for a way to work him.

"Where you from, Lieutenant?"

"Kentucky."

"*Kentucky?* Hey-y-y. Good old boy, all that shit. Right, sir? You should talk to Baby Cakes when he gets back. He got hit last night. Priority evac. He'll be back. He's from down there somewhere. Tennessee. Mississippi. One of them. And Bagger. He's from Georgia. And Cannonball. He's from one of them Carolinas. South, I think. Only he's—. Well, I know how you must feel about splibs, huh Lieutenant?"

"What's a 'splib'?"

"Splib. You know, sir. A neee-gro."

Hodges sensed he was being tested. He did not like Flaky, he had already decided. He looked icily at him for several seconds. "Fairchild, it's only been fifteen minutes and you already piss me off."

Flaky became immediately suppliant, retreating into his passive role. "I'm sorry, sir. No shit." He sought a means to change the subject, and finally held out his Instamatic camera to Hodges. "Sir, would you mind taking a picture for me? I asked some of the others and they all gave me a hard time."

Hodges shrugged absently, taking the camera. Flaky scratched his head excitedly and studied the field of dead men as if he were preparing to buy one off a rack. He selected a body that half-sat against the dike, shot in the face. "Perfect. C'mon, gook. We gonna take our flick together." He sat next to the dead man, adjusted the body so that its back was on the dike, then put his arm around it. Flies buzzed his face and he swiped at them, swearing. "O.K., Lieutenant. Knock yourself out."

Hodges stared through the lens at the smiling wisp of man, wondered about his sanity, and took three pictures. Flaky rejoined him. "Hey, thanks a lot, sir. Folks back home will never believe this if I don't send 'em flicks. They think we're all sitting around stoned, letting the B-fifty-twos do the killing."

Hodges gazed at the scattered corpses. "What are we gonna do with the bodies? They'll stink us out of here in a couple of days, won't they?"

Flaky gestured impatiently, immersed in his sudden importance as an expert on such things. "Ah, we move every couple days anyway. If we stay longer than a couple days in one spot the gooks figure us out and kick our asses. We'll probably move tomorrow."

"And just leave 'em here?"

"Hell, yeah. I mean, yessir. Villagers'll bury 'em. Or their buddies." Flaky stared almost threateningly at Hodges. "You think you're gonna get a Marine to sweat out there in the field to bury a gook that tried to kill him last night?"

Hodges walked slowly back to the perimeter, and then to his platoon CP. Last night's agonies were clearly visible. The rent poncho hootch of his predecessor still sagged where the mortar rounds had blasted it. There was a large scab of blood on the hard dirt next to it, and the ground was still littered with used battle dressings and tatters of clothing.

Ten feet away from the hootch he saw the man's boot. He almost retched. It appeared to be a bad omen to him. Walk a mile in my shoes. Hell, yeah. Flies buzzed through the air, landing on morsels scattered through the CP.

"Fairchild, I want a burn call. That hootch. All the battle dressings. Pieces of torn gear. That boot—"

"*Lieutenant.* Sir. That boot's got part of him *in* it."

Hodges felt the itchings of a deep rage crawling up his neck. He could not decide whether it was his dislike for Flaky or his threatening nausea. He put his face within a foot of Flaky's.

"If you want to save it, put it in your fucking *pack*. It ain't doing the man any good laying here feeding flies, is it? Burn call, Fairchild. Like now."

Fairchild grumbled off, daintily gathering bloodied pieces of clothing and the battle dressings. Hodges erected his own poncho hootch, carefully distant from the dead corpsman's and the departed Lieutenant and Kerlovic's. Then he sat near the platoon radio, pretending to study his map, but instead studying the clumps of men, browned by sun and dust, who now comprised his platoon.

They were a wild-looking bunch. He realized for the first time that the groups of dirty ruffians on Okinawa had been tame compared to the grunts. The ones down the hill from him were grubby and unshaven, motionless with apathy. Near one fighting hole, two deeply tanned figures played a bored hand of back alley, tossing cards and scoring as if the game were somehow a burden. Most of the others were asleep, exhausted from the night before, huddled underneath the shade of poncho hootches. Virtually all of them were stripped down to tiger shorts and boots because of the intense heat and the almost-barren hill.

They were, he decided, surveying them with a tentative affection, the kind who would say *no*. He found he could not define it further. They simply emanated a weird sort of stubbornness, not really hostile, perhaps not even conscious on their part. Like they've all been beat and one more *fuck you* to some mindless order isn't gonna sink them any deeper, and they know it, he mused.

He surveyed the squalid, ramshackle city of jerry-rigged poncho hootches that was the perimeter. Scavenged sticks and strands of bootlace supported makeshift poncho homes. Incredible, he thought. That the air-conditioned, stewardess-patrolled flight, that all the starch and salutes of Da Nang, that the huge tents and bunkers of An Hoa's regimental rear would boil down to this. And beyond him on all sides, the quaint repetitions of gentle ridges filled with treelines and villages, adrift in veritable seas of rice.

Twenty meters down the hill, across a plain of scraggled grass and brittle bushes, Snake was interviewing his new dudes. He talked with them, one at a time, assigning them to fire teams and trying to think of names for them. Everyone had a name. More often than not, Snake decided what it would be. Today there were four new dudes. He had already interviewed Shag (the name carried over from civilian days) and O'Brien (a name would come in time), who had become the property of a thoroughly bewildered Bagger.

He now peered at a man who was only slightly taller than he, and almost as wiry. The man was small-faced, with wild, active eyes. His hair was thick and curly, deep brown, shot with red highlights. His face and entire body appeared mottled with light freckles, over very light, almost pallid skin.

The small face parted in a devilish challenge of a sneer as the new dude dropped his pack in front of Snake. "Lurch already started calling me Wild Man."

Snake's eyebrows raised. He pushed his glasses into his face. "Lurch calls you that?" The man nodded, still grinning. "Why'd he call you that?" Snake pondered it a moment. "We already had a Wild Man. He wasn't like you." Snake sized the man up. "He got shot."

The man was unbothered by the omen. "Lurch already told me. So what, anyway?" The new dude shrugged impatiently. "Look, man. I couldn't give a shit, know what I mean? I came here to kill gooks. You can call me any damn thing you want." The wild eyes flashed a warning. The smile reappeared. "Long as you smile when you say it."

Snake remained curious. "Why'd Lurch say you should be Wild Man?"

" 'Cause I was gonna shoot him. Nah. That's not right. I just called him is all. M-sixteens. Across the tent. He wouldn't go. No balls."

Snake ogled him unbelievingly. "Nah-h-h. Did you really do that?" Wild Man-elect nodded comfortably, folding his arms as if resting his case.

Snake turned to his fourth new arrival, who sat near him, smoking nervously as he eyed the unfamiliar sights of the perimeter. "Did he really do that?"

"I'm sorry?" The fourth man had been rather dazedly scanning the perimeter, oblivious to the conversation.

"Well, don't be sorry, sweetheart, just answer my goddamn question!" Snake laughed and the fourth man seemed mildly stunned. "Did numbnuts here really do that?"

"Do what?"

"Call Lurch with his M-sixteen. In the rear."

The fourth man gazed briefly at Wild Man-elect and smiled exasperatedly, shaking his head. "From what I could hear while I was getting my ass out of the way, I'd say yeah. He really did that."

Snake took on an air of humorous excitement, reaching the level of a grudging respect. "Well, you're crazy as hell, you know that? Why'd you wanna do old Lurch? He's a Number One dude, man. Even used to be a grunt."

Wild Man shrugged easily, still sneering. "Didn't really *want* to. Dig? But he was pulling some lame shit, man. Really bugging me, know what I mean? Called me across the tent like I was his goddamn servant, just 'cause he runs the working parties. Like he was some kind of whip cracker. I don't mind working parties, but I couldn't let him get away with *that*. Corporal. Kiss my ass. Wasn't anything else I could do. Anyway. He said he was sorry. And I believe him."

Snake was convinced. He laughed almost enviously. "Whooeee. O.K. You are sure enough Wild Man. But don't pull any of that out here. I ain't got time to baby-sit you."

Wild Man grinned confidently, stroking his M-16. "I don't need no baby-sitter. You gonna have to run to keep up with me, Snake-man. I came to kill. Old Luke the Gook better be saying his damn Hail Marys."

Snake contemplated Wild Man for an instant, then decided. "I was gonna give you to Cat Man. But I think Bagger could use you. He needs help, man. You get on down to Bagger's hole."

As Wild Man departed, Snake eyed his fourth man and leaned back against his pack, lighting a cigarette. The man looked awestruck and childlike, swaddled in the bright greens of new-issued clothes and flak jacket and gear. His face had the air of a child viewing his first circus.

Snake nodded humorously to him. "So what are you 'sorry' about?"

The man scanned the perimeter, searching for some sort of order or structure in its apparent randomness. He warmed tentatively to Snake, laughing at himself. "Well, the last six months, for starters!" He motioned toward the lines and squinted to Snake. "Hey, man. This is scary. Where the hell are we and where the hell are *they*?"

Snake put his finger to the dirt. *"We* are here." He then made a circle in the air. *"They* are everywhere else."

The man still attempted to determine the reaches of the perimeter. Poncho hootches seemed scattered everywhere. He squinted again. "I still can't make any sense of it."

"Don't worry. We'll point you in the right direction in your fighting hole tonight." Snake dragged slowly on his cigarette, studying the man. "What's your name, man?"

"Goodrich. Will Goodrich." The man smiled faintly. "Like the blimp."

"Blimp."

"You know—the Goodrich blimp?"

"Your old man owns a blimp?"

"No. It was—"

"What the hell you talking about a blimp for?"

"It was supposed to be a joke."

Snake grimaced. "Some joke." He finished his visual examination. "You *look* like a goddamn blimp. How much you weigh, man?"

Goodrich's eyes danced and his fleshy face beamed good-naturedly. He pulled on a rubber nose and leaned forward. "Well, you see, that's why I decided to come to Vietnam. My doctor told me to stay away from rich foods for a while."

Snake begrudged him a tolerant smile. "You're about

three kinds of weird, you know that?" He flipped his cigarette across the dusty hill. "Shag says you been to college. Says you went to Harvard. That right?" He did not wait for a response. "We had a couple dudes with college, you know, like Vitelli, he had two years of it somewhere. He got killed last night. But what the hell is somebody from Harvard doing out here?"

Goodrich shrugged resignedly. "Oh, shit. I wish I knew."

"No, really."

"I failed philosophy."

Snake nodded slightly, able to empathize with that. "So how'd you end up in the Corps? Get drafted?"

Goodrich leaned forward and put a cigarette between his teeth. He lit it, grinning fraternally to Snake. "There was this recruiter, see?"

Snake nodded amusedly. "Roger that. They were gonna make you an officer and they screwed you, right?"

"No no no. They were gonna let me play in the band."

"The *band?*"

"Yeah. I play French horn." Goodrich smiled with perverse pride. "I'm really quite good. I was on scholarship. Three years. The guy says, 'Sure, kid. Sign right here. We got all kinds of bands.' And the next thing I knew I was a grunt."

Snake slapped his narrow thigh, laughing. "Oh, Jesus. You are a fucking original, you know that? We *never* had one of you before." He scrutinized Goodrich. "I gotta come up with a good nickname for you."

Goodrich was leery of being branded. "Why don't you hold off for a while, like with O'Brien? Hey, man. I'm *full* of surprises."

"Harvard. That's one of the places that gives us all these Senators and Congressmen and Secretaries that never know their ass from first base about what goes on in the street. Or over here. The only time you ever see 'em is in the goddamn papers. They must live under rocks. But you always see 'em in the papers. 'Senator Goodrich says the war must go on.' You gonna be one of them Senators some day, Goodrich? I bet you are."

"Well, my father's a lawyer, but—" Goodrich laughed embarrassedly, realizing he had actually taken Snake's jibe seriously.

"Well, that's it." Snake grinned devilishly. "Perfect. We got our own Senator now."

Senator chuckled helplessly and shook his head. "I guess it could be worse. I suppose you could have called me Blimpy, or something." He considered it. "Senator. Hmmm. It has a nice ring to it. Wait till I write home and tell them how fast promotions are in the Corps."

Snake put a hand on Goodrich's shoulder. "You go to Speedy's team, Senator. Better speak straight to him, 'cause he don't know much English. Dig?"

Snake turned toward a distant fighting hole and yelled. "Speedy! *Ve baca!* Got some new meat for ya!"

Speedy jogged up to Snake's hole, thick and very dark, his black skivvy shirt stained by patches of dust. He grinned widely to Snake. Snake gestured to Goodrich. "This here is Senator. He's all yours."

As Goodrich turned to leave, Snake grasped his shoulder, unable to shake one last premonition from his subconscious. "Hey, Senator. You're not a CID, are ya?"

Goodrich was caught off balance. "A what?"

"A CID. You know. C - I - D."

Goodrich was confused. "I don't even know what a CID is, man." The only connection he could make was *El Cid*. That can't be it, he fretted. "Unless it's a status that I'm unaware of, as opposed to a conscious state, I don't think you can say I'm one, no."

Snake peered at Goodrich as if he'd just spoken Chinese, then slapped his shoulder jocularly. "Whoooeee. They teach you that kind of double-talk at Harvard? Oh, well. You ain't any CID, I know that. Not even a CID could think up that kind of smoke screen. Hey, listen. You better be glad, Senator. We got people who like to do CIDs, know what I mean?"

Goodrich smiled uneasily, getting the general idea. "Yeah, I guess I'm glad I'm not one, too."

Goodrich walked with Speedy to the fighting hole. Inside it sat a tall, gaunt man with a shock of brilliant blond hair and a wispy yellow moustache, absently scrubbing his M-16 with a toothbrush. He turned a thin face up to Goodrich and quickly measured him, then smiled and wiped the end of his spaded nose with the back of his hand, catching a bead of sweat.

Speedy stood with Goodrich. "Burgie, this here is Senator."

Burgie raised his eyebrows, a greeting. "What's going down, anyway. Helmut Ottenburger. Don't ask me. It's my real name. Chicago. Dig it. I got drafted. Don't take any shit off the greaser here."

Speedy suddenly jumped into the fighting hole and threw Ottenburger's fresh-cleaned weapon into the dirt, in three pieces. The bolt rolled down the hill and disappeared inside a mat of grass. The two wrestled furiously, spilling out of the hole onto their gear. They swore at each other. Goodrich was startled, then realized that both were laughing.

Burgie was pinned to the ground. Speedy sat on top of him. "You fucker. I'll kill your ass."

"Hold it, man. Hey. Enough of this. Let me up."

"Tell Senator you're sorry."

Burgie laughed, trying to roll Speedy off him. "Hey, Senator. Use your influence. Get this greaser off my chest."

Goodrich stood awkwardly, watching them. He had not even set his pack down yet. Finally the burly Puerto Rican cuffed Ottenburger on the side of the head and let him up, then turned and smiled to Goodrich.

"Thinks 'cause he's six-three he's tough. Put your gear here, man. You know how to make a hootch?"

"Not like that."

"Get your poncho out. I'll show you."

They approached Hodges slowly, singly or in twos and threes, like hesitant, wild animals inspecting their latest zookeeper. It occurred to him, as he watched them pay a sort of reluctant homage to his poncho hootch, that he really did have the power of life and death over them. If I'm bad, he mused, while making small talk and tentative attempts at humor with them, they die. It's that simple. Remembering the stories from Basic School, he understood immediately why an individual would want to wound an incompetent officer with a grenade. It's not vindictiveness, he reasoned. It's self-preservation.

But he felt an immediate, visceral kinship with most of them, and sensed that it was mutual. He perceived the autocratic excellence of Snake from their first meeting.

The small, hostile man with the large tattoos on each arm seemed driven by a need to dominate this weed-filled existence that the others were merely submitting to. Snake was the least friendly to Hodges, and yet Hodges sensed that he was potentially a natural ally. Snake's self-image was at stake. For the others, it was merely their lives.

Hodges had asked Snake where he was from. Snake had shrugged, peering unemotionally into the center of Hodges' face.

"I ain't from anywhere, Lieutenant. It's me and Mother Green, the Killing Machine. Till death do us part."

Then the others, as in a procession. They were rough and wild and dirty, and they spoke a dialect that was geographically undiscernible, with minor variations of tone and pitch, as if they had all been recruited out of the same small town. Groovy. Wow. Number One. Number Ten. There it is, man. A bust for your dust. What a bummer. But it don't mean nothing.

And yet, with most of them it was an unconvincing toughness. Beyond the talk and the antics they appeared confused and vulnerable, unsure of their own existence and thus as malleable as clay.

Pierson's squad approached and left, in twos and threes. Then both machine-gun teams, curious and not yet willing to accept him. Doc Rabbit and Flaky, who comprised his entire command post after the action of the preceding weeks, languished near him. Flaky was ingratiating. Rabbit moodily ignored him.

And also Snake's squad. Speedy and Burgie paid him a perfunctory visit. They were a study in opposites: Ottenburger tall and thin, with white-blond hair and a careless, laughing manner, talking in quick sentences about truck driving, his great passion. Ramirez short, thickly muscled, and as dark as his black skivvy shirt, a contained, serious man who carefully measured his words and movements. Goodrich, who had come out in the resupply helicopter with Hodges, accompanied them but said nothing. He appeared deeply confused by his new surroundings.

Cat Man ambled past after picking up ammunition from Flaky for his fire team. He walked with a feline delicacy, and yet each of his movements conveyed a sure, muscular firmness. Like a mountain lion, Hodges mused, trying to categorize the small Mexican according to his nickname.

Cat Man had a quick smile, and said almost nothing, but his eyes measured Hodges continuously. They examined his face. They took in the muscle tone along his arms and back. They noted the calluses on his hands, and even the way he had laced and tied his boots. They missed nothing, and in a two-minute visit, without so much as a dozen words, Hodges knew that Cat Man had gone over his new platoon commander with the completeness of an enemy intelligence expert.

Some stayed longer than others. Bagger, who seemed to require Hodges' attention and approval, insisted on inspecting Hodges' poncho hootch for him, supposedly to ensure that it would not collapse. Bagger had a squatty, powerful build, with thick shoulders and arms that drooped ape-like in front of him as he walked. His toes pointed too far outward, giving him a curious, swaying waddle each time he stepped. From a distance he appeared ominous, but his face gave him away. It was wide and confused, a squinting child's, as if the world's riddles were a continual bafflement.

Bagger brought Hodges a cookie from a package his wife had sent, and then used the occasion to display a whole string of pictures. In five minutes Hodges had a history of their whole love affair, beginning with their first date after a football game his junior year in high school.

Bagger grew increasingly frustrated as he showed Hodges the pictures. He finished by shaking his head and stuffing the pictures back into the plastic bag he carried. "Lieutenant, she knows how bad I am. I ain't kidding, sir. I'll do my best, Lieutenant. You can count on that. But I ain't any team leader."

Then Cannonball, Bagger's sidekick, who had accompanied the squatty Georgian on the visit to Hodges' hootch. Cannonball wore only his camouflage tiger shorts and his jungle boots. He smiled good-humoredly to Hodges, and sat down in the shade next to his hootch, quietly watching as Bagger showed Hodges the pictures.

Cannonball was built tightly onto a tall, thin frame. A humorous, almost apologetic smile dominated his expression, as if he had just pulled off a highly successful practical joke. And the smile lit his hazel eyes: they too laughed. His hair was in a modified Afro, but was colored with mixed tints of brown, not black. His skin was creamy, the color of dry grass.

Cannonball seemed shy, almost painfully sensitive. Most of his remarks to Hodges were indirect, through a running, chiding criticism of Bagger.

And in a moment Phony, whom Bagger had identified as the coolest in the squad with a grenade—the "frag man." He had sauntered up, appearing to be anything but the cold-nerved battler that Bagger had made him out to be. He was the wearer of an angel's face: innocent warm brown eyes behind long lashes that batted almost effeminately when he blinked, a flawless, unbearded complexion, and the gentlest of smiles. His limbs and body were unmarked by muscle tone, covered with a prepubescent smoothness, a form of baby fat that seemingly blanketed his bones, even in his thinned-out bush condition.

As he walked toward them, Bagger whispered confidentially to Hodges, "Don't get uptight, Lieutenant, but Phony don't call nobody 'sir.' We had a dude, Wild Man Number One, who was in boot camp with him, and he *never* called any DI sir. That's what Wild Man said. He don't mean nothing, Lieutenant. He'll call you 'Lieutenant.' But don't let it get to you. He's been in more jails than I ever heard of, but he's solid when the shit hits the fan. He just don't like to call people 'sir.' "

Cannonball nodded, smiling wryly. "Yeah, you know, like Snake always says. Old Phony don't argue with *nobody*. You piss him off, he just *do* you."

On one smooth arm there was a red-devil tattoo. *Born to Raise Hell,* the devil intoned. Hodges grinned weakly, wondering how much of Bagger's and Cannonball's talk was hype.

Phony waved to Bagger. "What's happening, Bag-man?" He waved again, to Hodges. "Well, hey, Lieutenant. You see my gooks?"

Hodges squinted. *"Your* gooks."

"Yeah. The ones in the crater. I done 'em. Boom-boom."

Cannonball pointed toward the crater. "Yeah, Lieutenant. You should have seen it. Snake, he figured it, but old Phony done it. Ain't nobody can chuck a frag like Phony."

Phony smiled, chewing a wad of C-ration gum. "Boom-boom."

Cannonball nodded, grinning. "Boom-boom."

The sun began to fall into the western mountains. The perimeter of men gathered in small clumps about their four-man fighting holes, making dinner and preparing for another night in hell.

Goodrich sat in a tight circle with Speedy and Burgie, cooking his dinner. Finally he gathered the courage to ask.

"Burgie. What the hell is a CID?"

"A CID? A CID is a snoop, man."

"Is that all?"

"Yeah. Works for Criminal Investigation Division, something like that. Turns dudes in for stuff."

"Like what?"

"Oh. Just about anything. We don't like CIDs."

Bagger and Cannonball sat together, surveying the three prospective victims of his immaturity, his new fire team. Bagger appeared bewildered.

"Cannonball. Tell these poor bastards what the hell they're in for, with stupid me as team leader."

Cannonball addressed the group, again by chiding Bagger. "What can I say, Bag-Man? All that shit las' night, and you the only one in your team come away clean. You must be doin' somethin' right!"

Bagger shook his head miserably. "Aw, Cannonball. That ain't even funny."

Wild Man leaned forward eagerly. "Man, that must have been some real shit. That cat Baby Cakes—what a dude, man! Everybody's talking about him today. And the other one—Ogre, crawling in to get him. Then him running out there into all the gooks—I saw the crater—he must be some kind of cool, man."

Bagger agreed, a bit mournfully. "There it is. But you'll see. He'll be back. Him and Ogre. Then they'll get their teams back, and you'll see what it means to have a team leader. Shee-it. I wouldn't make a pimple on that man's ass."

Wild Man was still curious. "So Phony did the gooks in the crater, with the team on the other side. Some shot, man."

Phony was sitting twenty feet away, listening to his transistor radio and cooking up some C-rats. He called to Wild Man. "Ain't nothing to it."

"Is there any trick?"

"Nah." Phony stared at Wild Man for a moment, never

losing his smile. Then he walked to his fighting hole and picked up a grenade. "You just hold it like this—"

Bagger blanched. "Don't, Phony. Goddamn, we'll catch so much—"

"And let the spoon fly like this!"

"Oh, Christ!" Bagger lay flat, holding his ears. *"Fire in the hole!"*

There was a sudden boom inside the crater. Dust and dead flesh flew into the air. Along the lines, in the other parts of the perimeter, there were surprised, querulous howls. At the command post the radio screeched with interrogatories from the company commander. Snake and Hodges ran to where Phony now stood, nonchalantly grinning in the midst of a group of sprawled, surprised new dudes.

Snake confronted Phony. "What the hell is going on?"

Phony answered amiably, his head bobbing as he talked. "Aw, they was asking me about how I done it last night and the only way to tell 'em was, you know, to show 'em." He shrugged helplessly. "So I showed 'em."

Wild Man grinned hugely, his active eyes in awe of Phony. "What a shot! You are *crazy,* man! You are crazy as *hell!*"

Snake shook his head, glancing at Hodges, then took Phony's shoulder. "You keep it up, Phony, and somebody's gonna lock you in the brig."

7.

From the air they would have been barely visible, a half-mile string of burdened green ants, struggling up a kidney-shaped, foliated anthill.

In the weeds where the wind would not blow, Bagger sweated freely into his flak jacket, shirtless underneath it, and adjusted one of his pack straps. It was cutting deep into a shoulder. "If this is Tuesday," he drawled wryly to no one in particular, knocking a branch out of his way, "it must be Phu Phong four."

The ville, designated on American maps as the fourth hamlet in the village of Phu Phong, and hence, Phu Phong (4), was one of many frequent perimeters used by the Marines in their random wanderings across the valley floor. Four hundred meters across at its widest point, it sat on a high, kidney-shaped mound, covered with trees and shrubs and high weeds, scarred by years of bombing, and dotted with ragged, straw-thatched hootches.

From the heights of Phu Phong (4), Hodges got his first clear look at the layout of the Arizona Valley. To the west, beyond three other similar mounds that made a bumpy line toward the village, was the only prominent terrain feature in the valley: Razorback Ridge jutted bald and high and rounded, like the back of a huge pink hog, out from the blue-green gloominess of the wall of western mountains. In all other directions from the village there were wide seas of rice paddies, brown with harvest rice, dotted with lower villages and occasional treelines that floated like islands in the rice.

Far to the south, over the wide cut of an oozing river, Hodges could just make out the brick-red trail of dust that was puffing up from east to west, as if someone was sky-writing on the Basin floor. The morning convoy from Da Nang, twenty-five miles west and north, was grinding its way toward the regimental combat base at An Hoa. Far southwest there were the red scarred hills, the high claydust mist of An Hoa itself. Three, perhaps four miles away, but unreachable and thus irrelevant, except when it came time for resupply or artillery support.

The Arizona Valley was a veritable island. A northern river separated it from the calmer Dai Loc District, where there was access to Da Nang. The southern river cut it off from the rest of the An Hoa Basin, where there were two artillery bases—at Liberty Bridge and An Hoa—a Vietnamese Popular Force compound at Duc Duc near An Hoa, and a road capable of transporting the convoy. The northern and southern rivers came together at the eastern tip of the valley, where Liberty Bridge sat just beyond their confluence. And to the west, as all around the larger basin that held the valley, canopied mountains rose like foliated skyscrapers, unpopulated barriers that stretched all the way to distant Laos. The North Vietnamese owned the mountains.

Phu Phong (4) was the highest village in the valley, and an ideal fighting perimeter for the Marines. Hedges and holes would provide good cover and concealment. The draws of the hill, and the open, sweeping paddies would give good fields of fire if they were attacked.

The company went on line and swept toward the far edge of the hill, moving slowly past ragged hedges, clumps of hootches, clusters of junk and dented cooking pans, torn straw matting, stench-filled waterbull pens, and staring, stolid villagers. Hodges noticed the evidence of other warring units as they swept. There were dozens of fighting holes along the fringes of the hill, many so old that weeds had claimed them. There were old mortar pits, and dozens of burn holes and straddle trenches. Worn portions of the villagers' thatch roofs were often patched with C-ration boxes or strips of American ponchos.

As the company dug into its new positions Hodges strode the hill, examining it. At its very crest was a long, Z-shaped trench, chest-deep and as wide as a man's body. It was perfectly sculpted, the walls of the trench absolutely parallel. In the middle of the trench, just to one side of it, was a large, circular hole, four feet deep and about six feet across, with the earth left in the middle of it as a perfectly cylindrical post. It seemed to him to be a work of engineering genius.

He called Snake to the trench. "What is this? I've never seen anything like it."

Snake scratched a tattoo, bronzed and shirtless in the heat. "Everybody likes this hill, Lieutenant. That's the way the gooks set up." Snake jumped into the trench, demonstrating. "They don't need any circle. They don't need to protect all those radios and shit. If a man stands in this trench he can blow you away no matter which side of the hill you come charging up."

Hodges pointed to the circular post. "What about that?"

"That's a machine-gun pos. Prob'ly a fifty-cal. Maybe a twelve-seven. You put a tripod on the post and get down in that hole and you can fire three-sixty degrees, keep a bead on a jet coming and going, hardly even expose yourself."

"That's stomp-down amazing."

"Hey, Lieutenant." Snake measured his new Brown Bar carefully, not yet accepting him. "Old Luke the Gook don't screw around."

Snake sat comfortably at the edge of the NVA trench, peering steadily at Hodges. Finally he grimaced. "You shouldn't of made Flaky burn that boot. Sir. Bad style. It stunk."

"It would've stunk anyway."

"My new man Senator threw up."

"I was sick of looking at it. What a mess. Don't you ever clean up?" Hodges studied the man who had already shown himself to be the most proficient member of his platoon. "What would *you* have done?"

"I'da buried it."

"Then why didn't you?"

"Sir?"

"Why didn't you? You had the CP for half a day. You sat up there with all those flies and shit. You were acting platoon commander. If it pissed you off so bad, why didn't *you* bury it?"

Snake smiled slightly, surveying Hodges with fresh interest. " 'Cause I don't like dead stuff. I never touch dead stuff. I just leave it alone."

"Well, I don't like dead stuff, either." Hodges' eyebrows lifted and he offered Snake a grin. "That's why I burn it."

Snake shrugged, satisfied. "O.K. Lieutenant. I just never seen it before. It made my man Senator get sick, I told you."

"Yeah." Hodges sat across from Snake. He took out a pocketknife and cut himself a plug of chewing tobacco that had come in a Supplementary Pack, along with cigarettes, candy, and writing gear in the resupply. He pulled his map from a lower trouser pocket, and studied it, then looked to Snake.

"We're gonna ambush Nam An two tonight. Half the platoon. Your squad and a gun team and me."

Snake lit a cigarette, staring coolly at Hodges. "Did you think this up yourself, Lieutenant?"

"Are you crazy? I got nothing against Nam An two." The two men smiled at each other with a tentative fraternity. "Know any good places?"

Snake took out his own map, pondered it, then peered down the hill into the paddies, scanning the narrow string of trees across from them that marked a heavily used speed trail. Nam An two was one mile down the trail. "There's a little cemetery just off the speed trail, maybe a hundred meters from the ville. We could put a gun on the trail. Easy to defend in the cemetery. Might make a Number One ambush." He eyed his new Lieutenant. "Long as we gotta go."

"Yeah. Well, we do. Skipper's breaking me in, or something. Says we'll have a good shot at the gooks if they move down the trail toward the company tonight. Hell, I don't know. Says we should have first shot."

"He's all heart, ain't he?" Snake watched Hodges spit a stream of brown tobacco juice into the dirt. "You really chewing that SP tobacco, sir?"

Hodges nodded casually. "It ain't that bad."

"Bagger says he wouldn't give it to his horse for worms. If he *had* a horse. And it *had* the worms." They laughed together. "Only thing that ragweed's good for is feeding gooks who won't answer questions. *Fucks them up*, Lieutenant! One swallow of that and they sing like stoolies." Hodges shook his head, amused at Snake's quick humor.

Snake reached into his lower trouser pocket and pulled out a pack of Marlboros. "Here, Lieutenant. Have a smoke."

"I've been trying to cut back. Bad for your wind."

"You gonna worry about that out *here?* Hey, Lieutenant. We are *all* sucking wind."

Hodges shook his head, still amused, and took a Marlboro. He spat out the chewing tobacco and rinsed his mouth with canteen water. "Bagger's right. It tastes terrible." He casually placed the remainder of the plug into his low trouser pocket.

"You *keeping* the rest of it?"

" 'Course I am." Hodges grinned, his amused face thanking Snake for teaching him this latest Lesson Learned in Vietnam. "For gooks."

Phu Phong (4) had three good wells, deep concrete holes with raised portions of earth at the base. The French had built them for the villagers. They sat at the base of the village's steep hill, equally spaced along a wide, dusty trail that ringed the village on a paddy dike. The dike itself was thick and high, separating the village from the surrounding fields. Hundreds of smaller, lower dikes latticed the paddies in a maze that somehow held deep certainties to farmers.

Marines flocked to the wells in groups of twos and

threes, refilling canteens and washing. Village children gathered and gazed somberly at their frolics, standing off of the trail in the dry bush. The babysans were sickly and unwashed.

Goodrich leaned over a concrete hole, drawing water out of it with a half-gallon can that had once held apple juice supplied to the Marines. The can was left by some other company that used Phu Phong, and made into a bucket by the villagers. Goodrich worked the rope, pulling the can of clear, sweet water from the black hole, and poured it over his face, drinking thirstily. The move to the Phu Phongs had exhausted him.

He then turned to Speedy, handing him the can. "I really think those kids hate us." Goodrich spoke as though the feasibility had never crossed his mind.

Speedy tossed the can into the well and let it sink, then drew it back up. He found Goodrich's comments perplexing, naive. "We try to kill their papa, Senator. This whole valley VC." Speedy gorged himself on village water.

"That's a hell of a note." Goodrich forced a winsome smile. "It'll take a little getting used to. I just hadn't expected to be hated. Not by them."

Speedy drew another pail of water, mildly irritated. "Ah. It don't mean nothing, Senator." His wide, brown face went orgasmic as cool water poured over it again. "We get over to the Phu Nhuans, on the other side of the river, the kids are better. They hustle for you. Fill canteens, help wash you, stuff like that. We give 'em C-rats and cigarettes for it. It's all right." He attempted to console Goodrich, himself unconcerned with staring children. "It's better over there. You'll see."

Speedy scrutinized Goodrich, who was still studying the children, apparently lost in thought. It appeared that Goodrich was becoming upset. Speedy finally ran at the babysans, throwing his arms out threateningly. *"Didi,* you little fuckers! *Didi mau len!"*

The children stared at their attacker for an unfrightened moment, then turned and walked solemnly through the brush, back up the hill. Goodrich held the water can over one of his canteens, filling it.

"You didn't have to do that, Speedy. I didn't *mind* them, really. I just can't help feeling sorry for them."

Speedy's flat face cocked curiously and he grimaced to

Goodrich. "Make up your *mind*, Senator." He looked back through the brush. "Those little sons of bitches'll *do* your ass, I mean it." He took the bucket from Goodrich and tossed it back into the black hole of the well. "Don't feel sorry for 'em, Senator. You give 'em chow, their old man eats it tomorrow night. You turn your back"—the brown face splashed with water again—"they steal everything you got. Grenades. Everything."

Speedy took a long drink, then peered philosophically at Goodrich. "Those little babysans are devils, man. No shit. Devils."

"I still can't help it. I mean it. None of this is *their* fault."

"Well, none of this is *our* fault, either." Speedy stared solemnly at Goodrich. "Do yourself a favor, Senator. Frag yourself and get the hell outa here before you crack up. You don't belong here. Know what I mean?"

The stand of trees loomed like a low black cloud in front of them. Goodrich watched it grow larger, strained to find some light or movement that would disclose the great chimera that sat among the sunbaked branches, waiting to scorch him dead. The column seemed to jet along through the knee-deep rice. Goodrich fought reluctantly to keep the pace. Too fast, he mused loudly, the thought echoing through the chambers of his fear. We'll walk right into them and when we get five feet away they'll kill us all. I've heard the stories. Who the hell's on point? Doesn't he know they'll kill us all? What will I do? Can't hear anything but clonks of LAAWs and bandoleers and rice swish on my legs I'm thirsty need a drink. What if I just take out a grenade and pull the pin and hold it so when they start to kill us I can throw it at them how will I know where to throw it I can't see a fucking *thing* not even Burgie and I could reach out and touch Burgie he's that close look at the trees now we're so close we could die at any moment who the hell is walking *point?*

Thud. Goodrich tripped over Ottenburger, who was squatting in the rice. He fell down next to him, the echoes of his bandoleers a scream inside the ear horn that was his helmet. Burgie grasped him quickly and held him to the earth.

"Lay chilly, Senator. They're peeping out the treeline."

Goodrich sat very still, then turned his head slowly toward the trees. The whole column was kneeling, motionless, frozen like a picture, swallowed by rice. It was so quiet he could hear the distant booms of artillery shooting out of An Hoa with a clarity that seemed to come from just on the other side of the looming trees.

Four silhouettes crept soundlessly from the treeline then, rifles ready, moving toward the column. Goodrich felt his eyebrows raise and pointed his M-16. Burgie pressed the rifle back into the rice.

"Take it *easy*, Senator. That's Cat Man."

Cat Man set his team in at the edge of the treeline and moved to a low dike where Snake and Hodges were kneeling. He knelt next to them, pushed his helmet back, and leaned over. He addressed Snake, ignoring Hodges.

"Too much shit in there, man."

Hodges whispered. "It's the right trail, ain't it? We follow it for a click and we're there."

Cat Man shook his head. Snake looked coolly at Hodges. "Cat Man's right, Lieutenant. We take the trail, we may never make it there. Too many dogs and water bulls, shit like that. They'll start barking and grunting and the gooks'll hear us coming, blow our asses away. Don't take that treeline, sir."

Hodges nodded, acquiescing. Then, as an afterthought: "You can find the cemetery all right from the paddy?"

Cat Man measured him without emotion. Starting from a known point, his mind was its own map. "Yes, sir."

The column cut quickly through the trees. Goodrich moved inside them, was enveloped by the black haunt of empty hootches, mushroom trees, thick high sawgrass where every inch a shadowed ghoul lurked, waiting. Will I die tonight? How embarrassing that would be: to die on my first patrol. He softly clicked his weapon off "safe," then thought of tripping over Ottenburger again and accidentally killing him, and clicked it back.

Finally back into the open paddy again. He felt the welcome scrape of rice along his legs, waited briefly for the monster to attack and kill him from behind, then focused his fear to the front once more. The whole black night was a laughing killer, waiting for its moment.

Goodrich's ears were filled with clonking metal, whispered curses, and his own stomps from stumbles into potholes and low unseen dikes. Finally they reached the low mounds of the cemetery. He viewed its haunting isolation as a haven from the swishing madness.

Hodges placed the machine gun quickly on the mound nearest the trail. Snake began to position his squad behind various graves, making a tight perimeter.

Across the trail, a hundred meters distant, was a clump of trees shot with a dozen scraggly hootches. It was off the trail, an island in more rice, laced to the other villes by another narrow treeline. Nam An (2). Hodges peered intently at the ville. A small mote of light flickered inside the dark shadows of trees and hootches. He remembered that no lights were to be on in villages after sunset. The villagers know that, he mused.

Hodges approached Snake, who was setting in two men behind a mound. "That light mean anything?"

Snake squinted. His hands grasped clumps of grass on the mound. He bolted toward the unpositioned squad members.

"Open fire on that ville!"

The cemetery erupted as tracers reached toward Nam An (2). Rounds poured furiously for a few quick seconds, then there was a moment of silence: in their excitement, all had emptied the first magazine of ammo at the same time.

Hodges caught up with Snake. "What's going on?"

But now the ville responded, answering Hodges' question. Muzzle flashes by the hootches, high cacophony of AK bullets overhead, flash-booms of B-40 rockets, their large grenades a rash of second booms around the cemetery. A .50-caliber machine gun tore ragged holes in slow, heavy bursts above their heads.

"Fire the LAAW!" Speedy cut loose. There was a belch of fire on his shoulder, then a boom in the ville. *"Fire the LAAW!"* Another belch, another boom. A hootch in the ville was now in flames. Hodges could see urgent shadows near the flames, creeping to new places. What do you know, he marveled. Gooks.

Snake now had the whole patrol in place, firing steadily at the treeline with a slow, well-aimed pressure. Hodges peered at the ville for another moment, entranced. I never would have known. Then he remembered that he had an on-call target right on top of it.

Radio. He turned for Flaky. Flaky was gone. *"Fairchild!"*

Hodges searched for a moment and found him lying flat behind a mound, calmly oblivious in his cowardice. "Come on. Hurry up." Flaky came sullenly, like a dog with his tail tucked. Hodges grabbed the handset off the radio.

"Fire Alpha Delta four-oh-seven!"

A mocking hiss, unanswering, on the other end. Finally, "Who is this?"

Hodges swore. "Come on, goddamn it. This is Three Actual. Give me Six. Somebody. Hurry up. Contact mission." The .50-cal bullets cut lower now, just above the mounds.

The company commander came on the net. "Whatcha got, Three Actual?"

Hodges peered into the village again. Two hootches burned. Figures scampered near the flames. Two more LAAWs boomed in the cemetery. His machine gun poured tracers into the village in a low, steadily sweeping line. Be cool, he told himself. "I don't know." He thought another moment. "Gooks in a ville. I got an on-call right on top of it. Alpha Delta four-oh-seven."

The company commander was crisp, professional, removed. "Roger, understand four-zero-seven. Got a direction on that?"

Direction. Damn. "Wait one." He pulled his compass out and peered carefully over a grave, shooting an azimuth at a flaming hootch. He tried to read the luminous dial under the hootch's burn. South. Something like that. He thought to shoot a more accurate azimuth but a B-40 rocket slammed onto the trail just down from him and he ducked behind the mound again. South is fine. "Thirty-two hundred. Danger close."

"Roger, understand thirty-two hundred, danger close. How close?"

The .50 cal just above his head. Be cool. "*Real* close." Not good enough. " 'Bout a hundred meters."

"Roger. Stand by."

"Could you hurry?"

No answer. The radio was once more a silent hiss.

Goodrich half-lay, half-crouched behind a grave, reloading magazines. He pulled a clip out from his bandoleer, fit the charger guide into the magazine, then clumsily dropped the ammunition. He searched frantically in the high, brittle grass for the lost bullets, but felt naked stooping away from the sanctum of his mound, and abandoned his search. He pulled out another clip and jammed it down the charger guide, bending the clip in his petrified fury, and ten bullets bounced like pearls from a broken necklace through his lap, lost among the high weeds in the darkened night. He leaned over, trying to catch the last of them, and stared up at two spindly, tattooed arms that hung down from a crouching frame.

Snake grimaced impatiently, shaking his head. "You stupid shit. What the hell you doing? You shoulda loaded those before. Hurry up. Quit bagging it, Senator."

An AK-47 burst cracked on top of the grave, four digging rounds that threw up puffs of dust. Snake moved off to check the other positions. He took a couple of steps, then turned back to Goodrich. *"C'mon,* Senator. Put out rounds."

Hiss of the radio was finally broken. "Three, Six. Stand by for shot."

Hodges keyed the handset, peeping the ville. "Roger, Six." He screamed to the patrol. "Stand by for shot!"

"Shot out."

"Shot out!" A metallic double bang floated across the fields from An Hoa. They crouched low in the graves and in one instant a phosphorescent flash erupted just on the other side of the mounds, joined by another that smoked whitely twenty meters down the trail. The patrol was frozen behind the mounds now, staring uneasily at Hodges: you trying to *kill* us?

"Ah—add a hundred. Fire for effect."

An eternity that was perhaps two minutes. "Stand by for shot."

"Roger." Hodges screamed, *"Stand by for shot!"* The patrol hugged the bottom of the mounds this time, fearful of Hodges' talents.

The rounds impacted with steady earnest crunches that began just outside the ville and spanned its width. They threw up cloudlets of dust, pieces of flashing hootches. Snake and Phony nudged each other from behind one mound.

Snake nodded toward the ville. Another series of rounds dug into it. "See. I *told* you."

Phony popped a wad of gum, nodding judiciously with approval. "Well, whatta you know. Get some, Lieutenant Hodges."

Three repeats on the ville. Explosions saturated the trees, filling the air with a low layer of dust that had raised from riven fields among the hootches. The firing from the ville ceased. Hodges gloated.

Then there was a heavy burst, a dozen AKs spitting angrily far to their right. Across three hundred meters of reaching rice, another village rose on a low hill thick with trees and squatting bushes, Dai Khuong (4).

Snake tightened the perimeter into two-man positions and ordered them all to hold their fire. Then he crept over to Hodges.

"Hey, Lieutenant. We could really be in the shit. We better lay chilly til we scope 'em out. They could be moving on us. Might really do us if they get the drop on us."

"Anybody hit?"

"Wild Man. Tee-Tee. He's grooving on it. No sweat."

Hodges nodded. The AKs started from Dai Khuong again and he remembered he had an on-call on that village, too. Man, I am a *thorough* son of a bitch, he gloated.

On the radio. Dai Khuong was a repeat of Nam An (2). And, later in the night, Nam An (1), three hundred meters to the north, directly on the other side of the patrol from their first encounter in Nam An (2). The patrol passed the night under high, sporadic bursts from three sides, one man up and one sleeping at each position.

When Nam An (1)opened up Snake crawled casually to Hodges. It was the key he had been waiting for. "No sweat, Lieutenant. They're just screwing with us." It was three o'clock. "If they were really gonna try and *do* us they wouldn't be up there. It's too late. They gotta make their hat most ricky-tick." He allowed Hodges a small grin. "Nice job on the art'y. Sir."

"You ain't seen nothing yet."

Deep blue slivers in the eastern sky, mosquito slaps and grunts, weapons wet with dew. The last round of security checks on the radio. In the near ville an early rooster crowed lonesomely. Dawn. Hodges listened to the rooster, wondering how it had survived the artillery of the night before. Then he smiled a bit perversely to himself: let's see if it makes it through *this*.

Flaky lay against the bottom of a mound, helmet forward over his eyes, the radio handset stuck inside the helmet. There was a muffled squawk and he reached languidly for the handset and keyed it, speaking sleepily.

"Go, Six." Short pause. "Roger that." He turned to Hodges, who was watching the ville emerge eerily in front of the bluing sky, as if a great TV picture tube were slowly warming up. "Guns up on the T.O.T., Lieutenant."

"Tell 'em to go ahead."

"Yes, sir." Flaky keyed the handset again, still sprawled against the mound. "Six, three." Pause. "Let 'er eat."

Hodges strode to the rear of the cemetery and awakened Snake, who had curled up in the high grass inside his poncho liner. "Saddle 'em up. Let's go."

Steady thunks from miles away, a rhythm, interminable, of mortars popping out of tubes. Deep blue had surrendered to a mix of gray: the sun lurked just beyond the edge of the world. Nam An (2) became saturated with explosions, mixes of phosphorous and high-explosive shells that rained down like a steady hailstorm, raising jets of dirt like water spurts. Round after round, like the explosions of cylinders in a slowly idling engine.

The thunking tubes in the distance ceased, the last rounds still latent in the air, and the patrol moved out. Snake's squad made a wide line and Hodges and the gun team followed in trace. Snake paced just behind his squad, dispersing the advancing men, controlling the rate, keeping them on line. They advanced toward the ville, twenty meters apart, weapons pointed forward.

The last mortar exploded inside the trees and there was a moment of nerve-shattering silence. The patrol moved cautiously toward the gloomy mist of smoke and dust, watching for movement. In the ville the rooster crowed again, tentatively, as if his earlier effort had beckoned a falling sky. Hodges smiled tightly: how the hell did it make it?

Goodrich watched the phosphorescent fog anxiously, his weapon pointing forward from his waist. The gloom of the village prepared to envelop him. Twenty meters. Behind him, Snake chanted tersely.

"If they hit us it'll be most ricky-tick. If it moves blow it away. If it moves blow it away."

Something stirred in the brush to his right. Phony laced it with a short, perfunctory burst, not even breaking stride. It was a dog. It moaned like a fading record. OWW-W-w-ww. Phony chuckled softly and grinned. Ten meters from the outer trees.

In front of Goodrich a pajama-clad figure rustled and then crouched, on the porch of a burnt-out hootch. Goodrich saw a black sleeve and inhaled sharply, startled, then fired three quick rounds. The figure ran to the corner of the hootch. Goodrich fired a full magazine, spraying the entire hootch without aiming, and dropped heavily behind a near dike. The whole patrol then opened up on the village. This is it, thought Goodrich. Five feet away they'll kill us all now no using mortars on them no getting out of it we're *dead*.

The patrol had fired on full automatic, and all firing stopped as the squad changed magazines in unison. The gun team jogged cautiously up to a dike and prepared to fire. The ville was silent. No return fire. Snake called to the patrol. "Hold your fire!" He crawled over to Goodrich. "Whatcha shoot at, Senator?"

"In the hootch. Black pajamas. I dunno."

The patrol lay flat along the edge of the village, peering into it. Snake called loudly to the hootch. *"Lai day! Lai day, you motherfucker!"*

No movement. Snake screamed again and fired a round into the hootch. There was a whimpered answer from the hootch's corner. Mumble mumble mumble whimper *Khong biet* whimper mumble.

Snake called to Hodges. "It's a mamasan, Lieutenant."

"Move out, then. Be careful, though."

The patrol picked up, rushing past the first hootches, and set up security. Hodges put the machine gun on top of one family bunker, covering a tree-lined path, and walked into the burnt-out hootch. Goodrich and Snake stood in one corner, peering down at the woman. Speedy and Burgie were busily searching for contraband through random piles of burnt matting, pots, and mackerel cans.

The wounded woman was curled in a corner, weeping, holding one shoulder. Her coarse black hair was pulled into

a loose bun and her lips were stained red by betel nut,
making her look as if she had begun to paint herself up for
a welcoming party. Her teeth were purplish-black after
years of chewing the numbing betel nut. She turned pained
eyes up from her lined, puffy face and pleaded with the
hulking figures that stared down at her. Mumble mumble
mumble whimper *khong biet* mumble *honcho* mumble *bac
se.*

Snake leaned over threateningly. *"Dung Lai!"* She
stopped talking, continuing to whimper. "What did you
expect, Mamasan? You heard all the racket. You know—
bac bac VC? *Khong biet?* What the hell did you leave
your bunker for?" He shook his head, feigning anger. "You
lucky old bitch! You should be dead! That's right!"

Goodrich knelt next to her, mortified. A pool of blood
leaked down from her shoulder in a steady rivulet, dripping
off her elbow to the dirt floor of the hootch. "I'm sorry,
Mamasan. Really." He reached out to her, intending to
examine the wound and wrap it for her. She shrank back
immediately, mumbling rapidly to him. He cringed from
her. "Goddamn, Mamasan. I'm really sorry. *Really.*" He
began to unbutton the pajama top and she grasped it shut,
terrified.

Snake nudged Goodrich with a boot. "Don't be sorry,
Senator. She knows the rules. She shoulda been in her
bunker. It's her own fault."

Goodrich shook his head, his chubby face sagging in its
grief. He looked down at the bleeding, decrepit creature
whose most recent misery emanated from his very trigger,
and neared tears. "I should have looked more closely. I
was scared. It was crazy to shoot like that."

Snake scoffed contemptuously. "Oh, bullshit, Senator.
Don't turn yourself all around—"

Speedy interjected from the other corner of the hootch,
where he was going through mamasan's fireplace with an
intrenching tool. "Senator crying again?"

"—She coulda been a gook. She knew she was wrong.
Look twice and you're dead, Senator."

Speedy eyed his new charge with disbelief. "You're a
case, Senator. They going to carry you out of here in a
strait jacket."

Hodges yelled to the hootch from across the weed path.

"Forget mamasan. We'll take her back and have a doc check her out. Search the rest of the ville. I'm tired as hell."

The patrol moved through the village in a floating perimeter, two hootches at a time, following a tedious, standard practice. Call the villagers out of their earthen family bunkers, where they've spent their latest night in hell. Throw grenades into the bunkers to ensure there are no enemies still hiding in them. Then search them out. Check hootch areas and bushes for bodies, weapons, and contraband.

Bagger discovered a pair of bright blue pin-striped shorts in one hootch, a unique find. He held them daintily in his huge hands, his red face grinning mischievously, and walked over to the hootch's eldest occupant, a mamasan of perhaps thirty who stood under the thatch with five small children.

"Where's your old man, Mamasan? Huh? *O dau Papasan?*"

Mamasan smiled tightly, humoring the invader. *"Khong biet."* I don't know.

"Oh, I'll bet my ass you dunno, with all them babysans." Bagger loomed over her, grinning meanly. "Well, if you dunno, I s'pose it's all right for me to souvenir his britches, huh?" The stocky man laughed devilishly. "Gotcha, Mamasan. Catch Twenty-two. If he's around, you better tell us where, so we can liberate his ass. If he ain't, what do you care about his old shorts, anyway?"

Snake noticed Bagger, and called to him. "Bagger."

Bagger stuffed the shorts into his flak-jacket pocket. "Oh, I'll bet old papasan was humping a B-forty last night. Ain't that right, Mamasan."

"Bagger. Give 'em back."

Bagger finally acknowledged Snake. "I'm gonna wear 'em, man, instead of tiger shorts."

"It's against the rules. You know that. Give 'em back."

"So what do you care? Huh? You talking like a goddamn lifer, Snake. What's the rules to a pair of shorts?"

Cannonball called from the top of a nearby family bunker, where he was standing security. "Man, you know Snake, he goan' be a lifer. I been telling you that."

"Ah, screw you, Cannonball." Snake walked up to Bagger. "I ain't gonna get in trouble because of any damn shorts." He looked around for Hodges. "I ain't having any new Lieutenant or somebody run me in because you want a pair of shorts. Now give 'em back to the lady. Hurry up."

Bagger fished them out of his pocket. "Oh. Now she's a *lady*, too. Cannonball's right. My man Snake is gonna be a lifer."

One hootch over, Cat Man and Phony were patiently standing in front of an old man who was gesturing wildly in the air. They both grinned, shaking their heads in perfect time with the gestures. Hodges walked over to them, curious at the mimic pantomime of it, as if all elements were prerehearsed.

"What the hell . . . ?"

Phony eyed Hodges pleasantly. "Hey, Lieutenant. You can shoot some art'y, you know? Not bad. Oh. *Him?* He lost his *can cuoc*." Phony noted that the phrase did not register with Hodges. "His I.D. card." He put his arm around the old man's shoulders. "It's a lifer game. Find a dude without his *can cuoc* and he's s'posed to be VC or something, 'cause he ain't registered with the gov'mint."

Snake had joined the group. He addressed Hodges. "So every time we find a dude without one, we're s'posed to run him in. But it's like everything out here, Lieutenant. Nothing's what it's s'posed to be. All the VC have *can cuocs*. Half the villagers don't, cause when you lose it, you have to pay a goddamn fortune to get a new one. So *can cuocs* don't mean nothing, really. It's just a game." He grinned, poking the old man playfully in the chest. "But every villager has the same story. We ask where it is and they point up to the sky and tell us how the bombs blew it up, so we'll feel sorry for 'em and think it's our own fault. That right, Papasan?"

The old man smiled earnestly, his electric, beady eyes communicating as he ran frail hands through the air, simulating an air strike, then brought them together in front of himself and threw them up and apart, indicating the exploding bomb.

"And anyway," Phony shrugged absently, "they're all VC. Every ville out here is VC. Them *can cuocs* don't mean a goddamn thing."

Cat Man agreed. He nodded shyly, his delicate features intense, and addressed Hodges with carefully chosen words. "Wait till you sweep into a ville and it's flying a VC flag for you, Lieutenant. Papasan grins 'cause he thinks we're gonna stick him. If we were just moving through, he wouldn't even wave."

They found no bodies in the ville. There were numerous blood trails, a blend of blood that joined in a drag line toward the western mountains, a half-dozen dropped grenades, and one abandoned AK-47 rifle, lost in the dark as the enemy retreated.

Hodges was slightly disappointed. No victories without tangible monuments. He was also amazed at the lack of damage to the village. Two burnt hootches, several dozen new pockmarks in the dried earth, and one bleeding mamasan. All those mortar rounds, he marveled. And even the rooster came away unscratched.

The company perimeter was more than a mile away. Speedy and Burgie pulled a bamboo pole off one rended hootch, found a parachute that had once floated down above a huge Basketball flare, and fashioned a hammock-like carrying device for the whimpering mamasan. The patrol then straggled back across the sunbaked valley, walking in the sanctum of the treelines because it was daylight and there would be snipers, then finally cut across the wide, parched paddy that led to the southern tip of Phu Phong (4). Hodges radioed ahead, and a small patrol met them at the base of the hill, near one of the wells. The company corpsman, one of the Vietnamese Kit Carson Scouts, and a fire team for security awaited them in the scrubby shade of the well.

They filed up to the well, the patrol finished. Some walked immediately to it and doused themselves, cooling off from the hump. Others dropped into the shade, greeting the fire team, which was from the other squad in their platoon. Still others moved up to the perimeter without pausing, anxious to eat.

A dozen Marines ambled down from the perimeter when the patrol returned, curious about the previous night's happenings, calling and jibing friends from the returning patrol.

They gathered around the moaning mamasan. The corpsman took her pajama top and ripped it at the shoulder, then wrapped her wound with a battle dressing. She winced mightily, still whimpering.

The Kit Carson Scout sauntered slowly over and peered down unemotionally at the woman. Snake put his hand on the man's shoulder, pointing to the mamasan. "Dan. Ask her why she wasn't in the bunker. Why she in fucking hootch when Marines *bac-bac* VC."

Dan nodded solemnly, thinking for a moment, then asked her a question in Vietnamese that came out as a song. Mamasan whimpered, responding in a weakened rapid fire, a long, gesturing explanation. Dan pondered the answer, still emotionless, then sent her into tears with a short retort.

Snake leaned in front of Dan, smiling amusedly to him. "What did she say, Dan?"

Dan still stared down at her. His expression had not changed. "She says, Marines, VC *bac-bac boo coo* long time, she in bunker, gotta take shit. She say, wait all night, go outside to take shit, got *boo coo* bombs. Go back fucking hootch, Marine come, shoot her."

The crowd nodded, muttering judiciously. Mamasan still whimpered. Snake nudged Dan. "So, what did you say?"

Dan shrugged absently. "I say, now on, shit in bunker."

The crowd applauded in appreciation of Dan's wisdom. Dan smiled back impishly, acknowledging the praise. Then he coolly, persistently questioned the weary mamasan, prodding her, trying to discover information about the North Vietnamese unit that had been in her village the night before.

Goodrich watched Dan and the others and, attempting to understand and rationalize their callousness, discovered a basic truth about himself. Even as he searched for some humorous remark that would write off the incident, he knew that he could not accept it. He could understand, condone the massive use of force, but the terrors of its particularizations horrified him. A hundred NVA deaths tallied in a newspaper column would draw an absent nod, but one stinking, suffering old wretched woman who bled from his own bullet, who would be flown by helicopter to an air-conditioned hospital and saved, turned his stomach.

Whoo boy, he fretted, walking by himself up the hill. Only 387 more days of this. Time sure flies when you're having fun.

The mail had arrived on the resupply helicopter and there was a letter from Mark. Goodrich dropped his gear next to his poncho hootch and lit a cigarette, reading it.

You wouldn't believe the faces of my friends when I told them my old college roomy was a Marine! I think they believe I'm an FBI plant! It is kind of funny, you know—me *here* and you *there*. I see pictures of the patrols burning down homes, things like that and I just can't picture you there. But if anything I feel a little good, if you insist on making an ass out of yourself. It injects the tiniest bit of credibility to the holocaust. I mean, I sure can't see *you* burning people, or standing by while someone else does. *Pot,* maybe, but definitely not *people.*

The letter was the touch that bottomed out Goodrich's depression. He turned to Ottenburger, who was napping under his poncho hootch. "Hey, Burgie. Where do I turn in my letter of resignation?"

"Say what, Senator?"

Goodrich attempted a smile. "Where do I quit, man?"

Ottenburger snorted. "Talk to Bagger. He knows all about it. He quits at least once a day."

Speedy overheard them and called almost derisively, fed up with Goodrich. "Tonight, Senator, I'll give you a grenade. You pull your own pin. No sweat. One hand up in the air, *boom,* bye-bye Senator."

Goodrich grinned miserably. "Tempting. Tempting. But it might hurt."

8.

WILL GOODRICH

Mark went to Canada. Goodrich went to Vietnam. Everybody else went to grad school.

It was academic, like studying for an exam. The draft counselors schooled you and helped you determine your own best approach, and you worked on it, cultivated it, and usually it worked. After all, Harvard breeds achievers.

John Wilkins Grimsley the Fourth drove up to his father's hunting cabin on the Canadian border and locked himself inside for three weeks before the draft physicals, refusing to talk with anyone. He drove straight to the physical examination center, having stayed up for two nights without sleep, refusing to speak with even the gas station attendants along the way, and went berserk during the exam.

Temporarily, of course. John Wilkins Grimsley the Fourth was awarded a psycho deferment. Now he can go on to medical school. He will be a great doctor some day. Perhaps a psychiatrist.

Michael Murphy was large and slightly overweight. There was a pill that raised blood pressure and was not detectable in the urinalysis. Michael Murphy was declared 4-F for high blood pressure, which seemed a natural result of his size and weight. Michael Murphy can now be a lawyer, and uphold the standards of integrity, honesty, and obedience to the law.

Sol Levinowitz was a nervous, aggressive little man. He pissed into the cup and then threw his urine into the face of the Army technician. The Army technician sighed and went into another room, where he changed his uniform and washed his face. Sol Levinowitz was not the first person to use him as the object of his "overaggressive" angle. So Levinowitz was judged too aggressive to submit himself to the discipline of the Armed Forces, but he has no trouble submitting himself to the disciplines of the classroom. Sol Levinowitz will be a famous professor some day.

Tim Forbes was tall and thin, a soft-spoken scholar. Tim starved himself underweight, down to barely one hundred and twenty pounds on a six-foot frame. Tim worked very hard at it, with admirable discipline. At the draft physical, he expertly manifested carefully researched suicidal tendencies. Tim Forbes was rewarded with a Rhodes Scholarship for his diligence. Some day he will write speeches for great politicians. Tim Forbes will confess his boondoggle, and we will admire his honesty. He only did what everybody else was doing.

Mark Solomon and Goodrich lived in the "loony room." Mark cared too much, and Goodrich didn't care at all. For Mark, Vietnam was the most important political happening since the Russian Revolution, a symbolic event that could spell the final end to imperialism. Mark believed in Nuremberg, in the duty of conscience. He had joined several antiwar groups, and had written and distributed leaflets. Vietnam consumed him. He avoided the draft, deciding to go to Canada as an affirmative act, the only weapon in his arsenal that could have a definite, statistical impact.

Goodrich did not care about anything. He was at Harvard because his father and brothers had been to Harvard. He was a menopause baby, younger by fourteen years than his nearest brother. He grew up alone in a world of brothers who were uncles and a sister who was an aunt. He had been locked into prep school at fourteen.

He did not know people, other than the people of Harvard and Groton. He did not know girls. There had been no girls in prep school, and there were no girls at Harvard. Occasionally Mark would arrange a blind date for him and he would end up playing the "Harvard Genius" role. It was the easiest way to hide the fact that he could not, for the life of him, figure out what girls wanted to talk about. He had had one woman, a Manhattan whore who was a birthday present from one of his older brothers. He climaxed in thirty seconds. Other than her, the only women he knew intimately were inside the pages of erotic magazines.

He was twenty, a Harvard Genius, with a world he had never touched at his feet.

Leaving school was the first decision he had ever made completely by himself. His family was furious and his classmates considered him absolutely insane. He was unable to articulate why he had quit, or what he wanted to do. He tried the Peace Corps, and the interviewer gave him a battery of tests, then told him he was too militant to join. Goodrich had laughed incredulously, amused that anyone would think him militant about anything.

The interviewer explained that it had been Goodrich's response to the question on Vietnam. Goodrich had commented that he thought it was sensible to attempt to restrain an irreversible Communist takeover there, that issues such as elections and political repression in the South were red herrings when one considered the alternative of total repression by a Northern-imposed government.

The interviewer told him that it would be harmful to have people with such beliefs representing the country in under-developed areas. People fear the United States, the interviewer explained. They need to be assured. They need Peace Corps members who will tell them how wrong America has been in Vietnam. Otherwise, the Peace Corps might be considered a beachhead for further American aggression, the interviewer said. The interviewer told Goodrich that, if he felt that way, he should go into the military.

The idea appealed to Goodrich, and grew on him. His father had been a dollar-a-year man in the Navy during World War Two and was proud of his service. It would be a way to mend some fences.

He was an accomplished musician, capable of playing several instruments well. He had seen the Marine Band while it was on tour during his prep-school days, and had remembered the quality of its performance. He decided to enlist in the Marine Band, as a compromise to all competing emotions.

The recruiter could not *guarantee* the Marine Band on a two-year enlistment, which was the maximum Goodrich would sign for. "It all depends," smiled the recruiter, "on the needs of the Corps. But if you're *good*—"

"Oh yes," Goodrich assured the Sergeant. "I'm *very* good."

"Then you've got just as much of a chance as anybody else!"

Which, of course, was zero, equally shared.

9.

Finally, after three weeks, a platoon sergeant.

A Staff Sergeant. A Marine who had experienced the Corps before Vietnam filled its ranks with crass, uncaring civilians. Someone who had known parade fields, barracks that shone with polish and pride, firm-faced men older than their years who starched their utilities, shined their boots, and shaved their heads.

Into the chaos of forgotten formalities and jungle sores came Angus Austin. He appeared as the company was setting into the dust and ash of a new perimeter. The resupply helicopter dropped its netted load of food and ammunition, then touched briefly on the earth and excreted three men. And in five minutes the Third Herd had a new Papa Sierra. Like it or not.

He was a humorless, dry-voiced man, old for thirty-one, who had left a small town in Appalachian Pennsylvania, where his father was a high-school janitor, and had given the Marine Corps all of his thirteen adult years. He had enlisted after Korea, and was hopelessly frozen into the rank of Sergeant until Vietnam enlarged the Corps. To be a Staff NCO had been Angus Austin's dream. To make Gunnery Sergeant was little more than a wish.

But not beyond hope. He reported to Hodges, his thick hulk sweating profusely in the late afternoon heat, peppery cheeks coarse with a five o'clock shadow that made them appear darker than his shaved head, and dropped his Army rucksack into the dirt. The pack, which was considered too large and cumbersome by most Marines, bulged with unnecessary gear. It was Hodges' first warning that Austin was not a bush Marine.

Austin extended his hand. "Staff Sergeant Austin, Lieutenant. I'm your new platoon sergeant." Austin surveyed the platoon lines, where Marines were digging fighting holes into the latest perimeter. "What the Gunny says, this platoon hasn't had a *real* Papa Sierra in a long damn time."

"Well, no." Hodges scrutinized the stocky, frowning man. "Not a staff NCO, anyway." Hodges grinned. "Where the hell have all the Staffs been hiding?"

"Lieutenant, we all did this once already. That's where we been hiding. We were here in '65 and '66, when these kids were still in school.

"Where were you?"

Austin turned around. "Sir?"

"In '65?"

"Da Nang." Austin did a short stroll, a nervous pace in front of Hodges. "I landed with the Ninth Marines."

"What was your job?"

Austin appeared a tad embarrassed. "I was Police Sergeant at the air base. I was in charge of the administrative integrity of the perimeter."

Hodges chuckled. "You mean you supervised trash pick-ups?"

"Well, not only that. Sir." Austin had taken on a wounded, irritated look. "But what the Gunny says, you haven't had a real platoon sergeant down here in months. I hear you're new. Now, don't you worry, Lieutenant. We'll get this platoon squared away in no time. Is there anything the Lieutenant wants me to work on right away?"

"No . . ."

"Well, I know what we have to deal with. These people who end up in the grunts. Lieutenant, you wouldn't have believed the Corps before this Vietnam shit." Austin had sat down across from Hodges, and was taking out various comforts from his pack. His eyes had a nostalgic look. "Man couldn't have a goddamn *parking* ticket and get in the Corps before Vietnam. You wouldn't have believed the inspections we had, Lieutenant. And the discipline. A man couldn't even talk to his Lieutenant without going through the chain of command. A Lieutenant was *God*."

"Well, I'd just as soon do without all that, Sarge—"

"We'll have 'em treating you right in no time, sir."

"They already treat me right, Sarge."

Austin smiled comfortingly to Hodges. "Lieutenant, you don't know *how* to be treated right until you've had a proper Papa Sierra. In all due respect. Now I've heard you're a damn good Lieutenant, that you know your tactics and your supporting arms. The Gunny told me that, not five minutes ago. Sir. And I intend to make this a platoon you can be proud of."

"I'm already proud of it, Sarge. Hey." Hodges shrugged helplessly, smiling in mild bewilderment. "I can't handle all that. I'm a civilian, Sarge." Austin squinted at the heresy. "I'm just a damn civilian playing Marine for a couple years because there's a war. Know what I mean?" Hodges gestured out toward the lines. "So are they, most of them. Civilians, you know? A bunch of kids who got caught up in all the bullshit. They don't know a request mast from a walk in the woods. The only dress parade they'll ever be in was when they graduated from boot camp." Hodges grinned, pondering Austin's overstuffed rucksack. "Don't get me wrong. They know the bush, and they can buckle for your dust, Sarge. But don't turn them all around with that stateside shit."

Austin drew out a cigarette and studied his new platoon commander with a mix of disbelief and antagonism. He dragged several times on his cigarette, stunned speechless. His brows furrowed as he mulled Hodges remarks. Finally, he formulated a response. "Lieutenant. I'm a Marine. Every ounce of me. This is my Corps, and it always will be, and I can't stop being a Marine. And they're Marines. Whether it's for five minutes or fifty years. In all due respect, that is. And if a Marine is out of uniform, or he didn't shave, or he's disrespectful, then it would hurt me to my goddamn *heart* not to straighten the man out. You can't ask me to do that, Lieutenant. You can't ask me not to do the best job I know how."

It was Hodges' turn to be speechless. He lit a Marlboro, thinking of Snake's usual jest to nonsmokers (we are *all* sucking wind out here). He knew that Austin would take a complaint to the company Gunnery Sergeant, who would in turn inform the company commander, and that he would get an early reputation for running an undisciplined platoon. That would mean trouble for every platoon member from other staff NCOs. He was also confused and somehow moved by Austin's emotional defense of the Corps.

"No. I can't. But Sarge, I want you to know what my priorities are. What's important. We're all Marines. I'm sorry. I didn't mean that like you took it. But it's a different Corps out here." Austin's face set stubbornly, disagreeing. Hodges continued. "Out here uniforms aren't important. And when's a man gonna get a haircut, for Christ's sake? The company's been out here fifty days, now." Austin reached into his rucksack and displayed a set of manual hair clippers. Hodges shook his head in disbelief. "All right. There are *ways*. But clean weapons are more important. And digging deep holes. Staying spread out on patrol. Carrying the right gear."

Austin waited for aonther second, as if he believed Hodges would add to the list if enough time lapsed. Then he stood slowly, dusting off the seat of his trousers. "Aye, aye, sir. But begging the Lieutenant's pardon, the other things are important, too. Like General Westwood says, 'You show me a trashy perimeter and I'll show you a lousy fighting unit.' General Westwood relieves company commanders who have trashy perimeters."

Hodges gave up. Austin would learn in time, he hoped. Or maybe, just maybe, he would become convinced by Austin. "All right, Sarge. Who am I to argue with General Westwood? But it isn't as important as the other stuff."

Austin appeared vindicated. "Begging the Lieutenant's pardon, sir, it all goes together. Now. With the Lieutenant's permission, I think I'll go check the lines."

Austin walked immediately to Snake's portion of the platoon lines. Snake was digging in with Cat Man's team, which was the squad's middle position. The men were rotating their digging tasks, and Snake and Phony were lying back on their packs, resting, as Cat Man and Cannonball dug inside the holes. All four men were smoking and talking in the easy, relaxed manner of a close-knit family.

Austin stood before Snake. He wore no rank insignia, having left his flak jacket, which had small, black staff Sergeant's stripes on the pocket, at the platoon command post. He fixed brooding eyes on Snake and Phony and placed his hands on his hips, staring coldly at them as if he expected them to stand at attention. Then he nodded slightly, in what appeared to be mild disgust.

"And what are you two up to?"

Neither man had ever seen Austin, or heard that the platoon had a new Platoon Sergeant. They glanced conspiratorially at each other. Phony smiled with angelic innocence. "Why? You know something better to do?"

Austin scrutinized Phony with a dark glare. "Yeah. I can think of a lot of better things to do. Like picking up trash at the Da Nang brig."

Phony's eyes brightened. *"Da Nang!* Did this dude say he could get us to Da Nang? Oh, Christ, I don't know what the hell I got to do to get there, but let me know, man. *Get me out of here!"*

The others howled, even as Austin's face grew livid. Snake watched the new Platoon Sergeant's hands clench and loosen, and he cut short his laugh, attempting to attract Phony's attention. Snake had an antenna for trouble, and he suddenly realized that Austin was capable of producing it.

But Austin had already turned to Cannonball, who was standing knee-deep in the hole he had been digging, laughing mightily at Phony's humor. "You! Black Marine. Where's your fields of fire?"

Cannonball stared for a quick moment at what he believed to be a slur, then regained his amused grin, and glanced out across the rippling paddy to his front. "Aw, everywhere, man."

Austin continued, bolstered by this first direct response. "What do you mean, 'everywhere'? Where's your PDF?"

Cannonball scratched his head, squinting. "Say wha-a-at?"

"Your PDF. Principle Direction of Fire. Don't you have a PDF?"

Cannonball waved a lithe arm at Austin, ignoring Snake's attempt to silence him. "Awww, ma-a-an. Don't give me none of that boot-camp shit. You ever been overrun? We don't shoot no 'principle direction' man, we shoot gooks."

Snake finally was able to position himself between Austin and the others. He smiled a conciliatory grin. "Hey, listen. I don't know who you are but—"

"Who the hell are *you?*"

"I'm the squad leader here. Now—"

"Well, I'm *Staff* Sergeant Austin, your new Platoon Sergeant, and you *piss me off*."

Behind Austin, Cannonball dropped his entrenching tool and covered his head. Cat Man and Phony stood mute. Snake shrugged gamely, eyeing Austin with a tiny smile. "Hey, look, Sarge. The men were only having some fun. You know how it gets out here. Same old faces every day—"

"Well, I'm glad you all like fun, because now we're going to have some *real* fun. You think you should be treated different from other Marines just because you're getting shot at every now and then? Well, this shit stops today."

Austin turned back to Phony, still seething from his disrespect. "Get rid of that skivvy shirt."

Phony looked down. The skivvy shirt was among his most prized possessions. There was a large peace symbol on the front, with ACID written over the top of it. On the back was a crazed gargoyle head, its tongue hanging out, with FUCK YOU written over it. Some magic-marker genius in the company rear at An Hoa had customized the boring, combat-green for Phony.

Phony brought his hands to his chest, stroking the shirt, still grinning innocently. "Get *rid* of it?"

"That's right. You're wearing a uniform, Marine. You don't rate customizing it. Get rid of it."

Phony shrugged Austin off. "I ain't got another one, anyway."

Austin walked quickly to his gear at the command post and returned in moments, holding a bright green skivvy shirt, never worn. He walked ceremoniously up to Phony, who was digging inside the fighting hole, and grabbed his customized shirt in the back, ripping it off him, "surveying" it in the fashion of training-unit inspections when a hole was discovered in an article of clothing.

Phony had reached for Austin's hand, but missed. He darkened in his only display of deep anger since he had joined the squad. He tenderly removed the remains of the shirt from his neck, still staring ominously at Austin. Then, in mere seconds, he regained the innocent, acquiescent smile.

"You can't do that. You shouldn't have done that."

"Well, I already did. Didn't I?" Austin peered at all of them. "We're going into the Bridge in a couple days. It'll be tighten-up time, girls. We're gonna square you all away."

10.

The brown emerged from the western mountains, curled lazily in two separate streaks that marked the Arizona Valley's perimeter, then met in a wider, swifter gash that straightened out the curls and dashed along miles of sand and paddies in a deep rush to meet the distant sea. Just where the rivers met, one wade away from the implacable Arizona, was the Liberty Bridge compound.

Hodges looked at it as the company moved along the eastern banks of the Arizona, preparing to wade the northern river just above where the two rivers joined. He had never been to Liberty Bridge, except for his brief ride through it on the incoming convoy, but he had listened to his platoon members chatter about its desirable qualities for a week. The Bridge was a skating place, they had all agreed. Hot chow. Few dangerous patrols. Daily baths in the crystal currents of the river. Tents and cots. Sit-down shitters. Skate City.

The company waded toward the northern compound, on the more peaceful Dai Loc side of the river. It was a small perimeter, manned by two platoons from a grunt company, plus the mortar and command sections of the company. Its major function was to provide security for the two convoys that gathered on the northern shore on their way from Da Nang to An Hoa each day, waiting to cross the river. The mile-long, dust-spewing, raging mix of tanks and amphtracs and trucks had to cross the river, one vehicle at a time, on a small, line-pulled barge.

Because the Bridge compound did not have a bridge. Actually, it had two, neither of which functioned. Hodges stood on the red cut of convoy road next to the northern compound and examined them both close up for the first time.

The Old Bridge was a memory of blackened poles that reached fifty feet into empty air, topless but for a few charcoal cross beams. The French had built it decades ago, along with a railroad bridge five miles downstream on Go Noi Island, in order to open An Hoa Basin to commerce. Hodges had heard the story of the French efforts, and seen the vestiges of their attempts, during his earlier wanderings near the An Hoa combat base. In addition to marketing the rice, he had learned, the French had discovered coal at the Basin's western edge, just at the base of one jutting cliff, and had begun a coal community. They had also built a brick factory near what was now the outer perimeter of the combat base, turning what was now only claydust, clouds of powder in the air, into building blocks.

The Viet Cong had destroyed both bridges in the mid-1960s as a part of their "grass roots" campaign to isolate the Basin's villagers from the Saigon government. Hodges thought of the desolate Arizona villages he had just left, with their concrete wells that were evidence of attention somewhere in their hopeless past. The grass-roots campaign was a winner, he mused. And government "officials," the ones who dealt with Americans as "village chiefs," now did so from faraway Da Nang, sometimes venturing into An Hoa for brief, daylight visits.

Hodges remembered seeing the local "District Chief" appear in An Hoa while he was waiting to report to the company. The chief had landed at the airstrip in his own airplane. His wife was in a flowing *ao dai*. If they had wandered on the other side of An Hoa's barbed wire, Hodges grinned ironically, they wouldn't have lasted five minutes. Grass roots. The coal mine was clogged with booby traps. The brick factory sat under clouds of claydust. The Old Bridge loomed as the symbol of the Basin's isolation.

Hodges and his platoon left the convoy road and walked the concrete foundation of the second bridge, on their way to the southern compound. Seabees worked busily, occasionally glancing at the string of dirty, unshaved grunts who shambled by.

The Powers That Were had euphemistically christened

the new bridge Liberty Bridge. It was low, made of concrete, and as yet incapable of supporting the convoy. The Seabees had been working doggedly on it for several months, in an effort to once again link the Basin with the Other World. Once completed, it would sink under the monsoon currents of the joined rivers for two months of the year, but for the other ten months, the Basin would be privy to communication with the rest of Vietnam. Or so the Americans hoped.

They left the new bridge and walked toward the southern compound. A truck lumbered past them, covering Hodges with a veil of red dirt. He swore at the driver, spitting dirt from his mouth. For that moment, he felt privileged and awesome, a grunt returning to a safer haven.

He strode up a sharp hill. The southern compound sprawled before him. Properly termed the Bridge compound, it was a complete combat base, the only permanent base in the Basin other than An Hoa, some seven miles of ribbon road away. It sat on top of a large J-shaped hill that was eight hundred meters long and four hundred meters wide at the bottom of the J. It was the focal point for the operation of an entire infantry battalion, in addition to providing security for the convoy.

Hodges and his platoon walked the road into the compound. Reams of barbed wire and rolls of concertina reached down the hill on both sides of them. Inside the compound, Hodges noticed the dozen artillery pieces on the right side of the road, inside circular parapets. He passed a cluster of 81-millimeter mortar pits. There was a sandbagged chapel, next to a similarly sandbagged command operations center bunker. He entered a long road lined by dust-reddened tents, passed sandbagged bunkers, some positioned with 106-millimeter recoilless rifles, long and black and ugly, and .50-caliber machine guns. At the end of the road there was a high wooden observation tower. Jeeps and mechanical mules shot busily past him, covering him and the others with more of the red dirt that had claimed every fixed object on the hill, making every tent and sandbag as natural to the barren plateau as sagebrush on a prairie.

The Bridge. *All ri-i-ight!* He found the tents assigned to his platoon and settled them in. They were by themselves. He felt mildly honored that, with only a month in Vietnam, his company commander had trusted him to have the Bridge security platoon. The rest of the company would man the northern perimeter. Hodges' platoon would augment the defense that was shared primarily between his battalion's Headquarters and Supply Company and the Artillery Battery across the road.

Later that afternoon the company gathered in a weary, undisciplined clump in front of the Bridge compound's chapel. A dozen rifles were jammed by their bayonets into the red dirt, a rigid row of memories. A dirty, stubbled figure stood behind each rifle, holding a helmet. The battalion Chaplain read a name off of a piece of paper, and then chanted hauntingly, "Killed in Action." He did it twelve times. Each time, one dirty figure stepped forward and put a helmet on a rifle butt.

Goodrich sat in the dust that surrounded the sandbagged chapel, watching Cat Man solemnly place a helmet on a rifle. Shag. New dudes together. Shared awe in An Hoa. Coming to the bush on the same day. Sharing the delusion that the fresh, the combat-innocent, would be the last to die, hearing the stories but not really accepting that a man could endure all the training, all the tension, all the distances and culture warps only to die before he had had a chance to suffer.

Then, a few days earlier, on an uneventful security patrol, all delusions ending with two rapid cracks from an invisible, ubiquitous sniper rifle that caught Shag just below the ear, a perfect shot, as he sat smiling on a mound of earth while Cat Man's team checked out a nearby hootch. Eight hundred yards of open paddy to Shag's back, miles of wispy treeline near and far. They were nowhere. They were everywhere. Goodrich had been talking to Shag when the rounds went off. It seemed impossible. They were *everywhere*.

It was beginning to make less and less sense. Mark was beginning to make more and more sense. You just wander around trying to kill them until they kill you, he mused. Where the hell is the sense in that? It's insane.

All helmets were on the rifles. The Chaplain said a prayer. His voice was high and nasal. He spoke with a dry-throated Texas drawl. He sounded, thought Goodrich, as if he really believed there was a God.

Dear Lord, whose wisdom surpasses all understanding . . .

Goodrich turned to Ottenburger, next to him, and hoarse-whispered, "I just can't justify it."

Burgie shrugged. "So, who asked you to?"

. . . who so unselfishly laid down their lives for a greater good, a good which only You have a true . . .

"Don't get uptight, Senator. Won't change a goddamn thing."

Bagger was on the other side of Burgie. "Number Ten. I quit, man. I can't keep watching this."

. . . we ask You to look kindly on these young souls who have so recently joined You, fresh from the tribulations of an effort that is to Your greater glory . . .

Bagger grimaced. "Lord forgive me, but that man gives me the creeps. I keep wondering who gets the honor of being next."

Burgie nudged him. "Shut up. Don't even talk about that."

. . . who gave their lives so that other men might live in freedom. Amen.

Bagger peered at the Chaplain. Fresh clothes, unscarred boots, rolls of fat beneath his chin, a natural repository that seemed drained from the flabby face. "Well, what the hell does he know about it?" He fretted absently to himself, too numb to feel true repulsion. "Get some for God."

Goodrich was encouraged by Bagger. He leaned in front of Burgie, anxious to communicate. He felt deeply troubled. "It makes me believe in the randomness of things. Like existentialism. Suffering without meaning, except in the suffering itself."

Bagger nudged Ottenburger. "What the hell is Shithead talking about?"

"School."

The regimental commander joined the Chaplain. He had journeyed from An Hoa in a command and control helicopter, which waited like a setting hen on the small landing pad at the base of the hill. Bagger grimaced at the Colonel with a mix of disaffection and fear. He spoke with a tinge of awe. "Look at that man up there. He's got more power over me than God. To hell with the preacher.

Somebody better run up there and kiss his ass before he sends us back into the Arizona."

The Colonel stood starched and green and clean beside the row of dangling helmets, looking down at the clump of hollow, weathered faces.

. . . I want you to know how proud I am of the way you men have been fighting. Operation Allegheny Forest was a complete success . . .

"Goo-o-oood," drawled Burgie in a hoarse whisper. "Maybe he'll make a General now."

. . . five hundred eighty enemy killed. . . .

"And he's never seen a fucking body." Burgie again.

Goodrich joined him. "Why doesn't he talk about how many Marines were screwed up?"

Bagger nudged them both. "You guys shut up about my Colonel. You wanna get us court-martialed?"

. . . three hundred ten individual weapons . . .

Burgie persisted, the long face smirking. "It's the truth."

"Then *think* it. Shut up."

. . . always terrible when a man dies, but I want you to know . . .

"What does he know about it?"

"He fought in World War Two, probably Korea."

Burgie grunted, unconvinced. "What's he done *lately?*"

. . . First Battalion continues to lead the way. I've recommended you for another Meritorious Unit Citation.

Burgie smiled again, allowing it to melt into a sardonic grin. "Get some for the Colonel."

Goodrich agreed. He leaned forward, his fat face intense. "That's it, you see. When meaning becomes purely personal, so does glory. No great cause. It makes less and less sense."

Bagger leaned forward, his face suddenly lit. "Wait a minute! Did you hear that? We're up for a Meritorious Unit, man!" The ceremony was over. He stood and walked away. "God damn. An MUC."

Waterbull was back. He walked slowly down the scrape of road along one finger of the compound, counting tents. Dude said five tents on the left. Right here. He pulled the tent flap and entered the musty oven heat, blinking his eyes after the white-bright of noonbake, then focused and grinned. His faceful of farm-boy freckles danced in the dark. There he is. He crept to the cot and tipped it effortlessly, dropping Snake onto the pallet-box floor.

"Wake up, you little shit!"

Snake crouched quickly, dwarfed by the massive redhead, then smiled and popped him on the chest. "You ugly mother! Thought you'd died of the clap!"

Waterbull chuckled. "Hell, I almost did. How come you're not at the service?"

Snake scowled. "I don't go to those things, you know that. I don't like talking about dead people. What good does it do to talk about it? Won't change it. They didn't die for any goddamn Colonel."

Waterbull sat on a cot, dropping his pack and rifle onto the floor. "Colonel's a good head, Snake. Gave me a ride out here on his chopper. Came down to the LOC and said, 'Who's going to the Bridge?' and took us with him. Me and another dude." Waterbull pulled out a cigarette. "Besides. You better get yourself used to Colonels, being a lifer and all."

"Oh, bite my ass."

"Yes, sir. You are going to be a lifer. Back here ten years from now on your fourth tour, some kind of beer-drinking Gunny. 'The war must go on, says the Gunny.'"

"Yeah, and you'll be back on your farm, telling war stories, if you can get anybody to listen. Hey. What the hell are you smoking?"

Waterbull grinned pleasantly. "Good stuff. Wanna run one?"

"You trying to get me in trouble? You know I don't smoke in the bush."

Waterbull held it in, then grinned. "This ain't the bush. This is the *Bridge,* man." He took another hit.

Snake checked his watch: ten-thirty. "Oh, all right. It's been a long goddamn month, I shit you not." He took a deep hit, leaning back on the cot.

Waterbull was already high. It was his third joint that day. He slid out of his flak jacket. "Lots of dudes gone, huh?"

Snake nodded. Screw this, he thought. "Gimme my own." Waterbull complied. He took two deep drags. He could feel it already. "Hey. This is good stuff, Bull. Numbe One."

"Got it in Da Nang." Bull languished on the cot. "How's the new Lieutenant?"

"A grit. He burned Corky's boot."

"What?"

"Remember Corky?" Snake felt good, relaxed. He smiled. The top of his head began to tingle. "Good old Lieutenant Corky. Lost his leg, man. I had to check his balls."

"What?"

"He thought his dick was gone but it was hanging there, all right, but I had to check his balls." Snake giggled a little. "Hodges come in and Corky's boot was laying there, full of foot. Grossed him out. He made Flaky burn the boot. Bad style."

Waterbull was incredulous. "With the foot *in* it?"

"My new man Senator threw up."

"What is he, crazy?"

"Nah. He made it cool, man." Snake laughed, remembering. He was tingling comfortably. Bull glowed in the almost-dark. "I was dumping on him for it and he knocked me dead. Don't mess with him, Bull. He's all right. He asked me why I didn't do what I would have done. Oh, wow, I feel good."

"What?"

"He don't pull any lifer stuff and he calls in artillery. He keeps telling Austin to go easy on the games. Jesus. Austin."

"Who's Austin?"

"You'll find out. That same old face. Hey. How was it in Bang-clap?"

Waterbull chortled, sifting through his pack. He pulled out a string of pictures stuck inside a plastic accordion-style holder. "My wife."

Snake laughed for thirty seconds. Tears streamed onto the cot. It was the funniest thing he had ever heard. "No-o-o!"

Waterbull grinned dreamily. "Yeaaahhh."

Snake still laughed. "They'll never understand in Kansas." His comment seemed hilarious to him.

"She'll never see Kansas. Ah, we're not really married. I mean *married*. She just wouldn't screw unless I married her. Religion or something."

"So you did."

Waterbull giggled deeply. "I'da *killed* for a piece of that!" He stared fondly at the pictures, remembering. "Ohh, wow. Some kinda woman. Softest boobs. Quit laughing at me. Just check it out."

Snake grooved on the pictures in the dark, pondering each one dreamily. The girl smiled to the camera, variously dressed and undressed, shimmering black hair to her waist, rounded breasts inviting, wishing for caresses. Waterbull pointed to a picture of his "wife" sitting cross-legged on a bed, clad in bikini underpants, her breasts standing above crossed, lithe arms.

"Tell me you wouldn't marry that."

Snake pondered her. "I'm taking R & R in Bang-clap, Bull." He lay flat on his cot, laughing with anticipation. "I'm gonna marry her *too!*" He lay motionless, feeling lazy and peaceful. "Hey. You got Bagger's team. He don't groove on all this Marine Corps stuff. Only one other dude in it. Wild Man. He's crazy. Had another man O'Brien, got all screwed up the other day. You didn't know O'Brien. He won't be back. You don't know Wild Man, either. Where you been, Bull?"

"Took shots for two weeks to get rid of that clap. That was some bad shit."

Sergeant Austin held the tent flap in one hairy hand, bracing himself before entering the tent. It was three hours later. He took a deep breath, his lips tight, and finally threw the tent flap back and strode inside.

"Tighten-up time, girls."

He strode slowly down the aisle of the tent, examining its occupants. Four men on a near cot took a quick look up from their card game, then ignored him. Cannonball looked up from a letter as he lay on his cot, then returned to it. Bagger and Wild Man stared solemnly at him, almost insolent. He felt his blood rush. No respect anymore.

He looked around the tent in the semidarkness. Where's that—what's his name? *Snake.* He mimicked the word silently. Even Hodges calls him *Snake.* Like he's some kind of celebrity that can't be called by his last name or his rank. Snake. Snake my ass.

Snake was laying back on his cot, recently awakened from a nap. Still feeling pretty good. He noticed Austin and, with effort, rose and walked up to him. Now there's a same old face if I ever saw it, he joked to himself. Trouble, just waiting to unload.

As he neared Austin the Sergeant jerked a thumb in no particular direction, a gesture to indicate everywhere.

"Shaves."

Snake met his eyes, parroting his seriousness. "Shaves."

"Right now."

The entire tent looked at Austin in hostile silence. "I won't have you people walking around the battalion CP like bums. You're bad enough as it is." Still no response. "And by tomorrow afternoon I want to see skin on the sides of every head in this tent."

"Skin."

"Skin, Corporal. Haircuts. There's a gook barber outside the compound."

Austin strolled the tent, eyeing its sullen occupants. Fight a war with trash, he griped to himself again. He stopped in front of Phony's cot. Phony was chewing a wad of gum, reading a comic book. Bat Man. Hmmph. Well, it's a wonder he can read at all. Phony looked up from his comic book for one brief glimpse of Austin, then returned to it.

"Hey, Sarge. What's going down, anyway?"

Austin raged inwardly. What's going down, Sarge? Like I'm some kind of blood brother to this bullshit. Like I'm his goddamn buddy.

"*You're* going down, if you try to grow any more sideburns."

Phony guffawed, rubbing a cheek smooth as a baby's. "Sideburns? Hey, Sarge. I wouldn't know *how* to grow a sideburn." The tent filled with muffled laughs.

Austin examined Phony's gear, which lay in a heap by the side of his cot. His flak jacket covered his pack. On the back of the flak jacket Phony had scribbled in tall, black letters, *"Fuck it . . . just fuck it."*

Austin pointed to the flak jacket. "Get rid of that."

Phony grinned blandly at Austin for a moment, studying him, then emptied the pockets of the flak jacket. "O.K., Sarge." He picked it up and heaved it down the aisle of the tent, where it landed with a heavy thud near the door.

Everyone in the tent burst out laughing. Austin balled

his fists and screamed at Phony: *"I'll write you up, god-damn it! You wise-ass! Now go get that jacket!"*

Phony shrugged calmly, and retrieved the flak jacket. "You said get rid of it."

"Not the *jacket*, stupid. The shit you got scribbled on it. Scribble it *off* it. I thought we went through this the other day. What do you think that jacket is, a letter to a friend? It's a piece of military gear. You treat it that way."

"O.K., Sarge. Take it easy, huh?"

Take it easy. Jesus. Austin turned to Wild Man, the next cot down, who was fondly stroking the beginnings of a moustache.

"You a Corporal?"

Wild Man glared at Austin.

"When you make Corporal you can grow a moustache. Shave it off." He pointed to Wild Man's flak jacket, where he had written *Peace Through Fire Superiority*, and to Ottenburger's, the next cot beyond Wild Man, which said *If I die bury me upside down, so the whole world can kiss my ass.*

"Those, too. Un-fucking-military, girls. Get that shit off today. Understand?" The tent remained silent, unanswering. The hostility was so permeating that Austin felt his neck skin tingle. These people are Marines, he reassured himself. They're gonna be treated like Marines. He turned back to Snake, who stood expressionless where he had greeted Austin.

"I want this tent to be squared away. I'm coming through here twice a day. I want gear on top of racks, packs outboard."

Snake winced, holding one hand in the air. Somewhere, in the cobwebs of his memory: "—Outboard."

Austin shook his head. "Christ. Toward the wall on both sides." Snake nodded, remembering from boot camp. Ah. Outboard. Austin continued: "And I don't want all these magazines and cock books just laying around. Find a place for 'em. And don't forget. By tomorrow I want whitewalls."

"Whitewalls."

"Whitewalls. Haircuts." The tent remained silent.

Finally, Snake shrugged. "That it, Sarge?"

"For the tent. *You* come with me."

Austin led Snake out of the tent along the narrow finger that was the top of the J-shaped compound. Bunkers lined both sides of the finger. At the point, underneath the tall observation tower, there were four large bunkers, heavy with sandbags. Each supported a 106-millimeter rifle that jutted long and menacing toward the steep slopes outside the compound. The slopes were blanketed with barbed wire and concertina. Beyond them, on all three sides of the finger, were flat, bushy fields that extended for hundreds of yards.

Austin pointed to a treeline four hundred meters north and east of the compound, near the river. "You got the LP out there."

Snake squinted across the field. "Where?"

Austin was unspecific. "Out there. Where you can cover the treeline."

"You're shitting me."

Austin fixed his brooding eyes on Snake. "No, Corporal. I am not shitting you. Colonel's orders. That's your squad's LP while we're at the Bridge. Every night, one fire team on the LP. Where you put it is up to you. But it better be somewhere near that treeline."

Snake sat on a bunker and lit a cigarette, peering into the fields. He no longer felt good. His mind felt heavy, sullen. He sensed that Austin was enjoying his discomfort. He turned to the Platoon Sergeant, who had started to leave. "Hey, Sarge." Austin halted. "Why send an LP on the other side of a hundred meters of goddamn wire? How will it get back if we get hit?"

Austin stared stonily at Snake. "They'll walk."

"They can't. Hey, look. How're they gonna *walk* through all this wire, if there's gooners hitting the compound?" Snake shook his head. "They'd have to *fly*, that's what they'd have to do." Austin had begun to leave again. "I don't like it, Sarge. The whole thing sucks."

Austin stared impatiently at Snake. "I didn't ask you if you *liked* it, Corporal. I told you to *do* it."

"Enough is enough." Snake took a deep breath. "I ain't gonna do it."

Austin grew livid, walking toward Snake. "Who do you think you are, Chesty Puller? No one in the chain of command would risk your neck without a reason, Corporal. It's necessary to the defense of the perimeter.

Nothing like this is exactly dreamed up, you know. It came from the Colonel."

"I don't see him standing no LP. Let him do it."

Austin stood very close to Snake, looking down at him. His face seethed with fury. "You're on report."

"Huh?"

"You heard me. I've had enough of this wise-ass talk. You're on report for refusing an order to face the enemy." Austin pursed his lips, then tightened them. "I'm going to string you so goddamn high, Corporal."

"I wanna see Lieutenant Hodges."

"You aren't seeing anybody."

Snake grinned determinedly. "Oh, no, Sergeant. I got my rights. This is what you call your basic 'request mast,' know what I mean? I wanna see my Lieutenant. Right now."

"Well, what can I say? It doesn't seem right to me, either." Hodges sat on the point bunker, looking down into the fields. "I don't know why in hell I didn't figure it out before."

"Begging the Lieutenant's pardon, sir, it's been considered sound tactics to send listening posts in likely areas of enemy attack for—forever." Austin spoke flatly, knowing he had lost, but building a record for future arguments.

"Well, I'll tell you the rule I use, Sarge. The rule I use is, would I think it made any sense if I got sent out on it? And I wouldn't. So I don't like it."

"It didn't make any sense when General Shoup landed the troops at Tarawa, either, and lost two thousand in the first wave. But he did it. In all due respect."

Snake shook his head exasperatedly. "Come on, Sarge. This is *Vietnam.*"

Austin peered threateningly at Snake. "This is war. Vietnam, Iwo Jima, the Frozen Chosin Reservoir. The goddamn *moon.* War is war."

"All right, Sergeant Austin. You've got the LP tonight." Hodges stared evenly at his Platoon Sergeant, the corners of his mouth slightly upturned as he suppressed a smile.

"Sir?"

"You take it out tonight. Give me a report on how wise you think it is tomorrow morning."

Austin stared silently at Hodges for a long moment.
Then he gestured to Snake. "I'd like to see the Lieutenant
alone for a minute, sir."

Hodges nodded to Snake, who drifted along the bunkers until he discovered a gun team working on their
weapon, and began a discussion with them. Austin
watched Snake, waiting until he was out of earshot.
Then he turned to Hodges.

"In all due respect, sir, that was a cheap shot. I'm a
Platoon Sergeant, and I belong where the bulk of my men
are."

"They're *my* men, Sergeant Austin. And you belong
where I send you."

Austin's thin lips tightened. He peered across the mass
of barbed wire and concertina at the fields below. "I
don't make orders, sir. I only carry them out. I owe the
Corps my loyalty. If the Colonel decides there should be
an LP out there, I execute that order. Now, if the Lieutenant believes the LP shouldn't be out there, I suggest
he go talk with the battalion staff."

Snake and Hodges climbed down narrow wooden steps in
to the battalion command bunker, and entered a room
filled with a mass of radios and maps, built basement-
style underneath quintuple layers of sandbags.

Hodges approached a jowly, stocky First Lieutenant,
who apparently was running the command center, and
attempted to explain Snake's reasoning. The First Lieutenant glowered impatiently as Hodges spoke, alternating
his gaze from him to Snake. Finally he raised his eyes to
the ceiling of the bunker and lifted a hand, cutting Hodges
off.

"How long you been in Vietnam, Lieutenant?" He
emphasized the "Lieutenant" in an apparent attempt to distinguish his seniority.

Hodges shrugged unconcernedly. "A month or so."

The First Lieutenant scowled impatiently. "Well, look.
We've got more than four years of Vietnam inside this
bunker, just among the officers. We know what we're
doing. Don't tell us how to do our job."

"Look yourself. I don't care if you've been here all your
goddamn life." Hodges smiled calmly. "No disrespect to
the Colonel intended, you understand. But that don't

mean you can't take a suggestion. I think my man has a good point. LPs on the other side of this wire are crazy as hell."

The scowling man continued to alternate his gaze between Hodges and Snake. "All right. You made your suggestion. I'll talk it over with the Colonel."

"When will you let us know?"

"If he changes his mind, I'll let you know."

"All right." Hodges did not know how to force his point. "Can't ask for more than having the Big Six consider it, I reckon."

As they reached the top step of the bunker Snake pushed his hands into his trouser pockets. "Bullshit. He ain't gonna talk to the Colonel about this."

"Give the man a break. He said he would."

"Kersey hates our guts. And he's probly in there kissing the Colonel's ass right now. He won't cross the Colonel."

"You know him?"

"*Know* him? I know every freckle on his ass, Lieutenant. He was my Platoon Commander for two months. He's an asshole."

"I noticed that."

"Well, I guess I should tell you." Snake glanced quickly to Hodges as they walked. "He had a habit of sneaking up on people on the lines at night. Yeah. No shit. He liked to sneak up on people and then write 'em up when he caught 'em having a smoke or listening to the radio, or asleep. It got him points with the Skipper. Well, Wild Man Number One used to get really spooked at night. You can't blame him, you know? And he always swore that anything that moved on him was a gook. We told him about Kersey but Wild Man, he didn't care. He'd had the malaria, too. He was tired, and really flaky. And Kersey tried to sneak up on him. The company had been in contact every night for a week. Nobody knows for sure what was in Wild Man's head. But when Kersey started creeping up on him, Wild Man turned around and shot the shit out of the bastard." Snake's eyes brightened. "Pow. Twice. One in each leg."

Snake glanced again at Hodges, searching for a reaction. Hodges continued to walk next to him, apparently unruffled. "Yup. We all felt like putting Wild Man up for a medal. Anyway. Kersey's a biggy with battalion now. Him and the Colonel are tight. Nobody knows Wild Man did him. Everybody thinks he's a big wounded hero, shot by a gook. He knows, though. And he hates our guts, 'cause we know. He dumps on us every time he sees us. But he ain't gonna get us down. We *did* him. Wild Man did it for all of us." They walked a few more steps, silent. Snake shook his head. "But I never saw that man do anything except try to kiss a lifer's ass. As long as he's looking good to the Man, he couldn't give a rat's ass how many people are bleeding." Snake peered at Hodges one more time. "You gonna blow the whistle on old Wild Man Number One?"

Hodges shrugged, contemplating Kersey. He had met a dozen Kerseys in the Marine Corps already. They held all ranks, although to him they seemed to be mostly Majors. The Marine Corps exuded a special attraction for charlatans, out of proportion to their numbers in society: sour-faced, humorless men who actually believed that mere rank made a person more intelligent, compensated for personal deficiencies.

Hodges allowed himself a small smile, picturing the hulking Kersey sneaking up on a fighting hole in the black of night inside some steamy jungle perimeter, hoping to catch a malaria-shaken, angry, frightened Marine asleep or screwing off so he could court-martial the man and gain favor with the company commander. He snorted. Hell. I'd have shot the bastard, too. You can check out the lines without playing cat and mouse.

"Are you?"

"Huh?"

"Gonna blow the whistle on Wild Man?"

The Major's admonition from his first day, as he left An Hoa for the bush, still addled his reasoning. *They go crazy, Lieutenant. You will, too.*

"No." He grinned blandly to Snake. "I just wish the man had been a better shot."

The charred memory of the Old Bridge loomed above them, rising from the water on its blackened poles. Behind them, three hundred meters to the south, the Bridge compound sat on a red hill. A few hundred meters up-river the Seabees busily worked at the finishng touches for the new bridge.

The squad had just completed a reconnaissance patrol of the listening post site, and had stopped to cool off on the way back to the compound. They bathed and swam contentedly in the shallows of the river, combat gear and clothing in scattered heaps along the riverbank. Ottenburger sat on the sand bottom in two feet of water, holding a tiny mirror in front of his face, meticulously dragging a razor across an unlathered cheek. The others frolicked and washed in deeper currents.

Snake leaned against the water's force, feeling its mountain-cooled freshness massage him from feet to neck. He scrubbed his hair absently with a soap bar, and spoke to no one in particular. "Now that I seen it, it's even worse. It's no skin off Kersey's ass if somebody gets stuck out here."

Phony chuckled ironically. "I bet the bastard planned it. Payback for Wild Man Number One. He did it on purpose."

"Nah. Other units had it, too. That's what he told Hodges. It ain't because of us. It's because he's a dumb shit."

"Well, he'd probly groove on us getting it out here."

Snake rinsed his hair in the water. "So would Austin. He's really pissed at me for asking about it." He grinned at Phony. "He don't like you, either."

Phony's face lit up. "Yeah. Well, Austin has got to go. Hey. Gimme some soap." He grinned, catching the bar of soap that Snake tossed him. "Thanks."

Cannonball approached them, going underwater for a second to cool his creamy face. "Don' be such a one-way dude, Phony. You cain't do ever'body, man. Colonel say he wants a LP out here, it don' do no good to do the Sergeant. Like Austin says, man. We ain' gotta *love* it. We jus' gotta do it."

Phony nodded his head judiciously. "Uh huh. Well, I just gotta do *him*."

Bagger splashed in the water like a playful child. "Look. Why don't we just bag it, man? You know. Let's don't and say we did."

Cat Man smiled shyly to Bagger, moved to speech after having listened carefully to the discussion. "You don't know Kersey, Bagger. You got here too late for Kersey. He'll walk us to the wire every night. Just wait."

Bagger's turbulent face was a large squint. "So? We go down to the edge of the wire, find a nice ditch, maybe a bomb crater, and tune out."

Speedy interrupted, supporting Cat Man. "And get blown away by some H & I, or somebody flaky on the lines. No way, Bagger. We got to do this."

"If we could get Kersey to come out of that bunker after dark, I could do *him*." Phony.

"Do Kersey. Do Austin. Do the Colonel. Do me if I piss you off. You cain' do everybody in the world, Phony."

Phony grinned mischievously. "Don't piss me off, Cannonball."

"Do me. Do you. Dooby dooby do. That ain't the answer." Snake had emerged from deep thought. "I say the only way to handle this is to be cool. All of us go together to the Colonel, and play him off Kersey. You know, set it up like Kersey is the dumb shit he is, and let the Colonel decide it's stupid. Sort of a group request mast. Dig?"

Speedy studied Snake, then called to Goodrich. "Senator. Hey. Come here. We need some of your school, man. Tell us what happens if we all go to the Colonel about this."

Goodrich, who had been swimming at the fringes of the gathering, felt embarrassed to be relied on for an opinion. The reconnaissance patrol had left him with a shiver of panic when he turned around and measured the distant, wire-encircled compound from the LP site, but none of it made sense to him. Nothing had from the first day. This was merely more of the same.

He smiled self-consciously. "I don't really feel qualified to comment. I've never talked to a Colonel."

"Come on. Don't be an ass. What do you think?"

"We all hang, as I see it."

Speedy indulged him. "Why?"

"Well." He felt trapped. "If I were a Colonel, I'd think it was a mutiny. A squad of snuffies trying to tell me how to run my perimeter. The Army may be getting away with stuff like that, but this isn't the Army. We'd hang by our balls, maybe get bad discharges, too."

"Oh, bullshit." Snake held his ground. "Senator don't

know people. The Colonel would only do that if we put him on the spot. The angle is to put *Kersey* on the spot, and let the Colonel play Joe Cool and save us. Am I the kind of guy who looks for trouble? Hey." Snake attacked Speedy. "What are you using Senator for, anyway? You're the one always saying how he don't know shit about the bush."

"This ain't the bush. It's Colonels. And the man's got school."

"I don't care, really I don't." Goodrich was miserable at being the topic of debate. "None of this makes any sense to me. As far as I'm concerned, let's go to the Colonel and demand he send us *home*. If we're going to get into trouble, let's make it worth it."

Snake waved a hand at Speedy, vindicated. "See? Did you ever hear such a bunch of horseshit in your life?"

Waterbull waded over, dwarfing them all. "What the hell's got into you people since I been gone? An LP on Liberty Bridge, skate capitol of the Twenty-Fifth Marines, when you just spent two months in the Arizona. You all gone *dinky dau*? If we argued about every stupid thing we'd be screaming all day, every day. I think you're all pissed off just because it's Kersey and Austin, that's all."

Wild Man slapped Waterbull on the back, his thin frame skeletal in contrast to the huge redhead's. "Tell 'em, Bull. We'll take the LP every night."

Cannonball concurred. "I say do it."

Phony climbed out of the water and dried his smooth, unmarred body with his skivvy shirt. He started to put his trousers on. "O.K. Me too." He noticed Snake's disappointed grimace, and grinned blandly to his wiry squad leader. "But Austin's going, man. Boom-boom."

Hodges called into the tent and Snake ambled out, joining him on the road. They strode slowly toward the point of the compound, silent for several minutes, yet deeply comfortable with each other. Hodges lit his own cigarette, then Snake's.

"Thanks, Lieutenant."

Hodges nodded. "How's the LP?"

"They don't mind it. Everybody's had it one night, and they're used to it. Anything new from the Colonel?"

"Yeah. He says do it."

"Figures. Wonder if he's ever been out there. At night, I mean."

"You flat know he ain't. But we never been to Amphibious Warfare School, either."

"What do they teach at Amphibious Warfare School?"

"Korea."

"Ha. That's what I thought." Snake dragged silently on his cigarette.

Hodges snapped his fingers. "Damn. Almost forgot. You remember an operation about six or seven months ago, on Go Noi Island, where the company was working with some ARVN unit?"

"Oh, Christ. Don't tell me we got to do *that* again."

Hodges chuckled. "No. At least not any time soon. But there's gonna be a TV crew in here tomorrow morning. You know, network news from back in the World. And some correspondents. They want to ask some questions about the ARVN from people who were on that operation."

Snake grimaced darkly. "Fucking reporters. Goddamn leeches, sucking off of other people's blood. Sit like buzzards, watch us die for a fucking news story, then go back to Saigon and celebrate their story with a whore."

"You sound like you're not the man I need." Hodges grinned amusedly.

"What do you need?"

"Somebody from that op."

"Well. Me and Phony are all that's left, I think." Snake mulled it. "Baby Cakes and Ogre. But they ain't back yet."

"Well, the word is, get some people who were on that op, and let them talk. And tell them if they say anything bad about the ARVNs they'll get their asses kicked all the way from here to Hanoi."

"Ha." They had reached the edge of the compound. "You're right, Lieutenant. I ain't the man you need. But I got just the man for the job."

"Phony?"

"He'll groove on it."

Hodges moaned. "Yeah, but network news will never be the same!"

The interviewer had a Saigon tennis-court suntan and long hair. His utility uniform fit him like someone else's suit. His boots were unscuffed. He looked unbelievingly as Phony traipsed over to the camera, his head bobbing nonchalantly, three pieces of gum in his mouth. A First Sergeant called angrily to Phony just before he reached the interviewer, and he waved good-naturedly back, in his glory, and held the chewing gum in a dirty hand.

The interviewer did a short lead-in. Phony was the third man to be interviewed. The other two had given stock answers about the growing abilities of the ARVN. The interviewer addressed the same question to Phony, who scratched his head casually, contemplating it.

"Well. What they say is, they're all right. So I guess they're all right."

"What do you think, Corporal? You worked with them on Operation Minnesota Lake, which from all accounts was a great success."

Phony looked around him, grinning. There were more than a dozen Staff NCOs and officers staring expectantly at him. He waved to Austin, then to Kersey. "Hey, Sarge. Well. Minnesota Lake. Yeah. Go Noi Island. That was a couple months ago, like the other side of my life, you know? I was a new dude. We pulled a sweep and block on this river, and the ARVNs, they come up on the other side and we waited, you know, right on the water for two weeks till they come, and we couldn't even go down and get a canteen of water or nothing, except just at first light, 'cause we were the block and we were s'posed to be hiding. But you look at Go Noi sometime, you'll see there ain't even a damn tree, so how can we be hiding? But that was the rules, so we just cooked up there in the sun, looking down at that river. Damn, it was hot. I guess it was about seven months ago, 'cause Lieutenant Kersey, he wasn't shot yet. Ask him. He remembers, I'll bet. So we all got the ringworm and the hookworm from not washing and drinking all that bomb-crater water. It was a bust, you know? Then the ARVNs come sweeping up to the riverbank on the other side and just kept right on going till pretty soon the whole sweep was swimming in that river. I felt like opening up. Wild Man Number One, he had an accidental discharge from his machine gun and it come pretty close to one of them in the water. But it was like watching somebody screw your sister."

"Well, thank you—"

"But that was the only time I seen 'em, so I could be wrong."

On the way back to the troop tent, Phony was intercepted by Austin. "You're a dead man, Lance Corporal. You'll be a Private. You breathe wrong, you're going down. You understand?"

"Anything you say, Sarge." Phony shrugged helplessly, his face a bland, innocent smile. "They didn't want to know, they shouldn't ask."

11.

The concertina gate cracked open, then latched quickly shut, locking them out. They walked lonely, naked in the moon-dark, through the narrow break the road made in the field of jagged wire. Artillery boomed behind them, six howitzers firing far into the Arizona. The rounds crunched distant like a futile, muffled anger. Flares hung over Dai Loc, far to the front, like streetlights scattered on a placid hill. Just below, the river glimmered from the flares, narrow streaks of white across it. They moved heavily, bent like old men under flak jackets and helmets and weapons and ammunition. Two LAAWs apiece, five grenades, three bandoleers of ammo.

Speedy humped an extra twenty-five pounds: the radio. He whispered into the handset. "Three Charlie, leaving the wire."

They followed the outer wire, parallelling the finger that made the top part of the J. Back in the compound an 81-millimeter mortar mission fired. Tubes thunked and flashed behind them. Rounds landed like firing pistons far to the east, their front, in the Cu Bans.

They reached the point and broke away from the wire, seeking the streambed that would be their sanctuary for the night. It hid beneath waves of dry, scraping sawgrass that played their trouser legs like coarse violins as they fought it. The treeline grew in front of them, just visible below the blackening sky.

Finally the sawgrass dipped. Streambed. The treeline loomed now, a wall of puffy dark things, wide and impenetrable. Even from this distance, seventy meters, it emanated an ashy, dead odor of burnt-out hootches. They settled quickly into the streambed, knowing its contours: this was the third time Speedy's team had worked the listening post. Each man spread a poncho liner over the abrasive grass and lay inside the streambed.

Speedy whispered to the hissing handset: "Three Charlie, all set in."

Goodrich stretched out on the poncho liner. He took his bug juice from his helmet band and soaked his face and arms. He felt the tingle of it and was almost nauseated by the airplane-glue aroma. Whew, he mused. Bugs are almost better. He took a canteen out of his low trouser pocket and drank thirstily to wash the fear out of his mouth. He couldn't quite get it all. It lingered like bile. The compound was a hulking, warted silhouette, fire-flashing, boom-emanating, an isolated, impenetrable world behind them. Theirs was a four-man other world, of zoo-kept animals turned loose in the wilderness.

All stood the first watch together, lying side by side like moonbathers. They watched the treeline through the darkling sky, studying its outer edges when the flares creaked and dropped behind it, muttering to each other about mounds and points and dips.

Finally Speedy leaned across the streambed. It was nine o'clock.

"We give Smitty first watch. I take second. Burgie third, Senator fourth." Goodrich nodded, thankful: three straight hours to sleep. Number One.

Helmet off, beside him in the grass, he slept a fitful doze, face pushed against the poncho liner. Mortar flares creaked and whistled eerily over his head. Persistent mosquitoes orbited his ears, whining. Artillery and mortar missions left the distant compound with intermittent booms. Occasionally, he woke from the haunting silence of the dead village just beyond the trees. He smelled the ash that once was hootches and was chased by haunting visions through the reaches of his dozings: it was night and the villagers, mamasans and babysans and waterbulls and dogs, crept through the sawgrass toward the streambed, teeth bared, bent on revenge. But when he would awaken there was only silent blackness. Dead ash filled the air.

Finally, thankfully, he slept.

". . . I don't *know* what it is, Flaky. Put the Actual on. Hurry up, man." Speedy's dark eyes were fixed on the treeline. Goodrich rolled and immediately noticed the tautness that had strained the neck veins, squinched the eyes of the unflappable Speedy. He checked his watch. Eleven-fifteen.

"Roger, this is Three Charlie. We got noises out here." Pause. Speedy's eyes had not moved. "Sounds like somebody digging in. Right at the edge of the treeline. That's *most* affirm. No. I can't see shit. I don't *know* what it is."

Goodrich listened carefully, terrified. There were muffled whispers in the trees, clangs of metal in the brick-hard dirt. The metal worked a rhythm as the voices urged each other. Clang *clang* clang. *Clang* clang *clang*. Three entrenching tools, digging quickly just at the treeline's edge.

"About fifty, seventy-five meters. Roger. Right where we're s'posed to be. That's affirm." Pause, then a hoarse, louder whisper. "Well, listen, man. If you're gonna put a fire mission on it you better let me adjust. Negative. We are too *close* for eighty-ones. Roger. Maybe fifty meters." Another pause. "O.K. We'll just keep an eye on it."

Speedy woke Ottenburger, holding his head down on the poncho liner when he began to raise it. Burgie looked quizzically up at Speedy's face, then comprehended. Speedy then woke Smitty, on the other side of him, holding him down as well. He whispered as he put his meaty hand on Smitty's head. "Gooks. Shhh."

Burgie listened attentively to the spadings and grimaced, deeply upset. "Ohhh. They got something big out there, or they wouldn't be digging it in." He nudged Speedy. "Did you ask for a mission?"

"No sixties on the hill. We're too close for art'y or eighty-ones."

Burgie scrunched back into the grassy streambed and peered behind them, at the compound. It was an unreachable island, floating in a sea of concertina. Marooned. "You're right. We are *fucked*, man."

Twenty minutes. Thirty. Muffled laughings from the treeline, growing bolder. The insistent rhythm of the clang-

ing spades. The team hulked silently in the streambed,
afraid to leave or even move for fear of becoming instant
targets. They no longer dared even to whisper to one
another.

Every fifteen minutes there was a barely audible chatter
from the handset, which was now turned down to a whis-
per-silent volume. "Three Charlie Three Charlie Three
Charlie, Three Three Three. If you are all secure key your
handset twice, if not key it once."

One deliberate, angry squeeze.

Suddenly there were loud explosions across the river.
The northern compound literally erupted. Recoilless rifles
flashed and boomed, again and again, their explosions
raising clouds of dirt inside the compound. Machine guns
and small arms hammered at the Marines. The two-platoon
perimeter fought back. Red and green tracers interlaced,
careening into the black air, making weaving patterns in
the night.

The artillery battery on the Bridge compound reacted.
It turned its guns north and lobbed dozens of projectiles
across the river, seeking to silence the attack. New bright
flashes, hazes of dust, grouped around the northern compound.

Then a moment of anticipatory lull. Goodrich knew
what was going to happen. He wished he could tell them in
the Bridge compound. He wished he could dig a hole in
the dirt and come back out in California. Watch out, he
groaned inwardly, too afraid to cry. Oh, shit. Here it
comes. Right now.

An avalanche of mortar rounds, timed from a dozen
tubes to land together on the southern compound. Then
just above the stranded team the deep pops of a heavy
machine gun. Goodrich listened to himself whimper. He
could not stifle it. It seemed to him a scream that would
give them all away. But finally he realized that it was no
more than a scratchy, whispering whine.

The Bridge compound's defenders were caught unaware, having begun to feel like spectators to the northern
compound's furious defense. Bodies went flat inside bunkers, seeking cover from the mortar barrage. As they did,
streams of sappers poured through the outer wire, sliding
pipes of bangalore torpedoes to clear pathways through
the concertina. For a moment, they were unnoticed, the

explosions they created blending with the mortars. They broke through both sides of the J shaped hill, just at its hook, tossing satchel charges of explosives into the nearest bunkers. Half of the bunkers on the artillery side, unmanned as their defenders had helped with the firing missions on the northern compound, were quickly taken by the NVA. The rest of the perimeter swarmed with creeping, dashing sappers.

Two bunkers were lost just down from third platoon's last position. The sappers manned the bunkers after killing the occupants with satchel charges, and provided a beachhead on the lines. A stream of shadows poured into the compound between the bunkers. The first cell of NVA that raced past the bunkers burned an entrance with a whooshing flamethrower. It ignited the corner of a nearby tent, and drew bright-red answers from a host of rifles fired from nearby bunkers. There was no second whoosh. Its trigger man and his mate lay dead beside low smoulders from the torchlit tent.

Another sapper team crept quickly to the center of the compound and encountered two almost identical bunkers. In its haste it demolished the chapel, leaving the command center bunker unscathed. After the chapel exploded, in a detonation that raised a bright flash and leveled the bunker in a smoking heap, another fierce mortar barrage shook the hill. The North Vietnamese would attempt to take out more bunkers, consolidate, then retreat through the breaks they had made in the wire.

Speedy's team cringed in the streambed, unspeaking, wincing as the gun cut loose again. Its explosions seemed so close that one could reach a hand up and lose it to a bullet. Each man knew that if he made an untoward move, revealing himself in any way, the whole team would not last five minutes. Nowhere to go. Nowhere to hide.

It's a twelve-seven, mused Goodrich. I've heard the stories. They can cut down trees. He hugged the ground closer, conscious of the mere inches of dirt that separated him from the cacophony above him. It seemed almost logical to him that he was going to die. The worst part was not knowing when. Maybe I should get it over with, he pondered. Stand up and let them shoot me. Maybe I should charge the gun and try to take it out. Snake would.

He looked at the others. Nobody moved. He needed to scratch a mosquito bite. He tried to go to sleep.

Sappers danced and dived, quick shadows under phosphorescent flares and smoldering tents. Anything that moved was suspect. Steady rifle fire poured into the two overrun bunkers, having suppressed the NVA riflemen there. Other sappers were in the wire and inside tents and in ditches. They hid and crept throughout the perimeter, creating chaos.

Staff Sergeant Austin dashed across the perimeter. He zigzagged. He crawled. He finally made it to the bunkers, jumping into a sandbagged position near the NVA breakthrough. He knelt for a moment on the floor of the bunker, catching his breath. Jesus. He took his helmet off and wiped his forehead. He looked up then, and found Phony, Cat Man, Cannonball, and newly arrived Big Mac casually leaning against the bunker walls. Big Mac was watching tracers pour into the NVA-held bunkers as if it were on television. The others peered down at Austin.

Phony grinned, nodding to him. "Whooee, Sarge." He gestured toward where Austin had come from. "John Wayne woulda been proud of ya. No shit."

Austin stood. "How are you people holding up?"

Phony shrugged. "A-OK, know what I mean? The gooks in them bunkers been waxed." He pointed toward the command bunker, two hundred meters down the road. "Rest of 'em went thataway." He smiled unconcernedly. "We get rounds every now and then. But we're skating."

Austin nodded importantly, almost melodramatically, his swarthy face flushed. "Keep your eyes open. They're everywhere."

Phony bounced his head, nodding. "Sure, Sarge."

An explosion echoed on the road, just behind the bunker. Austin crouched, then jerked his thumb toward it. "See?"

"That was a mortar round, Sarge."

Austin's jowls split in a wincing frown. No respect. He looked both ways, watching creeping, distant shadows. Finally he jumped out of the bunker, toward the next position. He took five steps and dove to the earth, searching his front again.

Phony held a grenade in his hand. He pulled the pin, then casually let the spoon fly, never losing his bland grin. He tossed it expertly, five meters on the other side of Austin. Austin started to rise. *Boom.* He fell on his face, motionless.

Phony yelled loudly. *"Corpsman up!"*

Big Mac stared unbelievingly. "Jesus *Christ!* What did you *do?"*

Phony shrugged absently, watching Austin writhe. "Nothing." He allowed himself another innocent, bland smile. "What you mean, man? That was a mortar."

The officers inside the command bunker had assumed control of all tactical nets, directing the defense of the compound from their underground haven. Kersey, washed in the bunker's fluorescent brightness, worked from a large composite map of the compound and its surroundings. He communicated to the listening posts, and to radios positioned in various bunkers along the perimeter, attempting to determine enemy gatherings and strong points through such reports. With that information, he would advise the battalion commander as to possible artillery missions and air strikes.

Hodges, out on the perimeter, was reduced, in effect, to a radioman. He relayed reports to the command bunker concerning the status of his platoon's sector of the huge perimeter. At other times, he worked his way from bunker to bunker, as Austin had been doing, to check on casualties and ammunition consumption. Behind him dawdled a murmuring, cursing Flaky, with the platoon radio.

When Austin went down, Hodges was in the next bunker, thirty meters away. With him in the bunker were Snake, Waterbull, Wild Man, and Bagger. Austin fell between the two bunkers and immediately began to groan madly. Hodges, having been unaware of Phony's designs on Austin, did not read the knowing looks that passed among the bunker's occupants.

Snake glanced quickly to Hodges, catching his reaction, then smiled sardonically. "Ain't anybody gonna help Austin?"

Austin had tightened into a ball. A burst of AK-47 fire passed just over the bunker. Behind him the twelve-seven tore angry rents in the still night air. Thirty meters up the road three more mortar rounds impacted. Wild Man snorted. "Let him bleed a little first."

Hodges crawled alone to Austin. The grenade had gone off to the Sergeant's front and left, peppering him along his whole left side, except where his flak jacket blocked the shrapnel. He bled from his forehead. Several pieces had entered his chest and stomach where his flak jacket hung open. He clutched his stomach, still curled into a tight ball.

Austin cursed to himself as Hodges approached, seeming almost to revel in his bleeding. "Goddamn, Lieutenant. I never heard a fucking thing. Oh, Jesus." Austin's tight mouth experimented with its own versions of wonderment and disbelief. He managed a small smile, and stroked a slippery wet undershirt. "Sorry, Lieutenant. Looks like you're gonna have to get yourself a new Papa Sierra. I won't be back."

Hodges dragged Austin by the belt toward Phony's bunker. Austin screamed in painful protest to the tugs. "Hold on, Sarge. I'll get you a doc, man. And you *know* we're all gonna miss you."

Sickening crunches behind them, walking toward them, unstoppable, like a flash flood. Twirl*Boom* Twirl*Boom* Twirl*Boom*. Eighty-one-millimeter mortars, walking toward the treeline. Twirl*Boom* just behind them Twirl*Boom* just in front of them Twirl*Boom* inside the trees.

Speedy grabbed the radio handset and whispered urgently. "Cease fire! Cease *fire*, goddamn it!" Pause. "The mortars. Three Charlie. *Charlie!* You're blowing us away with your mortars! We're too close!" Pause. "I don't give a *fuck* about the gun, man! Start giving a fuck about us!" Another pause. Speedy turned wryly to Ottenburger. "It's Kersey. *Cabron.* He says it's for our own good."

Burgie grimaced tightly. "Lucky us."

A wounded sapper dangled in the wire, wrapped up in the concertina where the NVA had first broken into the compound. He was clearly visible under the illumination flares, thirty meters out, dressed in shorts and banded with strings of ropes on his arms and legs that isolated his blood in eight-inch instant tourniquets.

Snake studied him. His left leg was off above the knee and his midsection had been pierced. Snake wondered absently what had hit him. They were inside the compound before anybody had a chance, he mused. Stupid shit prob'ly got in the way of his own bangalore torpedo.

The sapper appeared comfortable, not attempting to disengage himself from the jags of metal, occasionally wiggling an arm to ponder its movement, now and again lifting his head to examine the bunkers full of Marines who peered back at him.

And every now and then he implored the shadows, almost comically, *"Chieu hoi,"* uttering those magic words of surrender as if he had ventured all the way to that barbed stopping point in order to defect. As if he had been wrongly demolished while crossing the wired threshold over to the Other Side.

"Chieu hoi!"

Snake shook his head, laughing at *Chieu Hoi* on the wire. On the far side of the perimeter Chieu Hoi's comrades fought fiercely, still controlling several artillery bunkers. There were booms, scattered bursts of weapons in the tent section; 106s and artillery boomed at clumps outside the wire; the 12.7 tore angry, ragged holes in the air.

"Chieu-u-u-u-u hoi. Chieu-u-u-u-u-u hoi." Illumination flares dangled over him and he hung delicately from his bed of wire, the banded stump of leg quivering. Chieu Hoi managed a smile. To his right another fierce eruption as a reaction squad attempted to root his comrades from their bunkers.

"Chieu hoi," he said, with urgent logic.

Finally Snake could endure it no longer. He screamed over to Cat Man's bunker. "Cannonball, shut that fucker up." Thunk *boom.* Blooper. The explosion sprinkled the sapper with new holes. He rocked slightly on his bed of concertina.

He moaned now. It was worse. He began a mumbling argument with himself, perhaps cursing the lying pamphleteer who taught him the magic phrase that did not work. He decided to try again. He looked toward the bunkers, smiling hopefully, and instructed them once again. *"Chieu hoi."* Then, very quickly: *"Chieuhoi."*

"Shut u-u-u-u-p!" It was unclear who yelled it. Someone

shot Chieu Hoi. Another rifle joined. Another. Finally they stopped. Down the perimeter the reaction squad still fought fiercely.

"Move?" Speedy was incredulous. "Where the fuck are we supposed to move *to?*" He listened for another moment. "Wait a minute." Pause. "Fuck the Colonel, wait a minute." He turned to the team. "Kersey says we gotta move. Says they're calling in eight-inchers from An Hoa to knock the twelve-seven out, and we're on gun-target line."

Smitty glowered in the dark. He had been in Vietnam a week. "I say stay, man. I ain't moving."

Ottenburger shook his head. "Ever seen an eight-incher land? We gotta move." He appeared drained, beaten. "We are truly fucked, man."

The gun opened up again, ragged rounds above their heads, as if to rankle them. Goodrich looked over to Speedy, trying to remain cool but visibly trembling. "Where?"

"I don't know. Two hundred meters left or right, he says. Two hundred fucking meters." Speedy lay flat, hugging his poncho liner in his misery. "Got any ideas?"

Ottenburger glanced over the narrow dip of streambed. He shuddered. "It ain't gonna work."

Speedy pondered it darkly, his wide face pushed into his poncho liner. Finally, he decided. "We'll crawl down the streambed. Stay low, find a good spot, lay chilly."

He grabbed the handset and keyed it. "This is Three Charlie. We're going to the left, down the streambed." Pause. "I don't know where it goes." He eyed Burgie ironically. "Probly to the gook CP." Pause. "Well, give us fifteen minutes. We're gonna be crawling."

Speedy tucked the handset into his helmet band and turned to Goodrich. "Get going, Senator. Stay low."

Goodrich did not want to leave. He began to fold his poncho liner. Maybe it'll be over by the time I fold it, he mused, comfortable with his irrationality.

Speedy crawled up and pushed him. "C'mon, stupid. Get going."

Smitty was still defiant. "Screw it. I still say stay, man."

Speedy was becoming excited. "Cool it, boot! We gotta go!"

The gun opened up again. Smitty lay flat. "I'm staying."

"Good-bye." Speedy nodded urgently to Goodrich. "Get going."

Goodrich began to crawl, staying very low, pushing the grass flat with one hand and dragging his rifle with the other. Every five or ten feet he stopped, listening to the front. Behind him Smitty rushed to catch up with the team. "Goddamn it, wait up!"

The gun opened up again, blasting the perimeter. Goodrich listened. It sounded far away, no longer threatening. He sensed that the team had at last evaded it, and came to his hands and knees, crawling faster. He wanted to reach the new position and stop moving.

Pop. An illumination flare burst above the team. Pop. Another. Pop. Another. Speedy called angrily in a hoarse whisper, "Get down, man! Freeze!"

They all lay flat. The flares burned brightly, swinging lazily on their parachutes, day-brightening the field. Speedy talked excitedly into the handset. "Tell 'em to cut the illum, man! We're sitting ducks out here! *Charlie!* Three Charlie!" Finally the last flare went dead. Goodrich lay flat for another moment, listening for movement. Speedy urged him again. "Get moving, Senator! Hurry up!" Goodrich moved to his knees and crawled quickly down the streambed.

On the point bunker of the compound a man sat beside a large, ominous weapon, staring determinedly into an L-shaped site, carefully cranking two wheels. He caught the movement, saw the shadows when the flare popped. He sighted in under the illumination, then waited for it to burn out so the backs would raise above the ditch again. His assistant gunner had been shot by the twelve-seven two hours before. Now comes payback, he thought grimly.

"Fire the one-oh-six!" There was a terrific boom, a white-hot flash of back blast. He grinned meanly. Take that, you gook motherfuckers.

And then a figure running along the ditch that connected the bunkers, hands in the air, screaming to the gunner:

"Don't fire! Oh, no no no! Didn't you get the word? That's the LP!"

White flash distant, heavy rush just after him, like a minisecond of violent hailstorm. Then an angry, rolling *boom.* Gunner was one inch of handcrank off. The flesh-ette round erupted just up the hills, its centerpoint in back of Smitty. Nine thousand dart-shaped nails saturated that portion of the field, filled the ditch, and drove Smitty and Speedy lifeless against the streambank.

Goodrich turned when the boom rolled down and gasped. They were both caught in the middle of a crawl, reaching down the streambed for the haven from the eight-inchers. He stared, feeling isolated and abandoned, and then remarked absently to himself, through stark terror, about the surrealism of it. They aren't even bloodied, he noted. It's as if a referee stepped in and blew a whistle, removing them from a game. Tweeeet. You're dead. You, too. You moved when a flare was up and you got it. Now in a *real* war . . .

But they were really dead. The darts had saturated them so quickly that they did not bleed, as if they both died in the middle of a heartbeat that never finished, never pushed the blood out of the myriad of holes.

Goodrich was in a frozen panic. That was our own gun. They're all trying to kill us. They want us dead. Everybody wants us dead. Speedy hated me and now he's dead. I'm not going to make it but Speedy's dead.

"Senator." Ottenburger spoke calmly, almost sleepily. "Hey, Senator. Give me a hand, huh?"

Burgie. Oh, God. How could I forget about Burgie?

Ottenburger lay, half-hidden by sawgrass, only three feet behind Goodrich. Goodrich turned slowly in the streambed, careful not to raise his body off the ground, and crawled the inches to Burgie's face. Burgie smiled winsomely under the thin moustache, his eyes pleading with Goodrich.

Say it isn't so, Senator.

"I can't feel either leg." Ottenburger continued to smile, the eyes begging Goodrich to perform some miracle. "It's all cold, man. Everything's just cold."

Goodrich stared back uncertainly, wishing for some word that would make the past two minutes go away. Burgie's arms and face were unscratched. Maybe, thought Goodrich . . . He parted the sawgrass where the blast had spun Burgie's lower parts. The grass was wet. Burgie was a dripping ooze from the middle of his waist to his ankles.

Goodrich inhaled the heavy rich blood odor, felt his

fingers slide along the oil-slick fabric over Burgie's legs, and gagged. He caught himself, and lifted Burgie's shirt to try to examine the middle parts. Then he could not hold back. He vomited into the grass, inches from Ottenburger's blood pool.

Burgie eyed him, still smiling, still hoping. "Pretty bad, huh, Senator?"

Goodrich kept his head in the grass. He retched again. I can't look at him, he thought to himself. There's nothing I can do. Can't tie him off. Can't patch him up. Can't get him out of here. Behind him, the gun opened up on the compound again.

Maybe I can call.

He inched down to Speedy's carcass and took the handset from under him. The radio was dead. He had known it would be. At least I won't have to look at Burgie if I play with it, he reasoned. He turned the knobs, banged it gently and absently keyed the handset, still petrified of the gun team in the treeline. No effect. The radio was shot to hell.

There were a lot of soldiers in the treeline. He could hear them whispering and he thought he could smell them. He thought they were laughing, celebrating, but he didn't know Vietnamese so it was just silly gook talk, up and down the music scale. He thought they stank but it could have been a waterbull pen in the ville. He thought he was bleeding all over, dripping off his crotch and chest, but it could have been sweat, or Burgie's blood, or his own vomit. His eyes burned and his arms hurt where they had scraped against the coarse sawgrass blades. He thought his arms bled, too, from the grassblades. But it could have been sweat. Or Burgie.

"Senator." The same soft, pleading voice. "Hey. Help me, man. Help me, Senator."

Goodrich turned and crawled back toward Ottenburger, pulling cautiously on the grass and pushing with his toes. Ottenburger eyed him sleepily, then burped up a stream of blood. Oh, my God, thought Goodrich. His stomach, too.

"It's all cold, Senator. Can you patch me up?" Burgie still grinned, sleepily.

The first eight-incher hit the treeline, with a terrifying, huge explosion that rent the earth, sending tree roots and huge clods dancing in the air. Goodrich and Ottenburger were covered with a veil of fresh-erupted earth.

"Help me, Senator." Then, with numb finality, "I'm gonna die, aren't I? You're just waiting for me to die." Burgie burped again. "Oh, God. Can't you patch me up?"

Goodrich peered into the ice-blue eyes, but could not hold them. "You're O.K., Burgie. You just need a doc, that's all." There was a moment of silence as all near firing abated. Goodrich felt certain that nearby enemy soldiers would hear them. "Now, hold it down, O.K., Burgie? No noise, man."

Burgie did not answer. He continued to stare at Goodrich through calm, heavy-lidded eyes. Goodrich was becoming unnerved, feeling damned by the dying Burgie.

"Patch me up, O.K., Senator? Help me, man."

"You need a doc."

Another earth eruption, an explosion so loud and close that it seemed to come from inside, to be a living part. Burgie still stared, oblivious to the dirt shower. His voice took on a fading, pleading tone, yet he still smiled hopefully.

"Can't you stop it?"

I'm in hell, thought Goodrich, over and over. I'm in hell. He crawled to Burgie's face because he was too afraid to whisper from three feet away. His own face was contorted in its fear and anguish. *"I can't."*

"I'm gonna die. Oh, Buddhist Priest. I'm only nineteen. It's cold, Senator."

"You'll be all right."

"Don't leave me, Senator. Oh, God. Don't leave me, man."

"I won't, Burgie. I won't leave you. Now, hold it down. O.K.?"

First light. The rubble of the chapel smoked lazily, little curls of gray still reaching from the heap of blackened sandbags. There was an occasional, isolated burst of rifle fire as the last of the sappers were rooted out of bunkers and tents. The mess-hall Gunny opened up his supply tent and found an NVA soldier nonchalantly chewing on a load of bread, like a stuporous rat. The Gunny cut him down, sending bullets through the rations. The soldier lay dead in a pool of sugared water from canned fruit.

Along the perimeter's edge, the wire held dozens of

charred treasures, blown to bits, scorched, decapitated. A mechanical mule drove along the dirt road, loading bodies to be buried later in a mass entombment outside the compound.

The concertina gate creaked open. A column of hulking, exhausted figures filed slowly down the narrow road. In front of them, the river shimmered red with sunrise. The patrol followed the outer wire and passed the inside hook of the J-shaped hill where one string of sappers had broken into the compound. There were more than a dozen bodies caught along the wire, like fish snagged randomly by a wide net.

A transistor radio cut into the silence. "Gooooo-o-o-o-ood morning, Vietnam!"

Hodges bristled. "Tell Bagger knock off the sounds."

The order passed quickly up the column. The radio went silent. The only noise now was the blunt scraping of sawgrass on their legs.

Finally Wild Man stopped. He was standing in a short ditch, among four poncho liners half-buried under clumps of dirt and branches. Hodges waved him on. "Left. Down the streambed."

Hodges peered into the looming treeline. The twelve-seven lay awkwardly on its side, half-buried under riven earth, one leg of the tripod jutting into the air. He felt his lips go tight. Well. They certainly got their twelve-seven.

Just beyond the poncho liners Smitty's helmet lay in the ditch, abandoned in his frantic crawl to catch the rest of the team. They followed the streambed for seventy meters more. Finally, the team sprawled before them, surrounded by the buzz of feasting flies and the cooked aroma of drying blood.

Wild Man halted by Smitty's corpse. The rest of the patrol bunched up behind him. They stared silently for a long moment, absorbing the gut-wrenching impact. Finally Waterbull spoke in a barely audible tone, as if he were mimicking a sportscaster.

"Senator's O.K. Senator made it."

Goodrich still sat next to Ottenburger, who lay dead over a large scab of blood that buzzed with flies. Goodrich's helmet was in the streambed and his head was between his knees, the forehead resting on one crossed arm. He looked up slowly when Waterbull spoke, then gazed numbly at the cluster that was peering mutely at him.

"I can't talk. Please. Don't ask me about it."

Hodges called to the compound for an amphtrac. Snake approached Goodrich and put an arm on his shoulder, offering him a cigarette. Goodrich pushed Snake's arm away.

"Leave me alone."

Goodrich stood with effort, and found that he was shaking uncontrollably. He reached down to pick up his weapon and stared numbly at Burgie's corpse. His lower intestines rumbled fiercely and he felt his anus spasm wildly and he dropped his weapon, running ten feet down the streambed as he yanked his trousers open. He squatted shakily in the sawgrass and excreted a gush of brown water that was odorous with his last night's fear. He held his head in his hands, not wanting to view the rest of the squad that stood nearby. Sawgrass scratched his ass cheeks. Flies discovered his excretum and buzzed lazily below him. The sun cooked up his moisture and he was surrounded with the stench of fear. He rolled forward to his knees and retched, great dry heaves that drained a spittle of bile from his already empty stomach.

Snake walked over and offered him a canteen of water. "Take a drink, Senator. You'll feel better."

Goodrich drank with effort, still shaking. "God, I'm so fucked up."

"Put it outa your mind, man—"

Goodrich began to cry. He shuddered, his chest heaving. "Put it out of my mind? Oh, shit. What do you know? You want to see me cry? There. See? Are you happy?" Snake reached for him and he backed away, still sobbing. *"Go away."*

"You need to get some chow inside you and catch some Zs."

"I'll go myself. I don't need you. Leave me alone."

Goodrich walked back toward the compound, sobbing, catching his breath. He retrieved his poncho liner from the abandoned LP site, getting his first look at the huge gun that had caused his terror. He saw limbs and uniform pieces scattered among the clods. It upset him more.

He couldn't think. His mind was scarred from fear, bludgeoned by a new self-hate. He cried and the red dust of the road stuck to his face. His sweat melted crusts of Ottenburger's blood on the back of his hands, making rivulets of pink run down his fingers. He threw his rifle into the weeds next to the road and walked several steps, then went mechanically back and retrieved it. Neither act required a decision.

The compound was in front of him. They were still throwing bodies onto trucks and hauling them away. The mortar crew was already firing new missions into the Arizona. Last night it had been an unreachable haven, but now it was a wire-encircled prison.

I'm in hell, Goodrich sobbed over and over. I'm in hell I'm in hell I'm in hell.

There was no patrol back to the compound. A few caught a ride on the loaded amphtrac, sitting on top after the dead men had been loaded inside. Others walked in twos and threes, at their own leisure. Snake and Hodges strolled slowly up the dust road together, kicking at its red powder layer, smoking pensively.

Finally Snake spoke. "A bummer, man. I never seen anything like it."

Hodges kicked at the dust. "I have to write letters."

Outside the wire, a caterpillar tractor was scooping up mounds of earth, preparing a mass grave for the dead NVA soldiers. Snake gestured toward it. "They better dig a deep one. I bet we killed a hundred gooks last night." He reconsidered. "Eighty, anyway."

"Yeah, but what can you say. 'Dear Mrs. Ottenburger. We got a hundred gooks and three Marines. Sorry about that.'" Hodges shook his head. "I just can't write the goddamn letters."

"Then don't. Sir." Snake put his arm on Hodges' shoulder for a brief moment. "I'll do it. I wrote 'em for Vitelli and Marston. Hey. Don't let it get to you, Lieutenant. If *you* start crying, we're in the hurt locker."

They reached the compound and Phony was sitting on a bunker at the edge of the road, popping a wadful of gum. "Hear the news, man?"

"What's that?"

Phony grinned ironically to Snake. "My man Kersey's gonna get himself a *Silver Star*."

Snake glanced at Hodges: was I right, or what? "For last night."

"That's affirm. Him and the Colonel."

Snake squinched up his mouth. "I'll bet they never left that bunker over there."

Phony grinned again. "Well, Kersey did. He just went down for chow."

"Hmmph. The only thing that surprises me is they didn't put each other up for the goddamn Medal of Honor." Snake considered it. "Prob'ly didn't have enough casualties."

Snake and Hodges walked through the tent area, toward the platoon tents along the finger of the compound. Kersey approached, his utility uniform still clean, carrying a mess tray filled with food. He glared at Snake.

Snake smiled blandly to Kersey. "Hey-y-y-y, Lieutenant Kersey. Hear you're gonna get the Big Star. Yes, sir. Some day you'll be a General. Yup. It's gonna look real nice up there with your—*Purple Heart*." He threw the final words like daggers.

Kersey scowled at Snake, his face washed with hate. They passed on the dirt road, then Snake shrugged ironically. "Yes, sir. That's another reason why."

"Why what?"

"Why I'd kill that man in a minute, if I ever had the chance."

12.

PHONY

Knock on the door and hide. If somebody answers, wait until the door is shut and make your bird. If nobody answers, knock again. Loud. Peep the neighbors out. If a neighbor comes to a window, wait until they go away, then make your bird. If nobody answers and no neighbors notice, go on in. Break a pane of glass. Shimmy a loose door. Ain't no biggy.

Don't take too much. Hard to carry. Hard to fence. They notice quicker and they remember more.

Find yourself a fence. They're everywhere. Some fences give you skag. Ask for a taste before you trade. If what you got is good enough, they'll give you a taste. But after that you better trade. If you don't, somebody's gonna do you.

Or play hit man. So many stupid people. It ain't hard. Catch somebody right, like when their arms are full. Hold you a knife or a gun if you got one and start to take their money. If they move, bonk 'em one. Do 'em quick. Don't cut 'em. Don't shoot 'em. Too much trouble if you're caught. If they get the drop on you, run away. Make that bird.

If you get caught, play scared. There's room for that, too. No sweat. They'll send you to a home, only it's a jail. Juvie Hall. Be good in jail. They're mean bastards, anyway. If they want a piece of you, be sweet. If you're good, they let you out. Foster home again. Be cool for a couple of weeks. Then you run away and find a door and knock on it and hide.

If you don't get caught, that's cool. Trade you for some skag and bring it back. Throw down a Twinkie and a Coke for dinner and then lean back against the bare wall, right there on the floor with all the dirt and roaches, and shoot up. Rip. Pow. It takes your breath and leaves you there all low and floating, there ain't any feeling like it.

That's living.

There were a dozen foster homes, where he'd learned The Smile. The early years of agonizing days spent under disapproving glances when emotions were unveiled, as if emotions, other than a pleasant front, were unnatural and condemnable. As if a cry for help were a weakness and, more important, an intervention and a bother. The only solution, the only workable attitude, was to keep The Smile in good repair, to be careful not to ruffle the Man or the Bitch, and then to fight like hell, any way he could, for what was his. Or for what he wanted.

At ten he started running. By thirteen there was no way in hell they could keep him in. He'd found the freedom of the street, and he dealt with its chimeras in the same way: grin at it until it turns around, then unload. And run like hell.

By sixteen, he was in the Federal narcotics farm, after having come down with hepatitis from a dirty needle. He was the youngest person on the farm. He was good. He played scared and innocent. He knew jails. The other inmates named him Phony.

At seventeen he was on the street again. Incorrigible. Heavy. Whatever it means. He had a probation officer. The man was worried about Phony's future. Phony had never had a job. He had a civilian record, the officer shuddered, that would make a Juvie judge break down and cry.

The probation officer decided that the only way to balance out Phony's record, to give him a fresh start, was for him to go into the service and come out with a clean record. A good discharge would give him a clean slate. He might even learn a marketable skill.

Phony had raised his eyebrows at that. Yeah. Like I could be a hit man or something.

The probation officer wrote letters. He emphasized that Phony had made a good adjustment since his latest release, and seemed desirous of making a contribution to society. He emphasized that Phony had come from a deprived background, and had not had a chance to become a responsible citizen. He made certain to point out that Phony's offenses were Juvenile, and should not be held against him.

The Marine Corps took him. The probation officer was elated.

And Phony did all right. He knew jails.

13.

April. *Already* . . .

Back in the villes again. Somebody said it was an operation with a name, but it had its own name: Dangling
the Bait. Drifting from village to village, every other night
digging deep new fighting holes, every day patrolling
through other villes, along raw ridges. Inviting an enemy
attack much as a worm seeks to attract a fish: mindlessly,
at someone else's urging, for someone else's reason.

They waded an opaque, muddy stream, fretfully picking
leeches off their arms and legs on the other bank, then
moved slowly, single file, Indian-style. The village sat like a
dark green knot in the middle of a wide, dirt-brown paddy.
Hodges scanned the fields. There were no cone-hatted
babysans lazing on the backs of water bulls. When water
bulls disappeared from the fields, it was always the first
sign that the enemy was near, very near, in large numbers. It reminded Hodges of the TV Westerns, when the
town cleared the streets before a gunfight.

At the edges of the village, all along the outer rim of a
paddy dike that surrounded it, large, loose piles of shit
glistened in the morning sun. The sun beat down on the
dozens of droppings and the air filled with their stench as
the platoon filed cautiously through the first trees that
shrouded the trail. Hodges noted the human dung and
halted his platoon, listening carefully before moving any
further. There was too much shit for such a small village,
and the people had eaten too well. That could only mean
enemy soldiers had sneaked down from the mountains to
that isolated village and feasted the night before, unless
they had taken over the village for a few days, as the
Marines often did, and were on some sort of operation
against the Marines. Either way, it meant trouble, and
Hodges cautiously congratulated himself for noticing it.

The village had been almost unpopulated two weeks before, when he had made a similar patrol through it. Now there was evidence of occupation: thatch in many of the roofs, and a dozen freshly dug family bunkers. And yet no people. The town was truly cleared for a gunfight. The platoon walked slowly along a narrow dust trail, their vision choked by weeds and brush. They passed a hootch every twenty yards. Cook fires still burned underneath the thatch. Empty red mackerel cans littered the porches. Rice balls sat half-eaten on chipped and broken china plates. The plates, apparent in every ville, always amazed Hodges: fine china from some other time or place incongruously scattered through the primitivity of the Phu Phans. He did not know that once, only a few years before, a railroad had brought such luxuries twice a week.

There would have been dogs. Or roosters. Hodges registered another reason for caution. If it were villagers remarkably reversing the momentum of flight and returning to resettle an empty ville, they would have brought animals. But the village was dead. No domestic animals, and the others had long ago fled the valley to the mountains that ringed it: the playful monkeys, the richly colored birds, all disappeared, driven away by constant artillery. A few rats skittered through the brush near some of the hootches. Only the rats remained.

Mounds of family bunkers reached high through the dry weeds, and craters from a hundred bombs dipped low. The trail detoured around a huge crater left by a five-hundred-pound bomb. The earth itself was swollen and distended from the daily beatings it was taking.

Suddenly (finally, breathed Hodges, after having added up his clues) there were screams from the point of the patrol, then random shots. Hodges ran forward and saw that the wide, dike-rippled paddy at the far edge of the village had filled with fleeing figures, sprinting for a bald, red ridge two hundred meters on the other side. There were dozens of them. Some were dressed in blue, some in green, some in white. Some wore conical hats and some were bareheaded. Most carried long cloth bundles.

The men moved with a quick certainty that always amazed him. They formed a line behind a wide, thick dike, and began firing furiously at the images that danced before them in the brown grass. Hodges remembered to place one fire team of three men to the rear, toward the village, lest they get ambushed from behind. He congratulated himself again. Very shrewd, Hodges. Two months and you're thinking like a gook.

The figures continued to run away. It angered him. He urged the machine-gun team on. Compos, the gunner, fired determinedly, his black eyes wide and his arms dripping streams of sweat on the stock of the gun. Cronin, the assistant gunner, shivered with recent malaria as he clipped ammunition belts into place and pointed out targets. Wolf Man broke out clean ammo from the boxes he carried, his garish tattoos gleaming in the sun. They worked with intimacy, stopping and calling to each other, four parts of the same machine. The gun ate the belt of bullets with an insatiable greed. Cronin poured LSA oil to cool the steaming barrel. Bodies dropped in the high weeds of the paddy.

But it was not enough. Still they ran. Hodges walked the line, urging his platoon to kill, screaming at the fleeing figures.

"Fight us, you bastards!! Come on! *Fight* us!"

Most of them disappeared over the ridge. It was unfair, mused Hodges, that they should flee after he had pursued them so skillfully, had read their clues so well. They never fought back until they were ready, but he had to pursue and attempt to engage every slightest vision. Not fair, and they were doing it again. Once on the other side of the ridge it would be their game, not his.

There were still a dozen running in the field. Hodges noted Goodrich lying forward on his elbows, his weapon impotent before him in the dirt.

"Put out rounds, Goodrich! They're skying out!"

Goodrich glanced at Hodges, then out into the paddy at the fleeing figures. "Those are kids, Lieutenant. Kids and mamasans. I saw the ponytails."

"If those are kids, I'll kiss your ass. Now open up."

Goodrich shrugged and decided not to pursue it, feeling that any additional comment would be pushing it. In the weeks since the Bridge had been overrun, he had continually flirted with trouble over similar incidents. He fired his weapon perfunctorily in the general direction of the fleeing mob. What the hell. He can court-martial me for not shooting, but he can't court-martial me for being a lousy shot.

Hodges knew what would follow. It was the worst part.

He had been able to anticipate them, but now he knew they would read him. No patrol like this was finished until the bodies were found and tabulated. Very important, he mused, tempted to fake it. Sheeit. If they're dead, they're dead. I had 'em but they wouldn't fight. It's their game, now.

The company commander called him and ordered him to count the meat and he studied his map for a quick moment, hiding behind a bush for fear of snipers who looked for such things in order to kill platoon commanders. He had to take the ridge, or they would waste his whole platoon in the paddy. Where is the ridge? Let's see. Phu Nhuan (8) over there. Phu Nhuan (3) right here. There it is. The ridge has no name. All right. He grinned. Appropriate. The battle for No-Name Ridge.

He didn't want to do it. He thought again about bagging it. But if he did it to the Skipper, some of his men would do it to him. Shirking danger was an infection that spread more quickly than the plague. He left half of his platoon in the village as a covering force, and moved with the other half into the paddy, on a wide, cautious line, sweeping toward No-Name Ridge. He walked behind them on a low, blackened dike that had been charred by a napalm drop in someone else's war a week ago, feeling that he was offering his body as a sacrifice in the name of not bagging a superior's order. Blind obedience. Here I am, God of Dumb. Take me quick.

He was so certain of what was to follow that he removed a LAAW rocket from its strap along his back and extended it, pulling the safeties out. He had figured them in the village but they had him now.

Then the roof fell in. The rounds erupted with their mocking pops, and before he could make a conscious decision he was hugging a charred portion of the field, mashing his face hard into the black ash. The rounds kicked up little ash spots all around him and he rolled onto one side and casually fired off his LAAW. Am I cool, or what?

Flaky screamed behind him. The radioman was shot. Hodges turned his head, keeping his body flat as dust and ash kicked up around himself and Flaky. Flaky peered back, terrified. One hand was a bloody pulp. Well, thank God it's him, Hodges thought absently. If anybody ever deserved it . . .

He had to move. The rounds were getting closer. He
crept back to Flaky to check his hand. Behind Flaky, at
the edge of the village, the other half of the platoon put
out a steady rate of fire at the ridgeline. Hodges had
brought a 60-millimeter mortar section with him and the
men were free-tubing an inaccurate mortar barrage along
the ridge, the gunner grasping the hot tube with a towel.
Goodrich was now firing madly at the ridge. Hodges caught
his eye and winked to him. Not bad for babysans, eh,
Senator?

Doc Rabbit crawled heavily over, helmet on backwards
because he claimed he saw better that way, strapped with
double bandoleers that held battle dressings instead of
ammunition. His corroded M-16 dropped to Flaky's feet,
useless, unfirable even if Rabbit cared to fire, even if he
ever thought to bring ammunition in the bandoleers instead of battle dressings. The rifle and bandoleers were
camouflages that misled snipers in their hunts for corps-
men. Or so Rabbit consoled himself.

And for all his camouflage, Rabbit now sat exposed
against the dike, impervious to the incoming rounds, wrap-
ping Flaky's hand. He looked over to Hodges, who was
flat against the dike to protect himself. "They shot the
radio right out of Flaky's hand, Lieutenant. Some shot,
huh?"

Radio. Supporting arms. Hodges grabbed the handset,
still huddled against the paddy dike, and pressed his map
into the dirt where the dike met the field, hoping the enemy
would not see it. As if they didn't know by now, he fretted
sardonically. "Delta Six, Delta Three! Contact mission,
Grid eight-niner-five, five-zero-three, direction five-one-
hundred, distance two hundred. Gooks on a ridge."

The firing stopped before the guns were up for the
mission. Hodges called the artillery anyway, unsure of
why they had stopped shooting and aware that at least
fifty of them had fled over the ridgeline. They know I have
to go into that paddy to check bodies, he reasoned, searching along the ridge as the artillery rounds impacted with
their haunting crumps. They could just be waiting.

He kept the gun up as he again moved half of the platoon toward the ridge. Behind him, the now-ecstatic Flaky
was writhing animatedly against the dike as someone took
a picture of him for posterity. A few minutes before,

Flaky had called in his own medevac and then announced that the wound, which was a ricochet, had paralyzed his hand until the date of his discharge.

They took No-Name Ridge and set up along it as security. The other half of the platoon, led by Staff Sergeant Gilliland, who had replaced Austin, swept along the fields where the enemy had fled. Hodges sat on the ridge, feeling irritated at the inconclusiveness of their efforts, and smoked his fifteenth cigarette of the patrol. On the far side of the ridge was yet another paddy, and another stand of opaque trees. Swarms of figures flashed and faded in the treeline.

Damn gooks are everywhere today, he fretted. He called another artillery mission on the trees, thinking ironically that if he used too many rounds the artillery people would demand he take his platoon over into the next treeline to check for more kills, and then he would have to call an artillery mission on the *next* treeline for his own safety, and have to check it out, and . . . well. It could go on forever. Fuck 'em, he decided. Just fuck 'em. Fuck everybody who doesn't come out here and do this. Let them go check that treeline. What do they know?

Sergeant Gilliland called up from the paddy. He was standing just below Hodges. He and a few members from Snake's squad held several rifles, and had captured a soldier. Or at least it appeared to be a soldier, if one used his imagination.

"Peep out, Mamasan!" Gilliland was lifting a cone hat off the man's head, then dropping it back on. Gilliland would lift it, and reveal the closely shaved head of a North Vietnamese soldier. Then he would drop it, and the hat would cover the man's face, and a ponytail would hang down his back. "And did you see her ditty bag? Poor Mamasan. We drove her out of her home." Gilliland held up a long cloth bundle. He shook it and an AK-47 rifle dropped out onto the ground.

The men on the ridge began screaming and cheering. Down the ridge one man moved off the wide dust trail, stepped down a paddy dike, and began to call to someone who stood near Gilliland. The claydirt belched loudly, a screaming roar, and the man slammed to the dirt, legless. He appeared asleep. Twenty feet away someone else now crawled on stumps of fingers, yelling for Doc Rabbit. He peered down at his hands and held them in front of his face, examining them as he squealed in terror. Marines ran immediately to help the two men, stepping cautiously toward them both to avoid possible trip wires from other booby traps.

Hodges sat down, burying his head between his knees. He was defeated. The very regularity of the actions, the fact that everyone knew exactly what to do, what words to say, and where not to step, was an indictment. The strained emotion that he kept just beneath his nonchalance was creeping through again. He wanted to cry. They would watch him and then wonder what kind of an officer he was, how he could give orders to them when he couldn't take it. He couldn't cry.

Rabbit walked past him. "How's Boomer, Doc?"

"He ain't got any legs. But I got him tied off."

Flaky had already called the medevac. A month before, Hodges would have insisted on doing it himself, but it didn't matter. They all knew how. The skipper would call it good training, but to him it was another indictment. The only real test of success anymore was how many came back whole from each patrol, and now he was again a failure. They got us again. They *got* us.

He hated it and he hated himself. He walked over and tried to talk to Boomer but Boomer was out of it. He started to walk toward the man who had lost his fingers, it was a new dude whose name he didn't remember, and Doc waved him away. They had bandaged both hands heavily so the man wouldn't have to look at his pieces of fingers and they were talking rapidly to him about the World, holding his attention until the morphone hooked him. Below him, in the field, the prisoner had done something, said something wrong, and two men were hitting him. It didn't bother Hodges. The prisoner was the only tangible enemy to focus their frustrations on. Boomer was a good man, and now he didn't have any legs, just because he tried to get a better look at the phony mamasan.

Somehow a chopper made it to the ridge. Someone popped a smoke grenade and red powder curled acridly around Hodges. Then the helicopter gobbled them up and fluttered off and he crawled underneath a bush and fought back his sobs and beat the ground, all the time wondering if he wouldn't set off a booby trap each time he pounded

the dust, but that was how paranoid he had become, and
he thought of all the others who·had become raw meat at
his direction after only two months, and he hated it and
himself more deeply and he pounded the dust some more,
making a vow of rage. He would not allow their blood to
have soaked into that unproductive dust merely for some
mad amorphous·folly.

He rejoined Gilliland in the paddy and as the patrol
made its way among the weeds he felt a surge of deep,
undirected anger and desire to kill. Kill everything, mused
Hodges. We're a floating islet waiting to be killed just because Those Bastards think we should be killed so they can
have more bodies on their tote boards when the react
pulls us out from where we never should have had to go.
Those Bastards sit somewhere with air conditioners around
them and Coca-Cola inside them while we drink this goddamn wormy water. We're closer to being gooks than we
are to being Them and yet here we are wanting to kill
gooks, any gook because of this ulcerous anger that eats
the insides of my guts and this is only Checkpoint Four.

Stork humped the radio now. "Call in Checkpoint Four."

"Yes, sir. Six, this is Three."

Hello Checkpoint Four you mother two more of you
and I'm one patrol closer to being out of this shithole.

"Roger, Six. Be advised we're at Checkpoint Four."

Shards of earth, broken trees, staring gook mamasans
and kids they're numb look at them numb from all this and
I look at them and wonder where their old man is. He
probably set the trap that just blew Boomer up the bastard
and the kids would like to kill us I don't blame them I'd
like to kill them too not the kids but who gives a shit anymore it's all the same too hard to draw lines seen too
many dead kids I don't feel bad for them anymore. They
hate me. They're pathetic as hell but their old man's trying
to kill me right now they'd just groove on watching me
crumple to the dirt that's right need another cigarette.
Here comes another paddy if they hit us again it will be in
this paddy it's too wide to cross without prepping I'm
going to put us all on line and call a mission Battery Three
if they'll give it to me Open Sheaf three repeats I'll blow
that treeline all to hell. There's mamasans and babysans in
there I know that but what the hell I didn't ask to do this

dangling and if I don't blow them away I'll hit a goddamn company of NVA and I'll never live long enough to be glad I didn't kill any mamasans besides they have family bunkers and anyway there you are again it's them or us and that my friend whether you'll admit it or not isn't any choice at all.

14.

From outside the lines came a racing whoosh, then overhead a wavy string of smoke. The green-star cluster popped, its burning capsules lighting a phosphorescent patch of scraggly hill inside the perimeter, and in a moment all was predawn dark again.

Doc Rabbit squinted toward the middle of the perimeter, where the burning capsules had landed, looking for movement. He grinned sleepily, sitting up in his bed of raw earth. That had to be Waterbull's team coming in, Rabbit mused. Bagger shot that green-star. Bastard gets closer every time. But if he ever really does set the Skipper's hootch on fire . . . Oh, well. That was his last chance before R & R, anyway. Skipper'll have ten days to forget about it.

Hodges had the last radio watch. The handset squawked and he braced himself, answering the call.

"This is Three. Go, Six."

Hodges held the handset away from his ear, making a pained face at Rabbit. Green-stars go *parallel* to the lines, the radio was saying. *Train* your men, it continued. Finally there was a waiting silence.

Hodges keyed in. "Roger, Six. Probably was the first time my man ever worked a green-star. I'll talk to him." Hodges shook his head hopelessly, sharing Rabbit's grin. A listening post with Wild Man, Waterbull, and Bagger. The Skipper was lucky they didn't start an imaginary firefight out there, just to wake everybody up. He looked across ten feet of weeds to Rabbit, who had fought his way out of his poncho-liner blanket and was sitting in a disheveled lump in the middle of an array of canteens, C-ration tins, and battle dressings.

"Crazy bastards. I better find a new game for 'em before we all get in trouble."

Rabbit nodded, stretching sleepily, then drank deeply from a canteen. The water was musky, alive with creatures from some leech-infested pool, but was cool from the night air. Rabbit liked to soak his canteen covers with water just before dark. The evaporation, and the night air, had a small refrigeration effect, and made each morning's drink a luxury. He finished drinking and held the canteen like a toy in his huge hands, pondering his choice for breakfast out of the C-ration tins that were scattered at his feet.

Rabbit should have been called Doc Bear. He was large and thick, with a layer of dark hair that covered his limbs and heavily bearded him. He had sad brown eyes and a sleepy growl of a voice that made his comments sound like afterthoughts. But he had been nicknamed Rabbit years before, because his top teeth were prominent, and he sported a rabbit tattoo on one bulky forearm.

Rabbit selected a can of fruit cocktail and began working a C-ration opener around its lid. "Rained last night, Lieutenant."

The sky was gray now. It was almost dawn. Hodges tore off a quarter-sized corner of C-4 explosive, lit one ragged edge, and dropped it quickly into a punctured C-ration can. The C-4 ignited and burned hotly. Hodges set his canteen cup over it, heating water for cocoa.

"I noticed. I dreamed I was taking a shower, and I woke up to turn on the hot water."

Rabbit chuckled. Hodges reached over and shook Staff Sergeant Gilliland, who was snoring loudly underneath a poncho. "Come on, Sarge. Up and at 'em. Today's the big day. Look like you love it, man."

Rabbit laughed again, eating his fruit cocktail. On the lines the first radio clicked on, meeting sunrise, piercing the still air like the first lathe in a factory that would soon be overwhelmed by noise and motion.

"Gooooooo-o-o-o-o-od *morning*, Vietnam!"

Gilliland's poncho flew into the air, and he sat on the piece of C-ration cardboard he had scrounged for a mattress. He rubbed his craggy, acne-scarred face, then ran a hand along the wet, packed earth at the edge of his cardboard.

"Rain."

Hodges nodded. "Yup. We were just talking about it."

A cigarette appeared automatically under Gilliland's bushy black moustache, and was lit by hands that needed no guidance from the eyes, which quickly scanned the perimeter, then the field and the village across from it, finally becoming satisfied that this would be a boring, empty morning, like so many others. They lost their molten look and Gilliland threw his match disconsolately to one side and sat smoking, staring bleakly in front of him. He quickly smoked the cigarette down to a nub, then flicked it in front of him, rubbing his eyes.

"Yeah. Rain. You ain't seen the monsoon yet, Lieutenant. We got to start checking feet. Wait till you see a man take a boot off and leave half his foot in it." Gilliland massaged the ground as if in deep thought. "It'll be another couple of months before it's real bad." He pondered the C-ration cardboard he was sitting on. "You know, if anyone ever asked me what the most important development of Vietnam was, I'd just have to say C-ration cardboard."

Rabbit nodded to Hodges. "The man's gone *dinky-dau* on his last day in the bush."

"No, I mean it. We sleep on it. We burn it to keep warm. The villagers put it in their thatch to keep out rain. They make hats with it. What the hell has done that much good?"

"Rubbers on R & R."

"Well, I wouldn't know about that. I saw my wife in Hawaii." Gilliland reached defeatedly for a C-ration box, coming up with a can of date pudding. "Shee-it. This gets old, you know, Lieutenant?"

Hodges eyed him, sipping cocoa now, and grinned amusedly. "That's a hell of a thing to say on the day a man re-ups, Sarge."

"Well. You can bet your ass I'm not re-upping for *this*. Two tours of this is enough. That's right. *You* worry about the monsoon. I'm gonna be dry."

The whole platoon had been ribbing Gilliland for days.

Hodges jibed him again. "You'll be back, Sarge. You got *expertise* now. They ain't gonna let you switch from the grunts."

Gilliland worked to open the date pudding. "I gave 'em ten years of this. Ten years and three Hearts. And for what? Now it's their turn. I want ten years of Motor Transport, something like that. I need some expertise I can retire with. What the hell can an old grunt do when he gets out?" He peered bleakly at Hodges. "It's not like I'm getting flaky on 'em after ten *years,* you know. I got to think of my future." He found a plastic spoon in one low trouser pocket, wiped it on a skivvy shirt crusted with sweat and mud, and ate the pudding in four huge, untasting bites. Hodges pointed at the pudding and grimaced: *"Date pudding?* For *breakfast?"*

Gilliland waved him off. "Ah. It all tastes the same."

Rabbit threw his empty can toward the trash hole, and continued to rib Gilliland. "C'mon, Sarge. You know goddamn well the Sergeant Major ain't gonna let you switch. Nobody leaves the grunts. It's sacrilegious to even *think* it."

Gilliland eyed Rabbit, then snorted. "He's a hell of a one to talk, ain't he? Walking round the rear with an AK-47, flak jacket all zipped and helmet snapped, like he's the toughest grunt that ever walked. Shee-it. You know what *he* did his whole career? You think *he* was a grunt? Hell, no, Doc. He was a damn office pogue. That's right. A Remington Raider. If that fat fucker tells me I can't switch I think I'll break his head." Gilliland pondered it, his face becoming intense. "Hell, no. I'll go you one better. I'll turn that son of a bitch in. Yeah." He grinned sardonically to Rabbit. "Yeah, that Sergeant Major's a real winner. Sitting back there in An Hoa, selling off our rations to rear pogues. You ever wonder why we never get beer and soda out here?" Gilliland snorted again. "Beer and soda per man per day. Right? That man is making a *mint* back there, on our rations."

Hodges nodded absently. He had heard the stories, but could not be convinced that such a thing would occur. It would be the greatest of heresies. "Well, good luck, Sarge. If it all works out for you we'll never see you again."

Rabbit grabbed a wad of C-ration toilet paper and

headed toward the perimeter's edge. "Yeah. And if it don't, remember you always got a home with us."

Gilliland lit another cigarette and begrudged them a grin. "Well, don't think it hasn't been a kick in the ass. Even if it hasn't."

Rabbit walked through wet weeds, stepped over a low paddy dike, and reached Waterbull's team, just in from the LP. "You crazy bastards. You almost did it. Six more inches and you'da burned a hole in the Skipper's ass."

Wild Man looked up from a canteen-cup of coffee. "Wasn't me. I was gonna use a LAAW."

Rabbit grunted: "Sure."

"It was Bagger again."

Bagger grinned awkwardly. "Only six inches from getting me a company commander? Hell. I just might stay out here an extra day and try again." He dragged ceremoniously on a cigarette. "But I kinda fucking doubt it."

"Where you going?"

"Hawaii."

Rabbit squinted unbelievingly. *"Hawaii?* You *married,* Bagman?"

Waterbull leaned over to Rabbit, gesturing ironically toward the muscled, baby-faced blond. "Where the hell you been, Doc? You mean you ain't seen Bagger's 'These Eyes' routine?"

Bagger's face deepened to a scowling blush. "Aw, knock it off, Bull."

Wild Man mimicked the song.

> *These eyes cry every night for you,*
> *These arms long to hold you again—*

"Come on. Cool it, turkey."

Waterbull guffawed. "The pictures, Bagger! Come on, now. The flicks!"

Rabbit rubbed his bearded face. "What the hell is going on?"

Bagger attempted to cut the others off. "Nothing, that's what. It's personal, and assholes here ain't got any right to butt in. So butt the hell *out."*

Waterbull ignored him. "Every time that song comes on, old Bagger sits down right where he is and breaks out the flicks of his wife. Then he just rocks back and forth and cries like a goddamn *baby! Every time,* man! We could be in the middle of a ville, on patrol, and old shit-head here would drop everything. Man. I can't believe you ain't seen him, Doc. Hell. We could be in a damn *fire-fight*—"

Rabbit grinned unbelievingly. "You're shitting me."

"No-o-o-o! Hell, it makes you wonder. Last night—"

"Well, what do you know about what it feels like, Bull? Huh? You and the others. Go on off to Bangkok and get the clap from some damn whore of a wife!"

"Oh, she ain't really a *wife*—"

"Well, you bet your ass she ain't! And mine is." Bagger took his wallet from its plastic bag and opened it, holding the picture up for Rabbit's perusal. "Now. Check out what the hell I'm missing, there, Rabbit. Tell me you wouldn't miss it, too."

Rabbit stared at the picture. It was slightly out of focus, and revealed a mildly attractive, rather stocky girl in pig-tails and a cheerleader's uniform, kneeling between two pompoms. He nodded judiciously. "Uh huh. She's real nice, Bag-man. I don't blame you." Bagger continued to hold the picture in front of him, as if demanding more. "Cheerleader, huh?"

"You better believe." Rabbit began to leave and Bagger flipped the plastic card holder once more, grasping his shoulder and extending two more pictures. One of them was the same girl with a small baby.

"A *baby?*"

"That's right. Jerry Dean Dolan, Junior." Bagger blushed again. "He's two months old. I ain't seen him yet, but she says he looks just like me. She's bringing him to Hawaii. Don't he look like me?"

"Say what?"

"Don't he look like me?" Bagger appeared mildly threatening.

"Huh? Well, it's hard to tell. I mean—" Rabbit eyed Bagger's expression. "Sure, Bagger." Rabbit considered the picture again, and shook his head helplessly. "Good Christ. Who'd have believed it. My man Bagger is a *daddy!* Poor kid."

"Hey. Now you know why I hate this shit so much, huh? I got something to go back to. I got responsibilities.

All you suckers got is yourselves. I got a wife and a baby to take care of. What the hell am I doing out here, anyway? Where's the goddamn ARVNs? Who needs this shit, huh? I ain't any hero. Goddamn John Wayne, anyway." Bagger appeared spooked, as if he were beginning to hallucinate or remember a nightmare. "What if I get *killed* over here, for God's sake? What are you gonna tell my kid? Huh?"

"Anything but the truth." Rabbit waved Bagger off, trekking toward the edge of the perimeter. "Don't worry, Bagger. He'll never find out."

"Ahh. Screw around. Nothing's serious, is it?"

Rabbit dug a cathole and squatted in the far weeds. He could hear Wild Man and Waterbull continue to taunt Bagger.

> *The hurtin's on me, yeah,*
> *I will never be free no my baby no no—*

Hodges lay in the oven heat of his poncho hootch, dozing absently while monitoring first platoon's patrol on the company radio. Captain Crazy, the company commander, was telling Rock Man to move into a village he had just taken sniper fire from. Rock Man, the first platoon commander, was arguing for an artillery prep before he moved in. There were resupply choppers in the air, and Captain Crazy was explaining that there would be no clearance for an artillery mission unless Rock Man was in bad trouble, since it would be necessary to down the helicopters.

Hodges admired Captain Crazy. The big, bluff Italian, who had been an ARVN advisor during his first tour, was an excellent tactician. He was too offensive-minded for most of the troops, pushing all of his activities to the edge of periphery—as at the moment with Rock Man—but he produced a lot of kills, and was uniformly respected. Hodges and the others considered themselves lucky. At least Captain Crazy knew what he was doing.

He wasn't nicknamed Crazy for his tactics. Hodges named him during the Captain's first week in the bush, because of two incidents. One was the Captain's insistence that any unpenned pig be killed in the villages they used for night perimeters. Captain Crazy was spooked by pigs run-

ning through the weeds at night, and he claimed troops
mistook them for gooks, and mistook gooks for pigs. So,
every new village saw its hog population slaughtered. The
other incident was Captain Crazy's wound in the back of
his head, from a B-40 rocket, in his fourth day. He refused to be medevacked, and instead led a small patrol
back to Liberty Bridge, where the Battalion Surgeon
shaved the Captain's head and placed a large X-shaped
bandage over the wound. The bandage was visible from a
thousand yards. The troops took to joking about the real
reason for the bandage. Bagger claimed it marked the
center of the bull's-eye for snipers. Wild Man maintained
it was where they changed the rocks in the Captain's
head. Hodges decided that any man who didn't accept a
medevac back to the sanity of Da Nang was nothing but
stomp-down crazy. And the name stuck.

Rock Man was the Lieutenant in charge of first platoon. Hodges had named him Rock Man because he
idolized the tactics of the Korean Marines, better known
as the ROKs. Rock Man emulated the ROK Marines on
all his patrols: he believed, as he had heard the ROKs
also did, that razing the countryside, brutalizing the villagers, was an effective way to pacify them. Rock Man
was hardly out of high school. He had taken one semester
of college and then enlisted. He went straight from enlisted training into officer training, and then to Vietnam.
You always know where first platoon is, Hodges was fond
of joking. Just follow the smoke from the burning
hootches.

Hodges laughed, listening to Rock Man and Captain
Crazy argue.

". . . Well, how about an air strike, then?"

"You don't *need* an air strike for one damn sniper
round."

"Three."

"Three what?"

"Five. Jesus Christ, Six Actual, let me key you in. Can't
you hear the shit we're in, now?"

Hodges could hear the firefight in the distance. First
platoon was perhaps a mile and a half way. There were
high stacattos of AK-47s, punctuated by the boom of B-40
rockets. M-16s and LAAWs returned fire. He sat, listening

alertly while monitoring Rock Man and Captain Crazy on the net.

Snake approached from the perimeter's edge, looking toward the village where first platoon was fighting. "They are in the shit *again*. Get some, first platoon."

Hodges nodded, staring also. "Yup. Them gooks don't like old Rock Man."

Snake scratched his tattoos, sitting next to Hodges. "Yeah, Lieutenant. I figure old Rock Man and his animals done *made* a lot more VC than they ever end up killing."

Hodges lit a cigarette, agreeing. "There it is, Snake. Now, when they get inside that ville, they're gonna burn it down. And we'll go through there tomorrow on the way to the Chau Phongs and we'll hit us a booby trap, thanks to first platoon."

Then he lit Snake's smoke, and they watched the rest of Someone Else's War a mile away.

Mamasan squatted barefoot in the packed dirt just outside her thatch porch, her narrow haunches only inches off the ground. Her knees were spread and her arms were between them, holding a large, flat basket filled with crushed rice. She moved the basket in slow circles, like a miner panning for gold, causing the chaff to separate from the grain and seek the basket's rim. She was stolidly intent on her task, motionless but for the slowly moving arms and her rolling jaw, which worked betel nut like a cud.

She was ageless, somewhere between twenty and fifty, though from the three dirty, numb, scarred children who played under the thatch one would estimate her age to be on the low end of that scale. All three were younger than five. Their heads were shaved but for tiny rectangular patches in the front, even the girl's head. The children huddled on the porch, staring mutely at four Marines who now walked past the hootch, shirtless and laughing, on the way to a nearby well. The hootch and well were both inside this latest two-day perimeter.

The Marines called to her, still laughing: "Hey! What's happening, Mamasan?" One tossed her a C-ration cigarette.

She ignored them until they passed, but after they

wound around the bushes out of sight, she snatched the cigarette as if she were afraid it would suddenly evaporate as a mirage, and lit it with her pack of C-ration matches, having spit the betel nut onto the dust in a lumpy red glob.

She rocked on her haunches, smoking contentedly, and Dan appeared. The Kit Carson Scout walked along the same dust trail, dressed neatly in camouflage shirt and trousers that had been custom-tailored for him and brought out to the bush by Hai, the other Scout, who had recently visited his family in Duc Duc. Dan's hair was growing long and he combed it down in front, in bangs as the early Beatles did, primarily in response to the urgings of some of the company command post Marines, who now called him Ringo.

Dan had never heard of Ringo. He only knew that his hairstyle amused the Marines, and that they appeared to be mildly envious because they had to cut their own hair whenever the opportunity arose, while he was free to become a Beatle. And if they laugh, Dan mused, it cannot be bad. They appear to like this Ringo.

Those who had known Dan intimately would have noticed that he was nervous underneath his calm mask. The only hint of nervousness in Dan was in the eyes. His wife would have noticed that they flitted anxiously along the trail, and had lost their usual acquiescence. But no one noticed today.

He walked up to mamasan and dropped three cans of C-ration meat at her feet, feigning casualness. Then he dropped a C-ration can opener, still in its paper wrapper.

"I bring you meat," said Dan. He stood rigidly over her, just on the other side of the basket.

Mamasan stopped sifting and stared at the treasure next to her, wishing to grab it and devour every gram of meat and fat. Then she looked up at the expectant rigidity of Dan's frame, at his suddenly hot eyes, and forced herself to resume the sifting.

"We do not eat meat," mamasan mumbled, hoping he would depart and leave the cans. He will not miss them, she thought. There is so much food for them.

Dan did not believe her. They are not so different, he reasoned in his provincial way. This is the other side of the

river from my home but they are the same. They look the
same as me, different from the Marines.

"If there was a water bull who died in your field, and
it was not of your village, you would fight to steal two feet
of its entrails," Dan asserted. "Would you not?"

"I would eat the entrails," said the mamasan. She was
no longer sifting. She stared down at her flat basket.

Dan shrugged, making his point. "This meat is better. It
is from young animals. It is tender." He shrugged again,
gesturing to the porch. "Give it to your children. They look
very bad."

"They *are* very bad," acknowledged mamasan, with a
heavy hint of blame in her voice.

"At least they are alive. The VC killed mine." Dan
used his dead children as a weapon, to counter her unspoken accusation and justify the customized uniform he
wore.

His thrust struck home. Mamasan shook her head, taking an apparently pained drag off her cigarette. She spoke
more softly. "I will keep the meat. For the children. Thank
you."

"You remind me of my wife." Dan still stood rigidly,
peering with hunger at her squatting, wasted hulk. "They
killed her, too."

Mamasan rocked on her haunches, smoking the last tobacco out of the cigarette, not yet looking at Dan. She
flipped the cigarette away and Dan dropped a full pack of
Lucky Strikes at her feet. She did not touch them, nor did
she yet look at Dan.

"Where is your husband?"

Mamasan did not answer.

"He is in the mountains, isn't he? Your husband is VC."
Dan laughed comfortably, trying to relax her. "I used to
hide in the mountains, too. It was very lonely. I would
dream of making love, spend all my free hours dreaming
of it. Do you get lonely?"

Mamasan still rocked.

Dan eyed her shrewdly, a tiny grin at the edges of his
mouth. "Oh, I spent many months back in the mountains.
I remember all the hiding places, all the camps. I could
lead the Marines to every camp. Even in the dark."

Mamasan looked quickly at him, too stolid to appear

startled, but nonetheless noticeably awakened from her mask of apathy.

Dan laughed softly. "I would not do that. It would be too senseless. I do not seek death." He eyed her once again, suppressing something that almost resembled mirth. "Oh, it would be a great battle, though." Mamasan appeared upset. "But, as with these others, it would solve nothing, would it?" He sighed. "It is such a game, this war. Sometimes I wish one side or the other would hurry up and win, just so it will be over."

Mamasan stared curiously at him now, still rocking. Slowly, as if she were reaching for a time bomb, she grasped the cigarettes and unwrapped the pack, taking out a smoke and lighting it. She puffed greedily.

Goodrich approached them on the trail. He walked morosely, dressed only in tiger shorts and jungle boots, carrying a green towel and a bar of soap toward the well. He did not notice them at first. He was contemplating his feet as they stirred the dust of the trail. Then he saw the babysans near the hootch, staring numbly at him like four dirty, stolid statues. He felt like helping them. He decided they needed to be clean. He stopped on the trail and motioned to them.

"Hey. *Lai day,* babysans. Come on." He exhibited his bar of soap. "You washy-washy me, I washy-washy you. *Khong biet?*"

The children did not change their expressions, or acknowledge him. Goodrich examined their sores from his distance. Capitalism, Goodrich thought. The only answer. "Hey. Look. You *lai day,* washy-wash, me give you chop-chop. O.K.?"

The children looked at each other, apparently comprehending. Goodrich became enthused, and raced back to his fighting hole, returning with several cans of C-rations. He was under orders not to give food to civilians, but he didn't care anymore. The babysans still huddled together next to their family bunker. He showed them the cans.

"*Lai day!* Come on. You washy-wash, I give you chop-chop. *Khong biet?*"

The children began to move, and mamasan stood up, curious about Goodrich's overtures. He turned to her, and noticed Dan. The Lucky Strikes and the food were between Dan and the mamasan. Dan smiled benignly to

Goodrich, but his face was irritated, his nod impatient. The woman looked down, masking her emotion.

Goodrich comprehended, studying the C-ration tins. He was angry at Dan, and wished he had not brought the food for the babysans, so he would be able to criticize the Vietnamese scout in front of the woman. He viewed Dan as a traitor in many ways. Dan grew fat on Marine food as his people starved. Dan brutalized his own people in order to eat well and not be brutalized himself.

He walked toward Dan, staring at the food and at the woman. "What are you doing?"

Dan shrugged and winked at Goodrich, putting on the jive act the command post Marines had taught him. Ringo in rare form. "Hey-y-y, man. Me got *coe,* you know, party time. You know, mebbe boom-boom."

Goodrich felt protective. "What does she say?"

Dan maintained his smile, and turned to the mamasan. "Do you want the food he has brought your children?"

"Yes."

"Tell them to help him at the well. Tell them to go with him."

The woman spoke abruptly to the children. They hesitated, then as a group joined Goodrich on the trail. Goodrich stared at Dan, and then at the woman, in mild disbelief. Finally he shook his head and walked with the children toward the well.

"Christ."

Dan turned back to the mamasan, standing over her now, very close. He pointed up the trail. *"Honcho,"* he said, with a forced sense of self-importance.

Mamasan carried the cans and the cigarettes onto the thatch porch and set them on an earthen ledge, next to her fireplace. Dan followed her and stood very close, his groin pressing slightly against the back of her. She froze for a moment, her head bent, trying to ignore him. Then he spoke, still not touching her with his hands.

"Go inside the bunker."

Gray slivers of light intruded through the two bunker openings, but otherwise it was dark. Resignedly she shed her bottoms and he took her on the floor. She was motionless at first, her insides dry. He attempted to kiss her and she turned her head away, refusing him.

But slowly she oiled herself and in minutes she was

pressing back at his thrusts, having to forcibly restrain her-self from a groan of ecstasy. Dan dared to crush her to him and she acquiesced and he marveled at it, could not understand it. But he felt a sense of total power from the knowledge that she despised him and what he stood for, and yet was unable to restrain her nether parts from seeking him.

It is the animal, he decided, just before he shuddered with explosions on her body. The animal seeks to satisfy its hunger before it thinks of games.

15.

DAN

War is as natural as the rains. There are years when there is no war and there are seasons without rain. But always war and rain return. There is no difference. It is the nature of things. Thunder booms and so does artillery. The sting of a rifle is deadly. So is the tongue of the viper. If a man steps on a booby trap he will die. So also if he falls off a ledge in the mountains. One brother died from cholera. One brother died from Marine gunfire. There is no dif-ference. Buddha turned his head both times and the broth-ers died.

So thought Dan. Life had taught him that.

The unpatterned clump of thatch hootches in the southern Arizona was choked by sawgrass and blue-green jungle foliage, steeped in sweltering heat. The rains had only re-cently passed and the sun cooked out the moisture from the dirt and vegetation and the wind would not blow in the late morning and the little field that Dan was working was a steam bath. He stood in the seedbed, dressed only in linen shorts, and leaned against his hoe.

He was short and thin, but tight-muscled. The muscles

of his back bulged out from the spine, making a deep river for the sweat to pour down as he stood in the steamy heat. His face was the definition of endurance, eyebrows slightly raised, the brown eyes acquiescent and unquestioning. There was no smile.

He had been preparing the seedbed. That afternoon he would plant the seeds. Later, when the rice plants grew large enough, he would take them one at a time from his seedbed and place them in the paddy with his hands. Each plant was a child to him. And in the paddy they would make rice. One could not grow a plant from seeds in the paddy. Dan did not know why. He only knew it would not happen. One had to plant the seed and nurture it in the seedbed and, when the seedling was strong, he had to dig it out and cup it in his hands and place it in the paddy. It had always been that way. One did not question why. There were no answers. And answers would not change it.

Dan grew tired in the sunbake and walked under the open umbrella of thatch that was his outer home and dipped out a cup of water from a metal pot. The pot was made from a rusted Marine gasoline can, and the dipper was an old C-ration can. The thatch was thick above him and it was cool in its shade and the water was clouded with dirt and rust but also cool. Dan dipped out two more cans of water, drinking slowly.

He spoke softly to his wife, who was sitting on a low wooden plank in the corner of the thatch, nursing a child. His voice was melodious, and as it played the singsong tones of Vietnamese dialect one was easily entranced by its strength and resonance. His wife nodded slowly, working betel nut between her teeth, rocking slightly as the baby nursed. Her teeth were beginning to permanently blacken from the betel nut. The baby would not nurse long. There was little milk. His wife was twenty-four and the milk was almost gone.

There were four other children. The next-youngest, a little girl not quite a year old, was sleeping inside the family bunker, behind the thatch. The other three played quietly on the dirt floor of the thatch. Two small boys, scarcely a year apart, were squatting, examining the little pool of urine that a dog had just left on the dirt floor. Dan kicked the dog. Even the boys knew to urinate outside the hootch. Neither of the boys wore bottoms yet. They wore old black shirts. They would not wear bottoms until they learned to control their bladders.

The eldest child, a girl of six, was staring with empty eyes at the stand of banana trees outside the thatch. She was slender, delicate and beautiful, and wore gold earrings. The earrings were the only things of value Dan owned. Her beauty was already marred, though, by ulcerous sores that grew on her legs and arms, and by the scars of sores now healed. The sores, which the Marines called gook sores, grew in deep circles that penetrated the skin. They oozed a clear liquid. They became very large. They lasted for months. Dan did not know how to stop them. In fact, he had never considered stopping them. They had always grown on people. They were as natural as mosquito bites.

The girl stood and walked quietly across the dirt under the thatch to Dan and wrapped a slender arm around his thigh. She then turned, standing behind him, and continued to watch the banana trees. Two men appeared, walking silently on the trail that emerged from the foliage near the trees and passed Dan's hootch. One was dressed in green and the other in dark blue. They both carried rifles. The man in green carried two rifles, an AK-47 and an M-14.

Dan set the cup down next to the watercan and greeted them. He had known them both for many years. They greeted him warmly and the man in blue caressed the girl's hair. She remained behind Dan, smiling shyly to the man in blue. He was older, perhaps thirty-five. He was the VC village chief, leader of the local forces.

The man in green thrust the M-14, barrel up, into Dan's chest. Dan took it from him, examining the weapon. It was his brother's weapon. His brother had taken it from the body of a Marine a year before. His brother had killed the Marine in an ambush. His brother had been very proud of the weapon.

The man in blue put his hand on Dan's shoulder. "Your brother is dead."

"I am sorry," Dan said, continuing to examine the weapon. He was not sorry. He had known his brother was dead as soon as he examined the rifle and recognized it as his brother's. He had known his brother was going to die for two years. His brother had believed too strongly and had tried too hard. He had already accepted his brother's death, and had already been sorry. The moment merely finalized the death.

"I am sorry," he said again, looking into the older man's eyes. "How did it happen?"

He did not care how it had happened. The man in blue did not care, either. He had not come to tell Dan how it happened. "His cell was ambushed last night," the older man said. "Four were killed. But we got the weapons. He died for his people. You can be proud of that."

"I know," said Dan. He was not proud of that. His brother had left his family to starve so that he could die for his people. Fights do not grow rice. Fights do not feed children. "I know."

Dan held out his arm, handing the rifle back to the man in green. The man kept his own hands at his sides, refusing to accept it. The man in blue stepped forward, his chin set and his body taut. "It is your rifle now, Dan. You must carry it with us. You must come to the mountains and take your brother's place."

Dan stared blankly at the older man, already beginning to accept the inevitability of it. They would kill him if he refused. They would kill his family if he ran away. "I have five children," he said slowly. "And I am a farmer. I do not know rifles."

"We all have families," the older man responded, his jaw still set. "And none of us likes to fight." Dan blanched inside at the untruth of that. His brother had liked to fight. Many of them liked to fight.

"There is the rice," Dan said. "Only today I am putting the seeds in."

"Let your father put the seeds in."

Dan smiled slightly, hoping. "My father is dead two years of cholera."

"Then let your wife."

"My wife is two weeks out of childbirth."

"Then let your mother."

"My mother is—"

"You come today. Plant rice when the war is over."

Dan shrugged. The war will never be over, he thought to himself. The rice will never be planted.

"Tell your wife good-bye. We will pass through soon. And we will help to harvest when we are able."

Walking down the dust trail to the mountains Dan felt a deep urge to kill the two men. He was carrying his brother's rifle. He debated for an hour about doing it. The man in green was in front of him and the man in blue walked behind him. Dan reasoned that he could kill the man behind him first, quickly and easily, and still have enough time to kill the man in front of him before the man could turn and comprehend the older man's death and shoot Dan.

But the rifle was unfamiliar in Dan's hands. He would probably do something wrong. And if he succeeded he could never go back to farming again anyway. They would seek him out and kill him and his family. He envisioned the oldest girl lying dead under the thatch and decided not to try. There would be another way.

In the mountains the men lived comfortably in caves and thatch shelters, carefully camouflaged so airplanes could not see them. They trained in grassy areas or slept during the day, and moved through the foothills to the valley at dusk. At night they would ambush Marine patrols and hold meetings in the villages far from Marine positions. When the North Vietnamese moved from base camps further back in the mountains to attack the Marines, Dan's unit supplied guides for them, moving them quickly through the speed trails inside the treelines, past Marine outposts.

Dan learned to shoot the M-14 well, and also became proficient with a submachine gun. But his heart was not in it. He would never make an adequate warrior. His leaders soon learned this, but they also quickly learned a greater truth. They watched the villagers become entranced when Dan talked to them at meetings. Dan was magnetic. He loved the villagers and he looked upon fighting with distaste. The villagers felt this when he spoke to them. And his clear voice played a melody when it worked the intonations of his language. Dan spoke and people listened. He smiled sadly and touched them when he spoke and his presence was very strong, very convincing.

Dan became a propagandist. At night he would filter with a cell of men into an Arizona village and the villagers would gather in a knot around him, old people and young women and children. And Dan touched them and told them beautiful fairy tales about victories over the Marines.

Be strong, he told them. It is almost over. We defeat them every day. Work the fields and give us rice and soon it will be over and your men can return to the villages.

At times he almost believed his own stories. He spoke, his voice like low flute notes playing up and down the scale, recounting great victories, helping the villagers prepare for the return of their men. But soon the fraud awakened him and he grew terribly depressed. It will never end, he decided. It will always be this way. Why can't I tell them that? Why can't I tell them how horrible it is, how many of us die? They know the horrors of malaria and cholera. Why can't they learn the horrors of this? There is no difference.

In three months the cell held a meeting in Dan's own village of My Le (1). He had difficulty lying to his own people. They sat in a cluster around him, gathered under one of the thatch porches, and Dan expounded a greatly subdued version of his speech. He spoke long and sadly of the ones who had died since the Marines came into the valley. "We kill many," he told them, watching wispy beards and crinkled faces nod slowly, seriously, valuing every word as if it were a piece of jade served up on a velvet pillow. "But we lose many, too. I will not lie to you. We lose more than we kill. But—"

He could not think of a justification. All reasons were like echoes bouncing off his conscience, unable to penetrate it and come out as words. War was like the rains. The French came and the French went. The Marines came and the North Vietnamese came and they too would someday leave. As surely as the monsoon brought its terror and abated.

There was nothing he could tell them. Finally he smiled sadly at the crinkled faces, loving each face for its suffering, and said: "—but that is the nature of things. Someday it will be over."

He saw his wife that night. She was strangely older and could not look at him without crying. The youngest child was dead. "How?" Dan asked.

"He would not eat." She stared at the dirt floor, remembering. "He would not take the milk and there was nothing else. He died a month ago. I give my milk to the girl now. She is weak also. We are all weak."

She looked at Dan, holding the eldest girl tightly to him,

the oil lamp making dancing shadows on the bunker wall behind them. "You make beautiful words."

Dan shrugged, immune to sarcasm. "It is better than fighting. I do not like to fight. Words hurt no one."

She disagreed. "Words are worse than bullets. Bullets kill. Words prolong the death by giving false hope. It is worse to prolong."

"It is worse to die." Dan stroked the girl's hair. "A dead man has no hope."

His wife cried again. "We will all die while you speak your beautiful words," she whispered.

Dan stared quietly at her. "Others endure. You must also endure. There is no other way."

The youngest girl cried loudly and Dan's wife put the girl to her breast. The child sucked hungrily. There was little milk. Dan rocked the eldest girl and watched his sons sleeping on the low board of the bunker. "Perhaps there is a way," he said, speaking softly. He set the girl onto the floor of the bunker and crawled to its entrance, looking carefully from his thatch porch, up and down the trail.

The trail and porch were empty. The Marines were firing Harassment and Interdiction rounds that night. The rounds crashed in unexpectedly all through the village, slowly, one round at a time. They were meant to discourage enemy troop movements. The villagers did not know that. They viewed the rounds as one would view a rainstorm. Some nights there were artillery rounds. Some nights there were no artillery rounds. It did no good to question it. Questions would not change it any more than they would change the pattern of rainstorms.

But that is good, Dan thought. My fellow soldiers will be in other bunkers. He stepped back down into the bunker and sat next to his wife, speaking softly. The littlest girl still sucked hungrily but there was no more milk. The wife stroked the girl's cheek, relaxing her, not pushing her away because it would make her cry. At the breast, even without milk, the baby would be silent. The mother did not wonder why. She merely knew that it was so.

"Would you leave your home?" Dan asked. "Would you leave this valley?" The wife did not understand. "I could run away. I could surrender. But you will have to leave the valley or they will kill you. We could live in Duc Duc.

Plenty rice. And the men come home in the day. They do not really fight. The Marines fight. It would be better."

"How do you know this?" the wife asked, already captivated by the melody of Dan's voice. Dan showed her a *chieu hoi* leaflet. There were many of them on the valley floor and in the mountains. The Marines dropped them from airplanes during psychological-warfare missions. They were safe-conduct passes for those who wished to surrender.

"There was a man in our company," Dan told her. "A corpsman. *Bac se*. We talked many times of the futility of it. He told me secretly of his plans. He made very careful plans. And then one day he surrendered to a Marine unit here in the valley and they went to his village and took his family with them before the VC could kill them. They sent the *Bac se* and his family to Duc Duc. Duc Duc is where all such families go."

His wife was not convinced. "How do you know of Duc Duc? Have you ever seen this village?"

Dan stroked the back of his youngest son, who had rolled restlessly on the bunker floor. "Some days I have duty on the southern riverbank. We hide in bunkers along the trees and stop the villagers from crossing the river to go to Duc Duc. Sometimes, after the Marines and the North Vietnamese have fought fiercely, there are dozens of people. They strap pans and clothes into bundles and put them on their heads—you've seen them that way—and they walk to the riverbank, hoping to find a boat that will take them across to Duc Duc. We stop them because they must grow rice. If they do not grow the rice, we cannot eat. If we cannot eat, we cannot fight." Dan shrugged. "It is such a game. I do not like to fight. I like to farm. And be with my family." He looked closely at his wife in the flickering light, stroking her back. "Would you leave your home?"

His wife had never been out of the valley. Once, when she was very young, she and three friends had walked for hours all the way to the eastern tip of the valley, over seven miles of paddies and ridges and treelines, and watched the bustle of Dai Loc across the river. It had awed her. It was the only time she had seen an automobile, although she had since watched tanks and amphtracs

lumber past her village. And at night when they would
dare to venture from the family bunker she sometimes
stood high on top of it, and watched the strange bright
lights hanging like low moons over An Hoa and Dai Loc.
She had no comprehension of electricity. She could not
envision life away from My Le (1). Her family had been
in the village for five hundred years.

But she and Dan had long agreed that this war would
not end in their lives. She would see Dan only like this,
every few months, for his life as a soldier. If he survived,
perhaps for fifteen years. She could not stand that thought.

She was terrified of Duc Duc. It was only four miles
away, but it would be filled with strange faces from many
villages, and there would be no land to own and work.
What does a family do when there is no land? She looked
at the little girl sucking on her dried teat and at the three
others, suffering quietly on the bunker's boards. And what
of them? They have suffered long enough. One child already dead. Who will be next? She decided she would go.

The youngest girl was finally asleep. Dan's wife laid her
on a board and moved to Dan. Dan held her closely to
him, feeling the strength in her back. He had missed her
terribly. He had never been away from her before.

"I will escape this morning," he told her. "We will leave
the village just before dawn to return to the mountains. I
will run from them at a good place on the trail and hide
until the sun is high and find my way to the Marine perimeter. They will kill me if I try to surrender to a patrol. That
is the nature of things. You must come to the perimeter,
too. Can the children walk to the perimeter?"

"Where are the Marines?" his wife asked.

"There is a company at Tan Phouc. A mile."

"We can walk to Tan Phouc."

"Good," said Dan. "Wait until the sun is high. If you
walk before the sun is up the Marines will kill you. All
people of the night are VC to them. It is the nature of
things. When the sun comes up walk to Tan Phouc. I will
meet you there."

Then Dan loved his wife on the boards of the bunker,
in between the sleeping baby and the restless boys. It was
good love. They had missed each other. Their suffering
from all things external to their relationship made the act
a deep and desperately emotional grasping. There was only

the family. And the land. But now they would lose the land. The love became a special signal of their coming isolation from everything but each other.

He slept fitfully. As the sky began to blue, just a deep touch low in the east, his cell leader called for him at the bunker's opening. He kissed his wife once more and picked up his M-14, fingering it slowly, remembering his brother as he walked out on the trail. His brother would have killed him for what he was about to do. Dan sighed. His brother had believed too strongly. Such is the nature of this game, he mused. That a brother would kill a brother who only wanted to be with his family and his land.

The cell of eight men walked quickly up the trail under a half-moon, the sky now dark blue over them. The trail bent close to a streambed and Dan broke suddenly from it, sprinting through a dozen yards of jungle thickness, and ran along the streambed. He knew the streambed as a man knows the rooms of his own home. He had grown up playing along it. He first made love to his wife beside it, when they were fourteen. They would not find him by the streambed. There were muffled shouts when Dan broke from the trail, then two quick shots. They would not shoot wildly. They did not have the ammunition to waste. And too many shots would bring the Marines.

Dan found a mudhole and lay flat along the streambed in it. The cell swept past him. He listened to the angry whispers as they fought the jungle growth. They would not bring him back to the mountains if they caught him now. They knew he did not do this to return to farming. He had been too friendly with the corpsman who surrendered earlier. He had not spoken well to his own people the night before. They would kill him if they found him. For the sake of discipline.

But they must leave soon, he reasoned, feeling the mud soak through his blue pajamas as he hugged the streambed. Soon it would be light and the Marines would be patrolling. They will be trapped if they do not make it to the foothills. They know that, he fretted. They must leave soon.

Then in the distance, down the trail, a half-dozen shots. Perhaps a few more. They came from My Le (1). He became bewildered. They would not do that. They will wait until nightfall and return, he thought. The way they did when the *Bac se* surrendered. They do not have the time to do that. They must take the foothills by first light.

He hesitated, shivering in the mud. Then he could no longer bear the tension. He crawled noiselessly along the streambed, remembering each bend, staying off the bank and away from the trail. He reached My Le (1) and the sky was gray. Soon it would be hot and blue. The cell would be well toward the mountains now.

He left the streambed and walked through mounds of jungle growth, finding his hootch from the back way. He crossed the still-unplanted seedbed, reaching the family bunker before he came to the thatch. It was silent in the bunker. A dog bolted from under the thatch as Dan walked toward the entrance. Around the trail, on the other side of the banana trees, a rooster crowed. The village was awakening with the sun. Dan could smell the cook fires from the other hootches.

But there was no movement inside his family bunker. Dan walked slowly, unwillingly, to the bunker opening. Perhaps she has already begun to walk to Tan Phouc, he hoped, knowing she had not.

He walked inside the bunker and the soft gray light that filtered in from the two openings confirmed his apprehension. The close air of the bunker was rich with the heavy odor of wet blood. His two sons lay dead where they slept. Their heads were blown apart. His wife had been driven into the corner of the bunker by the blast of a rifle. She still held the baby girl tightly to her breast. One of the bullets had passed through the baby and then Dan's wife. His eldest daughter lay dead at his feet. One of his former compatriots had ripped her earrings from her earlobes. There were two straight tears of red where the earrings had been.

Dan was sick with rage and grief. He could not bear to look closely at them. He ran out of the bunker and over the dust of the seedless seedbed and through the brush, already hot and close from the morning sun. He found the stream again and lay inside another mudhole, shuddering with misery.

Now there was nothing. The land was gone. The family was gone. Some dead of cholera. Some dead of war. There was no difference. But slowly the rage grew. There was a difference. They did not have to do that, he thought, again and again. They are wrong to think that any belief is worth doing that. What they believe cannot be right if it does this to them.

But the difference did not matter. He could not go back to them even if he believed they were right to do it. They would now kill him, too. For the sake of discipline.

The sun moved high over the trees, and the water in the shallow hole became hot. Dan climbed up the streambank and began to walk to Tan Phouc. He carried his rifle for a few steps along the bank. Then he stopped, holding it in front of him, studying it. If I surrender with my rifle they will believe my story more easily, he thought. But if they see me walking toward them with a weapon they might kill me. They are like that. They have much ammunition and they shoot very quickly.

He threw his rifle into the stream. They would believe his story. He was good with stories.

It was hot and there was no breeze. The mudhole water in Dan's clothes dried quickly and was then replaced by his sweat. He left the stream and walked steadily across a wide paddy toward the Marine perimeter. The scarred hill before him was covered with a mass of green ants that became tanned, shirtless figures dressed in green as he came nearer. Some sat languidly near hootches made of sticks and ponchos. Others walked or worked or rough-housed. Dan was afraid, but he did not consider turning back. They were his last hope. There was nothing to turn back to.

They watched his approach from the hill. He was a lone, steadily striding, stolid figure who was soon recognizable by his clothes and haircut as VC. They sent a patrol down to the paddy with an interpreter and apprehended him outside the perimeter.

Dan squinted his eyes from the sun, still walking with steady, measured steps, and walked up to the interpreter. He was relieved to see a Vietnamese face. He stopped abruptly in front of the interpreter and slapped his muddy *chieu hoi* leaflet into the man's hand. Then he spoke with melodious tones, looking stonily at the dirt of the paddy.

"It is such a game," Dan said.

"What did he say?" the Marines asked anxiously.

The interpreter smiled. "He say, 'VC full of shit.' "

Everyone laughed and the Marines slapped him on his back. They were very big and very friendly. Dan was surprised at their humor. One of them gave him a cigarette and lit it for him. Dan smiled softly, thanking him.

The Marines brought Dan to the company command post, in the center of the perimeter. He was amazed at the little city of fighting holes and poncho hootches and whip antennas from the many radios. And there was so much food, cans of it scattered about each hootch and hole. That is why they are so big, he thought to himself. So much food.

He squatted respectfully in the dust, where the patrol left him. The interpreter asked him if he was hungry. The interpreter was tall for a Vietnamese, and spoke with a nasal laziness that marked him as a learned man. He did not look like a soldier, Dan noted. He wore his uniform uncomfortably. Somewhere he has a business. Or perhaps he teaches. He is not meant to be a soldier. But, then, neither am I. I am like the water bull. I am strong but I prefer to use my strength in the fields. I am happiest with my children. And I startle when the gun fires. Like the water bull. But there are no more children and no more fields.

"Yes," Dan responded. "I am hungry."

He ate greedily, unheated C-ration meat straight from the can. He had not eaten meat in a very long time. Perhaps a year, he thought, trying to remember. A little fish, but no meat. Much rice. Without the rice we would all die.

Another Vietnamese approached Dan while he was eating. He was short like Dan, but heavier. He greeted Dan warmly and asked him many questions about the VC in the valley. He was quite familiar with their operations. He told Dan that he had served with the VC in the valley for two years. He was from Phu Loi, to the north. He served the Marines now, as a Kit Carson Scout. He seemed very proud of it.

"What do you do?" Dan studied the man's thickness. It was muscle. The man ate well. He seemed happy, too. Dan could not remember feeling the way the man seemed to feel.

The man's name was Hai. Hai smiled warmly, sharing his secret. "I do not do much. It is a good life. Sometimes I lead patrols. Sometimes I talk to villagers. Sometimes I do nothing." He spoke with a sense of self-importance. "There is nothing better to do. They pay me as a Sergeant.

Fifty piasters. It is so much better than serving in the
Army. In the Army they would hate me because I was VC.
Here I feel important. And there is so much food."

Dan shrugged miserably, confiding in the man, appreciating his openness. "It is such a game," he said softly.

"You should join us," Hai urged. "There are supposed to
be two of us. There is nothing better for you now."

"I have had enough of war," answered Dan. But the
vision of his family lying dead inside the bunker would not
leave him and already he was pondering Hai's invitation.

Hai shrugged. "There will always be war. You should
make the best of it. You will fight in the Army if you don't
do this. Or spend forever in a prisoner camp. Why did you
surrender?"

"Because there was nothing left."

Dan spent the rest of the day in the Marine perimeter. The
Marines were very friendly, accepting him as one of their
own now that he had surrendered. They are so naive, he
thought. The world is so simple to them. Yesterday I
served the VC. Today I serve them. I would rather serve
neither. They do not understand that. But, he thought,
hating the increasing redundancy of his conclusions, that is
the nature of things. And they seem kind. Strange to find
them friendly after fearing them and hating what they
have brought.

Dan was flown to the rear and interrogated and processed. It was easy for him because he had surrendered.
The Intelligence people were friendly and he cooperated
fully with them. They asked him a series of "control"
questions, ones they already had answers to, and found
him to be honest. He did not feel guilty when he gave information about his former unit. He hoped secretly that
they would all be killed.

He was processed quickly and took the oath of alle-
giance to the Government of Vietnam. He raised his hand
and renounced the National Liberation Front in his clear,
melodious tones, making the oath a song. It is such a game,
he thought, singing the oath. Governments are not real.
Rice is real.

He remembered Hai and the Marines and the memories
gave him an embryo of warmth. Nothing else did. He asked
to join the Kit Carson Scout program. The interviews

were easy for him: he was well versed in propaganda. He told the interviewers the same stories he used to tell the villagers. The only difference was the identification of the culprits. The interviewers nodded warmly, captivated by low flute notes, and Dan was accepted into the program. After a brief course of training he was assigned to the same company he had surrendered to.

There was friendship for him in the company. The Marines liked him. Dan was a warm person who smiled through his sadness. He soon proved to be a shrewd interrogator. He was fierce with prisoners. He was effective, if somewhat unpredictable, with the villagers. There were times when he remembered the valley as it was before a brother would kill a brother for the sake of discipline, and he was gentle and loving, one of them. But there were other times when he could not view a villager but as the wife or child or parent of one of the soldiers who had killed his family and driven him from his land.

All the men are in the mountains. Your man kills families. Shall I kill you?

16.

The tiny gray airstrip nestled French-style at the base of a string of mountains. One had to immediately wonder why the French had built it there, and then wonder further why the Americans had chosen to build the Basin's major combat base next to it. There was a temptation to excuse the French, who had not learned the lesson of Dien Bien Phu until after the airstrip had been in use for some months.

But there came an addled surge of déjà vu, perhaps only subconscious, when one stood at the old gray strip and peered into swaddles of blue-green cliffs that lurked to the south and east, and at the uncontrollable Arizona to the north, an easy mortar arc away. It was as if the only substantive change that fifteen years had wrought, aside from the increased ability of both sides to destroy the innards of the prize they sought to capture, was the composition of the fortifications. The French, considering their obligation more permanent, had built concrete bunkers, many of which still stood ten miles away in Dai Loc. The Americans, true to the "temporary" nature of their commitment, erected sandbag bunkers that decayed, sagging at the seams and finally bursting, oozing back into the earth, each monsoon season, and had to be continually replaced.

An Hoa combat base. Cities of tents sprawled from hill to barren hill around the airstrip, red as the claydirt that permeated the air. The perimeter jutted and sprawled in no identifiable fashion, resembling a badly gerrymandered political district. Units had arrived in the Basin in trickles, an artillery battery here, a tank detachment there, each passing month contributing juts of new perimeter in a burgeoning pastiche. Regimental command post, two separate mess halls, most of an artillery battalion, detachments of every kind: tanks, amphtracs, motor transport, disbursing, medical, supply. And the company rear areas. Home of the Twenty-Fifth Marines.

At the edge of the airstrip there was a sign: *WELCOME TO AN HOA—LITTLE DIEN BIEN PHU*. Rear-area personnel, perversely proud of the frequency of incoming rocket and mortar rounds, had erected the sign. Bagger, just off the resupply helicopter, pointed a rifled arm at the sign and nudged Cannonball. "Sure. And where the hell have we been for the last five months—downtown Saigon?"

They walked slowly up the hill toward the battalion area, past tents red with dust, the dust so deep inside the weaves that no amount of brushing or scrubbing would ever erase its color, past oil-barrel urinals, their screens dripping, choked with flies and cigarette butts, eddies of oil and urine odors surrounding them. Occasional jeeps and mechanical mules cloaked them with the red dust. The road was puffy with it. It rolled off their boot tops as they walked, as if it were a slightly viscid liquid. For those brief moments they enjoyed their dirtiness, the patches of gook sores that ate into their skin, their filthy, month-old clothes, even their relative gauntness. Those minor evidences set them off from the rear pogues who populated An Hoa, typing inside tents, chasing supplies in mules, or examining pay records.

They reached a pallet-box sidewalk and strolled languidly between a closer grouping of tents, into the company office. In the rear of the tent the First Sergeant sat among a gaggle of clerks, drinking a beer. He was huge and crew-cutted, a jovial disciplinarian who still carried a piece of shrapnel in his back from Korea.

The Top squinted slightly when Bagger and Cannonball walked in together, shoulder-bumping close, obvious friends. The racial polarity of the rear area made that a rare occurrence. He made sure that both were on the R & R list, then billeted them in the company transient tent. Finally he smiled sternly to the two scruffy bush Marines.

"You people look gross. Go to the supply tent and get some clean utilities. And get across the street to the showers before they turn the water off. You've got an hour. And *shave*. And tomorrow, get haircuts."

Bagger nodded wryly, remembering the ephemeral regime of Sergeant Austin. "Whitewalls."

The Top affirmed, still smiling, "That's right, Marine. Whitewalls. Welcome back to the Corps."

Bagger nudged Cannonball as they exited the tent. "Welcome back to the Corps. Christ. Will somebody please tell me where the fuck I been for five months?"

Cannonball shrugged nonchalantly, accustomed to hassles. His sharply featured, cream-colored face was totally at ease. "C'mon, Bagger. Didn't you know this is the *real* Corps?"

In the transient tent there were a half-dozen new dudes, green-clothed, faces ambiguous, as yet unaffected, who would join the company in the bush shortly. They crowded together at one end of the tent, suffering communally the miseries of the inexperienced. In the rest of the tent were a dozen other transients, back from the hospital, on the way to or returning from R & R, or merely slackers, playing an angle that would keep them in the rear while the days ran on their tours.

Bagger and Cannonball strode into the tent, found adjacent cots, and dropped their packs and weapons. A tall, spindly man with a full mane of jet-black hair approached them. He was grinning conspiratorially, and wore two strings of love beads, like brightly colored Indian trinkets, around his neck.

Bagger looked at the man as he approached in the shadowed darkness of the tent, then finally recognized him. "Way-ull. Kiss my ass. It's Stretch. Where you been, boy?"

Stretch's long neck bobbed affably. "Japan. Two months. Been skating for a fat man's ass. Uh huh."

"How the hell you make it to *Japan* on a stomach-ache?"

Stretch smiled proudly, massaging his stomach. "Had the hookworms, man. Had me a Number Ten case. Rode those mothers all the way to Yokosuka. They laid eggs in my gut and I took a two-month cure. Can you dig it? Coulda kissed each one of 'em."

"Did it hurt?"

"Had the shits, cramps, stuff like that. What the hell. For two months in Japan, I'd do it again." Stretch grinned his conspiratorial grin. "Matter of fact, I just might."

"Well, you won't have any trouble finding wormy water. Skipper won't have any water buckets sent in, and we're in the An Tams now. He says it affects our mo-bility. Yeah. There's plenty of wormy water."

Stretch turned to Cannonball. "Well, Cannonball. How you making it, *boy?*"

Cannonball smiled easily and tapped Stretch on the chest. His fingers lingered along the tall man's shirt front, and he stood very close. "You see a *boy*, you jus' go ahead an' knock him down."

Stretch laughed. "Yeah, old Cannonball. Hey. Homi-cide's back."

Cannonball's hazel eyes sparkled. "No shit? I been won-derin' where that bad-ass brother been. He been gone a hell of a long time fo' a slice up the side of his head. Where's he at?"

Stretch cocked his head, enjoying his informer role. "Well, he's in trouble. Uh huh. Reason he took so long is he decided to take him a vacation down in Dogpatch— you know, in Da Nang, there—when he got out of the hospital. Spent a couple months shacking with some whore down there when he shoulda been back in the bush. They caught him swiping a camera in the R & R center a couple days ago, sent him back here for a court-martial."

Cannonball shook his head. "Damn fool." He looked back up to Stretch. "So, where's he at, man?"

"He's over in the Black Shack."

"Say what?" Cannonball squinted up at the gloating Stretch.

"Man, you *have* been in the bush a long time. The Black Shack. Two tents down, in the back."

Bagger erupted into motion, taking Cannonball by the shoulder. "Well, come on. Let's go see the stupid shit."

Stretch leaned his narrow head back, mocking Bagger. "You better not go, Bagger. He don't want to see any Chuck dudes. He won't even say 'hey' to me when I see him on the road."

Bagger dismissed Stretch. "So what. Neither would I. C'mon, Cannonball. Let's go."

In the battalion area, two tents down from the company tent, one-quarter of a troop tent had seceded from the Marine Corps. Blocked from the remainder of that tent by a divider wall, and from the rest of An Hoa by a barrier of hate, it held six cots, although it had never been fully occupied. Four months earlier, Bagger learned, a group of blacks awaiting court-martial had seized it in the name of Brotherhood, and christened it the Black Shack. Periodically the occupants changed, but the Black Shack had remained: no officer or NCO, white or black, had had the fortitude to eject them.

Above the tent flap was a hand-lettered sign: NO CHUCK DUDES ALLOWED: THIS MEANS YOU. Malcolm X glowered from a poster on one wall. On another, Bobby Seale pointed a rifle at the camera. There were hand-lettered posters: KILL THE BEAST. DEATH TO ALL CHUCK PIGS. A table in the center of the tentspace was covered with stacks of Black Panther and Muslim literature.

The Black Shack was the place to come and rap about the horrors of racism and prejudice.

And Rap Jones was its guru. Bagger had heard of Rap Jones. The longtime private was infamous throughout the Regiment. Rap Jones had been in Vietnam more than two years, merely trying to complete a one-year tour: a person's brigtime didn't count toward completion. Rap Jones had been convicted of more than a dozen noncapital offenses, most of them petty, ranging from unauthorized absence to refusal to obey a direct order. Rap Jones, it was rumored, knew every dope pusher and deserter in Dogpatch, the thicket of tin shacks in Da Nang where such errant people dwelled.

Rap Jones, in the parlance, was a bad nigger.

And now Rap Jones stood at the entrance to the Black Shack, holding both tent flaps tightly, arms outstretched like a bronzed Christ, self-proclaimed martyr of the People, denying Bagger access to his friend. Bagger stared up the three wooden steps at Jones, torn between a natural impulse toward undirected, explosive frustration, and his desire to reach a harmony with the smirking malcontent so he could speak to Homicide.

Rap Jones pointed to the sign: NO CHUCK DUDES ALLOWED. "Cain't you *read?*"

Bagger glanced at the sign, then back to Rap Jones. "Homicide in there?"

"Uh huh. But he doan' want to talk to you."

Bagger tried to peer past Rap Jones at the inside of the tent. Bobby Seale pointed a rifle at him from the far wall, but Homicide was not apparent. *"Hey Homicide! Come on out here, man! It's me, Bagger! Me and Cannonball! C'mon out!"*

No sound or motion from inside the tent. Rap Jones nodded to Cannonball. "You comin' inside, Brother?"

Cannonball eyed Bagger, noting the anger that had tightened his friend's lips, burned his cheeks, driven his hands deep into his trouser pockets. He knew that Bagger had a tendency to explode when pressured. He looked at the narrowing eyes and comprehended that Bagger was ready to unload on Rap Jones, that he would start a race riot at any second, in an effort to see a black friend. Cannonball sensed the irony of that possibility, and suddenly felt trapped by the two worlds he would have to straddle in order to prevent its occurrence.

Desperate, Cannonball screamed into the tent. *"Homicide. Get yo' black ass out here. Hurry up, now!"*

Rap Jones taunted them both with a mocking leer. He jabbed at Cannonball. "You Whitey's nigger, boy? Goan' stand outside. Don't piss ol' Whitey off now, boy."

Bagger bristled. His fists came out of his pockets in two hard balls, ready to mash Rap Jones's face. "Why, you motherfucker—"

Homicide peered down at them, over Jones's shoulder. A jagged scar ran down his deeply black cheek from the hairline, vestige of his wound. His hair was combed out into a puffy Afro. His normally angry eyes were dulled by pills. Homicide was totally spaced out.

He attempted to focus on his visitors, finally recognizing them, and slurred out in a deep bass, "Hey, y'all."

Bagger glared at Rap Jones, vindicated: Homicide had spoken. "Goddamn, Homicide. What you been doin'?"

Homicide stared dully at Bagger for a long, motionless moment, then touched the scar on his cheek and spoke slowly, as if he were reciting a school lesson that he had just succeeded in memorizing. "Been bleedin' Whitey's war. Killin' brown folks, ain' no reason. Been dyin' fo' the Beast."

Bagger stared unbelievingly at Homicide, then uneasily over to Cannonball, who was grimacing, feeling more and more trapped. Cannonball felt Bagger's unspoken accusation and attempted to ignore it, turning back to Homicide. He studied the stuporous, expressionless face, the body draped in a black skivvy shirt, strings of love beads like a choke chain around the neck, a slave bracelet around one wrist.

Homicide, decided Cannonball, was beyond reasoning. But Cannonball nonetheless scolded him, attempting to reassure Bagger that Rap Jones's hate did not predominate. "C'mon, Homicide. What you sayin', man? You talkin' trash. Shut up, now."

As he spoke two faces peered down at him, one deeply black, round and numb, the other the color of polished leather, thin and angular, hating. Rap Jones spoke with finality, nodding to Cannonball. "You wan' talk with Homicide, you come inside. You doan' wan' come inside, you *slide.*"

Bagger's neckveins bulged and his wide face was turbulent, furious. *"We ain't talking to you! You shut your face. Hear?"*

Rap Jones seemingly ignored Bagger, but reached quickly inside the tent and came back to its entrance with a long, carved stick: short-timer stick. Bagger watched his antagonist pat the end of it against the flat of one hand and quickly realized that, in one swift motion, Rap Jones could pull the sheath and expose the hidden blade, and in another, pierce him with it.

But Bagger was beyond caution. He reached inside his flak jacket pocket and pulled out a grenade, straightening the pin. "You pull the cover offa that, I pull the pin outa this. You stick me you better be quick, nigger, 'cause this is going inside your skivvy shirt."

Both men froze, staring deeply, tautly, into each other's eyes. Homicide still peered blankly over Jones's shoulder, mumbling numb aphorisms about the Beast to a silently staring Cannonball.

Cannonball sensed that he had somehow caused the standoff by his waffling, and that Bagger would not back down of his own volition. To ask Bagger to leave with him now would be a futile gesture that would explode the powder keg. Rap Jones would prod Cannonball for being an Uncle, Bagger would attack Rap Jones, and somebody would die. Or at least bleed.

Ain' worth it, mused Cannonball. An' I did this. Doan' ask me *how*, I do'n know how, but I know I *did* this. Only one way out of it, too. He turned to Bagger. "Bagger, you book on out o' here, man. I gotta rap with a brother, hear? Catch you later, man."

Rap Jones smirked. Bagger glared unbelievingly. "You mean you're gonna go *in* there?"

Cannonball shrugged, trying to be nonchalant. "Yeah. You doan' understand, man. I'll just catch you later. O.K.?"

Cannonball walked up the steps. Rap Jones dropped the short-timer stick on a near cot and passed the Power to Cannonball in an overlong, exaggerated series of hand grabbing, celebrating his victory over Bagger.

"Heyyy, there's a Brother. What's happenin', now?"

"You what's happenin', Rap Jones. *An' the nevah-endin' struggle."*

"All right! An' what is Blood?"

Bagger watched, amazed. He bent the grenade pin back. The three men disappeared inside the Black Shack and tightened the tent flap behind them.

Bagger stood for a moment, watching after them, then walked dazedly back to the transient tent, muttering to himself. "Niggers. Jesus Christ. I never thought Cannon-ball was like that. Out in the bush, they need you, they're all right. Get 'em back in the rear and they turn to shit." He mimicked Rap Jones. "An' what is Blood? Well, kiss my ass. Goddamn spooks."

17.

The sun fell like a red balloon through the haze above the western mountains, streaking the mists with sheets of flame that made the hills appear to burn. At last it was cool enough to eat. Goodrich sat alone underneath the half-thatch of a burnt-out hootch, at the edge of the latest confluence of village and trees that had become their two-day home.

No one lived in the village anymore. It was filled with hootches like the one Goodrich sat under, blown apart and abandoned. Latticed trenches dug by the NVA zigzagged throughout it, connecting hootches and advantageous fir-ing points. Fighting holes from three years of Marines sur-rounded the village along the paddy dike that encircled it. Some of the holes were so old and the grass had grown so high inside them that they were unnoticeable unless someone fell into them when walking. Others, like the one Goodrich had just finished digging, were raw on their in-sides, walled with a clay that clung to a man each time he rubbed against it.

But you never use an old fighting hole, Goodrich re-membered, opening a can of Spiced Beef. Either it's booby-trapped, or the gooners know exactly where it is and can hit it with a B-40 blindfolded. Always dig a new one. He snorted helplessly. A few more times in this ville and we'll have a trench dug all the way around it.

Goodrich ate his dinner, surveying the ghost town that had once bustled with villagers. Sometimes, when he could shake the permeating fear out of his mind and focus on it, the futility of what they were doing overwhelmed him. Abusing the land until it became unworkable, killing and being killed, and yet nothing changing beyond the tragedy of the immediate event.

Those tragedies had accumulated in his mind like particles of silt in a filter, until they had completely plugged up his logical processes, preventing the saner portions of his existence from registering any longer. Every day, some new horror inflicted in the name of winning Hearts and Minds. It either numbs you or it infuriates you, he lamented. No wonder the other people didn't get uptight when I shot that old mamasan on my first patrol.

He tried to count the tragedies. The villages they had assaulted on line for fear of being ambushed when they crossed open areas: "reconnaissance by fire," Hodges called it. Shot dogs and chickens and hogs. Accidental wounds and deaths of civilians. They were a routine, almost boring occurrence.

Marines denying villagers their extra food, on the premise that the food would only wind up with the enemy. Destroying unused C-rations, punching holes in the cans and tossing them into burn holes with the trash. It had become a familiar sight, from some black-humored theater of the absurd, whenever the company pulled out of an old perimeter. The last part of the company column would still be on one side of a hill, or on one edge of a village, as a horde of tattered villagers massed on the other end, like an anxious army of rats. And the column hardly clear of the hill or village when the rats began to cover it, children and women and old men scampering about the trash holes, flicking out C-ration tins with long sticks. Occasionally, the company would mortar its own perimeter with White Phosphorus rounds after leaving it, to scare the scavengers away. But it never achieved more than a momentary effect.

Then denying the villagers their own food as well: not being able to distinguish between an enemy rice-collection point and a family's storage area, so taking all rice beyond a villager's immediate needs. Or, if no helicopter was available, destroying the rice by urinating on it or dropping smoke grenades in it.

The prisoners. Goodrich had come to Vietnam with a Miniver Cheevy view of war, believing that reason would rule over emotion, that once a combatant had been removed from the fray he would be accorded a certain sum of dignity. He had also thought the North Vietnamese soldiers and the fabled Viet Cong would face captivity with a sort of gallantry. It had confused and amazed him to see prisoners shit in their pants and grovel before him. And he could not get used to men being beaten and kicked, for no apparent reason.

And worse. He had watched Wild Man shoot a bottle off one prisoner's head, on a dare. The prisoner had fainted, then shit in his pants when he was awakened. He had seen Bagger try to talk a wounded soldier into killing himself, handing him a bayonet knife and placing the tip of it into the soldier's belly. He had been amazed to see Waterbull, normally a nonparticipant in the abuses, toss a prisoner into the water of a bomb crater when he had tired of carrying the enemy soldier, who had been shot through the knee. Waterbull then yelled jocularly that the prisoner was trying to drown himself. Goodrich had helped fish him out of the water, to the taunts of some of the others.

The pain of watching living corpses. The worst had been two North Vietnamese soldiers who had been either napalmed or hit by White Phosphorus, it wasn't clear which, and had walked to their perimeter to surrender. A villager had patiently guided them. They were scorched from head to foot, blinded, their hair burnt off and their skin pink and cracked, like a hot dog on a charcoal grill. Their throats were also scorched. They could not speak or cry. The villager identified them as enemy soldiers.

The insanity was not so much in the events, but that they were undirected, without aim or reason. They happened merely because they happened. The only meaning was in the thing itself. And what does it get me to know that, Goodrich mused bitterly, confused. Harvard shitbird. College turkey. Even Hodges calls me that. But Wild Man has college. And his father is a successful man. Some kind of business.

There was no outrage from the others. They just didn't care about anything other than the experience, for its own sake.

Help me, Senator. Can't you stop it?

Ottenburger. Every night as he stood watch alone in his fighting hole. He could not shake the steady eyes, the flat, resigned voice. They were their own metaphor for the futility Goodrich felt. He just bled and bled, talking like that, until he ran out of blood. Did I do it? I just had to watch him die.

It was growing dark. Snake approached, walking casually along a low dike from the squad area. Goodrich felt himself grow taut. He was still in awe of Snake's ability to master this insanity of dust and weeds, but he found the spindly, tattooed squad leader insensitive and overbearing. The perfect Marine, mused Goodrich. A vulgar, violent little shit with a chip on his shoulder.

"Make like a mole and get in your hole, Senator. We're gonna get hit tonight."

"Oh, good. Did you arrange it?"

Snake laughed at him. "Nope. Captain Crazy arranged it by setting up in this damn ville." On the lines someone was burning trash. Snake yelled at the man, "Put that fire out! It's dark!" He turned back to Goodrich, shaking his head in mild disgust. "Put us here with a dike in the front like that, treeline over there. What the hell does he expect? We got followed in here. You see all them gooks? Every time we crossed a paddy I could see 'em. Come on, Senator."

Goodrich rose slowly. "Oh, I can't wait."

Snake stopped and turned back to Goodrich. "You think we can? You think you're the only one that don't like this, don't you, Senator? Well, Buddhist Priest." Snake stared coldly into his face. "If anybody dies, I hope it's you."

Goodrich swallowed hard, unnerved. No one talked about that, not in the bush. "Why?"

" 'Cause you're a pissant crybaby. And you don't carry your own weight. When's the last time you did something for somebody besides yourself, Senator?"

"Do you realize how ridiculous it is? Can you truly comprehend, Snake? You're doing for each other and you're dying for each other. That's all. I mean *all!* And the lousiest thing in the world to die for is another sucker who's only dying for you. Do you get what I mean? The only reason any of us are dying is because we're *here*. It's like two scorpions in a jar. They'll kill each other, but only because they're in the jar. Do you get what I mean?"

Snake stared quietly at Goodrich for a long moment. On the lines, a man lit a cigarette. Snake screamed at the silhouette: *"Put out that smoke!"* He turned back to Goodrich and tapped him on the chest. "You get down in that hole, like most ricky-tick, or I'm gonna punch you in the mouth. *Make your hat, Chicken-man!"*

Goodrich picked up his weapon and resignedly followed Snake along a narrow dike, walking in the blue dusk toward the lines. In front of him, the treeline, a hundred meters out, somnolent in the darkness, suddenly went bright red with the flashes of several B-40 rockets. Green and red tracers followed as he watched, for a moment frozen in awe. Finally he dropped to the ground, seeking cover from the tremendous, instantaneous eruption that made him feel as if he were standing inside a cookpot that had exploded a thousand kernels of popcorn, all at once.

Goodrich crawled, whining, naked in the cropped dirt of an open field, between the old hootch and his fighting hole. The whine escaped him in a steady, involuntary gag, his vocal cords constricting tightly in his fear, causing him to emit a sound that was a child's cry. NNNNNnnnnnnhhh. He found the edge of the dike and leaned into it, safe. The rounds went over his head.

Curses in the field, raw with pain. Just out from him, in the open, Snake lay curled in a ball, holding one leg. Goodrich hugged against the dike. Snake writhed. Dust spots kicked up around him from the incoming bullets.

If I helped him, Goodrich thought suddenly, he would leave me alone. They would all leave me alone.

But his fear immobilized him. Die for Snake because Snake is out there dying for me? Makes no sense. He lay against the dike and contemplated it some more. But if I crawled out to him I could drag him back over here. Then I could help him and there wouldn't be very many rounds. They would leave me alone, then.

A quick, large shadow emerged as he watched, and Waterbull scooped Snake up like a steam shovel grabbing a lump of dirt. In one motion he picked up Snake and headed for the dike. He landed, rolling Snake over the top of him to cushion the fall, only feet from where Goodrich lay, still contemplating.

In front of them, the lines now poured a steady rate of fire back at the treeline. Waterbull reached for Snake's foot. A B-40 rocket slammed into the hootch where Goodrich had eaten his dinner, setting its half-roof of thatch ablaze.

Snake protested as Waterbull probed. "I'm all right, Bull. Lemme alone."

Waterbull searched along the leg Snake had been holding. A burst of AK fire interrupted his effort, throwing a veil of dust from the dike into Bull's face. He lay flat for a moment, then grabbed Snake's leg again.

"Goddamn it, lemme *alone,* Bull!"

Snake seemed in deep pain. "Thanks for getting me. I mean it. I just want to peep it out myself." He pushed his glasses back to the top of his nose. "Now." He reached tentatively for his foot. "I think I took a round in my toe."

Bull guffawed. "In your *toe?*"

"You think it's funny, shoot *your* foot and see how it feels, asshole." He began to unlace his boot. A string of mortar rounds walked slowly across the perimeter. Snake listened for a moment. "One tube is all. This shit's gonna be over before you know it." He grimaced as he started to pull his boot off, and noticed Goodrich. "Hey, Senator. Be a hero and get my helmet, will you? I need the battle dressing off it."

"I was going to help you. I was just getting ready."

"Good. Get my helmet."

The incoming rounds had stopped, at least for the moment. Goodrich crawled quickly out and retrieved the helmet, tossing it to Snake. It skidded across the dirt and stopped a yard away from Snake's face.

"Nice job, Senator. Silver Star, at least." Snake took the battle dressing from the helmet band, and, in one painful yank, pulled his boot off.

There was no blood. He felt the crusted sock, counted his toes. The sock was dry. All toes were present. Waterbull knelt, preparing to apply the battle dressing.

"Take the sock off, Snake."

"Don't need to."

" 'Course you need to. Come on. Take it off."

"I don't *need* to, Bull, all right?" Snake felt the bottom of his sock, finding a tear in it that was perhaps an inch long. "Gimme my boot."

Waterbull cocked his head, flabbergasted. "You mean after all *that,* you ain't even wounded?"

"The *boot,* Bull. All right?"

Waterbull reached along the dike where Snake had thrown the boot, and handed it to Snake. Snake examined it carefully, feeling the front with one hand. He shook his head in disbelief. "Look at that, will you? Check this out."

There was a small hole in the toe of the boot, where the bullet had entered. There was no exit hole. Snake cackled. "Somewhere inside this boot there's a bullet that went between my toes." He stuck his foot in the air, showing them the torn sock. "Can you dig it?"

Waterbull caught a glimpse of the tear from the glimmer of a distant illumination round. "Nahhh. I don't believe it."

Snake laughed, relieved. "I'll tell you, it felt like somebody put a whack on my foot with a damn sledgehammer. Knocked me on my face."

Waterbull nodded sagely, slouched against the dike. "You should call in a Heart for that, man. Yup. Definitely worth a Heart."

Snake shook his head, still laughing. "No blood. Not a drop. Forget it."

The three made their way toward the lines, Snake limping slightly. It was quiet now. Goodrich walked beside Snake. He spoke hesitantly.

"I was going to help you. I was coming. Waterbull beat me."

"The day I gotta count on you I'm hanging up my jock, Senator."

The perimeter was quiet as a tomb. Medevacs were safely out, one man up, three down in the fighting holes. The treeline and high paddy dike had been silenced hours before. Hodges sat next to his poncho hootch, standing radio watch. Every fifteen minutes he called security checks to the listening posts. At the end of an hour he would walk the platoon lines, checking fighting holes, rapping with those on watch, ensuring the lines were awake. But, other than that, a time to ponder, to ruminate, to plan.

He held his helmet on his knees and cupped a cigarette inside it, lighting it. Not supposed to, but screw it. It's three o'clock. The gooners are all in bed. Nonetheless, he continued to cup it as he smoked. There's always that chance. One sniper round can do it. Every now and then it happens.

Three artillery rounds impacted casually in the treeline.

H and Is. Behind him, the 60-millimeter mortar section
fired five more in the vicinity of the high dike. Then there
were quiet, elongated moments spent sitting under total
blackness, as if he were locked inside a strangely odorous,
mosquito-infested closet. So alone, so lonely like this.

And at night like this they visited him, those old ghosts
who had come alive each Sunday in his grandma's kitchen.
He had joined them. He was one of them. They descended
from the heavens, or maybe from the hollows of his memory, and they were real. He commiserated with them.
Sometimes they were so close he felt the swishes of their
passing. They tickled his neck. They brushed his arms.
They ached inside his own misery.

He stared into the blackness, dragging on his cigarette,
communicating with them. All my life I've waited for this,
he mused. Now I've joined you and your losses are a
strength to me. I ache and yet I know that Alec retched
with pain on the dust road that went to Corinth. I breathe
the dust and yet I know that Grandpa breathed the gas that
made a hero out of Pershing. I flinch when bullets tear the
air in angry rents and yet I know that Father, and three
farmer boys at Pickett's Charge, felt a cutting edge that
dropped them dead. How can I be bitter? You are my
strength, you ghosts.

And I have learned those things, those esoteric skills and
knowledges, that mark me as one of you. That loose-
boweled piles of shit, too much shit from overeating,
plopped randomly around the outer dikes of a ville, mean
trouble. Catching the aroma, seeing the groupings, watching flies dance lazily, rejoicing in their latest fetid morsel
that bends the low grass in a muddy glob like a bomb of
cow dung. Trouble.

I can tell from the crack of a rifle shot the type of
weapon fired and what direction the bullet is traveling. I
can listen to a mortar pop and know its size, how far away
it is. I know instinctively when I should prep a treeline with
artillery before I move into it. I know which draws and
fields should be crossed on line, which should be assaulted,
and which are safe to cross in column. I know where to
place my men when we stop and form a perimeter. I can
shoot a rifle and throw a grenade and direct air and artillery onto any target, under any circumstances. I can
dress any type of wound, I have dressed all types of

wounds, watered protruding intestines with my canteen to keep them from cracking under sunbake, patched sucking chests with plastic, tied off stumps with field-expedient tourniquets. I can call in medevac helicopters, talk them, cajole them, dare them into any zone.

I do these things, experience these things, repeatedly, daily. Their terrors and miseries are so compelling, and yet so regular, that I have ascended to a high emotion that is nonetheless a crusted numbness. I am an automaton, bent on survival, agent and prisoner of my misery. How terribly exciting.

And how, to what purpose, will these skills serve me when this madness ends? What lies on the other side of all this? It frightens me. I haven't thought about it. I haven't prepared for it. I am so good, so ready for these things that were my birthright. I do not enjoy them. I know they have warped me. But it will be so hard to deal with a life empty of them.

And there are the daily sufferings. You ghosts have known them, but who else? I can sleep in the rain, wrapped inside my poncho, listening to the drops beat on the rubber like small explosions, then feeling the water pour in rivulets inside my poncho, soaking me as I lie in the mud. I can live in the dirt, sit and lie and sleep in the dirt, it is my chair and my bed, my floor and my walls, this clay. And like all of you, I have endured diarrhea as only an animal should endure it, squatting a yard off a trail and relieving myself unceremoniously, naturally, animally. Deprivations of food. Festering, open sores. Worms. Heat. Aching crotch that nags for fulfillment, any emptying hole that will relieve it.

Who appreciates my sufferings? Who do I suffer for?

The mortar fired behind him, five more rounds at the high dike, and the ghosts were gone. Hodges stood slowly and dusted off his trousers, carrying the radio with him as he began to check lines.

He hoped that Snake would be awake. He felt like shooting the shit.

18.

Staff Sergeant Gilliland broke through the scraggly hedge-row from the landing zone, located the platoon command post, and walked quickly across a potato patch toward it, leaving an ashen, gray-powder wake behind each step. He ambled up behind Hodges, who sat in the dirt, dressed only in tiger shorts, writing a letter. Nearby, a transistor radio blared toward a baking sky. Gilliland swung his pack cavalierly in front of Hodges, dropping it. Hodges looked up and noticed an uncharacteristic grin lighting the scarred face, even lifting the sagging moustache.

"Well, kiss my ass. What's happening, Sarge? Didn't expect to see *you* back out here!"

Gilliland continued to smile, as if he had found some inner peace, some odd logic that made it all mean something. "Well, I won't be back here for very long, Lieutenant."

"Gonna be a Motor-T jock, huh?"

Still the smile. "No sir, I'm gonna be a fucking civilian."

Hodges started, almost as if slapped. "Come on, Sarge. Say it isn't so."

Gilliland folded his arms, sitting across from Hodges, the murky blue memory of a Devil Dog tattoo showing underneath the tan of one forearm. His molten eyes expertly examined this latest perimeter, noting distances between fighting holes, locations of machine guns, pieces of prominent terrain. "That's a hell of a good job on the perimeter, Lieutenant. We got an OP out there?"

"OP in the trees. I been bringing it back to an LP near that dike at night."

"Good idea. That dike is high enough to be a good B-40 pos. Know what I mean?"

Hodges grinned slightly, admiring Gilliland's bush sense. "Oh, it sure as hell was, Sarge. Last night. Didn't even have the LP out yet. Boom, boom. Two B-40s, right behind the dike."

Gilliland nodded sagely. "Figures. Gun in the treeline?"

"One mortar tube. Small arms. It wasn't much. Hey, Sarge. Quit putting me off. You ain't really gonna go be a civilian, now are you?"

"Oh, yeah, Lieutenant. It ain't no bullshit. Couple weeks I'm gonna be *Mister* Gilliland." Gilliland grinned frivolously. "Wanna buy a used car? How about some insurance?"

Hodges shook his head unbelievingly. "Sarge, you're *crazy,* man. You got ten years. Ten more, you can retire. Half-pay. *All* that shit." He scrutinized Gilliland, who still gazed unconcernedly around the perimeter. "Tell me, Sarge. Do you have medical insurance for your kids?"

"Nope. Course not. Marine Corps takes care of that."

"Do you have a—have you ever—do you think you're gonna get a *job* that'll compare, where you won't have to start at the bottom?"

Gilliland shrugged, unconcerned. "Maybe. Maybe not. I had reserve duty a couple years ago, and everybody kept telling me, you know, if I get out come on back and work. But Lieutenant, you ain't even asking the right questions, anyway." For a moment Gilliland looked searchingly at Hodges, then he regained his sardonic front.

"It ain't what's *waiting* for me on the outside. Not any more. Nope. It's the way things have changed." A cigarette appeared magically between his thin, now-somber lips. "It just doesn't mean anything to be a Marine anymore, Lieutenant. Vietnam did that."

Hodges nodded, grinning wryly, remembering Sergeant Austin's comments about Vietnam Marines. "You mean all the discipline is gone, all the spit and polish, blind obedience—"

Gilliland cut him off. "Nah. Sir, we got discipline. Only time the discipline disappears is when a man don't rate it anyway. It's one thing to ask for blind obedience when you tell a man to shine his shoes in a damn barracks. It's a whole new thing to ask for it when a man is gonna stand up and take a round between his eyes. Listen, sir. I was over here in '65, when the Old Corps invaded the Nam, know what I mean? Before the draft kicked in, when we had what they called 'true volunteers.' Well, we couldn't do what these kids can do. I mean it. We had a lot of hot shits on the parade field, and a lot of motivated sons of bitches, but there wasn't anybody in a company who knew how to fight a goddamn war! Couple gunnies, maybe, who remembered something about the Frozen Chosin in the Freezing Season. But that was it.

"So we did *dumb*-ass things. We hung grenades from our pockets by the spoons, like John Wayne, and then lost 'em in the dark because they fell off. We straightened the pins on 'em for quick action and then got so excited that we'd pick the grenades up by the pin and it would pull loose and we blew each other up. *Stupid* stuff. But then we learned. And now each kid that comes in is surrounded by people who know. Yup. They're all better grunts for it. And these kids. They are truly *crazy*, Lieutenant. They'll do things I never dreamed of doing."

Phony and Wild Man shambled by, waving absently to Hodges and Gilliland. Wild Man teased the Sergeant. "What you doing back here, Sarge? Uh huh. Just can't stay away."

Hodges laughed with them. He lit a cigarette. "Well, you're right about that much. *They* are *crazy*."

Gilliland watched the thin, retreating frames, amused. "Ah, they're pretty damn good. A little salty, maybe. But a man has to be a sucker to keep doing this. You don't go through this just for the fun of it. I don't want any more of it, Lieutenant. I've just *had* it with Vietnam. Call me flaky. Call me what you want. I've *had* it."

He noted Hodges's apparent perplexity. "I'll tell you a little story, maybe it'll make sense. When I came back from Vietnam the first time I went to the Reserve Training Center, like I said. It wasn't really big over here yet. We all knew it would get bigger, though, and we figured Johnson would call up the Reserves. We kept telling all the Weekend Warriors that they'd better get their shit in one bag, because they were going to war. Like Korea. And it got bigger, but Johnson didn't have the balls to call up the Reserves. Reserves can vote. And they drive airplanes for United. And they run businesses. Instead, Johnson just made a bigger draft, filled it with loopholes, and went after certain groups of kids."

"You said yourself the kids were great."

"It ain't what happens here that's important. It's what's happening back *there*. Shit, Lieutenant, you'd hardly know there was a war on. It's in the papers, and college kids run around screaming about it instead of doing panty raids or whatever they were running around doing before, but that's it. Airplane drivers still drive their airplanes. Businessmen still run their businesses. College kids still go to college. It's like nothing really happened, except to other people. It isn't *touching* anybody except us. It makes me sick, Lieutenant."

Gilliland moodily lit another cigarette. "We been abandoned, Lieutenant. We been kicked off the edge of the goddamn cliff. They don't know how to fight it, and they don't know how to stop fighting it. And back home it's too complicated, so they forget about it and do their rooting at football games. Well, fuck 'em. They ain't worth dying for."

"We do all right, Sarge. Fighting, I mean. The Corps."

"Don't get me wrong, Lieutenant. I *love* this green motherfucker. I wish you could have seen me the day I put on my staff NCO stripes. I never been prouder of anything in my whole goddamn life. I mean that. I thought, 'Now I'm really somebody. I'm a staff NCO in the United States Marine Corps, the President's Own, guardians of this country.' Now I wear my uniform back home and they look at me like I'm an animal. Wait till you go home. You'll put on all those ribbons—I know you, Lieutenant, you'll be the first sucker off that plane to run and buy 'em—and somebody's gonna spit on you for it. No bullshit. It happened to me in the L.A. Airport on the way back here. Some broad. I'm coming back to Viet—fucking—Nam because I'm a professional dedicated to protecting her prissy, babied way of life and she spits at me. Oh, I've had it. Let her boyfriend get drafted and come over here to take my place. Except he's probably found a way to bag it."

Hodges pondered Gilliland's tirade. He spoke flatly, with no attempt to prod the Sergeant. "Sergeant Major wouldn't let you be a Motor Transport jock, huh?"

The question seemed to give Gilliland momentum for another diatribe. "Called me a *coward!* Three Purple Hearts I got and that fat potato looked me square in the face and called me a *coward!*"

"Did you roll a frag under his desk when you left?"

Gilliland grinned excitedly, remembering. "Not quite. But I did the man a number, Lieutenant. I truly did. First I yanked his chain. I said, 'Sergeant Major, I been looking bullets straight in the eye for fifteen goddamn months all told, watching people die, digging holes to shit.' He says, 'War is hell, Gilliland.' I says, 'Yeah, but combat's a bitch. You wouldn't know that. How many cat holes have *you* dug since you been here?' He says, 'I dug mine in Korea.' I says, 'I didn't know you needed to dig any at Division headquarters in Korea in 1953.' Then I says, 'Sergeant Major, it looks to me like, if anybody's got anything to prove to anybody else about being a coward or not, you got something to show me.' He says, 'Gilliland, get the fuck out of my office.' "

Hodges indulged him. "Get so-o-ome, Sergeant Gilliland."

"That ain't all. Then I did the second thing. I says, 'Sergeant Major, I'm leaving. But first I want my ration.' He says, 'What the hell you talking about?' I says, 'Well, I been in the bush for something like three months this time around, and I ain't had my beer and soda ration. That makes ninety beers and ninety sodas you owe me.' He goes white as a turnip and he squints, threatening me like he's a mafioso. Says, 'I don't know what you mean.' I says 'O.K., forget it. I'm gonna request mast to my Colonel and ask *him* about it.' You *know* the Colonel and his staff ain't been missing *their* beer and soda, Lieutenant. Finally he does a truly stupid thing. He walks outside his hootch and unlocks a big Conex Box—you know, those big trash bins? He reaches in and gives me three cases of beer, Lieutenant, like he was dispensing manna from heaven. Three cases. That Conex Box was *full!*"

"Why the *hell* would he do a thing like that?"

Gilliland grinned ironically. "Well, I guess he figured cowards could be bought off because they don't have the balls to turn anybody in." Then he shrugged. "I don't know. Maybe he figures he's stronger than the Colonel, that he can weasel his way out of it even if I *do* blow the whistle."

"Did you take the beer?"

Gilliland laughed. "You bet your ass, Lieutenant!" He gestured across the potato patch, toward the landing zone. "Brought it with me. We can send a working party up to get it in a minute. But that ain't the *best* part." Gilliland continued to smile. "He gives me the beer, like he's making some kind of payoff. I'da asked him for the whole ration for the company, to start sending it out like he's sup-

posed to instead of selling it to rear pogues, but I woulda
tipped my hand. I thanked him, then I went straight over
to Regimental Legal and turned his fat ass in."

Gilliland beamed behind the sagging moustache.
"They're gonna investigate him!"

Goodrich worked the C-ration can opener around the
tin. It's common sense, he thought. Basic biology. Or
chemistry. Hell, I forget which. But flies like sugar and
shit.

The lid was off. Blackberry jam shone back at him
from inside the tin. A fly immediately buzzed in and
landed on it. He gloated. Goodrich, you're a genius. In a
day or two you're going to be in the rear, getting treat-
ments at the Battalion Aid Station.

He took the jam and rubbed some into a gook sore on
his stomach, filling the ulcerous hole, and also treated two
on one of his arms. He beamed. Com-pli-cations. Heavy.
Then he lay back, his shirt off, and decided to take a nap.

By the time I wake up, mused Goodrich, I'm going to
be a very sick man. I hope.

Cornbread, new to the squad, sat in the fighting hole,
cleaning his M-16. He had watched Goodrich curiously
during the whole process. "What you doin', Senator? You
crazy?"

"Crazy? Hell. I'm a *genius,* man. It's the smartest thing
I've done in at least a year."

"How you goan' git that outa the hole? I wouldn't rub
no jelly in my sore. You crazy."

"The flies are gonna eat it up, see? Maybe lay eggs in it.
In a day or two my gook sores are gonna be a *mess,* man.
A *real* mess."

"That's right."

"And I'm gonna get a vacation in the rear. Maybe even
Da Nang."

Goodrich rolled over and went to sleep, feeling exuber-
ant. In twenty minutes he woke up, his stomach on fire.
The gook sore was exploding. He looked down and discovered he had rolled over near an anthill. There were a
hundred ants working feverishly to move their anthill into
his gook sore.

He swiped at them. A dozen of them stung him, buried

in the jam. Cornbread howled with glee. Goodrich had to wipe the ants out with his skivvy shirt.

The flies loved the jam on his skivvy shirt.

Time, like an ever-flowing stream, bears all its sons away.
They fly, forgotten, as a dream dies at the opening day . . .

It echoed on the church walls in a piece of Hodges' memory, some old hymn from a saner portion of his past. Time was everything. Time kept them there, and time would let them leave. They were doing time, marking off the days, keeping track religiously of exactly how long it would be before thirteen months were up and the insanity ended. And yet the lulls and frenzies of the bush made it a timeless world. Each day counted as one when a man marked it off on his calendar, but a day could be a week, an hour could be a month. An afternoon spent under fire when a patrol was caught in an open paddy would age them all a year, tighten their faces until the eyeballs bulged, make them whine and leave them weak, yet when the patrol came back to the company perimeter it had been a year for them but only an afternoon for the ones who had not been on the patrol. And when the cruel sun fell below the western mountains, it still had only been a day. All that for a stinking day.

It was the most important part. Time *was* Vietnam. But it became so immeasurable in a man's emotions, some days so long and some so short, that it was irrelevant, except for what it did to the face of a calendar.

Hodges grinned whimsically, dripping streams of sweat as he lay listening to his radio in the oven of his poncho hootch. How long have I been here? Well, let's see. I've got almost ten months left to do. But that don't mean a goddamn thing. I've *been* here forever, man. For—fucking—*ever.*

The resupply helicopter that brought Gilliland also brought ice. The platoon commanders were called to the company command post. It was a serious occurrence. Hodges had not seen ice in the bush during his whole time there.

The company supply sergeant had stolen a piece from the mess hall in An Hoa and put it in a metal ammunition box. The ammunition box had sat on the resupply strip next to the runway for several hours. By the time it reached the field, the piece of ice was the size of a large grapefruit.

Five representatives gathered solemnly at the company command post; one for each rifle platoon, one for the weapons platoon, and one for the company headquarters personnel. Ceremoniously and exactingly, under the security of the five men, the company commander divided the ice into five roughly equal chunks. Hodges received his. It was the size of a golf ball.

He raced toward his platoon lines, the ice cube melting quickly in his hands. It was deliciously cold. He had felt nothing so cold and inviting in months. The air was oven-hot and the cube was disappearing as he jogged. He was tempted to eat it. No one knows why I went to the CP, he reasoned excitedly. I could just throw it into my mouth and no one would ever know. The inside of his mouth was dry. He was sweating and hot. The cube was passing quickly, coldly, through his fingers.

He kept his head, and did not eat the ice. He called to Gilliland as he reached his platoon command post. "Get the squad leaders. Quick, man. Oh shit. *Hurry up!*"

Gilliland jogged to the lines, knowing it was important, whatever it was. Hodges did not get excited without reason. Hodges placed the ice cube under his poncho hootch, in the shade. By the time the squad leaders had assembled in front of him, it was the size of a quarter.

Hodges motioned toward it. "We got ice. Anybody got any ideas how to pass it out? It's so small now, I don't think anybody could divide it. It should go to one man."

They could not decide. They debated as the cube melted away. Finally Hodges picked up the now nickle-sized piece and nonchalantly tossed it across the perimeter. He laughed, shaking his head in amazement at his earlier panic. He still felt the luxurious coldness on his fingers. He sucked them. "Jeee-sus. Who ever sent that out was a damn sadist."

19.

Hodges stared boredly at a fleeting speck that came only near enough to sprout stubs of barely discernible wings, that stayed only long enough to display one quick flash of rounded, all-weather nose before it screamed away, back to the Other World. From its orbit in the heavens, a thousand feet above reality, the Beacon Hop had struck. The waggle of a stick, the simple pressing of a button by an unsweating, air-conditioned hand, and the mission was complete.

He grinned ironically. Two more points toward that next Air Medal, eh, Major?

And in the treeline across scraggly squares of empty paddies there had been a short, unsettling scream as the jet passed over, then a deep volcanic roar, a flow of fire and metal quick and hot as lava. Twenty-eight 500-pound bombs, erupting in the space of a few unfightable seconds.

Hodges was sitting on a bed of sawgrass a half-mile away. He still could not hold back a mighty wince as the impact of the explosions sailed across the empty field. He had watched large jags of shrapnel dig into the dirt, even as far from the treeline as his knoll.

And then had waited, ticking off the minutes, knowing they would come. And the field filling with them, little specks at first, like termites gushing from a piece of old wood that had been mashed, destroying their home. Little white dots oozing into the unkept rice field, swarming slowly toward the Marine perimeter, not understanding the connection between this latest volcanic eruption and the circle of dirty, sun-hard men, but collectively knowing, mutually in awe of the fact, that these strange men had the power to invoke such wrathful gods. And had the power, as well as the means, to help mend the newest gaping holes that the froth of fire and steel had left them.

The termites fought the paddy grass, stumbled over

215

dikes, moving slowly toward the perimeter. They reached a wide stretch of sand, a low dip that would hold a deep stream when the monsoon filled the river, and approached the strip of village that loomed across it, home of the Marines. They walked steadily, women and children and old, old men, starkly etched, colorful figurines of agony, plodding through a long moment of white, relentless desert. They carried three stretchers.

Finally they were close enough. Hodges gathered a patrol, summoned Dan, and moved to the edge of the perimeter to meet them. They struggled across the treadmill of loose sand, reaching him in groups of three or four. There was no terror in their faces. Their faces were incurably sad, hopelessly numb. The pains were too regular to invoke terror. They could not fight it. It did no good to fear it. It was as inevitable as old age.

Hodges watched them absently as they approached, no longer interested in examining the individuals, having undergone this ritual so many times that each figure became a caricature: the monkey-faced women in their flour-sack tops and dirty black pajama bottoms, hair pulled back into severe buns, lips and teeth stained by betel nut, who began whining the moment they came within earshot. The frail old men, always dressed in white to ensure they were not mistaken for VC and shot at from long range by an anxious trigger, apologetically smiling behind wispy beards and high, crinkled cheeks. The stolid, half-clothed children, conical hats made out of discarded C-ration cases, unspeaking, covered with ulcerous sores.

The first group reached the patrol. There was a low wail from a mamasan. Dan cut her off with a sharp, gutteral word and she stifled herself, whimpering. She and another ageless, beautiless hag took a bamboo pole off their shoulders and eased a parachute-wrapped figure to the sand. The parachute was stained with blood. Inside it was a girl, perhaps fourteen years old. She was unconscious, and bled from her midsection.

The villagers gathered before the Marines. There were perhaps thirty somber persons standing wearily at the edge of the sand, staring up a bush-filled bank at Hodges. The other two stretchers were placed next to the dying girl. There was an old mamasan with an unidentifiable welt that had swollen half her face, and an oozing wound in one thigh that had saturated a bandage made from an old shirt. A small child lay in the other parachute, unconscious from a severe head wound. It was obvious that the child would soon die.

Doc Rabbit checked the small child first, then shook his head negatively, declining to work on him. He began redressing the older girl's wounds. Hodges watched Rabbit for a few minutes, then nodded to Dan, gesturing toward the patiently waiting group.

Dan eyed the villagers. They were from Le Nam, several miles east of Liberty Bridge. Ten miles from his former home in My Le. Dan did not know Le Nam. He felt nothing for the villagers. He spoke strongly, almost arrogantly.

"What do you want?"

One mamasan dared to answer, groveling before Dan while shrewdly eyeing Hodges. When she finished, Dan continued to stare at her, his face almost sullen.

Hodges prodded him. "What did she say?"

Dan still eyed her. "She say babysan get *boo-coo bac-bac* bomb, same-same K.I.A. Say *honcho* mebbe souvenir chop-chop."

Hodges squinted unbelievingly at Dan. Is she for *real*?

Dan continued. "She say mebbe one case C-rats same-same one babysan."

Hodges turned to the mamasan, studying her. How in the name of God can she prostitute her grief, declare a clean slate, for twelve C-ration meals? Did the kid mean that little to her? Or has she merely accepted the inevitability of it (they *are* going to die, eventually, all of them) and attempted to wangle the most realistic deal? Or is she starving? He studied her flesh. She was thin but not emaciated, definitely not starving. Hungry, perhaps.

He shook his head. "Hey, I ain't *believing* this. Dan, tell her no chop-chop. VC end up with it."

Mamasan played her trump card. She leaned over and deliberately stroked the dying child's swollen head, then spoke pleadingly to Dan. Dan still stared directly at her, emotionless. "She say mebbe one poncho same-same one babysan."

Hodges shook his head, rubbing his knuckles into one thick palm. "Look. Tell her we're sorry as hell her kid's screwed up. Tell her we'll try to get it to a hospital. But no goodies." He grimaced. "We're not the goddamn Salvation Army."

Dan translated. The crowd, which had been awaiting Hodges' decision before daring to voice other claims, broke into resigned mumbles, intermittent whines. Hodges watched them, noticing at the same time that Dan had grown cold, almost angry with their agonizings. The thought emerged once again: what the hell right do they have to bitch, anyway?

He nudged Dan. "Tell 'em if they don't like it, they can always leave." Dan cocked his head inquisitively at Hodges. "Tell them if they don't like getting shot at they can move to the resettlement village." Dan still did not understand. "Tell them, no like mamasan, babysan *bac-bac, didi* Duc Duc, got *boo-coo* rice, fucking hootch, no VC." Dan nodded, smiling. Ah. He translated once again.

There were knowing, ironic looks among the villagers. A very old man with a thin nose and shocked eyes pointed to Dan and spoke slowly, gesturing toward Liberty Bridge and An Hoa, both unreachably far away. Dan nodded, again and again.

"He say, no can do. Got VC, Cu Bans, La Thaps, stop mamasan, papasan, say go back home." Hodges appeared skeptical. Dan remembered his own experiences as a VC in the Arizona, and the days he was posted along the riverbank with the same mission. He nodded affirmatively. "No shit."

Hodges pondered it a moment, staring at the beaten, suffering faces, a few of which were actually daring to hope as they watched him in thought. All right, he decided. I'll call their damn bluff.

"Tell them to go get their gear. We'll put 'em on a helicopter. You know. Same-same medevac."

Dan appeared skeptical, but dutifully translated. The villagers mulled the proposition, attempting to gauge Hodges' sincerity, then set out in half-lopes back toward the treeline, which still smoldered here and there from the recent Beacon. Dan watched them depart, envious of the ease in which they were escaping. It would have been so easy for me this way, Dan thought, remembering.

Dan addressed Hodges without looking at him. "They

say, fucking A, *honcho* Number One. Back most ricky-tick."

Warner, from Pierson's squad, stepped up beside Hodges and watched the spindly mob struggle across the barren sand. "Can we really do that, Lieutenant? Evacuate a whole ville, just like that?"

"Why the hell not? That's what we're here for, ain't it, Warner? Hearts and Minds, all that good shit."

Warner was tall and slightly meaty, with a sensitive, open face. He had enlisted after two years at a small midwestern college, where he worked forty hours a week frying hamburgers to pay for his school. He was the only member of the platoon who spoke consistently of national objectives, communism, or winning a war. But even he had recently ceased such speculations: in the bush, they were irrelevant.

Now Warner smiled, though, his thin lips ironically parting. "You better watch it, sir. A couple days like this and I might start believing again."

Hodges eased down the embankment into the sand. "Don't do that, Warner. It's been nice having you sane." He approached Rabbit, who had just shot the old mamasan with morphine. "How are they, Doc?"

"Babysan's dead. That girl there has shrap metal in her gut. I'd say she hasn't got a prayer. Old mamasan here is gonna tough it out."

The patrol surrounded the makeshift stretchers. Warner knelt down next to the unconscious girl and stroked her hair. "God. She's such a pretty thing."

Maye, also from Pierson's squad, snorted. He was stringy and tough, coal-digger tough, a stolid, accepting boy-man who was too realistic, too knowledgeable for sentiment. "Three years she'd be like all the rest of 'em. If she's lucky she'll live through this and stay in Da Nang when she gets out of the hospital. Then maybe in a year or two she'll make a good whore."

The girl was indeed beautiful, naturally so, her face calm and smooth in its unconsciousness. The lips were full, and underneath the pajama top were the sproutings of delicate breasts.

Warner looked sharply at Maye. "C'mon, man. Knock it off."

Maye grinned, knowing he had rankled Warner. "Wonder if she's grown a pussy yet? She's about old enough. Know how long it's been since I seen a pussy?"

"Well, however long it's been, it's gonna be a little while longer, Maye."

Hodges stared calmly at both of them.

"Ah, Lieutenant. Just a peek. She won't even know."

"Sure. And the next time you'll want to cop a feel, maybe get a stinky finger. And after that you'll want a ride."

Maye shrugged absently, giving no ground. "So what, Lieutenant? She's gonna be a whore, anyway!"

Warner's fists clenched. "Goddamn it, Maye, you never let up, do you? The whole world's your damn whorehouse."

Hodges nodded toward the dying girl. "Take her up to the perimeter. We'll see if we can't at least preserve her alternatives."

"It won't work, Lieutenant." Gilliland grinned mischievously.

"It's *got* to work, Sarge. Don't be such a goddamn cynic. Just because you're a short-timer—"

"Hey, Lieutenant. I'm so short I got to look up to look down."

"Yeah. O.K. I know. But don't be so *negative* all the time."

"Now, Lieutenant." Gilliland still flashed a secret, knowing grin. He dragged ceremoniously on a cigarette. "You know there's nothing I'd rather leave you with than a good attitude. Really." Gilliland lay back on his poncho, his head resting on his pack, staring at the roof of his poncho-liner hootch. "Couple weeks I'm gonna be laying in a real rack with my woman, trying to decide if I want steak or lobster for dinner. Least I can do is try to leave you with a good attitude, for Christ sake." He rolled his molten eyes, a humorous smile lighting his face. "But it ain't gonna work. I know."

"You've got a friend—"

Gilliland laughed, enjoying the mystery he had provoked. "That's right. I got a friend. He's the Gunny for the regimental Civil Affairs Section." Gilliland raised his eyebrows, a gesture of finality. "Lieutenant, the resettlement ville is full."

"Full? That's goddamned impossible. I *saw* it a couple months ago. It wasn't even half-full. Hell. A *quarter-*full. It can't be full."

Gilliland grinned ironically. He flicked his cigarette into the grass. "Oh, it ain't *really* full. It's just full on paper. But you won't get any ville full of people into it, I guarantee."

"I don't get it."

"C'mon, Lieutenant. You gotta think crooked. District Chief says he's got five hundred bodies in the ville when he only has two hundred. Government sends him five hundred rations of rice. He feeds two hundred people, then sells three hundred rations of rice on the black market. Pretty tricky, huh? Him and the Sergeant Major would make a gruesome twosome."

Hodges was stunned, unbelieving. "There's got to be some way to stop that. Why doesn't somebody blow the whistle?"

Gilliland explained, teasing Hodges with overbearing patience. "Who you gonna blow the whistle *to,* Lieutenant? This is what they call one of those 'Civil Affairs.' The Vietnamese run it. We just coordinate it. If the Man says the ville is full, then the ville is full. You might scream to the Province Chief, but he gets a cut off the rice, you can bet your sweet ass. Only thing to do is get it while you can, whenever they feel like letting a little go. But you ain't gonna get any whole *ville* in there."

"I'm gonna try like hell."

"I'll bet you a bottle of booze you lose. Jack in the Black."

No bet. The request was called via the battalion radio channel, and came back within a half hour: the resettlement village was full. Hodges sat moodily at the edge of the perimeter and watched the termites fill the paddy once again, a narrow string of them this time, each figure balancing a large bundle on its head. They approached, fighting the bog of sand, holding clothes and pots and baskets and small babies, and assembled in a tight, faintly hoping group outside the perimeter. The faces were the same: beaten, forever saddened. But there was an electricity among them, a sense of preparation.

Hodges summoned Dan and took a fire team down to the edge of the sandstrip. The group of villagers studied his face, noted the hesitation in his stride, and as if by command the electricity died. They knew, he decided.

He turned to Dan. "Tell them, no can do. Tell them, maybe in a month or so."

"No understand 'month.' "

"Tell them to walk. And to take the dead babysans back to the ville with them."

Dan told them. The group walked slowly back across the sand, crushed into numbed apathy. They carried two bamboo-pole stretchers. Hodges watched them carry the dead girl past him and noted, with fury that her pajama bottoms were pulled down to her knees. He swore: Maye would pay.

Warner stood beside him, watching also. "She was such a pretty little thing."

20.

STAFF SERGEANT GILLILAND

JUST OUTSIDE CAMP PENDLETON, CALIFORNIA. Joseph Frederick Gilliland, Staff Sergeant, USMC (Resigned), exited the Camp Gate, seabag up on his shoulder, and walked ten steps to a sign that read GIVE A MARINE A LIFT. He dropped his seabag next to the sign and pushed his piss-cutter hat low onto his eyebrows, sparing his forehead the agony of the sun. Then he allowed himself one last glance back inside the gate. The eyes grew molten and he shrugged resignedly, as if to shake the military nimbus from his shoulders, and he turned his back to it with finality, staring down the road.

So long, Mother Green. Hello, world. *Mister* Gilliland is back.

He had not even had a chance to put his thumb out when a car cut sharply off the road, just in front of him, and braked to a halt. A curtain of dust went into the wind and settled like snow over Gilliland's clean uniform and shined shoes and his seabag. He spit and wiped his mouth to clear the dust, then grabbed his seabag and went to the door of the car.

It was a new car, a Monte Carlo. Gilliland looked across the wide seat at a gruff-spoken, scowling old man who told him with two words to get in. He obliged the old man, throwing his seabag into the back and climbing into the front, next to him.

Gilliland had sweated freely into the crispness of his uniform while walking the Last Mile from the processing center to the gate. The car's air conditioner was clean and cool against him, and he opened his coat, waving it in his hands to bring the cold air inside his clothes.

He pulled out a cigarette and lit it in his automatic, magic way, a C-ration match appearing from nowhere and needing no guidance from the eyes that remained on the driver, studying him. It was obvious to him that the man was an ex-Marine. He was crew-cutted, thick and stubborn-looking, with a fat squinched-up face that still scowled out at the road. He wore a tattoo that had faded into his arm so that it was unrecognizable, but Gilliland had an identical one on his own forearm, now fading also, so he knew what it was. Once it was a bulldog, fierce and colorful.

Gilliland completed his inspection, then nodded to the man. "Hey, thanks, Top." All the old-timers became Top or Gunny, he remembered humorously.

The man nodded, apparently pleased to have been recognized as a former Marine. "Sure thing, Sarge. You a little old to be hitch-hiking, though, ain't you?"

Gilliland shrugged, then smiled winsomely. "You're never too old when you're broke. Besides, ain't you a little old to be picking up strange men?"

They laughed together, reaching a pugnacious rapport.

"Where you headed?"

"Pismo Beach."

The old man grunted. "That's a damn long way." He considered it. "I'm going up to Tustin. I'll let you off on the freeway there. I know a pretty good place."

"Much obliged, Top." Too old to hitchhike, Gilliland mused. A little old to be with three kids and no damn job, too. He began to doubt himself again, remembering the security and the good experiences of his ten years in the Marine Corps. Then he forced himself to shrug it off. Like old Snake used to say, don't do no good to think about it when you can't change it. I am a fucking *civilian*. Like it or not.

He consoled himself with thoughts of Pismo Beach. It had been his wife's idea. He had never been to Pismo Beach, but his wife had spent several vacations there as a girl. She had written him as soon as he had definitely decided not to reenlist, and informed him that she was leaving the children with her mother and meeting him at Pismo Beach, money or not, job or not. He smiled again, appreciating her more than ever. That woman knows me like she has a hot wire to the inside of my damn head.

She had written about the beach and the pier, where he could rent a pole and fish if he desired, and the blocks of arcades where he could play games and pinball machines. She had known, even more quickly than he himself, that if he went straight home it would be too much.

The old man had inspected his uniform. "Three Purple Hearts, huh? A man's gotta be some kind of crazy to go through that." The old man was visibly impressed.

Gilliland smiled complacently. "Well, I ain't crazy, Top. Matter of fact, I just quit."

"You *quit?*" The old man seemed stunned. "The whole Marine Corps? Nah. Ain't anybody quits as a Staff NCO."

Gilliland chuckled, shrugging helplessly. Marine Corps logic, he thought. I'm crazy if I stay and I'm a disloyal son of a bitch if I leave. Can't win. "Well, I gave 'em two tours, Top. Two tours and three big Hearts. And what the hell did it prove? Nobody in this goddamn country gives a shit. I've had it."

Top begrudged him his right to be a traitor. "Been pretty bad, huh? Hard to tell sometimes, from the papers. They're just so against it."

"Yeah, it was a bad trip, as the troopies say. And it was worse this time than it was the last time. Can you believe that? Everything we put in there and it just gets worse. Kind of crazy."

Gilliland looked out the window and watched the people in the other cars, trying to get used to being back. It was all he had thought about for months, the major topic of conversation in the bush. Life's goals reduced to ground zero: stay alive long enough to leave.

"You're pretty young to be a Staff Sergeant. My day it took twenty years to make Staff."

"Yeah, but it meant something then. Hey, Top—" Gilliland grinned conspiratorially to the old man—"I wouldn't make a pimple on a good Staff Sergeant's ass!"

The old man liked that. It reminded him of a story. He told the story to Gilliland and Gilliland laughed and told the old man a story that he in turn was reminded of. Then they talked about Vietnam and World War Two and how scared they were and how many people they had seen killed. Gilliland liked the old man's honesty and he felt close to him, as if each had touched the devil and could talk about it because the other person had also touched him. The devil was on the other side of a grotesque culture warp and Gilliland realized for the first time that he was afraid to face people who had not experienced such things. He was afraid they would not understand him. He didn't know what civilians talked about.

They reached Tustin and the old man dropped Gilliland off at the ramp he had mentioned, and told him where to change freeways to get to Pismo Beach. When he pulled away Gilliland felt deserted, as if the umbilical cord had finally snapped. He buttoned up his coat and mashed the piss-cutter down over his eyes again, then balanced his seabag up on his shoulder, like a native girl carrying a water jug.

He walked up to the on-ramp sign and stood under it, feeling isolated and abandoned. The cars whizzed by and he studied the flashes of people that passed him. Some were driving to the beach. Some seemed to be working. Some appeared to be merely driving.

He began to feel deeply depressed. It hasn't even *touched* them, he mused darkly. All the broken bodies and the nights in the rain and nobody even gives enough of a shit to give me a damn *ride*.

Finally a pickup truck filled with lumber pulled up. There were two men in the cab. They allowed Gilliland to sit in the bed of the truck with the lumber. He straddled his seabag, on top of a mound of two-by-fours and two-by-eights and one-by-fours. Neither man had mentioned his uniform when they stopped. The edges of the lumber were splintery and uncomfortable. The wind messed his hair, and he was beginning to smell himself through his uniform coat.

She wouldn't mind. She had never minded. She had always taken him just as he came. She took him right off the roads in the early years, when his hands were dusty and black under the nails and his body was soaked with sweat and dirt. And she hadn't minded his tattoos. And she was not uncomfortable with a body scarred by mortar rounds, a smaller leg shot through and through by an AK. She could handle a stinking uniform.

The truck left him at Anaheim and he stood on the off-ramp, trying to remember the old man's instructions about how to get to Pismo. Finally he hefted the seabag to his shoulder and crossed the street to where the next on-ramp was. The seabag weighed on him, even when it was balanced properly. When he reached the entrance sign he dropped the bag and sat on it and lit another cigarette.

His uniform was heavy with sweat, and had lost its crispness. He pondered taking the coat off and loosening the tie, but something inside him would not let him do it. When I get to Pismo, he mused, I'll throw the damn thing away. But I wore it right for ten years, and I'm damned if I'll stop now. He snorted, examining the Staff Sergeant chevrons he had once been so proud of. The President's Own. Guardians of the Free. He remembered an old troopy jingle as he watched cars whiz by. Doing the impossible. For the ungrateful.

A bottle flew at him from a passing car and smashed next to his seabag. Somebody in the car yelled something at him. Fascist. Something like that. Gilliland lit a cigarette, pensive behind the gash of moustache and the scarred cheeks. The molten eyes watched car after car drive by, but after the bottle he did not follow any car with even a movement of his head.

They're scared of me. The uniform. He pondered the irony of that. Things don't make any goddamn sense at all. I beat my head against a wall for these fuckers and they're scared of me. Wasn't like this a few years ago, I'll say that. I never waited longer than a half a cigarette for a damn ride.

Fifteen more minutes. A yellow Volkswagen turned off the road and stopped for him. It was a convertible and the top was down. A black-haired, bearded man was driving. He was thin and his hair exploded from his head in every conceivable direction. A chubby, long-haired girl sat beside him. She was wearing white short-shorts and a red halter that showed most of her breasts from the top. Her nipples stood through the fabric. She had very large breasts.

The driver was spaced-out. He smiled ethereally to Gilliland. "Hey, man. Where you going?"

"Pismo Beach."

The driver mumbled it to himself several times. "Pismo Beach. Pismo Beach." He looked over to the girl. "Where the fuck is Pismo Beach?"

She had a protective way of handling the driver. She stroked his leg and said comfortably, "North. *Way* north, sweetheart." Then she turned to Gilliland. "We can take you as far as Hollywood. If you think you want to go to Hollywood."

Gilliland grinned winsomely, happy to have a ride. "Oh, yeah. I always did want to go to Hollywood."

She giggled as if he were Bob Hope and he threw his seabag into the back seat and climbed in with it. He sat it on its end on the seat, like a fourth passenger, as they drove.

The car entered the freeway and the girl pulled out a large brandy snifter full of something crimson from under the dashboard. She took a long drink and laughed loudly, with her head back, and gave the snifter to the driver. He took a long drink, too. Then she turned around and offered the snifter to Gilliland.

"Want some? It's dynamite, man. Really dynamite."

"What is it?"

"Oh, it's—just really dynamite." She giggled uncontrollably.

"No, thanks. I got a long way to go today."

"Well, it'll take you there." She was still giggling.

"No, thanks. Really." Gilliland was becoming uneasy.

She ignored him after that. She and the driver continued to drink out of the snifter. The driver then casually reached over and caressed the insides of her thighs, up very high. She laughed in her throat and moved against his hand. Gilliland could not see the driver's hand, but he caught facefuls of the girl's long hair as she undulated, and could tell that her nipples had become hard.

He was afraid. He stared tightly at the driver's face, ready to grab the wheel if the driver forgot what he was doing and lost control. This bastard wants to kill me for a damn finger-fuck, he thought grimly. The driver started to take his hand away and she held it there. Gilliland wondered briefly whether she was a nymphomaniac. Fucking Hollywood, he mused. The whole place is X-rated. He took a Marlboro out and the driver noticed and pulled his hand away from the girl and grinned. "Hey, man. Wanna do a number?"

Gilliland looked the man in the eyes, through the rear-view mirror. "What's a number?" Is this guy queer, or what?

"You know, man. Don't you smoke dope? I thought all you dudes smoked dope. I heard the Nam was the best dope in the world, man." It was the first hint that the driver was even aware Gilliland was back from Vietnam.

"I'm too old to smoke dope." Gilliland looked uneasily into the mirror, upset by his entry into the Real World. He barked almost sullenly. "I'm twenty-nine."

"Twenty-nine? No shit. You don't look that old."

"I feel eighty."

Hollywood was deliverance. Gilliland jumped from the back of the car and stood on the roadway and held his head for a full minute, relieved to have made it alive. He groaned as the Volkswagen screamed back onto the road, toward a different freeway. And *that's* what I been bleeding for? Why didn't somebody tell me?

It was midafternoon. He bought a hamburger at a Big Boy's restaurant and walked back to the freeway ramp. His back ached from the weight of the seabag. The weight of it reminded him of the bush. He knew that someday he would have to stop relating all his actions, every anguish and pain, to the bush. But he could not help it just then. The bush was still realer than Hollywood.

He pondered the miles he had walked in the bush, aching under the flak jacket and pack, feeling the heavy weight of the rifle in his hand and the cut of the pack in his shoulders. The only ones it touched were us. And I went twice so these bastards wouldn't have to go at all. The garish absurdity of Hollywood made him feel profoundly hostile. He felt used, irrelevant.

Cars and trucks passed on the ramp and he lit another cigarette, waiting. The trucks belched huge clouds of black smoke as they inched up the ramp's hill. The black settled over him. There was no wind and he felt slick and oily and dirty in his uniform. A car passed by, filled with kids in bathing suits. They stared at him as if he were Clarabelle the clown, dressed up in his monkey suit.

A large truck pulled over. The driver was hauling a trailerload of vegetables to Seattle. He told Gilliland he would take him all the way to Pismo Beach. Gilliland climbed into the cab, throwing his seabag before him and then pulling himself up with his hands, placing his feet into the metal stepping places.

It was high and comfortable in the cab. They drove alone the coast toward Santa Barbara and Gilliland could see the frothing waves and the pockets of surfers out in them, grouped in the special good places for surfing. It looked tranquil. It calmed him. He called across the cab to the driver.

"Is the ocean like this at Pismo Beach?"

"Better. No rocks. Not so many people."

The driver did not fit Gilliland's image of a trucker. He seemed too thin, as if he would be unable to shift the gears, and he wore glasses with thick black frames.

The driver peered over to Gilliland, then looked back at the road. "You like the Marines?"

"I just quit. That answer your question?"

"I don't blame you." The driver shifted gears. His whole body labored to do it, but he did not have the trouble Gilliland had imagined he would. "You was in Nam, though, huh?"

"Two tours. Too long."

"Yeahhh, I was in the Army. Korea." The driver paused, remembering. "I hated it. Did you hate it?"

Gilliland pondered the question, feeling naked in his new

status as a civilian. "Sometimes I did. Sometimes it was all right. The people, anyway."

"No, I really hated it. Somebody always bugging you to do something. Somebody always playing God." The driver checked his rearview mirrors. "I drove trucks. We ran convoys up to the front. They say there ain't any front in Vietnam. That right?"

Gilliland shook his head yes, then no. He smiled hopelessly. "Shit, man. I don't know. I know we used to like to get back to the rear. There was a rear. But we were never on any front, or anything. We just roamed around the bush, or went somewhere on an operation for a while and then left. We just moved in circles, mostly."

"Sounds crazy."

"Well, it was. It was crazy as hell."

"Do you think we're winning?"

Gilliland thought about it for a moment. He lit a cigarette and took a drag and thought about it some more. He was somewhat shocked, not by the question, but by the fact that he'd never considered it in his entire second tour. They had never talked about it in the bush. It had nothing to do with being in the bush and fighting gooks. They had talked about good contacts and bad contacts and Getting Some and Bummers. But not about winning.

"Christ, I don't know. You probably know more about that than I do. I don't know anything about it."

The driver seemed to take offense at Gilliland's answer. He glanced over at him as if he had been rebuffed, then turned on the radio. The radio played country music and Gilliland found himself listening intently to the commercials rather than the songs. He hadn't heard commercials in months.

Mountains rolled like gentle waves near Gaviota, in varied shades of brown and green, and Gilliland examined them. His gaze caressed knolls and crevices with professional authority. Each shadowed draw and naked finger had deep meaning to him. I would walk there, he decided. I'd follow that finger to the top. And I'd put another squad on the finger to the right, and one on the finger to the left. Hodges'd like that. He'd say something like, "Sarge, you are a savvy dude. I shit you not." Kind of miss those guys. Then we'd move real slow up that mountain, like leapfrogs. No ambush that way. Put Snake's squad in the middle. Cat Man on point.

He searched the deep gray shadows along the top of the mountain. And I'd set up there. We could put a whole platoon up there. Maybe a company. It's a bare-ass hill but we could dig in real deep and we'd be spread out enough that they could mortar us and we'd do O.K. And at night I'd put an LP down that main finger, 'cause the gooners would come up that way, too.

He looked away and lit another cigarette and was overwhelmed by an emotion that was somewhere between a sense of loss and of rebellion. Hell. I'm just an old grunt. That's all I'm good for. What the hell am I gonna do? Ten years I played that silly game and up till five days ago it was the most important thing in the world—You Bet Your Life—and now it's gone. Walk through the gate, stick out your thumb, and the whole world changes. I'll never set a squad into a hill again.

Still he could not shake the thought that a squad set in at Gaviota Pass was more real than a fishing pier at Pismo Beach.

He suddenly realized that, on top of everything else, he was afraid to meet his wife at Pismo Beach. I'm counting too much on it being good, he fretted. What if it isn't like that? I been planning this too hard. I'm about to the point that if there isn't any fishing or the water's too cold to swim in I just might have a damn fit. *Something's* gotta be the way you think it's gonna be.

It grew dark and Gilliland slumbered in the truck. They reached Pismo Beach and the driver pulled off to the side of the road, just beyond the off-ramp, and Gilliland climbed out. He waved briefly to the driver as the truck pulled back onto the highway. Its exhaust covered him with new slick smells.

He stood in the dark next to the highway and felt a cool breeze wash against him. He sucked it into his lungs. So this is Pismo Beach. Smells good, even from here. Smells like sea and fish and food. He put his seabag onto his shoulder and began walking toward the ocean. The seabag beat at him, bouncing as he walked. He felt older than twenty-nine. Maybe it's the jet lag, he reasoned. It's only eight o'clock, but I been up all night, Vietnam time. Maybe it's me.

He walked past a drive-in restaurant before he reached the motel. The lights flashed harshly at him, hurting his eyes. There was an electric contraption that hung like a lamp and zapped every time a bug flew into it. The first time it flashed he jumped. It looked like a muzzle flash from a rifle, and his mind had been wandering. Inside, the jukebox moaned:

> It wasn't me that started that ol' crazy Asian war
> But I was proud to go and do my patriotic chore—

Four hippies sat at a table outside the restaurant. They wore faded blue jeans and rough-cut shirts and their hair was long and two of them had beards. They must be hippies, mused Gilliland. Ain't anybody would hire a man dressed like that and looking like that. But he doubted himself. Hell. I'm the weird-looking one, not them.

They leered at him as he walked past, struggling with his seabag. He kept to the sidewalk, but they were only a few feet away. One of them called to him.

"Evening, hero."

He ignored them. Another spoke loudly, so everyone in the restaurant would take notice.

"Hey, how was your *war*, Killing Machine?"

He crossed the street, careful not to look back. He was too tired to fight them. There were too many of them, and he didn't care anymore.

The desk clerk at the Shore Cliff Lodge had been in the Navy during World War II. He had driven landing craft for the First Marine Brigade in the Pacific. He had fought at Saipan and Tinian and Guam. He told Gilliland all about it as soon as he saw Gilliland's uniform, before Gilliland could ask him what room his wife was in.

The clerk took notice of the Purple Heart with its two gold stars and nodded expertly. "You're just back from Vietnam. Man, I just wish they'd let us *win*, you know? Craziest thing I ever saw." The clerk was bigger than Gilliland, and meaty.

Gilliland nodded, wiping sweat off of his moustache. He was tired. "Yeah. Now what room is—"

"We should just bomb 'em back to the goddamn stone age—"

"I'll tell you, Chief, we been doing that pretty damn—"

"*Make* Hanoi a parking lot. I mean it. How can you fight a war with your hands tied behind your back is what I want to know, Sergeant."

"You don't. You quit." Gilliland leaned over the counter and looked coldly into the clerk's eyes. The Vietnam War was over. It happened only to individuals, and it had ceased happening to him. "Can you knock off your bullshit and tell me which room Mrs. Gilliland is in? You wanna talk about the war, you go write a letter to your Congressman."

21.

A violent, thunderless noon rain scudded across a blue sky and soaked them thoroughly, even as the untroubled blue peeked around its edges. Then it suddenly abated, leaving them inside a thin, steamy mist. In minutes the resupply helicopter powered through the mist, driving it away with rotor wash, whipping the mist as winter wind drives chimney smoke. And they cringed, naked on the terraced hillside, feeling new horizontal rain that was driven by the helicopter's blades, lifted from long leaves of greening sawgrass.

Then the bird was gone, the moment of brief, fierce communication with the Other World had passed, and they were again abandoned. And mercilessly scorched, under an unharnessed sun. It was they that steamed now, clothes and poncho liners and packs reaching for the hot blue sky in hundreds of wispy, individual fogs.

A clump of burdened men trundled down the hill, jumping each hand-molded terrace like children descending grassy giants' steps. Shoutings accompanied the jaunt: an argument, many hours old, was being waged along the hillside.

Goodrich looked up from cleaning his weapon, an M-16 bolt in one hand and a toothbrush in the other, and stared curiously at the group that had been deposited by the helicopter. There were six men in the cluster. Goodrich recognized Bagger and Cannonball, now back from R &

R, who were laughing mightily, along with two pale new dudes, at the two men who were arguing. One of the arguers was tall and blond, splendidly muscled, with a narrow, jutting face and a thin, broken nose. He walked quickly, seemingly angry, attempting to be rid of the other. The second man, obviously the antagonist, was short and squat, square-faced, with a drooping, too-long moustache, sagging, amused eyes, and a nose like a hawk's beak. The short man followed the other, leaning forward in a crouch, attempting to address him. His face was lifted by an incessant, patient grin.

The tall man ignored his squat antagonist, walking quickly up to Goodrich. He squinted once, an attempt to recognize Goodrich, then looked along the perimeter for a familiar face. Finally he turned back to Goodrich, speaking in a forceful, unbelieving drawl.

"This is third platoon?"

Goodrich nodded, still awestruck by the suddenness of the clown show's arrival. The squat man crouched around and peered up to the blond man's face, still grinning mischievously. Blond man ignored him.

"Where is everybody?" Then, "Where's Snake?"

Goodrich pointed. Thirty meters down the lines, Snake lay sleeping inside a poncho hootch. "He's crashed. Right over there."

The tall, muscular man marched directly over to the poncho hootch, accompanied by the crouching, grinning clown. The others, including a now-curious Goodrich, followed closely after. Blond man nonchalantly dropped his helmet on Snake's back. Snake coiled inside the hootch, and appeared on the other side with the helmet in one hand, ready to throw it into his assailant's face. He went motionless, dumbfounded, on the backswing.

The tall man spoke, still unsmiling. "Hey, Snake. Put this crazy bastard out on an LP by himself, will you? Without a radio." Then he grinned hugely. Snake jogged around his hootch, his thin lips in a generous smile, tattoos dancing on the narrow arms. He threw the helmet into his assailant's stomach. It bounced off harmlessly.

"Baby Cakes! You skating mother! I thought you had a job in the company mail room! What the hell you doing back out here?"

Baby Cakes peered over at his clowning, squatting nemesis. "Never mind what. I'm here. Now, get me away from this asshole, will you? Every time I get around him I get in trouble. He gets me shot, he gets me the clap, he gets me written up." He shoved the squat man in the face, pushing him off balance. "Get away from me, shit-head."

The ugly dwarf laughed. "Ah, don't mind him, Snake. He's just a little pissed off. It was his own damn fault but he won't admit it." The Ogre had returned.

Snake guffawed. "You never done a wrong thing in your life, have you, Ogre?"

Ogre was stoned. Ogre was usually stoned. He grinned affectionately to Snake, his eyebrows slightly raised. "Hell. All I did was tell him about Mine Warfare School. You know. That he should go."

Baby Cakes pushed Ogre on the top of his helmet, fell-ing him. "Sure." He turned to Snake, as if presenting a case. "Here I was, had the skatingest job in the company. Sorting mail, Three months left on my goddamn tour, a bad enough Heart that Top didn't make me go back to the bush. And in comes this fucker—"

Ogre interrupted, giggling. "It wasn't like that."

"Shut up. Asshole here comes diddy-bopping in from the hospital. Made it all the way to Japan, takes three months, almost, while we're out here fighting the War—"

"How many gooks you been killing in the mail room, Cakes?" Ogre sat in the grass, still laughing, now shaking his head as if Baby Cakes' story was outlandish.

"I told you to shut up!" Baby Cakes turned back to Snake again. "He comes into the company office, starts telling me about all the whorehouses in Da Nang, like he knew every one of 'em personally, and I think he did. Seems he had a little trouble finding An Hoa after his va-cation in Japan—"

"Couldn't find the convoy."

"I'll bet. You were too goddamned stoned to give a shit." Ogre shrugged: entirely possible. "So he comes in and tells me all about it. Here I am—"

"Fighting off gooks with his letter opener." Ogre howled.

"Cut it out. Here I am, haven't seen a woman in *months* and he's telling me you can get it every night in Da Nang. Says he could take me to five skivvy houses

blindfolded. Says it wasn't any sweat, that they were clean,
nobody cared. Now, what the hell was I supposed to *do?*
Go into the head and beat off, thinking about it?"

Snake scrutinized Baby Cakes. *"You* went AWOL?"

"Hay-ull no! I'm not the kind to get in trouble, man.
You know me. I always try to do my job. I ain't any
troublemaker." He lit a cigarette and dropped his weapon against his pack, which now lay on the grass with his
helmet. "I talked with the Top. He likes me, you know.
Says I'm a good old boy, all that shit. I talked Top into
cutting orders to Land Mine Warfare School for me and
Ogre. He said I'd have to go back to the bush, though.
Battalion rule about people who been to school. Hell. I
figured it'd be worth it for another R & R. That was the
way asshole here made it out to be."

Ogre grew a tad more serious, and slapped Baby Cakes'
thigh. "It wasn't my fault, man. Who can tell about
MPs?"

Baby Cakes knocked Ogre's hand away. "Ahhhh. MPs
hell. First he takes me to the worst skivvy house in Da
Nang. They were ugly as a mud fence, every one of 'em.
I never saw such ugly girls in my life."

"You just weren't as horny as you let on to be. If you
were *horny* enough—"

"I *was,* Ogre! I *was!* I was so goddamn horny I signed
away my mail-sorting job! *Tell* me about being horny!"
Baby Cakes ignored Ogre once again. "Second place, when
the MPs come, the son of a bitch won't try to sky out
with me. I go back and bang on the door, yelling, *'Ogre!
Ogre!* MPs, man!' and he just says, 'I'll be there in a minute, uh, huh, I'll be there in a minute,' like I was telling
him he was gonna miss the bus or something. Then we
both got caught, and I had to give away my gold tooth
—you remember that gold tooth I took out of that gook's
head? The day Squeaky lost his eye?"

Snake nodded.

"That tooth. I was saving it to show my grandkids.
Now some boot MP who'll never even *see* a goddamn
NVA is gonna have a war story, thanks to asshole here.
All because he wanted to finish off a smelly old whore."

Ogre grinned, unabashed, appealing to the amused audience. "You ever try to pull it out in the middle of a
stroke when you know you can't put it back? *Huh?* I just

figured as long as I was gonna get caught, I may as well get what I was *coming* for!"

Applause. Cheers. Ogre had won them over.

Baby Cakes renewed his attack. "God*damn,* I'm sick of you! That ain't all. We get back to the troop area and we get written up for being out of bounds, anyway. They catch us coming over the fence."

Snake shook his head, commiserating, trying to suppress his grin. "I never heard anything like it. What a bust."

Baby Cakes warmed to the slight encouragement. He rolled Ogre onto his head, then pushed him over. It was a quick, effortless gesture that brought new cheers from the onlookers. "And *that* ain't even all of it! In a couple days I got the clap so bad I can't even take a leak. My gut's so stretched out from trying to hold back pee I'll *never* look the same! And here I am back in the bush. And we almost didn't even get *here!*"

Ogre stood up, his ugly head drooping. "Oh, that. He'da never known, Baby Cakes."

"Well, you're mighty lucky." Baby Cakes looked around for lifers, and found none. "We're on the convoy coming back and we're in the truck bed with this Lieutenant who's on the way to the bush. It was about four days ago— remember when An Hoa was getting rocketed so bad, and they wouldn't allow choppers in? Oh, hell. A lot you all care about rockets in An Hoa. Anyway. It was a big thing in An Hoa. And we had to ride the convoy in. We're in the truck bed with this Brown Bar, and Ogre gives him a loaded Salem, starts rapping with him, you know, telling him sea stories about what they do to officers—"

Snake smiled slightly. "Hear about what Phony did to Sergeant Austin?"

Baby Cakes grinned knowingly. "I heard it was a mortar. Anyway, Lieutenant's scared shitless to start off with, but by the time we reach the Bridge he's stoned out of his mind, and he doesn't even know it! Keeps talking about how beautiful everything looks. Ogre slipped the man about four joints."

Ogre shrugged, grinning slyly. "He needed to relax."

"Yeah. Uh huh. And you're lucky he wasn't smart enough to let *you* relax in the goddamn *brig!*"

Ogre waved him off. "Ah. Lieutenants don't know about shit like that. And the ones who do don't care."

"Could have been a CID. The way you are, you prob'ly got CIDs watching every move you make. They could clean up Da Nang, just closing down every place you stop at on an average day, Ogre." Baby Cakes had concluded his diatribe. The crowd had departed. He turned back to Snake, comfortable in the knowledge that the squad now knew of his sufferings at the hands of Ogre. "Speaking of Lieutenants, how's ours? In the rear they say he's all right."

"He's a hillbilly. Like you. He don't give anybody any shit and he don't take any shit off anybody. Austin was gonna write me up on the Bridge and he took that bastard apart. It was so cool. I told him about Wild Man Number One doing Kersey and—"

"You *told* him?"

"And he said he wished Wild Man had been a better shot. I think he'd do Kersey hisself if he had the chance. He's a goddamn grit, I tell you."

Baby Cakes grinned easily. "Whoooeee. He wished Wild Man had been a better shot. That's heavy."

"And he cried the night Boomer lost his legs. He don't know I know. He was on radio watch and I went up to talk to him and he was sitting there, shaking his head, crying. I went back to my hole. Later he came on down and we shot the shit about Boomer. He likes to shoot the shit."

Baby Cakes seemed impressed. Snake had fought the other Lieutenants. "Sounds like you *like* the man."

"Yeah. I do. He's one of them, watcha-callits—" Snake grinned, referring to the slogan often used on recruiting posters—"Leaders of Men." He nudged Baby Cakes, pointing to his gear. "Pick up your trash. We gotta report you in. You got a team again, Cakes. Take Ogre—"

Baby Cakes grinned again. "Oh, no. You take Ogre. I've had it with him."

"Come on, Cakes. Don't start in on that again. Ogre's O.K. in the bush."

"Sure. Got me shot—"

Ogre interrupted. "That was your own damn fault."

Baby Cakes hesitated dramatically, then acceded. "Oh, all right. But you're gonna be the death of me, you goddamned toad."

Snake continued. "And you got Senator and Cornbread. Cornbread tries to act dumb, but he ain't. Senator ain't really a Senator. Yet. He just tries to make you think so."

"That's the Harvard dude, right? Top was talking about him one day. He's got about a hundred-and-fifty I.Q. Hell. I won't even know how to *talk* to the man."

"It's easy, Cakes. You talk real straight, 'cause he's a shit-bird. You say, 'Senator do this,' and 'Senator do that.' And if he gives you any of his jack-shit you say, 'Senator, you got point.' It's the only thing he understands. He's scared to death of walking point. He's scared to death of everything." Snake looked coldly toward Goodrich's fighting hole. "He let Burgie die."

Baby Cakes seemed surprised. "I thought they were blown away by a one-oh-six. Blown all to shit."

"They were. But Burgie bled to death, man. We got out there the next morning and Senator was sitting right next to him. Hadn't even put a tourniquet on the man. Burgie was all fucked up. But he bled mostly out of his legs. I seen the ground where he bled. All of us saw it."

Baby Cakes shook his head in disbelief. "Well, what kind of a man is that? What you giving him to me for, Snake?"

" 'Cause if he screws up I know you'll break his head. And I didn't want you to get bored. If you get bored, Senator can tell you about anything you ever wanted to know about. Just ask him. He can tell you about the tiger cages—"

"What the hell is a tiger cage, except a cage for tigers?"

"Ask Senator. And he can tell you about the Geneva Accords—"

"So what about it?"

"Ask him. Ask him. You're gonna come away a genius, Cakes!"

"I think I better work on coming away *alive*."

The perimeter was almost motionless under the close, windless swelter of the afternoon heat. The ragged, overgrown hill that had been carefully shaped into terraces some centuries ago, that had held manicured gardens only years ago, now hosted a hundred chest-deep holes, a city of jerry-rigged poncho tents, a tribe of nomad warriors. In two days they would leave it raped and scarred by their survival needs: scorched by trash fires, pitted by new fighting holes, reeking and maggoty from a half-dozen straddle trenches. And perhaps, if Buddha turned his head again, pocked by new ravages of war.

The sun beat down relentlessly. Men stripped to tiger shorts and boots, and sought the shaded ovens of their hootches. They listened to transistors. Some wrote letters. Some played back-alley card games. Some slept off the watches of the night before.

Ogre and Baby Cakes paraded the perimeter's fighting holes, seeking familiar faces. They found few. They were stripped to tiger shorts, and Ogre wore a wide-brimmed bush hat, pulled low over his ears in a carefully coaxed, bush-Marine style. The rear pogues wore them curled up, like cowboy hats worn sideways.

Both were pale after months away from the scorching sun that fired the bush. They proudly, consciously modeled deep scars from their earlier wounds: Baby Cakes the long pink gash, like a strip of cord laid from his midback to his neck, Ogre the deep crisscrossings in his calves and thighs that disappeared under his tiger shorts.

A large peace sybol hung from Ogre's neck on his dog-tag chain. Ogre had made it out of C-ration wire, carefully shaping the design with powerful, stubby fingers, making the more difficult bends in the strong wire by pushing it through the flash-suppressor opening at the end of his M-16 barrel. Such skills came naturally to Ogre. He had once made similar items for a living. Under a massive thatch of scraggly, unwashed hair, wrapped inside a stained, musty Indian blanket, Ogre had sold wire trinkets in the parks of San Francisco. Until one day, totally stoned, Ogre got curious, and the next thing he claimed to remember clearly was getting off the bus at boot camp. Now he called himself the Hippy CIA. Just peeping out the other side, grinned Ogre.

Cannonball looked up from a back-alley game and smiled at the passing figures. "Man, that was some kind o' shit." He surveyed the scars, then nodded to Wild Man. "You ain' never seen shit like that night, Wild Man. Dudes droppin' everywhere, gooks in between us, Ogre runnin' through 'em, Baby Cakes runnin' back out. Shee-it."

Bagger tossed a card onto the poncho liner that was their table. He was not yet comfortable with Cannonball

again, after the incident in front of the Black Shack, and
had rarely conversed with him since. But now he agreed.
"There it is. I was out there on that LP, thinking I was
gonna die, radio all blown to shit, stuck in that old fighting
hole we found when the shit blew up. I never seen the
platoon as fucked up as that night. Nobody knew where
anybody else was. We had rounds going out just over our
heads, rounds going *in* just over our heads, grenades going off all over the place. Then here comes Baby Cakes.
He picks up Vitelli and turns around and asks us if we
want to come back with him, like we were out there sun-
bathing on a beach or something. That dude has *balls*.
I wasn't gonna leave that hole for *nothing*. He just shrugs
and says, 'Well, fuck ya then,' and takes off. What a
dude. Just to save Vitelli."

Wild Man watched the sauntering, scarred figures, in
awe of Baby Cakes. "I never knew Vitelli."

"He was already dead. Don't ever tell Baby Cakes."

Phony leaned forward and took the cards on the poncho liner, shuffling them. "Yeah. Baby Cakes is gonna
get a medal for that. He rates it, too."

Cannonball nodded. "No lie. Ain' it good to see him,
now?" He stretched like a wary cat, smiling over to
Bagger, hoping to regain a portion of their damaged
friendship by speaking to him around persons Bagger
was comfortable with. "Hey, Bag-man. You never did tell
us about your R & R. You make another baby?"

Bagger put a meaty hand on his forehead, groaning.
Then the confused flat face broke into a grin. "Don't
even *think* that, man. I must of changed a hundred diapers.
She said it would be *good* for the kid. You know, to get
to know his day-uddy and all."

Wild Man laughed. "Sounds like she foxed the hell outa
you, Bagger."

"Ah, so what if she did. I thought about that, too."
Bagger shuffled cards. "You know, I gotta admit something. I hate the bush. I hate this bullshit. But all the time
I was with her, all the time I was walking that phony
beach where all the Beautiful People were laying out getting their just-right tans, all the time I was stuffing myself
with food I couldn't afford, I kept thinking about the
bush. Like I belong here, and all the other stuff is only
important because I *earned* it here, because it's a part of

being *here.* Like I been here all my life, and the people in the bush are real, are my people. Like nobody in the world except for us understands this, or gives one flying fuck about it, but that's all right, because it matters to us."

Cannonball eyed him narrowly, smirking. "So as soon as you got back to An Hoa you extended."

"Jesus Christ, don't even say that, Cannonball." Bagger laughed back.

Phony leaned over, his innocent face nodding in agreement. "Well, I know what you mean, Bagger. I never had a home in my life till I came out here." Nowhere to go back to. Stay forever.

Wild Man grinned ironically to Phony, then called over to Goodrich, who was sitting several yards away, under a poncho-liner hootch, reading. "Yeah. This shit's just like college. Right, Senator? Sit around the frat house with all the brothers, planning parties, having fun. Ain't that right, Senator?"

Goodrich had despaired of meaningful communication with the others. He had written home, and his parents had sent him several paperback volumes of philosophy. He was afraid his mind would deteriorate if he did not exercise it with strenuous reading.

"I didn't hear you." He had been reading Schopenhauer on genius, from *Wisdom of Life. As a rule,* wrote Schopenhauer, *a man is sociable just in the degree in which he is intellectually poor and generally vulgar.* Goodrich liked that.

"Out in the bush it's just like college, I said. Sitting around jiving with all the brothers, planning parties, all that shit."

"We went to different schools, Wild Man."

"Hey. That's right. I forget, you know. You looked so familiar."

Well, I won't be an ass, thought Goodrich. "If you want to know, I get the feeling this is kind of like Russian roulette, myself. Just as senseless. And the players aren't excused until the gun goes off in their face, so you get new players but the old ones can't leave until they lose. So the more times you put the gun to your head, the cumulative chances of its going off are—" He shrugged helplessly. "Well, how many people do you know who rotated without getting hit?"

Cannonball scowled quizzically at Goodrich. "Say what?"

Bagger peered at Wild Man. "What's he talking about?"

Phony answered. "School."

22.

BAGGER

The team. Everything's the team. You work hard with them, early in the morning when everybody else is still asleep. You work hard with them in the afternoon when everybody else has gone home. You take showers together and on the field it's like a battle. You do all these things for each other and with each other. Not for yourself. For the team.

When you play tackle, your glory is in yards gained through your hole. You don't score points. Somebody else scores points through your hole. You don't win games. The team wins games.

You stay together in school. Eat lunch with each other. Walk around with your letter sweaters in groups. Everybody stares. There goes the team. Not Jerry Dean Dolan. There goes our left tackle. Good luck, guys. You all stomp 'em Friday night. You hear? Yeah.

You party together. Screw around on the bus going to the away games. Cut farts and light 'em. That's cool. Sing songs. After the games with the girls. Cheerleaders are the best. They like the team and that's what you are. Part of the team.

So what can you say when the team decides to enlist? Four years together like that, and nobody's going to college. Not Jerry Dean Left-Tackle Dolan. For sure for sure. Had enough of that.

They drove to Athens in two cars. Eight of them. They found the Marine recruiting office and startled the recruiter with the ease of it. No sales pitch, man. Sign us the hell up. You just got the Bowman Rebels football team. The whole first team of graduating seniors. Can you handle it?

Can I *handle* it? The recruiter was in euphoria. Somebody lock that door before these gents change their mind!

Later that day. He slammed the car door, furious and afraid at what he had done. The penful of beagles out back bayed mournfully, announcing his arrival. He walked up the cinder-block path to the trailer, feeling blocks wiggle under him, and stared up at the door. She was standing just inside the screen, the screen filtering her, softening her features, giving her a picture-book attractiveness that did not filter out the animal in her. The animal exuded, embraced him as he climbed the steps. Cheerleader. Uh huh.

She smiled, the eyes dancing happily, mischievously, invitingly. Beads of water ran down sandy strands of hair and plopped on the top of a generous breast, then trickled through the warm, entrancing abyss, finally melting into the terry-cloth fabric of her loose-wrapped robe.

"Caught me in the shower, Jerry Dean. I bet you planned it that way." Hair clung wetly to her cheeks and down her neck, drops of shower water resting in the hollows of her face. She cocked her head, leaning on the door. He looked fully at her through the screen door, exploring all her secret parts with his eyes. She smiled back, still inviting him, enjoying his visual embrace. Got herself a left tackle. Uh huh.

"Did you all really go to Athens?"

"Oh, yeah."

"And enlist?"

"Oh, yeah."

"Well, you all are *crazy!*"

"Don't I know it. Hey. It's hot out here."

"Well," She pushed the screen door open and turned. "C'mon in."

He followed her into the living room, eyes fixed on the sturdy, well-shaped hips that clung tightly to the terry cloth each time she strode. She stopped and turned, looking him full in the eyes, smiling bold and mischievous.

He walked up. She didn't budge. Met his movement, pushed into him with that meaty firmness.

"Where's your mother?"

Open smile, widened to a knowing grin. "At work. You know that."

"Where's your sister?" She pulled on the robe's terry-cloth belt. Rich flesh exploded from the middle of her. Still the devil smile.

"She won't be back." She took his hands and put them on her breasts. "You gonna be a big bad Marine, Jerry Dean? You'll miss me, you know that."

That did it. In the pen the dogs were restless but had ceased their baying. Inside the trailer it was quiet with rhapsodic, animal enjoyment.

A throated, laughing voice. "You just a big old teddy bear, J.D."

"Uh huh. Your teddy bear got one of *these?*"

Graduation. Left tackle marries pregnant cheerleader. The team departs for war. The calamities of adulthood have overwhelmed Bagger.

23.

"Cat Man's got something in the trees."

Snake gestured with his head toward a mat of overgrown foliage just off the trail. Sweat flew off his face when he moved it. He was bare-chested underneath his flak jacket, and rivulets of perspiration poured down his trunk, gathering in his soaked trousers. "Over there, he says."

The platoon knelt or sat on the trail. Several men guzzled from canteens. Hodges peered across the field and saw an old abandoned hootch and a clump of banana trees. He shrugged, and queried Cat Man. "What?"

Cat Man's roving eyes met Hodges' for one brief, stolid flash and then returned to the field. Beyond it was the Thu Bon River, down a steep bank. "The banana trees."

Hodges looked at Stork, his radioman, who shrugged confusedly. He turned to Snake. "What?"

Cat Man pointed cautiously. "Stalks are gone." The old hootch was an empty, broken skeleton. The banana trees next to it were lush green, like an oasis in the brown field. Cat Man was right. Several stalks were gone. Beware banana trees, remembered Hodges. NVA seek their shade, lay on their broad, cool leaves, sometimes eat the younger stalks like celery.

"All right. Let's check it out."

Phony shook his head disgustedly, his face deep red from the heat. The platoon had been on patrol for several hours. "Ah, Lieutenant. Peep this out. Peep that out. We could find old Ho Chi Minh hisself back there and it wouldn't make no never-mind."

Hodges lit a cigarette, and raised his eyebrows to Phony, a rebuke. "You can stay back here on the trail if you want."

Phony put his helmet back on his head. "Yeah. Old Luke the Gook would love that. Christ. Cat Man and his damn bent grassblades."

They moved toward the old hootch, the whole platoon on line. It was a bored, perfunctory sweep. They fought the high weeds, weapons carried loosely in one hand, more worried about the high grass than the object of the sweep.

BBBBBRRRROOWWWW. Two bursts of automatic rifle fire, unaimed, a wide spray that encompassed the whole platoon. The banana clump was only fifty yards away, but no one was hit. The front men of the sweep returned fire quickly and Hodges knelt, lost in the high grass. He looked cautiously around him. He knew that all portions of the old villages such as this one were latticed by deep, grass-hidden trenches, that the platoon could be completely surrounded and not even become aware of it until the enemy began firing. For a moment, he considered retreating back to the trail, but he realized that there would be no protection on it, no guarantee that it also was not covered. On its other side, there was more village, more matted fields, other trenches.

He grimaced. We are the bait, dangling. "Assault to the riverbank!"

They moved immediately forward, firing from the hip.

It amazed him every time. They were so young in so many ways, so vulnerable, and yet an order filled with that kind of unknown was always obeyed almost before it was uttered. They did this part so goddamn well.

No other fire from the banana clump. The front of the sweep reached the riverbank and automatically set in, watching their front.

Big Mac passed the banana clump. He stopped, and peered down at a Marine ammunition box, half-buried in the dirt. He called to his team leader. "Hey, Cat Man! How'd you miss this!"

Big Mac reached over and lifted the ammo box, to show it to Cat Man. He straightened, the lid of the ammo box in hand, and—disappeared. At one moment he was stooping, grinning caustically to Cat Man, and in the next there was a violent rending of the earth, a belch of smoke and dust that sprayed half the platoon, the equivalent of a large artillery round impacting underneath him as the pressure-release detonator set off the booby trap. He did a full flip in the air. His rifle spun into the distance, a black baton. He landed where he had stood grinning to them only a half-second before, but now he was a scorched, decapitated ash heap that reminded them all of how very close they stayed to death, even on a boring day.

Pieces of Big Mac pattered on the leaves and grass for several seconds, like gentle rain. They had not noticed Phony staggering nearby without direction. Finally he screamed, high-pitched and confused. "DOC! Doc! They got my arm, Doc! They got my arm!" There was nothing underneath his right shoulder but a ragged tear of red that pulsed jets of blood with the rapid beating of his heart. His arm lay near him, in perfect shape, and as Phony staggered it seemed he did a voodoo dance over his severed limb.

"Doc! Snake!" Snake reached Phony and made him lie down. "They got my arm, Snake."

"Lieutenant!" Someone on the riverbank. "Jesus Christ, there's gooks everywhere!" The front of the sweep opened fire toward the river. Cannonball's blooper thunked and boomed flatly down the bank.

From below a wail of fire, aimed at the banana clump, where several Marines had gathered to help Phony.

Phony still screamed. Hodges called for Stork, and bolted toward the riverbank, where the platoon was firing madly.

He burst through an old hedgerow, half-jogging, and it erupted just behind him. He felt himself sail forward from the blast, so totally shocked by its unexpected force that he did not register what was happening for several seconds. AK-47 rounds passed over him with their stacatto pops and he heard the platoon firing back and when he looked up Rabbit was near him, yanking out a dozen battle dressings, trying to choose between him and Phony and Stork and apparently a few others.

Then he noticed the ooze that covered his arms. He felt it in his hair and along his neck and on the back of his legs and at the base of his back. He tried to sit and gushed blood from the seat of his trousers, then rolled over on his stomach as Rabbit finished Phony, whose screaming had given way to an incoherent babble.

Phony pointed toward Rabbit's morphine sticks. "Gimme another one, Rabbit. Ha hahh. Ha *Hahhh*. It don't matter, man. They got my fucking arm."

Somebody said that Stork was dead. Hodges didn't look for the tall, gawky radioman. Cat Man crept over and helped Rabbit dress his wounds, his normally emotionless face angry and confused. Rabbit dripped sweat in his face.

Snake was directing the fire of the platoon. He crept stealthily to Hodges. "They got a goddamn hospital or something on a little island out there, Lieutenant. They're making their *didi* over into the Arizona. They can wade it. I think they're just fucking with us till they get out of there."

Compos and Wolf Man worked the machine gun methodically. Hodges tried to lift his head. "Getting any?"

Snake shrugged. "A few."

"Put some artillery on the far bank. Blow 'em away."

"Ah. It's too late." Three minutes more, and the firing ceased. "We gotta get your ass out of here, Lieutenant."

The morphine was hitting Hodges. He felt good, warm and weak. The shrapnel holes had felt like bee stings, down deep inside, but they didn't hurt anymore. He listened as Snake called in the medevac request. Two emergencies, two priorities, two routines. Two dead men.

"Who's hit?"

"You are. Sir." Snake lit a cigarette. "And Phony. And Stork. And Big Mac. Two others. Big Mac is *all* fucked up. Hey, Lieutenant—" Snake grimaced pensively—"this really sucks."

Cat Man called to them from where Stork lay. He seemed apologetic, uncertain. He held the radio handset. "Lieutenant? Snake? They want the Actual."

Hodges was floating on the morphine. Snake dragged on his cigarette, and nodded to Cat Man.

"Who?"

"It's the Six. They want a Mine and Booby Trap Report." Phony was still babbling. Cat Man spoke haltingly. "They told me all the things. Ah, hell, man, I can't remember. Who am I? They want to know what kind of round went off, was there a trip wire, how far we were dispersed—"

"Oh, Christ."

"They want to know how it was camouflaged—"

"Tell 'em if we knew all those things we would have found it, instead of tripping the motherfucker. Tell 'em to come out here and *kiss my ass!*"

Hodges laughed softly, eyeing Snake. "Uh huh. You thought there was nothing to being a platoon commander, didn't you, you little shit? You didn't know about the paperwork."

"Now, Lieutenant, how the hell can we answer any of those questions? And what the *hell* difference does it make, once it goes off?"

"Make something up. That's what I do. Ever want to get back at a lifer? Make a story up that'll blow his goddamn mind. Tell 'em to come out here and see for their goddamn selves. Tell 'em that. What the fuck do they know."

Snake nodded to Cat Man. "Tell 'em we ain't got any report."

Cat Man walked away, avoiding both of them. "You tell 'em. Who am I? I don't even talk right, man."

Snake watched the medevac helicopter ascend. It was a high and distant deus ex machina that now left them again abandoned in the wilderness. Baby Cakes sat down next to him. They sat quietly, drawing on cigarettes, the rest of the platoon in a hasty perimeter that had secured the landing zone.

Baby Cakes broke the silence. "So what do we do now, Platoon Commander For A Day?"

Snake watched the helicopter. It had become a speck in the distance. "Burn down Vietnam." Phony's arm lay nearby, reaching for him.

"Hodges'll be back."

"Think so?"

"Sure. They'll send him back. He's hit about like Ogre was that night. He'll be back, Snake."

"He's got four months in the bush. They won't send him back to us."

"We better get out of here. There was a lot of gooks crossing that river. This ain't any place to get hit."

Snake stood up, placing his helmet back on his head. He loaded a fresh magazine of ammunition into his rifle. "No, I think you're right, Cakes. He'll be back. He likes it. I mean us. You know, I been in trouble all my life, man, 'cause I never been able to work for anybody. I can work for him. I *like* the son of a bitch. And I just know he'll come back."

"Yeah. And Phony'll be all right, man. He's tough."

"Yeah. He's tough. Now, Squad Leader For A Day. Get your ass in gear and let's get the hell back to Henderson Hill."

The column stretched wearily back toward the company perimeter, several miles away. Behind it, like random torches, the hootches of the nearest village spent themselves in orange rages. The flames rose anonymously, but it was the platoon's collective act of passion, a substitute for not being able to fight the enemy that had ravaged them. The hootches burned like funeral pyres. That one is for Big Mac. That one is for Stork.

Finally they reached Henderson Hill. It was low and flat, deep-red clay dust marked by huge craters and a steam-shoveled inner perimeter, the vestige of a Great Experiment. Years before, a Vietnamese Popular Forces unit had been ordered into the An Hoa Basin, and had built a compound on the hill. It had seemed an ideal place: less than two miles from Liberty Bridge, easy access to the convoy road's supply train, readily defensible. But the notion of a localized Vietnamese unit operating on a permanent basis had aroused the ire of the local Viet Cong, and the hill had been repeatedly attacked, regularly overrun, until the Popular Forces unit had refused to remain. It was withdrawn, the sandbag bunkers were plowed under, the towers felled and burned, and the wire around the perimeter abandoned to enterprising VC units who pilfered great sections at night.

But the hill itself remained an ideal company position, and it was used for short periods by many Marine companies operating in the Phu Nhuan villages. And the villagers around the base of the hill had remained peacefully ambivalent about the warriors who continued to ravage the Basin. With the exception of the Duc Duc and Mau Chanh villages, which hugged the wire at An Hoa, the Henderson Hill villages housed the most friendly, most cooperative civilians in the Basin.

The children greeted the patrol as it wound along the high, wide paddy dike that joined the village at the northern edge of the hill. Cheerful, doting faces, calling out to favorite Marines in husky, gutter English. "Hey-y-y, Wattaboo, you need washy-wash, O.K.?" "Hey-y-y, Wi'-Man, you Numbah One *bac-bac* VC, huh?" "Hey-y-y, *Bac Se*, you gimme cigret?" The platoon chided the children back, trading friendly insults, clowning with them as they danced along with the movement of the patrol.

Bagger slipped off his flak jacket and dropped it onto the shoulders of a small, thin boy. The jacket reached the boy's ankles. He laughed, calling to the other children, and jogged proudly, keeping pace with Bagger. He growled convincingly. "Ahhh! Me *bac-bac* VC!"

One small boy in a wide-brim version of a bush hat had alternately stood and walked next to the column, somber eyes squinched, searching. Finally he saw Wild Man. He skipped along next to him, tugging at his flak jacket, and spoke intensely. "Where Phony, ma-a-an?"

Wild Man did not address him. He twirled his finger in a circular motion indicating a helicopter medevac. The boy was genuinely upset: Phony was his "washy-wash" Marine, his personal responsibility when it came to drawing buckets at the well, for which Phony had been lavish with C-rations and cigarettes. He shook a fist.

"Aw-w-w, ma-a-an. VC *bac bac* Phony? Numbah fucking One Thousand. Phony come back, he *bac-bac booo cooo* VC."

Wild Man waved him away, on the verge of a snarl. "Get the fuck away from me."

Goodrich watched the parade of children. He liked their friendliness. And the villagers around Henderson Hill were almost worth fighting for. Or over. Or about. Whatever the hell we're doing, he grumbled. Real villages, as he had first imagined Vietnam would be. Cultivated gardens, pecking chickens, and penned hogs that even Captain Crazy did not see fit to slaughter. People who smiled. It was the only area Goodrich had worked in where the Marines dared venture outside their perimeter during the day, to sit under shade trees, run a secret joint, visit with the villagers. Anywhere else, they would be ambushed within fifteen minutes.

The two booby traps had shaken him. The victims were selected so randomly. You could be 100 percent right and still be 100 percent dead, or permanently scarred, like Phony. There's not a goddamn thing you can do about it, either, mused Goodrich. It enforced his sense of the complete randomness of it all. Like existentialism, he thought again, climbing the hill. Suffering without meaning, except in the suffering itself. But no one would understand that if I told them.

He had finally despaired of being the "duty moralist" of the platoon. He had personally refrained from setting fire to any of the thatch hootches as they burned the village on their way back, but he no longer spoke to any of the others about their actions. He had decided to maintain his own standards, to preserve a sense of sanity in spite of such events, but it would only have enraged them more deeply to try and stop them. A vote against burning a hootch would have been a vote against the memory of those who had been hit.

He could sense Snake's deep depression. It was obvious that Snake had been closer to Phony and Hodges, with the possible exception of Baby Cakes, than to anyone else in the platoon. To lose them both together, in addition to the other deaths, the continuing frustrations, had scarred the spindly squad leader's normal toughness. Snake had gone immediately to his poncho hootch when the platoon reached Henderson Hill, waving off the Vietnamese children who normally could count on him for several minutes of frolic.

And Cat Man had retreated inside a stolid, uncommunicative wall. For one brief moment, after the helicopter ascended with Hodges and the others in it, Cat Man had cursed himself for noticing the banana clump, blaming his own proficiency for what had happened. But now he spoke with no one. He returned to his fighting hole, broke out a piece of hairy, salted pork his mother had sent him in a food package, and began to make a stew. He studiously contemplated his C-ration stove when others passed him.

Noticing their frailties, Goodrich for the first time thought them human.

There was a new platoon sergeant, still in An Hoa. They had received word the day before. And tomorrow, they would leave the relative peace of Henderson Hill for a month of roaming through the killer weeds. Goodrich shivered with new fear. He had only heard the stories. Wide, flat, treeless fields of elephant grass. Acres of desolate cemeteries. Whole villages of stone-sad faces. And chest-deep holes that hugged each trail, where a point man all but stepped on his ambusher before he found him.

Tomorrow it would be Go Noi Island.

24.

CAT MAN

The fields are wide and flat, filled with dust. In the tractor you feel as if you are alone, lost in the ocean, with the dust as fog. It surrounds you and you cannot see beyond it. You turn the soil before it is irrigated and planted. Later you help harvest. In the afternoon the winds blow, sometimes from the sea and sometimes from the desert, depending on the season. On the tractor you live in dust-filled wind.

On the weekends there are parties. Wine and marijuana. There are girls who mature early and make love young and have children quickly and are old before they are thirty. They grow heavy and they acquire faith. But before they do, there are parties.

You have friends. You like to laugh. You seem shy outside your circle because you are self-conscious. But you will kill a man over an insult. You do not sue a man who insults you. How much is honor worth? You destroy him.

All the first days. Add them up. They made him Cat Man.

The first day in the town of dust and fog, in from Mexico with his family, ten of them sharing a three-bed-room house with his uncle's family of five. The first day in the fields, twelve hours, ten dollars, and the glow on his father's face when Tacio handed the money he had earned over to him. When there is a home I will keep the money, Tacio had explained, scowling fiercely as he had imagined a man should.

The first day in school, unable to speak a word of English past Hello and Thank You, smiling warmly as a counselor instructed him to report to Special Education. Not understanding a word the counselor had said but feeling that it was important to show no ill will. Reporting to the classroom, filled with rebels and retardeds and a nucleus of persons like himself who could neither speak nor read English, but were too old to start at kindergarten. Special Education. No education. The students throwing paper balls at each other, shooting spit wads across the room with rubber bands. The young, unruffled teacher sitting calmly at her desk, reading a novel to herself, so absorbed in her book that she did not even notice Tacio as he stood before her. Shyly addressing her, he a very serious boy who had been told he must leave the fields to learn. Handing her his slip of paper and announcing with sobriety, I have come to learn to read and write English.

And she looking blankly back, with mild curiosity, unable to understand a word of Spanish beyond Hello and Thank You. And Good-bye.

The first day he became a man. Inside the shed behind the house, among old newspapers and tires, his cloister from the crowded house, learning secretly to smoke. He was thirteen. Lighting a cigarette and sitting in the semi-darkness and wondering at the changes that becoming a man were causing him. For some time he had been excited by the sight of a woman's flesh. To see a woman like that girded him, with a feeling that was mixed with strength and despair. The strength was from his conviction that to experience such things would be a great and natural pleasure, which he was eminently suited for. To watch the gentle bouncing of a well-rounded breast created deep sensual certainties inside him. The despair came from his inability to realize such pleasures. He saw the invitation with every bouncing breast and curved hip. He understood the invitation. He simply did not know how to accept it. He was thirteen.

But sitting in the shed, dreaming in the darkness, and the partially closed door filling with a rounded figure. She was fifteen. It was nearly summer and there was a cool ocean wind and she was braless, underneath a gray sweatshirt. He watched the roundness stretch the fabric and felt the certainty again.

She asked him for a cigarette. She walked to him and joined him on the floor and leaned back comfortably against the rough board wall. She lit the cigarette he gave her, from the end of his own. "I watch you," she said. "Why do you always come to the shed?"

"To think," he answered.

She leaned back and he could feel the softness of her skin as it moved beneath the sweatshirt. He felt an unexplainable surge. "What do you think about that you must come here to do it?" Her voice was low and musical, baiting him. His head was humming slightly. It is the smoke, he thought. No. It is not the smoke.

"I think about becoming a man. I will have many women. I think about that."

She smiled knowingly then, standing and walking back toward the door. He felt a deep frustration. I do not know how to bring this thing about, he commented to himself. Then she slowly pulled the door until it was tightly shut. I have done it. Don't ask me how.

Thin slivers of daylight pierced through the cracks in

the boards that made the door, but otherwise it was black. She returned to him and sat very close, her body firmly touching him in many places.

"Put out your cigarette," she said. Tacio ground the cigarette into the dust and turned to her. He was not afraid. He was meant to do this. She placed his hand underneath her sweatshirt and he felt the soft warmth of her stomach and needed no further guidance. His hand moved up and experienced the fullness of her breasts. They were round and full and very firm. He felt a surge of warmth inside himself that made it difficult for him to breathe.

"Now you have to kiss me," she told him. And she leaned to him. In the darkness he learned the pleasures of the deep tongue that asked for more than mouth. He learned as naturally as a baby learns to eat.

In a few moments she drew him to her and he murmured in his quiet voice, "I am still small."

"You are large enough," she answered.

And he found he was.

The first day out of school, quitting the day he turned sixteen. As he left the building he felt the elation that a prisoner feels when he has been paroled, and is exiting the prison gate. It did not matter that the fields were also a prison. A prison entered out of choice is not a prison, no matter how small the realm of choice. There was no choice in entering school. And it did not relate to work. Therefore it did not relate to life.

Then, finally, the first day he knew he must go to war. The friends had dwindled from the fields, some drafted quickly because they were not in school and were thus deemed more expendable, but others enlisting readily, excited by the thought of battle. There would always be the fields. They were eternity. Tacio himself becoming incensed, and enlisting in the Marine Corps. I am meant to do these things, he thought warmly, feeling the anticipation lighten his body. It is the *machismo*. I am meant for this.

As indeed he was. He was the eyes of the platoon, quiet and delicately featured, a prowling cat. His eyes and his natural instincts combined to notice the smallest inconsistency. Old Snoop and Poop. Cat Man and his damn bent grassblades.

25.

It took a day to walk the eight miles from Henderson Hill to the near edge of Go Noi Island. The company assembled on the hill's bald crown and left it in a slow column, moving eastward one man at a time, until a half-mile column of burdened men struggled along the valley floor.

They passed through My Loc (3), at the edge of the hill (the children waving) and out to the convoy road, where the clay dirt painted every glistening, sweating part of every man brick-red as they walked along it. A short jag on the road and then they left it, reluctantly, for they would not find another, and crossed wide, moist paddies on the huge dike that would take them to the Phu Lacs. Past the Phu Lacs, dark, tree-filled islands in the rice, portentous, empty of motion, then along a little mud-filled stream that took them to the La Thaps. Quickly through the La Thaps—sparse, severe, hostile. Situated on high mounds, identifiable by nicknames. Over there was Dog Bone, shaped like some cartoonist's depiction of a short femur: two terraced, bulbous hills connected by a narrow shaft of ridge. And here was Christmas ville, where the company had celebrated Christmas with the ghosts of present evil, under a horrendous mortar barrage.

La Thaps to the Cu Bans—great, cratered thicks and tangles, rows of trees torn by their roots, hootches demolished and abandoned, whole hectares chewed by years of bombs. There were no people in the Cu Bans, only nightmares. And huge booby traps made from the occasional bomb that failed to detonate: the Villager's Revenge.

Then on to Le Bac, an island surrounded by sand beach and occasional strips of finger lakes that would be streams when the rains came, a fortress, high and ominous, that guarded the edge of Go Noi. A thousand wounds had stained the sand at Le Bac. And its people had the rigidity, the numbed, stolid hate, that existed only in Go Noi and the Arizona Valley.

They straggled tiredly through Le Bac, soaked by then in the steam baths of their own sweat. They had humped for eight hours, in the worst heat of the day. A collective tension seized them as they strolled through Le Bac's desolation.

Goodrich felt himself go tight as he passed the rows of brittle-thatch hootches, the deserts of brick-hard, unkept fields, the villagers with their etched, impassive faces. They're just waiting, he mused fearfully. They want to see me die. The villagers squatted, rocking on their haunches, sucking smoke through ragged twists of tobacco or working betel nut in slow rolls, like cows chewing cud. The flies were busy, deep inside their sores. And they were waiting.

Goodrich disliked moves, any kind of moves. He hated patrols. He hated ambushes. He feared even the relative security of the company moves. The column was long and always awkward if anything happened. Nobody really seemed ever to know where anybody else was. One sniper with his shit together could hold up a whole company for hours.

He felt vulnerable, exposed, on the moves. Worse, he thought. Senselessly exposed. He chided himself. I should have tried for the Army band. At least then, when the recruiter screwed me, I could have ridden on choppers. He snorted. If the Army was going into Go Noi today, they would have loaded up the birds and dropped the troops. Ten minutes, no casualties on the march, ready to fight. We walk all day, waiting for snipers, booby traps, and ambushes, and by the time we get there we're too exhausted to do anything but curl up and go to sleep.

On the other side of Le Bac there were jungles of high elephant grass that walled each man off into his own helpless world. It was Goodrich's first taste of Go Noi's mile-wide killer fields. He felt abandoned. He was afraid he would get lost in the grass and never find the company again. It could happen, he fretted. One wrong turn and I'd never find them again.

The grass ended and the high bank dropped to the waste of sand again. They crossed a murky finger lake, filled with weeds and huge, scurrying leeches. The water crept to their chests and they held their rifles above their heads as they crossed.

On the far bank was another stretch of sand, another sandy hill. Then they formed a hasty perimeter in a field of elephant grass. That mass of grass that reached high above their heads, that held the wind from them and sucked their strength with each drip of sweat, was Go Noi.

They'd come to find the Holy Grail. Goodrich shook his head, feeling hopelessly beyond the others. No one had understood his quip. Actually, they were to search for the Phu Thuan Market. Actually, persisted Goodrich, no reason whatsoever. The word had come down from Regiment that Phu Thuan was operating on Go Noi. Which was roughly the equivalent, mused Goodrich, of saying that a submarine is now cruising, underwater, in the Atlantic.

There was a band of budding capitalists from nearby Dai Loc who marketed goods to the North Vietnamese Army. Some goods were essentials, such as canned fish, and black-market commodities that had been issued to care for refugees who, on paper, had filled the resettlement villes, but who, in reality, remained in their own. Others were luxury items: sheets of plastic for hootches and ponchos, tobacco and peppercorns. The market would surface in a village, or near a convenient trail intersection, at dusk on some evening, sell goods to NVA "supply patrols" through the night, and depart back to Dai Loc at first light. There was no way to predict where the market would surface without good intelligence information. There was no good intelligence.

So, thought Goodrich sagely, it's just another excuse. We'll troll across the fields like bait because no one knows what else to do with us. We won't find any Phu Thuan.

We'll just find trouble.

Rounds again. Steady bursts. *Cracks* of AK-47s, maybe three of them. Up high. *Boom.* Grenade went off. *Boom. Boom.* Two more. M-16s rattled back. A moment of anticipatory silence. *Boom boom boom.* More *cracks,* short bursts.

Point platoon was dying up the trail.

They lay and sat on the trail, facing high grass walls, listening to the personal battle, someone else's war, at the head of the column. The trail was like a narrow alleyway running through tall buildings: it was almost impossible to leave it. The company followed it. Thus, its meanderings became predictable. And ambushable.

Bagger lit a cigarette, his wide face troubled. More M-16s cut loose up the trail. He winced, then smoked sulkily, staring at the mass of jutting green grassblades. More *cracks*, lower, lost in the grass.

"Hope they don't bring us up there. We'll never make it. We'll get lost in the grass. They'll hear us coming and do the hell outa us."

Wild Man drank from a canteen, then stared inside it, absently measuring his last drops of water. "They won't. First platoon'll handle it."

"First platoon's fucked up and you know it. They couldn't fight their way out of a thick fog."

Wild Man shrugged, apparently unconcerned. "Even if they bring us up, the gooks are in those holes." There were neck-deep holes along the trail, just next to it on both sides, spaced all along it. They were narrow and held only one or two men. "They'll be watching on the trail, not in the grass."

Bagger's eyes were becoming haunted, hollow. His lips were rigid. "Yeah, but where are their buddies?" A cacophony of *cracks*, a half-dozen *booms*. "Oh-h-h this shit is *bad*. We got point next." Point was methodically rotated among platoons, squads, fire teams, even individuals, on Go Noi's killer trails. Share The Risk. "I feel like somebody playing Russian roulette."

Wild Man quietly studied Bagger, watching him fiddle with his cigarette. "Bagger, you getting flaky?"

Bagger stared at the high grass. One AK cracked over their heads. More *booms*. "Oh, you bet your sweet *ass* I'm getting flaky. Who ain't flaky about getting set up to be blown away?"

The spider holes were silent. First platoon had won the Battle of Latest Trailbend. The company inched forward to secure both ends of the battleground so the medevac helicopter would land. The point man had been killed. Three others shot. Three NVA were dead.

Bagger and Wild Man stood, deploying a few feet into the grass as security. Wild Man grinned under a droopy, red-flecked moustache. It was a resigned grin. "Don't do no good to get flaky about it, Bagger. Won't change a goddamn thing."

Two hours later, three hundred meters down the trail, Wild Man got his. Same thing. That unceremonious, instantaneous *crack* that startles you, jets the adrenaline, totally surprises you no matter how many times you repeat to yourself that it will happen around this turn, right here it will happen, it's got to happen just around here, I'll get the bastard first—

An unseen burst and Wild Man was down, curled in a little ball, holding his stomach. He thought to shoot, knew he should respond, but could not let go of his gut. Behind him Bagger flopped to the ground, his eyes protruding in terror, his face taut. He hugged the dirt, frozen by fear. Gook popped out of spider hole, took a shot at Bagger's supine frame, and missed. Waterbull rushed to the trailbend and tossed a grenade uptrail to keep the ambushers' heads inside their holes, not knowing where they were. *Boom.*

Snake had them figured. He grabbed Baby Cakes' team and pulled them through the grass just off the trail. There were old cemetery mounds near the ambushers. He bunched the team behind the first mound, five of them huddled in a tight knot—Baby Cakes, Ogre, Senator, and Cornbread, plus himself. He schooled them. "Next time they open up, listen for where they are. When I say so, toss a grenade. Everybody. Keep it away from Wild Man. *Soon* as the grenades go off, we jump out of here and grease 'em. Got it?"

All nodded in response. Goodrich crouched low, petrified. They'll kill us all this is *crazy* they'll be waiting for us as soon as we step out they'll mow us down like—

Crack just on the other side, maybe five meters away. Waterbull had tried to reach Wild Man. Wild Man was now the bait, the lure that would draw more targets near the spider holes. *Crack* just on the other side of the trail. Two holes.

Snake nodded, his lips set into a firm line, eyes clear, analyzing. *"Now!"*

Five grenades over the mound. Short pause. Incredible, interlocking *booms,* a pulsing explosion. The booms still rang. Snake jumped up. *"Now!"*

He sprang quickly around the mound. Baby Cakes

jumped from the other side of it. Ogre and Cornbread followed. Goodrich clung to his grassy haven, waiting to hear the shots that would mow the others down. A rifle. Another. Outgoing. M-16s. He felt suddenly abandoned, was terrified to be alone in the high grass, and ran after the others.

The ambushers were dead. One sagged inside his spider hole, his head blown apart. The other was draped outside, across the trail. They had watched Wild Man, certain that the grenade barrage was preparatory to an attempt to drag him to safety. Snake and Baby Cakes had caught them from the side, just in back of where they were watching.

Wild Man groveled in the dirt, still clutching his stomach. Bagger stood up and peered at the ball of agony that was Wild Man, and could not control his anger. He walked to the trailbend and gazed at the dead ambushers. With a violent grunt he kicked one sprawling body back into its spider hole. Then he stood over the hole and fired a magazine into the body, eighteen rounds of automatic fire that sprayed all parts of the carcass.

Bagger's face was drained. "You gook *motherfucker!*"

Snake approached Bagger, putting an arm around his shoulder. "Save your ammo, Bagger. I think we're gonna need it."

Staff Sergeant Sadler, the new platoon sergeant, strode up to the point. He was tall, mahoganied black, thick-set, with bulging buttocks. Like so many other staff NCOs, he was an infantry veteran, on his second Vietnam tour.

Sadler congratulated Snake. "That was a hell of a job, Snake."

"Thanks, Sarge." Snake tentatively liked Sadler. The Sergeant seemed to have his shit together. Snake shook his head, showing hints of frazzles that wore on his lips and eyebrows. "When's this shit gonna let up, huh?"

Sadler squinted ironically. "Well, they keep this up, they goan' run outa ammo before too long."

"Don't hold your breath, Sarge. We might run outa people first."

The perimeter, this latest one-night home, sat hopelessly adrift in a sea of sawgrass. The sawgrass had many advantages over the miles of elephant grass that the company had struggled through to reach it. In fact, if one stood he could even see over the top of it.

The resupply chopper had brought mail. Inside the mailbags, someone had thoughtfully inserted newspapers. Baby Cakes leafed through a two-day-old issue of *Stars and Stripes*, his craggy face intent.

"It says here," he noted, "that folks are pleased with the progress of the last few weeks."

Ogre nodded, forcing himself to appear ruminative. "No-o-o-o shit?"

Baby Cakes continued, holding the newspaper in front of him. "Yup. Says things are going re-e-al good. Says there weren't any, you know, 'big battles' all last week. Says old Charlie's done run outa gas."

"Somebody better go tell Wild Man before he tries to claim a Purple Heart. Know what I mean, Cakes?"

"Yeah. Well, that was what they call an 'isolated incident.' Says right here there was a bunch of them 'isolated incidents.'"

Ogre grinned ironically, lying back on his poncho liner. "Yeah, uh huh. That's the way we been ever since I came to this company. Isolated, waiting for incidents."

"Funny man. We gotta get you on 'Laugh In.'"

"Well, I'd settle for Goldie Hawn in a plain brown wrapper, if they'd mail it to me." Ogre considered it. "Hell. I'd take that little old lady about now."

"You done worse than her in Da Nang. And here's a flick of the *moon*. Hey, Ogre! You know they put a man on the moon?"

"I already heard about it on the radio." Ogre seemed uninterested.

Baby Cakes squinted at the picture, examining it closely. "I be damned. Hey. Don't you want to see what it looks like?"

"I know what it looks like. It looks just like the Cu Bans."

Baby Cakes studied the picture again. "No. There ain't any trails."

The night was wholly black, very low, just above the grass. Rain fell steadily, big drops like explosions on the ponchos. Fog rose from the ground, which was still hot from the penetrating sun of hours before. Each huge drop of rain sent a part of itself, as steam, back into the dead night air.

Waterbull leaned against the back wall of his fighting hole. Behind him, Bagger and Little Mac slept fitfully under a low poncho hootch. He wore the third poncho. It would be rotated with the watch. The poncho hood was over his ears, underneath his helmet. He did not hear the night. He heard himself when his body rustled. He heard the rain's explosions when he stood still.

Well, they won't mortar us, he reasoned. And if they do we'll hear those bloopy short rounds, 'cause the increments will get wet and won't ignite, and we'll hear 'em blow up their own people. Listen to 'em scream like that night out in the La Thaps. He chuckled, in spite of his discomfort. Happens like that when it rains. People don't think gooks screw up, people think they're Supermen and all, should have heard 'em *that* night.

He peered in front of him. There was a wall of steamy grass, four feet high, well over his head as he stood inside the fighting hole. He and Bagger and Little Mac had matted down a few feet of the grass, primarily in order to dig cat holes to defecate in. But I can't see a damn thing, Waterbull lamented again. May as well not be standing here. Don't do no good. Besides, no gook in his right mind would go out in this stuff. Old Luke the Gook ain't dumb. He knows when to come in outa the rain. How the hell they gonna find us out in the middle of all this damn grass, anyway? I know where we are, and I couldn't find us if I went out past that cat hole right there. Like Cannonball says: they ain't no wa-a-a-a-ay, man.

His mind wandered. He began to think of his Bangkok whore. The freckles danced in the dark. His fat face grinned hugely, mindless of the splashing rain that beat against it. That little gal sure—well, there just *ain't* any other word for it. That gal could just plain *fuck*. He remembered the delicate body, the breasts that filled both his massive hands, springy, soft as velvet. The responsive nipples that rose when touched. The way she would moan comfortably when he rolled the nipples with his tongue. The firm, tight hips that danced crazily, seeking him. The warmth, the tightness of her liquid insides.

He was hard. He fondled himself underneath his poncho, remembering the first time with her. He set his rifle down inside the fighting hole and reached for his wallet. Maybe I can see that picture if I hold it close enough. He grinned, stroking himself. Hell. Everybody does it. Like they say: it ain't much, but it's better than a wet dream.

He pulled the wallet out, unwrapping it from its protective plastic bag, and found the transparent picture holder. He flipped through it until she stared back at him in the dark. Her legs were crossed, the magnificent breasts standing firm and beautiful, aching to be touched. He held the picture inches from his face, still fondling himself. Oh, man. To bite those tits right now.

In front of him, two short strides away, a man shivered in the wet grass, feeling his adrenaline pump explosively. He had been watching Waterbull for several minutes, waiting. The perimeter had not been difficult to locate. There was the trail, then the mattings of sawgrass: recent, ephemeral paths that led to the perimeter. And even though the rain washed the air continuously, there had been the odor from the cat holes: a hundred odorous droppings, ringing the perimeter like a stench-filled moat. The man inhaled deeply, curled his legs like a cat preparing to leap, and charged.

There was an instant of thrashing to Waterbull's front, like a deer breaking cover. Waterbull lowered his wallet from just before his eyes, and for an agonizing, elongated moment stared into the face of an equally terrified, resolved attacker. Each feature of the man luminesced in that instant, as if he glowed from inside in the foggy dark. Waterbull came to know his attacker's face as well as he knew his own. The heavy eyebrows, arched, the taut, tight skin, the narrow bridge of nose that flared down to wide, fat nostrils. The thick lips set firmly, determined, over a long, narrow chin. The whole face, wildly determined.

In the millisecond that seemed an hour to Waterbull, the time it took for his grimacing attacker to take his first revealing stride, he thought to do a dozen things, wondered why his body could not perform each desired act. He managed to drop his wallet. He even attempted to reach his weapon, lying two feet, a million hopeless miles, beyond his grasp. He reached for it and the bolting figure triggered his own weapon, hitting Waterbull in three places with a burst of automatic rifle dealt from perhaps four feet away. One burst. His attacker dashed past him and was inside the perimeter, lost in the high grass.

Bagger had been slumbering fitfully just behind the hole. His sleep had been mere dozings, interrupted by the fear that had turned his eyes gaunt, brought him to the edge of explosion. He had started when the attacker smashed through the grass toward Waterbull, and instinctively rolled from under his poncho hootch into the grass beside it. He lay dumbstruck, groping for his weapon, as Waterbull was shot. Now he hid, still silent, as a dozen other forms rushed past him.

Another automatic blast ripped through the low poncho hootch. Little Mac was shot through both legs. He thought to grab his weapon, to shout a warning to the rest of the perimeter, but observed the shadowed string of soldiers running past him and wisely lay still, pretending death.

The shadows disappeared, deep inside the perimeter. They crawled in the sawgrass, undiscoverable. It was impossible to organize a defense against them. They mixed among the Marines, concealed in the grass. In the middle of the perimeter there was a clearing, but even it was clouded by thickets of bushes, clumps of grass. The attackers hid, tossing grenades at positions from inside the lines, harassing command posts. Each position was isolated in its own grassbed. Wild rifle fire crisscrossed the inside of the perimeter, aimed at shadows, imaginary ghouls.

The perimeter was tightly drawn, its fighting holes very close in the choking sawgrass. Ten meters down from Waterbull, Snake squatted in a fighting hole, next to Cannonball. Cat Man was in another, just next to them. They had heard the cracks of rifle fire and comprehended that Waterbull's team was being overrun, but remained deep inside their own holes. In the killer weeds, any man who moved might be shot.

On the other side of Waterbull, Goodrich knelt in his hole with Cornbread, peering into the black interior of the perimeter. Next to them were Baby Cakes and Ogre, a few feet away.

Goodrich searched for movement, listened for cries from Waterbull's position. He was terrified beyond words. *Help me, Senator.* Rifle fire burst randomly. *Can't you stop it? Grenades from unseen places. You're just waiting for me to die.*

He turned to an equally terrified Cornbread. "Do you think we should try to help them?"

Cornbread's eyes were round and luminescent inside his wet black face. He answered in a hoarse whisper. "Ah cain't do it."

A grenade dropped near them from nowhere, and exploded a few feet in front of them. It boomed loudly, although most of its shrapnel was absorbed by the soft, wet dirt. The two were silent for a moment, watching, their rifles pointed toward the center of the perimeter.

Finally, Ogre leaned over from his hole. "One thing you ain't is *dumb*, Cornbread." *Boom.* Another grenade.

The sappers gave the impression of being ubiquitous. There were explosions, crimson trails of tracers everywhere. Bagger still lay frozen in the grass, too petrified to crawl five feet over to Little Mac, much less to examine Waterbull. Little Mac still pretended death, too frightened to call Bagger. The perimeter was small, and totally overrun: a shout would bring the Boogeyman.

For three hours the sappers terrorized the company. No supporting arms were called: the only option would be to call artillery on their own position, and there were not enough casualties to justify such a desperate measure. Artillery illumination was used, but it merely heightened the shadows, increased the volume of anxious tracers aimed at nothing.

Finally, on their own volition, the sappers left. They gathered, overran a machine-gun position on the far side of the perimeter, took the gun with them, and even dragged two Marines twenty yards into the weeds.

The perimeter quietened slowly, even after the enemy soldiers had left. Grenades went off, tracers flew, aimed at imagined targets, shadows in the weeds. Bagger lay for another half-hour before he dared to speak to Little Mac. His voice was constricted, guilt-ridden at its own terror.

"Mac. Hey. Are you O.K.?"

Little Mac also spoke hesitantly, remembering the string of burdened soldiers that had all but stepped on him a few hours ago. "I need a doc, Bagger. Can you get me a doc? Go get Rabbit."

Bagger hesitated, shivering in the wet grass, then

crawled slowly, reluctantly, toward the command post.

Baby Cakes had found Waterbull. The huge redhead was unconscious, but still alive. Baby Cakes tore the poncho off Waterbull, feeling in the rainy dark for his wounds. He spoke ironically as he worked. "Got your peter out, huh, Bull Man? Can't get enough of that whore. Lucky you're so damn big. Bid dude like you would take a year to bleed to death. Wake up, Bull."

Lieutenant Rock Man was among those killed by the sappers. The medevac helicopters would not take the dead out until daylight. Lieutenant Shaw, who was Rock Man's best friend and the commander of the weapons platoon, came out on the morning helicopter, returning from a visit to Da Nang that he had somehow wangled out of Captain Crazy.

Shaw had not known that Rock Man was dead. He trotted off the helicopter and began jogging toward the company command post, fighting the swaying sawgrass, holding onto his helmet as he ran, and he bumped into two Marines carrying Rock Man's corpse onto the waiting chopper.

Rock Man was waxy and stiff. Shaw stared at his dead friend in disbelief as the two men lumbered past him. Then he threw up. The helicopter rotorwash flung his vomit back onto his clothes. And Lieutenant Shaw flung himself back into the helicopter. They would not see him again. Two days later there would be a message from the company rear that Shaw was now on the regimental staff.

They swept the high grass of their own perimeter in the humid morning heat, a half-dozen squad patrols combing the weeds for enemy. They found five sappers, two of them alive. The two prisoners were brought to the company CP. One had been shot in the midsection, a bullet having pierced his stomach lining, leaving a tear where a part of his intestine now bulged, as if he wore a foot-long sausage near his belt. The other had been shot through the hip and through the shoulder. His uniform was soaked, top and bottom, with blood.

They gathered around the prisoners, a continually changing group of perhaps twenty men. They wanted the prisoners to die. If they died there would be two more kills, parity for their own deaths the night before. If the prisoners lived, they would not make the tote board that tallied ratios.

The prisoner with the bulging intestine jabbered deliriously through the morning, his voice high and nasal, a child's. He pleaded with them to mend his innards. He referred to himself as "babysan," at which they uniformly jeered. Yeah. Babysan, my ass. You seemed like a babysan last night.

Finally just after noon, he died. Dan ceremoniously placed a cigarette between the chilled lips, then withdrew the dead man's penis from his trousers and placed it in his stiffening fingers. The gathered Marines laughed contemptuously at the dead soldier.

The other soldier still clung to life when the resupply helicopter arrived in midafternoon, and was medevacked.

A group from Snake's squad watched the helicopter churn toward Da Nang. Snake grimaced. "They should of shot the fucker when they found him."

Ogre agreed. "There it is, man. Shoot him before you touch him, he's a kill. Touch him first, you got to wait around for him to die."

"Well, he just might make it." Goodrich.

"You better hope not, Senator. That's the game out here. That's what we're here for. To kill gooks." Baby Cakes grinned whimsically to his charge.

"Funny. I thought there was more to it."

"There is, Senator. There is. But it all goes together. Kill gooks, and make it home alive. Once they're dead they leave you the hell alone."

"Well, Bagger's got a team again."

"Come on, Ogre. That ain't even funny." Snake dropped a card onto the poncho liner. Ogre leaned over, bronzed again, shirtless, and picked up the trick. He peered into his hand, selecting another card, and dropped it.

Baby Cakes tossed his card onto the blanket and admonished his friend. "Yeah. That's enough of that kind of talk. Old Bagger's about to go *dinky-dau*, man. This nickel and dime stuff is driving him there. Don't make it any worse than it already is."

Fifty feet from them, Bagger slept in the speckled

shade of the bullet-ridden poncho hootch. He had sulked for hours, refusing to converse or even eat.

Goodrich felt he understood Bagger. He had watched the stocky Georgian go through the same withdrawal he had experienced after the Bridge incident. Bagger's bitching attitude came the closest to his own of anyone in the squad. Baby Cakes was too gungy. Ogre was a spaced-out ass. Cornbread was a mimic, a master at avoiding unpleasantness. And they don't like me anyway, mused Goodrich. Snake told them. Bagger might understand.

He wanted out of the team. He could live with Bagger's complaints. He could live without Baby Cakes' boasts and bravado. Goodrich called to Snake and the others from his fighting hole.

"Listen. Why don't you put me in Bagger's team? *We* have four men. It isn't right to leave him by himself."

Snake shrugged absently. "We're getting new dudes any day."

Baby Cakes pondered it. The only question in his mind was whether Bagger could put up with Goodrich and retain his shred of sanity. He was delighted to unload the Senator. He looked at Snake. "Hey. I don't mind, Snake." Then, under his breath. "I done learned all about Genevas and tiger cages. Let somebody else get smart."

Snake smirked at Baby Cakes, picking up the deck of cards. "O.K., Senator. Pack your trash and get on over to Bagger's hole."

Cannonball and Cornbread sat facing each other, cleaning their weapons. Cornbread measured Cannonball, then grinned confidentially. "Man, las' night that big blond Chuck—not Baby Cakes, you know, the fat one, Senator—he was sayin', 'Mebbe we should go on over an' try an' he'p Bagger an' Lil Mac.' You know, when all the shit was happenin'? Bagger an' Lil Mac, they ain' even he'pin' each other an' we s'posed to go on over an' he'p. Ah keep thinkin' 'bout dyin' fo' some Chuck who ain't even doin' fo' hisself—" he chuckled, rubbing a rag along the outer barrel of his M-16—"Ah jis' say, 'Ah *cain't*,' you know, like Ah'm too dummmmmb. One o' you smart-ass Chuck dudes show me how to get yo' ass shot off."

He and Cannonball laughed fraternally. Cornbread grew earnest. "You think he be screamin' 'bout he'pin' *you* if you was layin' in the grass all shot to shit? You think he wanna crawl pas' all them gooks, get his ass shot off to he'p *you?*"

Cannonball mulled Cornbread's assertion, growing serious. "Ahhh. Senator, man, he was jus' talkin'. Senator doan' do shit except he talk, you know, like he really give a shit. But you got it wrong, man. You ain' been out here long enough. Rest of us, we *tight* out here. Ain' nobody goan' treat you different. Ain' nobody goan' let you die."

Cornbread's round face grew lively. He came to his knees, looking to his left and right to ensure no one would overhear him. "*Aw*, man! You think they try an' he'p Rap Jones when he was hit up at Hue City? You think they try to come out an' he'p Homicide when he hit in the head out in the Arizona? Shee-it. They goan' let you die, be glad of it. One less Brother they goan' have to fight, come the Revolution. *Ah* ain' goan' let that happen to 'me, man. Uh-uh. Ah gettin' *out* o' this shit. Hey, Why you stayin'?"

Cannonball became acutely conscious of the contrast between his and Cornbread's color as he stared down at his hands. His own hands, so light they were the color of canned milk, lighter than many of the tanned whites in the platoon, lighter than the wheat color of dry grass. Cornbread's deep ebony, glistening in the swelter of noonbake, slightly adulterated from the black of pure Africa but nevertheless, very dark.

Once again the pulsing contrasts, the mixed blood that insisted on battles, both bloods a part of him, had trapped Cannonball. Inarticulably, sensually, he understood that in this war within a war, he himself was his own battleground. He swore inwardly. Shee-it. Here we go again. The man thinks Ah'm tryin' to be white because Ah ain't chasin' after Bobby Seale or somebody.

"They full o' shit, Cornbread. Rap Jones a lyin' motherfucker. An' Ah was *here* when Homicide got it. Baby Cakes run all the way out there, pick up Vitelli, tol' 'em to come back with him. Baby Cakes come back. Homicide an' Bagger lay chilly till first light. Homicide done it to hisself."

Cornbread challenged Cannonball. "*See?* How come Baby Cakes take Vitelli? He was a white motherfucker. Homicide hit in the *head,* man."

"Awwww, ma-a-an! Vitelli was *all* fucked up! I *seen* it.

He *died,* man. Homicide walk back in by hisself at first light. Him an' Bagger. They even fragged some gooks that was already dead."

Cornbread eyed Cannonball skeptically. "That ain' what Homicide tol' us in the Black Shack."

Cannonball went back to cleaning his .45 pistol. Cornbread was too far gone to convince. He shrugged. "I seen it, man. Ask Cat Man. Ask *anybody.*"

Cornbread remained unconvinced. "Anyway. I'm skyin' out o' here."

Cannonball began to reassemble his pistol. "Go 'head. Ain' nobody stoppin' you. Doan' hurt y'self, now."

Goodrich walked along the lines in his tiger shorts, his large, loose-skinned body dripping with sweat. Other than the tiger shorts, he wore only boots, his helmet, and his flak jacket. The rest of his gear was wrapped up inside his poncho. He carried it like Santa Claus over one shoulder, a great, drooping bag.

He was making the Great Migration to Bagger's hole, fifty feet away. The others in the squad seemed to studiously ignore him as he paraded past. No one called to him or chided him, the way they did when Snake sauntered along the lines. They don't like me. Oh, this is insane. And I'm hardly a third of the way through it. Four and a half months. Oh, Christ. Only two hundred and fifty-three more days of this absurdity. Goodrich felt as if he had been in the bush for years.

He observed the others. Seven left, not counting me. Snake. Ogre. Baby Cakes. Cat Man. Cannonball. Bagger. Cornbread. Where the hell is Cornbread? He watched them individually as they lounged in the midday heat. They're so damn good, at least at this, and what does it get them? This squad has the best head (Snake sat writing a terse letter), the best eyes (Cat Man browsed over a Mexican comic book), and the biggest set of balls (Baby Cakes laughed heartily at a clowning Ogre) of any sqaud in the company. And what good does it do? We take twice the casualties that even Pierson's squad, in the same platoon, takes.

Goodrich pondered that, nearing Bagger's hootch. That makes more sense than it would first appear. Who's made it out? Flaky, with his skating ricochet of a Purple Heart, now hiding somewhere in the rear, soaking every minute out of it. He'll make it. The Black Shack's occupants, from what Bagger says about them. They might get court-martialed but they aren't going to get blown away. Sergeant Gilliland, who hung up his jock and quit. He's safe. And Mark and his thousands, who refused even to expose themselves to it.

He reached Bagger's poncho hootch, still brooding over his discovery. Goodrich dropped his pack and flak jacket next to Bagger's dozing frame. Bagger rolled over, looking at him edgily. "What do *you* want, Senator?"

Goodrich experimented with a shrugging, pre-Vietnam grin. "I'm in your team now."

Bagger grunted, then rolled away. "You sure you want to take the chance?"

Goodrich sat down on his flak jacket, peering under the poncho hootch. He grinned again, feeling a rapport with Bagger's obvious misery. "Watch it, Bagger. People are going to say you're acting like me, for Christ sake."

Bagger started mildly, then peered at Goodrich, his confused face squinting. "You really know how to hurt a guy, Senator."

Goodrich felt comfortable with Bagger. No pretensions, he thought. "Yeah. Well, it was a hard thing to say."

Bagger struggled to a sitting position, his head stretching the center of the poncho roof so that it resembled a pyramid. "Sorry I been red-assing you, Senator. I got nothing against you." He pondered Goodrich. "You can be in my team. Matter of fact, you can *have* my team."

"*What?*"

"You're team leader."

Team leader. Decisions. Dealing with Snake. No way. "I can't be your team leader, Bagger. You have two months bush time on me!"

Bagger waved Goodrich off, his eyes gaunt and tired. "That don't mean a goddamn thing. I couldn't give less of a damn. I ain't telling *any*-damn-body to do *any*-damn-thing *any*-damn-more." He grunted. "I never did like it. I wish I never joined this Green Motherfucker. John Wayne. Shee-it. I ain't no military man. If you want to be with me, you gotta be team leader. Dig?" Goodrich sat stunned, unanswering. He had not escaped Baby Cakes in order to deal with Snake head-on all day, every day. "Now. I'm gonna catch some Zs. Wake me when you want me to do something."

Sleep, mused Goodrich, fretting over Bagger's snoring frame. The great escape.

There was a loud *boom* just outside Baby Cakes' hole that ripped through Goodrich's thoughts. Someone howled. OWwooo. OWwooo. In a moment, Cornbread came scampering into the perimeter, almost dancing. His head was back and he howled, as if at the moon. He lifted his knees high as he ran. Both hands were pressed against his bulbous buttocks.

He screamed again, looking warily for Snake and Baby Cakes. "Ah ain' hit! Ah ain' hit!" He raised his hands in front of him, noting gobs of blood. "Ah'm hit! Ah'm hit!"

Bagger awoke and looked out knowingly from his hootch, actually gaining strength from the weakness shown in Cornbread's actions, which were similar to what he had been contemplating for days. "That fucker fragged himself. I'll bet a month's pay."

Snake and Baby Cakes shared knowing expressions of contempt. Snake ambled up to Cornbread, who now stood in one spot, jumping up and down, still holding his buttocks. He spoke mockingly. "What happened, Cornbread? Some gook do you out there?"

Cornbread bounced, looking straight ahead. "Ah doan' know, man. Ah was out there fixin' to take a shit an' all of a sudden it went off. *Boom!*" He glanced at Snake. "Coulda been a gook, Ah jis' doan' know." He noticed Snake's grimace. "Probly was a booby trap, though."

Snake folded his arms, peering sagely up at Cornbread. "Well, I guess we better go out in the weeds and find the trip wire so we can call in a Booby Trap Report. Where were you when it went off, Cornbread?"

Cornbread was being cool now. Rabbit was dressing his wounds, and had indicated he would be medevacked. "Shee-it. Ah doan' remember, Snake-man. Ah was walkin' so fast. It happen so quick. An doan' know."

"Where'd you drop your E-tool?"

Cornbread's face went startled for a quick moment. He peered sideways at Snake. "Say what?"

"Your E-tool. How were you gonna take a shit without

digging a cat hole with your E-tool?" Cornbread was
thinking hard. "You weren't just gonna shit on the grass
out there and smell up the whole squad area, were you?"

Cornbread had it. He grinned slightly. "Oh, yeah, Ah
jis' can't remember every time. Ah probly woulda come
back in an' got it when Ah got to where Ah was goan' dig
the hole."

Snake shrugged helplessly. Don't Do No Good. "Hell of
a place for a booby trap. Out here in all this grass."

The medevac was on its way. Cornbread suppressed a
pained grin. "Yeah, man. That's jis' what Ah was thinkin'."

Cornbread walked stiff-legged toward the landing zone
to await the medevac. He passed Cannonball and
clenched his fist, smiling slyly through pained lips.

"You be careful, hear?"

Cannonball clenched his own fist perfunctorily, then
smiled and shook his head. "Doan' worry 'bout me. *You*
stay outa trouble, man."

Cornbread chuckled, speaking rapidly to Cannonball, as
if he were deeply humored. "Ma-a-an, they want stupid
niggers, they'd all *pay* to see a dumb-ass nigger. That's all
right. Ah ain' goan' get in any trouble. Ah'm too *dumb* to
get in trouble!"

26.

CANNONBALL

A thin, winding strip of asphalt, choked with roadside
weeds. Wide, flat fields of tobacco. In late summer the
fields would go all golden, as if the plants were throwing
back the sun into the sky, and the mule carts would wind
along the rows, he and two brothers turning leaves, starting at the bottom of the plants. Later they were hung to
dry inside a paintless shed.

His mama. Junk Lady Washington, they called her.
Fat, warm, and freckled. A laughing, religious mix of

Indian and African and white, narrow-nosed and thin-lipped. She worked homes in a nearby town and her employers had a habit of giving her the items they no longer needed, always assuming she did not have enough, until eventually one entire room of their tiny house was so filled with furniture and old vaccum cleaners and small appliances and clothes that they could not use it. The room became the supply point for the whole rural neighborhood, and Mama became Junk Lady. She never threw a thing away. Somebody might be needing.

He wasn't the first to go. The Army had already ruined his brother. That was what his mother maintained. His brother had been drafted three years earlier, and had left home, excited and ambitious, filled with dreams of marching and spit-shined shoes and discipline, and had come back with hot stares and angry words, out early on a discharge he had been too embarrassed to define. Ruined, Junk Lady had maintained, crying. His brother had stayed at home for a month and then moved to the city. Washington or Baltimore, he had said, although he had not written or called since. His brother's words had been so ambiguous, so filled with hate for the Army and the officers and whites in general, that it had been impossible to discover what had happened. His mother had finally decided that it was the Army. And when it came his time to go, he wanted no part of an Army that had so destroyed his brother.

On Sundays there was church. He needed it. The world was changing so rapidly, every week a new advancement and a new crisis, that he could not comprehend his place in it. Black people marching. He saw it on the television, and heard about it on the radios. He could feel it. Five years before, if he had not called some people "sir" they would have been after him. Now, those same people seemed embarrassed when he called them that.

It was too much to digest and he needed the Reverend's words. He would sit and watch the man's intense, sweating ebony face, the black eyes reaching for him, the rich baritone words speaking about the Lord and he would feel his spirit move right up there with the Reverend and he would just have to say Amen. It wasn't because anybody else said it, everybody else said it because the Reverend had reached down inside them, too.

The man would talk about the Lord but he was talking about the People, too, and Roland needed that. The Reverend wasn't anybody's man but his own self and he wasn't anybody's servant except God's and the African Methodist Episcopal Church's.

The Reverend dug Martin Luther King early on and he told his people the right way to be on that, too. He would scorn Cleaver and Carmichael and Brown from the pulpit. "There's only one race," the Reverand would sing, "and that's the human race. And what you got when you burn down the ghetto? You got a burned-down ghetto." Amen.

It was the Reverend who advised him to enlist in the Marine Corps. He had received his draft notice shortly after turning eighteen, and had been terrified of the Army. His mother had wept off and on for a week. "I don't want you goin' in no Army," she had moaned, remembering his brother. And there was only one person who could tell him how to be.

The Reverend had grabbed him by the shoulders, and he could feel the power flow into him. Those warm black eyes had owned him. "You don't need to do no runnin'," the Reverend had intoned. "You don't like the Army, well, go sign up for somethin' else. You go be the best one there, my man, and you ain't gonna be in any trouble. You can do it. You can be the *best*."

But it wasn't the Army. He learned that quickly. It was the Revolution. In boot camp, there were small hints of the problems that had ruined his brother. In infantry training they had blossomed. In Vietnam's rear areas they had exploded. Group reactions to discipline. Group hates. Group concessions. The merry-go-round was spinning full-speed. Be a Brother or face the risk of being alone, rejected by both groups.

What you got when you burn down a ghetto? A burned-down ghetto. What you got when you hate everybody but yourselves? Hate machines.

27.

Villages survived on Go Noi, great wasted remnants of the old towns that once sprawled thick and wide as railroad stops in French times, now flattened and redone in thin, scattered groups of humpbacked hootches where the remnant families hid from what it had all become. Stone pagodas stood here and there, left over from the railroad days, now pockmarked with machine-gun memories and broken by dead bombs. When the railroad ran, the stone was cheap and each village built its own pagoda. Now the railroad bridge was a blackened memory and the wooden track ties held up the insides of family bunkers and the stone pagodas died a little bit each battle.

And the most notable remark that one could make of Go Noi was how fine the family bunkers were, with railroad-tie supports.

The villages began just beyond the first great sea of elephant grass. From that point they twined and intermingled with the grass, like islands. They were as bleak, as desolate and deprived, as the Arizona. The shattered, dirt-floor hootches appended to a mound of earthen bunker, surrounded by uprooted trees and huge pocks of rended earth, populated by motionless, staring zombies, permeated with trains of scurrying rats. Experiencing them was as enriching, as stimulating, as strolling through the empty, blackened caverns of the moon.

But better than the killer grass. It was a relief to reach the villages and walk their relative openness. The hootches and the mamasans, the pecking chickens and the wire-haired, ugly dogs, struck comforting chords, even in their misery. They were recognizable, familiar sights.

For three weeks the company wound slowly through the villages, across more sawgrass fields, and through still other villages, searching absently for some sign of Phu Thuan, looking more closely during the days for some corner that had good fields of fire, where they could spend the night.

On this day, Third Platoon had Tail-End Charlie. No big trip, as Ogre said. They sauntered along mindlessly at the rear of the column, confident that all danger was well forward of them, that any initial contact would be made by the point. Tail-End Charlie was a skate.

For all but Cat Man. He was in such harmony with the subtleties of combat, was such a natural master of those things that others had to struggle to assimilate and use, that he would have had to force himself not to prowl. He walked with his head slightly tilted, his sensuous, small-boned face constantly in motion, examining bends and crevices, piles of litter around hootches, contours of bomb craters. The regularities of even devastated earth were so understandable to him that they could be suspicioned and inspected.

The village ended and a sawgrass field began again. Just at the edge of the ville, next to a bomb crater that had scooped out a deep sawgrass divot, under melted shards of earth, there was a flat-green stretch of metal. Unnatural. It just broke the surface of the earth, as if the earth were a huge brown sea and it had floated to the top like a dead fish, and now showed a small stretch of belly.

Cat Man glanced at it, then called ahead. "Hold it up."

Slowly, like an accordion expanding, the half-mile of men halted. Most of the column rested uncomfortably in the middle of the field. Sergeant Sadler moved back, and Snake forward, to where Cat Man stood.

Cat Man pointed to the smooth underbelly. "Bomb."

Sadler stared at it, and was tempted to leave it. It was late afternoon and the company would have to be dug into its new location by dark. But he knew that abandoned bombs provided explosives for grenades and booby traps to the enemy. The bomb was a 250-pounder.

Sadler decided. "We better blow it in place. I'll call up fo' the Engineers."

Snake spoke tiredly, anxious to be moving. "Let Baby Cakes do it, Sarge. He's had Mine Warfare School." Snake nodded ironically over to Baby Cakes. "Hell. That's why Top sent him back out to the bush."

Sadler shook his head decisively. "He doan' need no

two-fifty to break in on." He mulled it for a moment. "We need security back here, anyway. Leave him for security an' he can watch. He can blow the next one." There would be others. Dud rounds were scattered like toadstools on the Basin floor.

In a few moments the engineer wound his way to the rear of the column from the company command section. He walked jauntily, a cigarette dangling out of one corner of his mouth, a box of blasting caps carried in the breast pocket of his flak jacket. He carried a large green bag of explosives that swung freely under his shoulder, on a strap. He recognized Sadler and nodded nonchalantly. "Where is it?"

Cat Man pointed. The engineer walked over, knelt down next to it, and caressed its exposed parts expertly. "We'll have to dig it out a little and get a charge under it. It's pretty deep." He poked the dirt tentatively, like a surgeon examining a prospective patient, then turned to Sadler.

"Better get the company out of the way, Sarge. This thing is gonna blow up and out. I'd say two hundred, maybe two hundred fifty meters. Better get 'em out of the way now. I'll set the fuse and catch up."

Baby Cakes and a grinning, fascinated Ogre joined the engineer. Baby Cakes provided an entrenching tool. Ogre watched curiously, making periodic comments about the engineer's expertise.

"You ain't gonna blow us up, now?"

The engineer nodded importantly. "Nope."

"You sure this ain't a booby trap?"

The engineer peeped Ogre. "Nope. I ain't sure. We gotta dig it out some more."

"Well, kiss my ass! I ain't gonna stand here while you dig around any damn booby trap!"

Baby Cakes slapped Ogre on the chest. "Shut up, man. If you wanna learn how to do this, just watch the dude, O.K.? *He* ain't gonna blow us up. If you don't pay attention, next time *you* might, though. Just watch, shit-for-brains."

The company crawled forward, out of the blast radius of the two-fifty, leaving the engineer, Ogre, and Baby Cakes. Third platoon sat on the trail in the sawgrass, waiting for the three to catch up.

Five minutes. Nothing. Ten minutes. Snake peered anxiously at his watch. God*damn*. Wish they'd hurry up. Five o'clock already. We gotta find a new pos, make a perimeter, figure out night acts, dig the hell in, and *eat*, all before dark.

For a moment he cursed Cat Man's proficiency. Like Phony used to say, Old Snoop and Poop and his bent grassblades. Then he reconsidered. Cat Man was worth his weight in dope.

Boom*Boom!* Down the trail there was a large explosion, followed by a huge secondary, uninterrupted by a pause. That should do it, thought Snake. He scanned the trail. Still no Baby Cakes and Ogre. Well, he reasoned. They prob'ly found a hole next to it so they wouldn't have to trip all the way back down there if the fuse went out on 'em. Pretty good thinking.

Five more minutes. Still no Baby Cakes. Snake had become uneasy, but would not allow himself to think the gruesome thought. He fought it for a few more minutes, and then had to admit it. Christ Almighty, he grieved. They done blown themselves to bits.

Snake scampered over to Sadler. "Something's wrong, Sarge. We better get down that trail, right goddamn *now*."

The platoon mounted up and rushed down the trail, leaving the company to move to its night position without them. Two bends in the sawgrass and the village revealed itself before them. At its near edge, where the bomb had been found, the air was lightly hazed by dust and smoke. And in the air, clinging to each particle of haze, settling with the dust on grass and tree leaves, was the rich, wet aroma of recent blood.

But there were no bodies. And the bomb had not been blown. It lay ominously where Cat Man had discovered it, partially excavated toward one end, but undetonated. For a moment the whole platoon stared numbly at the empty scrape of dirt before the bomb, as if they had collectively discovered a haunted building or a ghoul itself. The undercurrent ran through all of them like a shiver: what the hell is going on?

Sadler was mystified. If it was gooks, he reasoned, there would have been a firefight. And what about the second explosion? And where the hell are *they*? He became spooked, and yelled to Snake and the other squad leaders.

"Set up security! Hurry up!"

The platoon deployed into a perimeter, and began searching out the area. There were few clues. The dirt in front of the bomb was raw, but there were no blood trails, no signs of the three men. Nor were there any mattings in the grass that might be followed.

Snake walked slowly around the grassy edges of the dirt area, massaging scraps of cloth in the fingers of one hand. The scraps clung like fuzz to the grass. In a moment Cat Man brought him a dark green strap that he had found on the other side of the bomb.

Snake approached Sadler. "I'll tell you what happened, Sarge. I'll bet my ass on it." He showed Sadler the scraps. "Some gook fragged 'em, getting ready to hit 'em, and he got a secondary off that engineer's goody bag."

Sadler pondered it, intense. It sounded logical. "So what happened to 'em? Couldn't have blowed 'em *all* to bits."

Snake calculated, his chin in one hand. "Nah. There was maybe five or six pounds of C-four in that bag, plus the man's blasting caps. Prob'ly did a royal job on the engineer. But there couldn't be any shrap metal." He looked at Sadler. "I bet it didn't do nothing but knock Baby Cakes and Ogre out from the concussion. Yup. I'll bet it didn't. And I bet those gook bastards picked up all their trash and skyed out with 'em."

Snake looked amazed, as if he had never contemplated such a fate. "Jesus Christ. They're POWs." He scanned the narrow ville, and the seas of sawgrass that ran virtually unbroken for five miles to the mountains. "Well. They can't be *very* far away. It's only been fifteen minutes. We better chase 'em."

Sadler scanned the impenetrable, unsearchable sea. "If they want to keep 'em alive, they'll take 'em to the mountains. If they don't, well—" He shook his head, still mystified by the whole occurrence. "And anyway, we better hurry." Sadler checked his watch: five-thirty. "We'll sweep on up to the edge of the ville real quick, maybe check a couple trails, too. If we doan' find nothin', we'll come back tomorrow. We'll call Division, too." He noted Snake's disappointment. "I'm sorry, Snake-man. That's all we can do."

"Hey, Sarge, you better come over here!" Wolf Man, from guns, held up a helmet. He and Cronin were straddling an unviewable object in the sawgrass. "It's the engineer. He is *all* fucked up."

The god of night pulled his shade across the sky, unleashing all his demons as the gray set in. The platoon moved quickly down the sawgrass trail, racing him, hurrying to beat the black. The black belonged to those others, the night god's children, who frolicked, even murdered under the romance of starbright. Night for the platoon was hiding time, time to dig deep holes and wait in fear for the loneliest of deaths, the impersonal, shattering projectile that would just as soon kill tree or air as man. In their middle, dragged between two poles, was the mangled body of the engineer. Back in the village, or in the grass, or maybe only in their memories, were the other two. No trace of them was found. Ogre and Baby Cakes had evaporated.

The next morning two platoons from the company searched the village, hootch by hootch, and followed the trails toward the mountains. They found nothing. Word was passed to all operating units in the area to be on the lookout for signs of the two men. There was no immediate response. Helicopters and observation aircraft patrolled, swooping low, seeking possibilities inside the sawgrass. There were none. Baby Cakes and Ogre had vanished. It would take a miracle to find them.

In the company perimeter the squad gathered at Snake's hootch, as if summoned, upon its return from the exhausting, many-houred patrol. Snake sat in the grass next to his poncho hootch, smoking a cigarette, mechanically throwing a bayonet knife into the dirt. He would throw it into the dirt, look at it for a frowning, contemplative moment, then slowly retrieve it and repeat the process. The others sat, stripped to tiger shorts or utility trousers, shirtless, watching him. Bagger drank thirstily from a canteen. Cat Man lit a smoke.

Finally Snake threw the knife hard. It entered the dirt up to its hilt. He took a long drag on his cigarette, and surveyed the four men who were left in his squad. Cat Man, sitting stolid as a gook, deeply upset because another of his discoveries had gone afoul. Cannonball, sweating profusely from the patrol, now drinking the remainder of Bagger's canteen. Bagger, his face completely drained, looking as if he had lost twenty pounds over the past three weeks. And Goodrich, nervous, egocentric even at this moment, fretting over an ulcerous gook sore on his arm. All of them, each in his own way, awaiting Snake's wisdom.

Snake picked the knife up again and studied it as he spoke. "We been together a long damn time. And we're all that's left." Names and faces flashed in every mind, unspoken. All the dozens that had poured through the conduit, now down to five. Drop by drop, drained down to this sediment, these exhausted dregs. We're all that's left. Out here, forgotten but for momentary hurricanes of helicopters, left to be killed or maimed, dreg by dreg, for the honor of possessing Trailbend or Banana Clump or nothing.

Snake lit another cigarette. No one said anything. "We can't leave Baby Cakes and Ogre out here." The tenor voice was soft, reasoned, modulated, but filled with underlying strength. "Baby Cakes ran straight at ten damn gooks to try and save Vitelli. Baby Cakes would *still* be out there looking for *you*." He stared at each man. Each man nodded self-consciously, agreeing. "Well. As long as there's a chance, we gotta try and find 'em."

Cat Man shook his head bitterly. "It's my fault, man. I always see too many things. I see bananas and Phony gets blown away. I see a bomb and Baby Cakes is gone. I should never see these things. It don't do no good to try, man. I quit. I don't try no more."

"It ain't your fault, Cat Man. Don't let it get you down."

Bagger eyed Snake hesitantly. "Well, what can we do? We're only five damn people."

Snake threw the knife back into the dirt. "We been on Go Noi almost a month. Company's pulling out of here tomorrow or the day after. We gotta get another look at that ville, maybe talk to the mamasans and babysans. If we can get some good scoop outa somebody, we might be able to help find 'em." He scanned the group again. "Who knows? They just might be out there in the weeds somewhere."

Bagger shook his head negatively. "No way. We can't do that by ourselves."

"Sure we can. If Sadler and the Skipper will let us. Matter of fact, it might be the *only* way to do it. We'll take us a little killer team out there tomorrow, just at first light. Take Dan with us so we can talk to the villagers. That'll be six people. We can really snoop around with six dudes. Any less than that, we might be hurting if we get hit." Again he peered at each man with the intense stare. "Is everybody in?"

They mulled it silently. Goodrich was incredulous. The man is absolutely crazy, he marveled. Six people out there? *Whatever* happened to Baby Cakes and Ogre, it's clear that whoever did it had their shit *together*. They'd eat us up.

Help me, Senator. No, no. They can't even be alive. A full day. No sign of them. We took that ville apart today.

I'm only nineteen.

All right, all right. If somebody else says they'll do it, I'll say I will. I'm not a leader. I could fuck up a wet dream.

You're just waiting for me to die.

"All right. I'm in. I'll do it."

Snake's eyebrows raised in mild amazement. "Senator? All right."

Cat Man and Cannonball measured each other, then nodded affirmatively.

Bagger studied Snake, and then the others. "What if we get hit. *Huh?* What if we get ambushed on the trail, like when Wild Man got it? What if they hit all of us coming into the ville? What can six people—" He considered Dan "—five people and a goddamn *gook*—what can they do?" He snorted. "I think it's crazy."

Cannonball measured Bagger, his head tilted unbelievingly. "Ma-a-an, am I hearing you right? You was goan' *kill* Rap Jones just 'cause he wouldn't let you see Homicide. Homicide was only a little fucked up. These dudes are *dyin'*, man! What'sa matter, Bagger? You doan' like white folks?"

Bagger felt his anger rise, then realized that Cannonball was attempting to affirm his friendship. He nodded, won over. "Rap Jones just pissed me off, man." He pondered that. "I'll just have to get pissed off at the gooks that took Baby Cakes and Ogre." He thought another moment, convincing himself, almost forgetting his fear. "Goddamn it, I *am* pissed off at those gook motherfuckers!" He looked back to Snake. "O.K. You're right. It's the only way. We owe it to 'em."

Snake retrieved the knife and held it tightly, his mouth set in a rigid line. "Good. I knew none of you dudes would flake out on me. We been tight too long. I'll clear it with Sadler and line up Dan."

He brightened slightly, his face fiercely determined. "Tomorrow we find Baby Cakes."

Along the trail the sawgrass whispered with their passing, stroked them at the trailbends, leaned out and brushed them with every breath of wind. They walked quickly, unspeaking, knowing each other's tendencies and movements after months of naked closeness, one body that had six parts in perfect, conditioned harmony. The fog clung to them, making morning as isolated and personal as night.

At last they reached the village. It did not suspect their presence as it would a company, or even a platoon. They crept along its edge, past the place where Baby Cakes and Ogre had melted into nowhere, walking toward the gathering of hootches. The hootches sat like visions in the mist, emanating rancid, moist smoke from their cook fires, ammoniated, dung-filled mud from waterbull pens, ashen death from inside the thatch. Somewhere a papasan was puffing on a twist of tobacco. Faint whiffs of it floated across to them.

They left the trail without command and walked a wet grass field, coming into the first hootch from behind, around its family bunker. Its inhabitants, a papasan of perhaps forty-five and a somewhat younger mamasan, were genuinely startled. The Marines filled their thatch porch and they sat motionless, panicked eyes peering toward the next hootch, looking for an avenue of escape.

Snake turned to Dan, who watched the villagers solemnly. "Tell 'em they help us, they won't get hurt."

Dan translated. The expressions of the Vietnamese did not change. Snake pulled out a picture of Baby Cakes, taken months before out in the Arizona. He showed it to the terrified papasan, and employed a sort of sign language as he talked. "Couple days ago. Right out here. Him and another dude, took away by the NVA. Understand V.C.? *Khong biet?* O.K. Where'd they take 'em?"

Dan translated again. He was already becoming angry. He sensed that the man knew exactly what Snake was talking about. He also sensed that the man was not going to help, no matter what he knew. The man's eyes peered straight into Dan, seemingly inoffensive, but asking him a harsh, unarticulated question with their very passive resistance. Why do you fight for them? Why do you help kill us?

"*Khong biet.*" the man answered.

Dan spoke rapidly, his flash of anger surprising even Snake. "I know you are lying to me," Dan responded. "If I find out you were lying I will kill you. You have one more chance. What happened to them?"

The man was terrified, but his eyes continued to peer coldly through Dan's. He shrugged, a seemingly helpless gesture. "I do not know. Sometimes there are VC. Sometimes there are Marines. But I do not see VC with Marines."

Dan appeared furious. Snake grabbed him by the shoulder and smiled to the papasan. "O.K., Papasan."

He asked Dan softly, "Is he lying, Dan? Papasan bullshit Marines?" Dan nodded, breathing quickly, upset by the confrontation, the battle over hostages, that reminded him of his own loss to the VC.

Snake ignored the papasan for one second, then turned quickly, striking him in the face with the back of his hand. Papasan's head jerked madly from the blow.

Snake walked to him, showing him the picture again. "Now, motherfucker. Take a good look. *O dau*, huh? Where'd they go?"

Papasan talked quickly, his hands at his shoulders in a helpless shrug. On and on he babbled, motioning with his hands, pouring out his frustrations.

Finally Goodrich cut him off. He rubbed his own face, peering uneasily down the village trail. He was wishing he had not come on the patrol. He wanted to hurry up and end it. He felt certain they were going to be ambushed if they stayed out very long.

"Come on, Snake. We're out here to find Baby Cakes,

not to beat on gooks. If you think he knows something, let's take him back with us and send him in."

Snake still stared angrily at the papasan, who was eyeing Goodrich hopefully. "And what the fuck good would *that* do, Senator? He'd be interrogated for three days and we'd be outa here tomorrow or the next day and Baby Cakes and Ogre would be God knows where by then. Nope." Snake peered intently at the men. "He knows *something*. Dan says so."

Goodrich grimaced, nervous and unimpressed by Dan's conclusions. "How the hell does he know?"

"That fucker just *knows*, man. If you grew up with gooks you'd know, too." Snake pondered it. "Oh, well. It might be better to let him think he's off the hook and then come back to him. But we'll have to sneak up on him, or he'll sky out. Let's go peep the others." Snake winked to Dan, giving him a reassuring grin. "Tell him 'thanks.' Tell him I'm sorry I hit him."

Dan stared coldly at papasan, translating. Papasan was still wary, but visibly relieved. He nodded quickly, nursing the side of his head. The killer team departed, moving to the next hootch.

Bagger motioned back toward papasan's hootch as they left. "You know what I don't like about him? He ain't *old*." He asked Dan in a hoarse whisper. "He VC, Dan?"

Dan pondered it, and answered judiciously: "Mebbe."

There were more than a dozen hootches scattered through the ville. The squad crept up on each one, interrogating villagers, showing them the picture of Baby Cakes, seeking information. They found none. Each villager was properly, almost dutifully fearful of them, but none volunteered information. Several hours passed. They probed the outer reaches of the village, following trails into the grass, looking for clues that did not exist.

Finally Snake had had enough. He tilted his helmet back and addressed Cat Man. "I say we go back and pick up old papasan and take him to the scene, man. Go over where they were blowing the bomb and walk out in different directions and play Hot and Cold. You know, peep him out, see what scares him. That old dude knows *something*."

Bagger agreed. "He ain't old. I'll bet he's a gook. No shit."

They crept back toward the first hootch at the other end of the ville. Papasan sat on his porch, rocking on his haunches, smoking. He saw them approach when they were about fifty feet away, and rose as if to run.

Snake called to him. *"Dung Lai,* motherfucker! You ain't going *any*where." Papasan froze resignedly. Running was for younger men. He was too old to make it to the sawgrass.

Cat Man grabbed him. Snake walked up. "You come with us." He noticed the mamasan, who was surveying them with a suspicious bitterness. "You come, too, you old hag. C'mon! *Lai day!"* Mamasan howled, complaining as she walked out from her porch to join them. "Shut up, bitch."

Bagger squinted at her. "She's a gook, too. How come she's got no kids? I'll bet she's a damn nurse or something."

Cannonball took her hands and turned them palms up. "Look at this shit, man! She ain' even got a callus! Not one damn rough spot on her hands! She ain' no mamasan. Bagger's right. I'll bet she's a damn NVA nurse!" He lifted her lips. She tried to turn her head away, staring hotly at him. He slapped her hard on the cheek, raising an immediate welt, then pulled her upper lip again. "Look at these teeth, ma-a-an. She ain' even chewed betel nut! How can she live out here an' not chew betel nut? Ain' no way, man. She's a goddamn nurse."

Snake called to Dan, then pointed to the woman. "She VC?"

Dan walked slowly to her, examining her as he approached. The skin too white, too unpocked to have survived for forty years on Go Noi. The hair pulled into a villager's bun, but almost rich, not as coarse. The eyes, surveying him with an intelligence, a knowing hotness that understood more than a suffering mamasan could ever comprehend.

He reached for her breasts. She intercepted his hands. He hit her hard in the face, then continued his quest. He stared directly into her eyes, feeling the breasts, remembering his own wife's withered set, even before she bore him children and drained herself to sustain them. Too much milk. She has eaten too well when younger, thought Dan. She is not a villager. She could not be from Go Noi.

Dan continued to stare directly into her eyes as he spoke. "She VC. Fucking A, uh huh. No shit."

Goodrich, already fearful of being ambushed, was becoming uneasy with the increasing anger of the other squad members. It had become worse with every frustrated attempt to gather information. He wanted out. If he had thought he could make it safely, he would have bolted from the patrol and made his own way back to the company. But the mile of killer weeds . . .

He attempted to speak calmly. "Look. Let's take them back, so some trained interrogators can work on them. I *know* the company will stay another couple days if we get something out of these people. Come on. Let's get the hell out of here. I'm getting flaky."

"You been flaky all your life." Snake walked slowly over to the papasan and stared coolly at him. "We're right on the verge, Senator. I ain't leaving now. Look at him. He's shaking like a drunk with the DTs." Snake laughed shortly, remembering mornings with Old Bones. "Fucker looks like my old man." He felt the man's muscles. "Bagger's right. You're a gook, all right. Har-r-r-d-core. So's your old lady. *You VC*, huh?"

The man shook his head frantically, and produced a *can cuoc* identification card. Snake laughed. "Ohhh, good thinking, Papasan. Even got yourself a *can cuoc*." He slapped the man on the back of the head. "Oh, I'll bet my *ass* you know where Ogre and Baby Cakes are. I'll just bet my *ass*."

The hootch was at the end of the village. It was the nearest living space to where the incident had occurred. Snake pushed the papasan toward the spot where Ogre and Baby Cakes disappeared. The others followed. Cannonball prodded the mamasan with his rifle barrel. She now frowned tightly, her face rigid with hate. They stood at the spot for a few moments, Dan pumping both captives with acid, angry questions. Neither showed a revealing emotion.

Snake stood in the parched earth where the engineer's explosive bag had erupted, totally stumped. He examined the faces of papasan and mamasan. They both wore masks: mamasan, cold and hating, daring to be disgusted, as a woman may. Papasan, attempting to acquiesce just enough to survive the interrogation, shrewdly misunderstanding the harder questions. *"Khong biet,"* said papasan, over and over. *"Khong biet."*

Finally Snake grabbed papasan by the nape of the neck and pushed him back toward his hootch. "Come on, Luke. We gonna take a look around your house." They walked back in their cluster, once again through the back way.

Cat Man noticed it first. Just the slightest drop. There in the soft dirt of a corrugated potato patch, the rows perfectly aligned, the powdery gray dirt holding wilted sticks that jutted out crookedly toward the baking sun. Two dips, like saddles, where the rain of the night before had settled the dirt. Unnatural.

Cat Man walked into the patch and stood before the dips. The dirt of the dips was wetter than the other portions of the patch. It slumped, cracked at the top from having settled.

Snake squinted, walking toward the hootch. "Whatcha got, Cat Man?"

Cat Man stood silently, glaring at the dirt, not wanting to accept the possibility, yet vibrating from its very feasibility. "Get a shovel."

Goodrich searched the hootch and found a spade, his own insides electrified. He jogged out and handed it to Cat Man. The others moved solemnly to where Cat Man stood. Cat Man extended the shovel to papasan. "Dig."

Papasan eyed the dirt warily. He feigned ignorance again. *"Khong biet—"*

Cat Man, the calm one, exploded. He kicked the man in the ass, then swung his rifle butt and struck him in the head. The man cowered in the dirt, his hands before his face. Cat Man grabbed him by the shirt and lifted him off the ground and shook him mightily, swearing at him in Spanish. He threw him back to the dirt, dealing him several kicks in the stomach, then picked up the shovel and threw it at him.

"Cabron! Hijo de la chingada! Dig!"

Papasan bled slowly at the edge of the welt the rifle butt had made on his head. He eyed Cat Man fearfully, fetched the shovel, and began to dig in the wrong place. Cat Man exploded again, rushing the man, striking him again in the head with his rifle.

"You mother*fucker! Here! Do* you think we are *blind?*"

Papasan comprehended. He bled doubly from his head, slow rolls of red that oozed down his neck and disappeared along the ridges of his back muscles. He walked to the first low place in the dirt, eyed Cat Man one final, petrified time, and lifted out spadefuls of earth.

The others also comprehended, and were silent.

Scoop by scoop the earth revealed a long prone form, lying facedown underneath a row of plants, stretched comfortably as if at rest. He still wore his flak jacket. The helmet was gone, as were his pack and weapon and all ammunition. The waves of blond hair were matted and black in the back of the head, and strangely flat.

Bagger leaned down and began to turn the body over, then recoiled at its rigidity. Finally he took a shoulder, and Cannonball the boots, and they lifted Baby Cakes out of the ground as if he were a board. They rolled him onto his back, and Bagger gagged. Baby Cakes' skin was tawny, as if burnt in a frying pan. His eyes were gone. Squarely in the middle of his forehead was a bullet hole. The matted black behind his head was where the bullet had blown the back of his head away.

Papasan was digging out the other body, now anxious to appear cooperative. In a few minutes Ogre lay comfortably inside his own shallow grave. Goodrich and Cat Man rolled him out. He also had been shot in the forehead. His handmade peace symbol still hung on his dog-tag chain. Ogre grinned an eyeless, ironic grin.

Snake stood with Dan and the mamasan, waiting. Mamasan appeared absorbed in papasan's effort. She did not look at the bodies. Snake glared at papasan, who now stood alone with his shovel. He spoke calmly, his face seething with murderous rage. "You motherfucker. You piece of shit."

Papasan raised his hands in another futile gesture, babbling to Snake. He finished, looking expectantly to Dan. Dan spoke disgustedly, his breast heaving with emotion. "He say, not my fault. He say VC *bac-bac* Ogre, Baby Cake, make him bury. He say, no VC. He say, mebbe mamasan VC."

"So he says it wasn't him, huh? So it was his buddies. Oh, I'll bet he really laughed his ass off to see two Marines get shot between the eyes. I'll bet he really got his rocks off. Well. We're gonna send your buddies a little message."

Goodrich looked up, nauseated from staring at the decaying forms that once were Baby Cakes and Ogre, and comprehended what Snake's "message" would be. He started, standing quickly, his eyes going round. "Ohhh, no. Let's get *out* of here. We found 'em. Let's get back."

"We'll be leaving in a minute. Senator."

"I came out here to find Baby Cakes, not to kill civilians. *No.*"

Bagger erupted. "I said all along that motherfucker was a gook. He just *looks* like a gook." He walked up to the man. "Yeah. Well, we ain't letting you get away with *this*, sweetheart." He grabbed papasan by the neck and bent him down over Ogre's body. Papasan resisted, but Bagger possessed massive strength. He bent papasan nearer and nearer, until the man's bleeding face was only inches above Ogre's corpse. "Yeah. Take a *good* look, gook. You think we should let you go after *that?*"

Goodrich took off his helmet and rubbed his fleshy face with one hand. "*No!* Don't do it, man."

"You don't care, do you, Senator?" It was Cat Man, still so angry he was flushed, trembling. "It don't bother you that they done that to 'em."

Guilt. Goodrich admitted inwardly that his greatest emotion at seeing the bodies was repulsion, a wish to be done with them, to get back to the perimeter and be away from them. And irritation that carrying them back would increase the chance of ambush.

"It does bother me. Just not enough to kill civilians."

"They *ain't civilians*, fucker!" Bagger.

"You didn't even like Baby Cakes. You couldn't wait to get out of his team. You thought Ogre was an ass. I seen you, Senator." Snake glared through him with razor eyes.

Goodrich felt himself backing away. They had all turned on him. "That wouldn't matter. I mean, it's not true, but it wouldn't matter, even if it was."

"We been baby-sitting you *too long!*" Snake grew fierce.

Cannonball smiled curiously. "You doan' like to kill, Senator? Ol' Senator, so goo-o-oood an' smar-r-rt. He doa'n like to kill. You killed Burgie, Senator. You sat on yo' fat ass two feet away from the man an' let him die. I *seen* it." Cannonball lost his smile. "Mebbe you only like to kill Marines. These gooks friends o' yours, Senator? You like what they did."

Help me, Senator. "Oh, for Christ sake! *Leave me alone!* Just leave me alone."

"Cannonball." Snake called them off. "Well, Senator. We're gonna do what we think we have to. You do what you think you have to. If you don't like this, leave."

Leave. Killer weeds. A mile. "You know I can't."

"Then go up by that hootch." Snake ignored him now. He instructed Dan and Bagger. "Put 'em in the same graves they put Ogre and Cakes. Make 'em lay down."

Goodrich walked quickly away. He heard Snake count behind him.

"One."

He went under the thatch porch and sat, looking out at the fields of sawgrass.

"Two!"

I'm in hell. I'm being punished. How did this ever happen to me?

The mamasan yelled something. Dan yelled back. Shots cut through the heavy air. A lot of shots. Goodrich held his head. He felt wronged, humiliated. He had told them not to and they had not listened.

Goodrich did not return to the grave sites. He waited for them in the hootch. They worked in the field for a few minutes. He could hear them conversing. He heard the spade pitch dirt. Then they returned to the porch. They were somber, spent, like after making love. Dan smiled faintly.

Only Snake spoke to Goodrich. "You keep your mouth shut, Senator. Know what I mean?"

They tore sections off of the thatch porch and made two sledlike stretchers. Baby Cakes was loaded onto one of them, Ogre onto the other. Then they wound slowly back through sawgrass fields, two men pulling each stretcher like somber pallbearers, a gut-wrenched funeral procession that had avenged the murders of its kin.

And, when they returned, the Spot Report to regiment read: 2 VC KIA.

28.

CAMP HANSEN, OKINAWA

Hodges stood at the base of the low, flat hill and felt a dry, insistent wind confront him as he stared up at the Officers' Club. He stood uneasily in the raw wind, no longer used to the elements after a month of Japanese hospital beds and wards, and questioned reality again.

Am I *really* on my way back to Vietnam?

It was a difficult truth to accept, after all the days of shots and probing rods and gouging scalpels, all the doctors peering over him as if he were a specimen on a book page or pickled in formaldehyde, all the pain. He thought of the days of warm floating and then falling into valleys of excruciating pain. Days when warm and pain were the total conscious focus, his mind nothing but an image on the ceiling, and thought could not be considered. Only little blurbs flashing through, like a slide show on the ceiling. Booby trap. Rabbit over him, dripping sweat into his face. Blood gushing from his arms and through his trousers. Picture faded. Booby trap. Grandma's lips are set, her eyes in tears. We all so proud of you. Picture faded. Booby trap. Picture of father, cap at a cocky angle, footlocker behind it. *I'm not afraid.*

Then pain would chase the slide show off the ceiling, leaving only red throbs that flashed from behind his eyebrows. Warm and pain and uninvited slide shows. It was terrible and he felt he could not go through it again.

But dreading it was not that easy. He had developed a numbing ambivalence that prevented him from feeling any real bitterness about being sent back. He enjoyed his status as a wounded infantryman. He missed the people in the bush, more than he had ever missed any group of people in his life. There was a purity in those relationships that could not be matched anywhere else. A person's past was irrelevant, unless it affected his performance. A person's future was without exception bright: the Great Reward for doing battle awaited all of them in the World. There was a common goal, and a mutual enemy. And the stakes were high enough to make each minor victory sweet, each loss a cause for grief.

Hodges scratched his head, climbing the hill. I hate it. It's terrible. It's destructive. Nobody gives a rat's ass whether any of us live or die. They've sold us out back in the World. It makes me cry every time somebody gets screwed up. The damn civilians are all VC. It's so stupid any more I can't believe it.

But *damn* it, I can't wait to show Snake my scars.

Nothing in the Club had changed and that alone reminded him of how different he had become. He entered through the game-room doors and watched anxious young Lieutenants drink and play pool and shuffleboard. The electric tension of the uninitiated dominated all their motions.

Not young, he thought. They were his age. Merely different. Green. The thin green line, he mused, allowing himself a small grin. He had met several of them, had even allowed himself a war story or two, but he did not yet enjoy exploiting their greenness. He would fly back to Da Nang with them. The bush was still too real, too much a killer to be laughed at. He liked the honored place his scars and experience accorded him, but most of all he found them naive and boring.

He walked through the dining area, heading for the bar. He quickly scanned the tables, searching for her, but it was midafternoon and the dining area was empty. He moved into the bar area, nodding to the scattered groups of men at the tables, and sat alone at the bar.

He bought a bourbon-and-water and tipped it straight up, draining it quickly. He bought another and sipped it slowly, waiting for the buzz to hit him. It was his greatest solace. His tongue and lips went numb, then his face. He bought another drink. He was watching himself in the mirror, but he was seeing Vietnam. He felt vaguely like a wounded cock being re-razored and tossed back into the dust arena. His only option was to win another fight, for the glory of the owner, or to die.

And yet . . . And yet. Once the cock gets the taste of

it, mused Hodges, you may as well throw him back into the arena. He isn't good for anything else because the fight is in his blood.

And he missed them. He missed the abrasive, deeply dedicated companionship of Snake. He wondered about the misguided antics of Wild Man and Waterbull, and whether anyone had heard from Phony. He even missed the complaints of Bagger, and the morose lamentations of Goodrich. It was all a part of it, he reasoned, drawing on his fourth bourbon-and-water. It all made the whole thing.

He addressed his drunken image in the mirror. The image stared searchingly back at him as he spoke. "I hate it. Goddamn it, I *hate* it. But I miss it."

He could see the dining area through the mirror, and presently he noticed the waitresses begin to prepare tables for dinner. Their way of walking was no longer entrancing to him. Rather, it appeared timid, restrained. He was used to Oriental women after a month in Japan. During his last ten days in the hospital he had been an ambulatory patient, and had emptied his anxieties into a half-dozen Japanese whores.

But he had thought of her continually since his medevac to Japan, knowing he would transit through Okinawa on his way back to Vietnam. He remembered her freshness, her hesitating innocence. Her earlier reluctance was its own attraction. She was young, fresh, untainted by the spoilings of the others.

Finally she crossed the mirror, her deceptively curved body hidden by the waitress uniform, her face a study of emotional control. Her presence was a hand that lifted him from his chair and pushed him into the dining area, seeking her. He was alone and confused and she was almost an anchor, a part of his pre-horrific past. Walking toward her, he could not help but marvel at his own earlier conquest. My God, she's *dynamite,* he thought.

She was preparing a table in the far corner of the room. She saw him coming and half-smiled, as if embarrassed, then looked around herself to ensure that the other waitresses were out of earshot. Her doe eyes watched him impishly as he approached and he felt light, buoyant, a part of something clean and electric that had shot between them.

No time for formalities. Vietnam in three days. He started to take her arm and her eyes grew large and she backed away, looking around the room. "No-o-o! You *crazy?*"

He remembered. Resist. Pressure for equal time from officer observers. Image of purity. He backed away, not wanting her to feel cornered or embarrassed. "Please see me tonight."

"No can do! I got Okinawa boyfriend now." She became the slightest bit coy, straightening already straight silverware. "You say four months, you come on R & R."

To him it was an admission. "I couldn't. I was hit."

She stared curiously at him. "What is 'hit'?"

He rolled down his collar, unveiling ropelike welts of scars along his neck and lower head. He secretly reveled in her expression as she squinched her face, on the verge of nausea. Along his back was an ineradicable message that he had endured and conquered an unsharable hell. The ultimate message, mused Hodges drunkenly, that transcends all language barriers. One scar is worth a thousand wasted words.

"I'm on my way back."

"Vietnam?"

"Yeah." He shrugged helplessly, his voice a whisper. "I'm scared."

She softened, staring into gray eyes that had shone at her in the dark room months before, while he filled her insides for the first time with the stuff of love. Vietnam. Again.

"Please. Tonight."

She shook her head, upset. "No can do." He still stood nakedly before her. "Mebbe tomorrow?"

Tomorrow. No time. Tomorrow could be next year or never. The way flights into Vietnam were handled, tomorrow could be Da Nang. "No tomorrow." Hodges walked away from her, back to the bar. Got to think about it, figure it out. He felt the stares follow him, from other waitresses and officers at the bar. Screw them. All of 'em. What the hell do they know.

He sat in her area at dinner. He said almost nothing, looking dumbly at her with an empty face. Tomorrow. Bullshit. As he rose to leave he touched her arm and stopped her in one of her journeys to another table.

"I'll wait for you outside tonight." She said no again and walked away.

He sat in the dark on the fence railing, whipped by the dry, insistent breeze, thinking of the other times he had waited for her, and of the intervening months. He no longer understood himself completely and the very fence on which he sat was where he had begun to lose his comprehension.

As he dragged on his tenth cigarette she became a gliding shadow in the dark. He hopped down from the railing and stood in front of her. "Mitsuko."

She stopped abruptly, staring into him. He was unable to tell whether she was angry or merely upset. He stepped toward her and she lowered her head. "No-o-o! Boyfriend come now. Pick me up in front. You go!"

Tomorrow. No time. "Tell *him* to go." He sensed the wrong in his demand as soon as he issued it. It asked too much in the name of uncertain memories.

Remarkably, she compromised. "Come my house later. Ten-thirty. O.K.?"

He took her shoulders and kissed her full on the mouth. She kissed him back, charging him, then walked quickly away. He returned to the bar and had another bourbon and then swore it off for the night, feeling he had abandoned his only friend for her. After that he took a long, sobering walk through the camp and into the village. It was dangerous to walk alone. The camp and Kin village had spawned their own myriad of battlegrounds, shadows and bushes where violent men would gut you for the dollars in your wallet. Americans behind the gutting knives. But still he walked, quickly, impervious.

It was time. He bounded down the lighted street to her apartment, knowing the way by heart, retracing less-burdened footsteps of his former self. He knocked quietly on the door and she answered it, filling the door with a fresh innocent radiance. He stepped inside and closed the door and she looked achingly at him and asked him what he wanted but she knew what he wanted because she craved it, too. He crushed her to him and felt her breathe more quickly and then there was no need to crush her because she was holding him so tightly that he could feel her urgent pressing from knee to shoulders.

The *futon* was unfolded but it was too far away, a whole room away, and he had no time to walk it. No time. He pulled her to the kitchen floor and somehow her happy-coat was gone and he reveled in the silky tightness of her skin again, having dreamed of it so many thousand times that he had to remind himself that this was real. She talked to him in low moans and he said his only Japanese words over and over, *Ichi Ban, Ichi Ban,* and he was inside her, she was hot mercury for him. He grasped for every part of her, wanting to absorb it all, and then exploded, sobbing from spent emotion.

And then was still. They held each other tightly on the kitchen floor, the light still on, the wonderful misery of memory now a melancholy joy of rediscovery. But Hodges was already thinking of when he would leave her again, and he embraced her more tightly, a murmur deep inside him saying that he would not lose her if he somehow held her close enough.

She smiled shyly and left him for a moment and when she returned he grabbed her and wrestled her to the *futon.* They laughed, still wrestling, then abruptly she held him very tight, her face into his chest. Billows of raven hair were a blanket on his middle parts.

Then they began talking, using gestures and half-words to convey experiences and thoughts. He watched her give so much of herself merely to be understood, and was overcome by the innocent beauty of her effort. She talked to him with small words, and with her hands, and with her eyes, telling him how much she had missed him, her voice almost in awe that he was now in front of her. He grabbed her to him, grinning. Words, he decided, are so empty. *This* is what you call *communication.*

He tried to tell her about Vietnam. She was too used to Marines to fully appreciate it. She saw the combat-innocent going in, and the survivors going out. She thought it was terrible that he had been hurt, and stroked his ropelike knots of scars as he spoke, gently massaging each one, trying to rub the hurt away. But she could not appreciate all of it. He stopped talking about it. There was no way she would ever even comprehend.

She mentioned something about her Okinawan boyfriend that he did not understand, and he waved her off. "Hey. Forget the man, Mitsuko."

She laughed. "O.K."

"No, I mean *really*. You wanna get married? All right. Marry *me*."

She started to laugh and then stopped, trying to read his face. Finally she pursed her lips, her eyebrows furled, and scolded him.

"You crazy. American, Okinawan get in trouble all the time. I know. Forget it."

He lay back on the *futon*, his hands behind his head, smiling comfortably. He felt better than he had since— well, since the last time he had been with her. "Everything I've ever asked you to do, you've said no first. Then you've always done it. Do you realize that? Well, I'm gonna marry you. I just made up my mind. And I'm not gonna let a little thing like you not wanting to get in my way!"

She studied him back. She had not understood everything he said, but she comprehended that he was serious about it. Or at least believed he was. She spoke with absolute finality. "No. Can. Do. No way. You no got family tomb."

He grinned quizzically. "What the hell has a family tomb got to do with you and me?"

Slowly she explained. The family tomb was the center of worship. When one dies he is remembered at the tomb. To marry a person who had no family tomb would be to condemn yourself to an afterlife of loneliness, without memory. Parents would never allow it. And her parents' blessing was important.

She shrugged with finality, eyeing him hopefully. "Understand?"

He nodded, then lay still, pondering her explanation, trying to figure out a way around it. There's got to be a way. Finally he hit it. He remembered all the Sundays talked away with Grandma, learning of the ghosts, the trials and the sacrifices of the ones Grandma simply called "us." Right here on Okinawa, he thought. Pick a war memorial.

"Hey." He caressed a silky arm. "Tell 'em I have a family tomb. Tell 'em Camp Hansen is my family tomb. It's the biggest one on the whole damn island!" She laughed, low and velvety, thinking he was teasing her. Then he attempted to explain it. The way he was brought up. Bullets in the creek beds. Daddy in the back shed. She mulled it for a few moments, not really understanding, running her fingers gently over his recent wounds, and pulled him to her. Neither mentioned it again.

They loved again. He sought to draw out every moment, to find infinity in the passions of her womb, to cling to her and thus avoid the rawness of what awaited him. She seemed to him the rightest thing in a world gone totally wrong.

They met again the next night and he sensed that he had confused her life as nothing else had or ever could. He had made what appeared to be an absolute promise, but he did not understand the Okinawan ways. She was still uncertain of his sincerity. She did not know what to do about the Okinawan, who had been pestering her. She was afraid that her parents would condemn her.

As they talked, Hodges sensed that her parents were the key. If they gave their blessing, there would be no screams from the Okinawan suitor. If he approached the parents, she would no longer doubt his sincerity. If the parents approved, all doubts about such things as family tombs would disappear. He convinced her to trade days off with another girl. "Tomorrow," he assured her, "your parents will fall in love with me, too. How can I miss? A fine American like me."

He walked out to her apartment in the wind-blown morning air, dancing along cluttered streets that seemed so quaint and harmless in the daylight, night's gutting shadows now bright and sunstruck. They caught a taxi ride to Gushikawa City, where she had been born, and where, she explained, her parents kept a business. He held her as they rode. Watching the traffic and signs and the little cluttered shops, he remembered their first taxi ride months before and renewed his vow that, someday, he would understand it.

In Gushikawa City, the cab wound randomly along packed streets until she stopped it abruptly in the middle of a block. He looked around and saw only shops and dozens of busy people. He paid the driver and she took his hand and led him through the crowd, much as a loom weaves fabric. They walked a waving path, careful not to touch other figures on the crowded sidewalk, and he felt the faintly hostile stares from passing Okinawans. They were not happy with gold holding white. He noticed that Mitsuko was wearing the same emotionless mask that she wore while serving Marines. She ignored the stares.

She turned off the main thoroughfare into what appeared to be an alleyway. It was one lane wide, and cluttered shops overflowed onto it, narrowing it further. As they walked he was surrounded by the clutter and the closeness and he sensed that he was entering a sort of inner sanctum. It was a close, bustling world of Okinawans, untouched and unvisited by Americans, devoid of cars and bars. He was amazed, not only that it existed, but that it thrived so near to the larger arteries that he had come to know as Okinawa. Cars and jeeps ground fifty feet behind them, but this was a walking world.

She turned again, into an even narrower walkway. The shops were as small as horse stalls now. The walkway was so narrow that the roofs of the stalls almost touched across it. They walked together, she bravely squeezing his hand in the face of rejecting stares, he lowering his head to avoid occasional low rooftops, absorbing strange smells and sounds of a patch of earth unchanged by the conqueror. He perceived that, for the first time, he was seeing her people. He smelled and listened and watched and he saw the certainty in her eyes and he knew her better, comprehended all the resistance. And as he was swallowed by the odors and the darkness of the shops, he felt drawn into a netherworld.

Finally she stopped. He stood in the middle of a mass of shops and cluttered goods and people, wondering at the darkness of the open-air stalls, the only light being small shafts that crept past the angled roofs. She nodded at one of the shops then, giving him a secret smile that was a wish.

He turned and faced the shop and peered through stacks of clothes, dozens of dull colored shirts and trousers, at two narrow aisles that were perhaps ten feet deep. The aisles met in a U in the back of the shop and there was a man sitting barefoot on a low wooden platform where they met. He was smoking a cigarette and sipping green tea that steamed lazily from a porcelain teapot on the platform. And, incongruously, watching a small color television. Hodges grinned. Culture clash, even in the netherworld. Except for the man, the stall was empty.

The shopkeeper sensed Hodges' presence and hopped quickly from the platform. His narrow, wrinkled face wore an emasculated smile. He was small, gnarled, and beaten. All old Oriental men seemed like that to Hodges: the forever vanquished. He walked toward Hodges, his smile as much a mask as Mitsuko's emotionless, empty face of a few minutes before.

Then the old man saw her. He stopped and stared at their joined hands and the mask disappeared and he was no longer vanquished. He was a father more than he was a vanquished warrior. Blood, mused Hodges, is more real than flags. The man spoke low, urgent sentences to Mitsuko, his eyes alternating between the joined hands and her face. She met his gaze at first, then looked to the ground, her head lowered. But she did not let go of Hodges' hand.

Her father had ignored Hodges from the moment he saw Mitsuko. He asked a series of staccato questions and she answered with hushed acknowledgements. Rapid-fire question. Soft, velvet *"Hei."* New question. Another *"Hei."* Finally, he turned to the rear of the stall and called commandingly. A tiny lady walked through the curtain, smiled widely when she noticed Mitsuko, and then assumed a querulous mask as she listened to the staccato of her husband. She did not look directly at Hodges, either.

Hodges watched their wailings and once again sensed the intrusion he was making into lives he did not understand. The shriveled parents spoke urgent words to their erring daughter, she surprisingly docile in the face of their lamentations. She did not meet their eyes. Her answers were a soft hush. But she continued to cling tightly to Hodges' hand.

He was frozen by his lack of understanding. He did not want to increase their frustrations by forcing his presence on them, but he was not comfortable standing docilely by while Mitsuko caught the abuse that he had caused her. Finally, he compromised. He diplomatically made a low bow, his head only inches from the father's narrow chest, and held it until the man ceased talking. Then he smiled to both parents and spoke softly, cautiously, trying to avoid the casual, arrogant manner that had given his kind a bad name.

"I love your daughter very much. I will be good to her forever." They looked curiously at him, not understanding his words and still not accepting his presence. He turned to Mitsuko. "Tell them what I said." She hesitated a moment, then interpreted, still not looking at them.

They peered at Hodges, somber and unanswering. He continued, and Mitsuko slowly translated. "I've known your daughter for five months. I really love her. I want to marry her and I'd like to have your blessing."

Mitsuko squinted her nose, staring uncertainly at Hodges. "No understand 'blessing.' "

Hodges smiled, amused. The parents sensed their closeness and exchanged concerned frowns. Hodges rephrased. "I'd like to say it's O.K." Mitsuko nodded and looked at her parents as she translated, her face hoping.

Her father looked from Hodges to Mitsuko, pondering his answer. Then he spoke with what appeared to be frankness. Mitsuko translated. "How can I say O.K.? I do not even know you."

Hodges felt a roll of slight elation deep in his chest. An equivocal answer seemed to him a major victory. Then her father continued, eyeing Hodges. Mitsuko translated again. "If you marry, where you live?"

The answer to the question was so obvious that Hodges had never even considered it to be open. He was slightly amazed that her father had even asked. "America."

Her father spoke a staccato sentence and then bowed slightly, turning back to the rear of the stall. Mitsuko murmured, her eyes following her father's exit. "No can do. Daughter stay on Okinawa. Family on Okinawa."

Hodges watched the wrinkled old man curiously, amused by what he perceived to be the parody in his actions. This old shopkeeper ain't getting *my* goat that easy. Does he think he has the right to bargain over his daughter like he's selling off a hog? Does he want *money?* Hodges purged that thought. Nahh. Hell. I just don't understand these people.

Finally he grabbed Mitsuko by the elbow, startling her, and stood before her father at the rear of the stall. Her father ignored them now, pouring himself another cup of green tea. He sat down on the bench and adjusted the television set. There was a Japanese commercial on the television. I don't understand, Hodges fretted.

He bowed again, cutting the man off from his television. The father reluctantly acknowledged his renewed presence. "I'd like to get to know you. I'm gonna come back again, soon, to see you. I intend to marry Mitsuko."

Mitsuko was tense and looked to Hodges again, her eyebrows raised. "No understand 'intend.' "

Hodges put an arm possessively around her shoulder. "I'm gonna marry your little girl, Papasan."

Her father grunted, shaking his head, and ignored them.

Mitsuko went to her mother. They had a long, though quiet, discussion, their voices hushed in deference to her father, who had dismissed both the issue and them. Mitsuko and her mother wore identical pained expressions, obviously understanding each other. Hodges walked over to them and placed an arm around Mitsuko's mother and kissed her on the forehead, wanting her to accept him and instinctively caring for her. She looked down, embarrassed, then took both of them briefly into her tiny arms, assuring them of her support with the gesture, and firmly pushed them toward the entrance of the stall.

The disapproving stares were all the more real to Hodges as they walked the narrow corridors of overflowing shops and bustling people back to the main street. He grunted ironically to himself, thinking of his earlier optimism. Uh huh. A fine American like me.

And the main street seemed a highway after his brief touch with the netherworld.

They spent the rest of the day on a taxi tour of Okinawa, which Mitsuko proudly conducted. She took him to the southern end of the island, where they drove past hundreds of family tombs, shrines, and monuments. She impressed him with her pride, and her grasp of Okinawan history, awakening him in her quiet way to the realization that Okinawa really was a separate entity, which had magically survived centuries of delusions by great, ephemeral warlords that owned it.

They drove to the site of the old Shuri Castle, which had been crumbled to the dust by the big guns of Ameri-

can battleships in World War Two. In its place was a
university. The castle gate had been re-erected from the
rubble, though. Above it was the sign that had been a
part of Okinawa for four hundred years, a guidepost and
a comment: *Shurei No Kuni.* The figures were translated
by Mitsuko: "Nation of Courtesy."

She carefully explained the warlord origins of the sign,
how the Chinese dubbed them that while exacting tribute
hundreds of years before. She told Hodges of the old
double-winged castle that helped stave off destruction
when the Japanese decided they wanted to rule Okinawa,
too. Hodges marveled at the ingenuity of the old islanders
who had decided to pay two warlords tribute rather than
subject their people to a double onslaught by the two
great powers. They had even constructed two separate-
but-equal wings of the castle to receive their two masters
simultaneously. Here You Are, Sir. Your Very Own Receiving Area. Don't Worry About That Other Warlord.
Nothing To Get Upset About. Certainly Nothing To
Fight About. Especially Here On Top Of Us.

Then she took him to the Shinto shrine at Nami-no-ue,
on the bluffs overlooking Naha. She carefully explained,
painfully searching for right words and gestures, how
mothers and wives had come to pray each day during the
earlier wars, beginning with the Sino-Japanese War. It
had been the first Japanese adventure Okinawans were
called to fight in. They're new at this, mused Hodges. Less
than a hundred years.

She glanced to him shyly, her eyes on his war-scarred
neck. They prayed, she noted with hesitation, that sons
and husbands would be found unfit for military service.

No samurai on Okinawa.

Hodges watched her through all those hours and sensed
that, in her delicate, indirect way, she was telling him
something. But the power of his ghosts, all the pride that
made him Hodges, would not let him listen.

He spent the next day in a large, dim warehouse, putting
his initials on dead seabags.

The seabags came from all the reaches of Vietnam's I
Corps, to be collected in the warehouse and shipped home
in groups. Each one represented a casualty who could not

carry his own seabag away from the war, and who had preceded the seabag either in a coffin or on a medevac flight filled with the gravely wounded.

Seabag duty was reserved for officers awaiting flights into Vietnam. Sort of a—reacclimatization process, noted Hodges drily as he strode across the camp toward the warehouse where he would stand duty.

It was a boring day. Hodges sat at a field desk in the front of the warehouse, talking away the hours with supply clerks and fantasizing about that evening, when Mitsuko would get off work. Occasionally a clerk would drive up in a motorized forklift and unload one or two seabags, presenting a casualty ticket and the seabag's tag for Hodges to verify. After Hodges signed the verification, the bags were placed on shelves in the rear of the warehouse.

The huge racks of seabags behind him began to bother him as the day progressed. The forklift worked unhurriedly, yet brought him a steady stream of dead bags to join the high, long rows that loomed in the darkness to his rear.

He found himself checking the names carefully as he certified the bags, at the same time hoping that he would not have to go through the agony of certifying the bag of one of his men, or an Officer classmate from Basic School. The dead bags became dead people. The forklift was bringing him coffins. Each bag was the same on the outside, like a coffin. And each held its own collection of belongings, sizes that fit only the man who had packed the bag, individualized—like the tragic innards of a coffin. The bags pulsed with personality, and he became overwhelmed by the long, dark rows of dead men.

Dead men. Yes, that was it. He walked the rows as if he were strolling through a cemetery. The bags reached the ceiling, shelved on racks, blocking the overhead lights and making mournful shadows on the floor. Occasionally he stopped, reading the tags, noting the man's rank and unit, as if reading the inscription on a gravestone.

They had existed. They bled and died. There was no monument to their effort in Vietnam and there would be little impact back in the World outside of their own homes. But here, in the dark rows of the warehouse, they came together for a day or week, a whole room of testimony. They had once existed, and now they did not exist.

A slow month, the clerk had informed Hodges earlier. It had been a slow month while he had been in the hospital. You could tell by the seabags. And how did you die, wondered Hodges, fingering a tag. A firefight on a slow day outside Dong Ha? A mere platoon overrun in Arizona? A booby trap on a boring squad patrol near Da Nang?

He found himself reading every tag, trying to find someone he knew. He dreaded the discovery, but he felt he needed it as an affirmation. All the misery, all the blood and death. Surely it could produce one seabag out of the room of bags, one affirmation of his own endeavors. He walked faster. He reached higher. He was lost in the dark rows, swallowed by hundreds of dead bags, each carefully tagged and certified. But there was no one he knew.

Finally he gave up, and returned to the field desk. In the very mortuary of affirmation, his platoon and his friends did not exist.

"Lieutenant Hodges, reporting as ordered, sir."

"Hodges. Come on in."

"Aye, aye, sir." Hodges walked the three steps to the Major's desk, and stood at attention. The Major was the Personnel Officer. Hodges had seen him every evening at the Club, and had often discussed the Twenty-Fifth Marines operations with the Major. They had gone so far as to have dinner together on several occasions, and it was apparent to Hodges that the Major knew he was seeing Mitsuko.

The Major held a green three-by-five card. Hodges knew it was his flight card. He had watched it inch its way toward the top of the Processing Clerk's stack for a week. After having stood seabag duty, he knew he had a day, or at best two days, before he would transit back to Vietnam.

The Major tapped the flight card on the palm of one hand, contemplating Hodges. "How'd you like to stay on Okinawa?"

"Sir?"

"That's right." The Major smiled. "Jesus, Lieutenant. I thought you would have jumped over the desk by now. I'm on the level. We just had a billet open up over at

Special Services. Recreation Officer. A Lieutenant rotated early on an emergency leave. He had less than ninety days on his tour, so he'll be reassigned from the States. I have the authority to fill the billet from the transients who've been In Country already. You're ideal. Combat time, hospital time. Would you like it?" The Major jibed him, grinning. "Good duty. Lots of free time. Stick around, Hodges, and we'll turn you into a whore-mongering drunk."

Hodges smiled weakly, assessing both the Major and his offer. Why me, he wondered. What the hell does he care? Hodges thought of the warehouse filled with seabags. Rather than repulsing him, they had reinforced his own sense of guilt. He had not yet contributed enough. His platoon had endured a month, was still enduring, while he frolicked every night against the silky skin of Mitsuko.

The Major shrugged, still smiling. "What the hell. I don't think I need to explain myself, for God's sake. Take it or leave it. It just isn't often that a Personnel Officer can do something for a grunt."

Hodges stared at the card as it moved in the Major's hand. All the way from the bottom, hundreds down, to just below the top, then whisked out of the pile by the arbitrary whim of a man who had been impressed by his war stories. He found that he resented the Major's kindness, because it forced him to face himself. Until now, it had been unavoidable. But, with a simple yes, he had the power to make it all go away. A simple yes, and the war would be over.

But so would everything else, and for the first time he confronted that truth. Yes, Major, thank you, sir, and the rest of his life would be anticlimax. There was nothing on the other side. What does a man do when his war is over, wondered Hodges, except keep fighting it? All expectancies then lived, and if not fulfilled, well, at least confronted.

The bald, red hills with their sandbag bunkers, the banter and frolic of dirt-covered grunts, the fearful intensity of contact. It was too deep inside him, and he had not yet done enough to be free of it. He suddenly felt superior to the Major, a creature apart, capable of absorbing combat's horror without asking for quarter. Down South his men were on patrol, or digging new perimeters, or dying, and he was nothing if he did not share that misery.

He stared deep into the Major's face, enjoying the one moment of nobility that his months of terror had allowed. "Thanks, Major. But I didn't come halfway around the world to referee basketball games."

29.

An Hoa. A space of earth, a collection of bald clay hills. Tents and sandbagged bunkers. Guns and tanks and trucks. Strange odors of excrement and rot. People. Brickdust like red mist. At this moment so vibrant, so powerful, that it dominated the Basin. Nerve center. Possessed of guns that could reach to every hill and tree. Collector and dispenser of sustenance. Sanctuary. The Rear.

And yet tenuous, ephemeral.

An Hoa was totally American. Its tents housed Americans. Its mess halls fed Americans. Its guns killed for Americans. Its miles of barbed wire and concertina fenced Americans in, and Vietnamese of all bents out. An Hoa was a moment of total power, foreign to the brickdust soil. It sat like Troy on the bald red mounds.

They struggled up the thin road from the helicopter pad, tired but relieved, electric with anticipation, looking forward to a promised four days of turnaround time in An Hoa before they beat the bush again. Snake's remnant of squad shambled off one helicopter and joined the string of people that headed toward the company troop tents.

Hodges watched them, waiting at the troop tent. Bagger, gaunt and hollow-eyed, but already starting to unwind, walking with his sturdy yawing steps, his rifle over one shoulder like a tramp's stick, held by the barrel. Goodrich, plainly morose, avoiding the eyes of the others, walking alone, his chubby face a miserable scowl. Snake, Cannonball, and Cat Man, a dusty threesome, smoking and jiving, happy to be back in the rear.

Hodges smiled excitedly and called to them. They collectively brightened and walked quickly to him. He greeted each of them as a long-lost friend.

Snake smiled relievedly. He looked as tired as Hodges had ever seen him. "Oh, Lieutenant. I never been so glad to see somebody in my whole damn life. You our Actual again?"

Hodges grinned back. "Yeah, well you all are lucky as hell. They tried to make me a Special Services officer on Okinawa, then a battalion supply officer. But I told 'em I *needed* the bush, man."

Bagger squinted, taken aback. "When did *you* get so gungy, Lieutenant?"

"Well, what kind of hello is *that*? Besides. You wouldn't want me as a supply officer, Bagger. I'd fuck it up so bad you'd starve."

They laughed fraternally. Cannonball grinned slyly. "Hey, Lieutenant. Come on. Show us yo' scars."

The privileged ceremony of the grunt: Hodges took off his shirt and proudly showed them the ones on his triceps and neck. "The ones on my ass are private." As they commented approvingly, he surveyed them. "Whoooeee. *Man.* You all look like hell, I shit you not."

Bagger shook his head. "Aw, Lieutenant. It was the worst shit I ever been through. Nickel and dime. Nickel and dime. They ate us up."

Cannonball agreed. "There it is. We never caught 'em in *one* good firefight. They just keep fuckin' with us. Phony an' Big Mac over here, Wild Man on the trails, Waterbull in the weeds, Baby Cakes an' Ogre . . ." His voice trailed off.

Snake eyed Hodges. "How many new dudes we got?"

"About half a tentful."

"Well, where the hell they been?"

Hodges grinned ironically. "Well, you see, we gotta go back into the Arizona next." He brightened, lifting his eyebrows sardonically. "They been saving 'em for the Big Op."

Cannonball grunted. "Yeah, I like that. They should save all of us fo' the Big Op. I ain' seen no Big Op to be saved *fo'*."

Cat Man and Goodrich had stood silently on the fringe

of the gathering, Cat Man because of his natural shyness, Goodrich out of a brooding disaffection from the others since the shootings. Hodges called to Cat Man. "Cat Man. How you holding up, man?"

Cat Man brightened perceptibly, but still appeared disillusioned, mildly confused. "Not too good, sir. It's a bummer."

"How 'bout you, Goodrich?"

Goodrich came sullenly from his doldrums and scrutinized Hodges. He had been faintly hopeful when he first saw the Lieutenant, but had been immediately turned off. Show me your scars, Lieutenant. Let's play John Wayne and model our scars. Hey, here, Lieutenant. I got a Number One gook sore that some ant shit in a while back. Want to hear the story on that one? Then we can all sit around and talk about the people we've killed. "I need to take a shit." Goodrich walked away from them, toward the troop tents.

Hodges shrugged. "Well, the Senator's his same old happy self, I see. Hey. Get yourselves some racks. Top's got a cookout going this afternoon, and we already got the showers turned on." He grinned one final time. "Better relax while you can, 'cause in a few days we are gonna be busting some ba-a-ad caps."

The square, low-ceilinged room was lit only by awkward slants of sky that filtered through slits of high screen just under the roof. It held twelve showers, six along each outer wall. The room and the showers teemed with filthy, screaming, happy grunts. The water was hot. Snake and Cat Man shared one nozzle, taking the first hot shower either had experienced in several months. Snake soaked under the shower head, his face into a gush of water, greeting each hot jet with something bordering on ecstacy. Cat Man soaped himself in the middle of the room, standing in a river of dirty water that sought a nearby drain hole.

He stared disgustedly across the shadowed room, past a score of naked bodies, to a corner shower. Two young Vietnamese men scrubbed together, taking advantage of the infrequent water hours. They operated the only Vietnamese concession on the Combat Base, a barbershop.

They had played together in the corner shower for ten minutes, while a throng of dirty grunts waited in a line outside to enter the shower. One of the barbers masturbated gleefully as he scrubbed. The other saw him, shouted an exclamation, and joined in.

Cat Man watched them busily soaping their private parts, oblivious to the crowd of Marines. He nudged Snake, scowling with disgust. "Look at that, man. Goddamn gooks."

Snake jumped out of the water and began washing his hair with a bar of soap. "Yeah. They're like that, you know? Ever been to Da Nang? Christ. The fuckers act like they own the place."

Two dust roads met in the middle of the battalion area, making a clearing half the size of a football field. The company gathered there, around huge outdoor cookstoves that the First Sergeant had scrounged somewhere, made from oil barrels cut lengthwise. No one asked the Top where or how he had obtained the barbecue stoves. Questioning a First Sergeant about logistical sources caused the sources to disappear. They ate freeze-dried B-ration hamburgers, and frozen hot dogs obtained in the same manner as the stoves. They drank gallons of beer. They got smashed and roughhoused and forgot about all the miseries outside the wire of An Hoa, one easy mortar arc away.

Hodges was shit-faced. He walked blearily around the gathering with Snake and Cannonball, who were totally stoned, in the middle of the two men, one arm around each. He was so drunk he forgot to eat. Snake was so stoned he was overcome by the munchies and could not stop eating. Hodges felt desperately close to the ones who had been with him since the beginning, as if they were the lone survivors of some ongoing, never-ending calamity. He felt possessive of them, as if he was their big brother, which was exactly the way they treated him.

On the far side of the clearing, near the company tents, a group of blacks crowded around a small tape deck that blared out soul music. In the still dusk air they danced shirtless on the road, their dark sinewy limbs flailing, their bodies sweating, working out their anguish through the music's conduit. Cannonball began bouncing under Hodges' arm, then jived across the dust clearing.

"Catch—you—later—suh!"

One of the company office clerks brought out a guitar and began strumming it. Goodrich approached him. "May I?"

The clerk shrugged. "Knock yourself out."

Goodrich was also drunk. There was no excuse to stay sober and there was no such thing as maintaining decorum anymore. He found a wooden ammunition box and sat on it. He tuned the guitar for a few minutes, strumming it fretfully, then exploded in an unending catharsis. He played the guitar expertly. His chords were melancholy parts of his own frustrations. Dozens of people were drawn by the mournful strings. They gathered in a knot around him.

He began to sing. He had a clear, strong baritone that cried for all of them. He sang every antiwar song he could think of. He sang every Dylan protest song he could remember. They loved it. He had reached them with music in a way that his words and arguments had never approached. And, more important, he was re-energizing after months of agony, pouring out his bitterness in sweet, melodious words.

He was a natural entertainer. He strummed between songs, enjoying the attention, the requests. He seemed to know every popular song that anyone wanted to hear. He played "Galveston" and "Stand By Your Man" for Bagger, who wept unashamedly as he listened, peering at a set of pictures of his wife.

Hodges appeared, walking next to Snake. Goodrich spoke loudly to the crowd, gesturing to his platoon commander. "Wait a minute, folks. I have to dedicate one to my Lieutenant, old Grit-City himself. Robert E. Lee Hodges! Can you possibly dig it?"

Snake stepped forward. "Be careful, Senator."

Goodrich eyed Snake with a small smile, strumming on the guitar. "And for my squad leader—well, there's only one song for a lifer." Goodrich picked his chords. "From the . . . *hell* of Montezuma, to the . . . *hell* of Tripoli. We will . . . *die* for stupid reasons, on the land and on the sea."

There were a few laughs, a few claps from the dozens of men around Goodrich. He nodded graciously to them. Snake smirked.

"Real cute, Senator. Bring that guitar with you out in the Arizona next week, and sing it to Luke the Gook. He'll love you."

Goodrich stopped, afraid of rankling Snake. He strummed the guitar, still smiling, pondering Hodges. "Now, my Lieutenant just got back." He continued to strum, his words coming out as a melodious introduction to another song. "Yeah. They asked him to stay on Okinawa, drinking beer and screwing off. Yeah. But my Lieutenant, he's a dedicated man. Yeah. It's in the blood, they say. There's no peace on Okinawa when there's war in Vietnam. Yeah. Cause there ain't any . . . kills on Okinawa, and there ain't any . . . gooksores junglesores ringworm hookworm diarheeee-a!" The Marines applauded and cheered. Goodrich strummed faster. "No. And there ain't no day acts night acts LPs Ops ambushes or . . . pa-a-trols." His audience cheered again, laughing at Goodrich's fat-faced mimicry. Goodrich grinned intently, strumming slower. "So I just have to sing a little song for my Lieutenant, who likes this bullshit so much he came back for more."

Goodrich sang slowly, looking mournfully at Hodges. It was a popular song, a favorite of the Marines.

> *I'm not scared of dyin'*
> *And I don't really care*
> *If it's peace you find in dyin'*
> *Well then let my time be near*
> *If it's peace you find in dyin'*
> *When dyin' time is here*
> *Just bundle up my coffin*
> *Cause it's cold way down there*
> *And when I die*
> *And when I'm gone*
> *There'll be one child born*
> *And a world to carry on—*

A large hand squeezed the neck of his guitar, killing the chords, then a massive arm wrenched the guitar from

Goodrich's grasp. Goodrich looked up and Bagger stared ominously, drunkenly down at him. Bagger kicked the ammo box, as if testing the strength of the wood before kicking it out from under Goodrich.

"The song is over, Senator. Who the fuck do you think you are? That was an asshole thing to do. An asshole thing."

His former audience stared silently at him. They often sang the song among themselves, but the pointed introduction had been too much, like a gallows wish.

"It gets better . . ." People began to walk away from him. Bagger kicked the ammo box again. Wordless and embarrassed, Goodrich rose and walked away.

Midnight. Hodges, reasonably sober now, strolled through the platoon tents one last time before returning to the officer's tent. Snake and Cannonball slept peacefully, Bagger sat on his cot, still steamed, mumbling to a sleeping Goodrich. Goodrich was snoring. Every time Goodrich snored, Bagger mumbled. "Shut up, Senator." Hodges watched for thirty seconds, amused.

Finally he spoke. "Hey, Bagger. Why don't you go to sleep? Then you won't notice."

Bagger startled, then smiled in the darkness of the tent. "Oh, hey there, Lieutenant." He nodded toward Goodrich. "I can't go to sleep. Asshole here snores too loud."

"Then wake him up and tell him to stop."

"Oh, shit. Then I'd be up all night while he told me about the science of how you snore. Hey. Sorry about that song tonight, Lieutenant."

Hodges sat next to Bagger on the cot. "Ah, it don't mean nothing, Bagger. The man's uptight. I guess that's how they let off steam at Harvard."

Bagger busily fumbled through his pack, and finally produced a plastic bag. "Got some new flicks of my wife, sir. From R & R. Looky here." He flipped out an accordion-style plastic holder filled with Instamatic pictures, then quickly put his hand over one of them. "Oops. You can't see that one."

Hodges indulged the stocky Georgian. "Yup. That's a real nice gal you got, Bagger."

Bagger was singing, a drunken whimper. *"The hurtin's*

on me, yeah, I will never be free no my baby no no no . . .
Oh, Lieutenant. God, I hate it. I ain't gonna make it, sir.
Something bad's gonna happen. They're being too nice to
us. It's always a bad sign when they're nice to us." Bagger
sobbed again and looked up to Hodges with mild reproof.
"How does it feel to know you didn't really have to come
back?"

"Shitty."

"Then why'd you do it?"

"Christ, I don't know. Style, I guess."

Bagger sniffed. "That don't even make sense."

"You're telling me." Hodges was thinking of another
song, one he had heard in the officer's tent while trying
to sober up. Songs, he mused. They were emotional umbilical cords that fed a man the World for a few minutes,
even in Vietnam. And some were omens. *I see a bad
moon rising,* the song had intoned. *I see trouble on the
way.*

Hodges patted Bagger on one thick shoulder, intending
to cheer him up, but the song bounded through his fear
and deflated his gesture. *Don't go out tonight, it's bound
to take your life. There's a bad moon on the rise.* He
released Bagger's shoulder and pointed toward an empty
cot.

"Where's Cat Man, Bagger?"

"Cat Man, Cat Man. Cat Man passed out about two
hours ago."

"Where?"

"Well, I don't remember, exactly." Bagger pointed
thoughtfully. "But it was one of three ditches."

30.

"Get 'em on the road, Snake-man. It's oh-eight hundred
now."

Snake pulled the poncho liner off his face and stared in
the dimness of the troop tent at the figure looming over
his cot. The man was very black, round-faced and heavy-

shouldered, with a small bulge over his belt and thick bulbous buttocks. He stood, hands on hips, leering amusedly at the stringy wisp of man he had awakened.

Snake thought to shake his head and clear it. He moved it to one side, and found that it only set it into further spinning. He sat on the edge of the cot, his brain tingly, his whole self relaxed, and was almost angered that he had to activate his senses enough to respond to the man's order.

He eyed his platoon sergeant, who still smiled amusedly at him. "Hey, Sergeant Sadler." He rubbed his face, trying to remember why he was being awakened. He found his glasses underneath the cot, put them on, then rubbed his face again. "Uh—I s'pose I should know the answer to this. But what's going down? Why you want us on the road?"

"You knew las' night. We had a *good* talk las' night." Sadler chortled. " 'Course, you were 'bout halfway to the room. I'll give you a hint: you ain't done it in a *long* time."

Snake grinned, finally awakening. "No shit. Gotta hand it to you, Sarge. When we get to the rear you think of everything."

"Yeah. I *think* about it. Doan' hold yo' breath about any o' *that*. Now, get yo' ass outa the rack an' get yo' people on the road. We got platoon formation. *Now*."

Snake had slept in his boots and trousers. He reached down for his flak jacket, staring unbelievingly at Sadler. "Platoon formation? Aw, come on, Sarge. You're shitting me." Faint memories of Staff Sergeant Austin's interrupted regime floated through the cobwebs of his mind.

Sadler stood over him, still amused. "Man, you a salty little shit, you know that? Where you think you *are?* Back on the block?"

Snake shrugged absently. "I was just wondering about what the hell was going on."

"I told you las' night."

"I forgot."

"Well, if you wanna know, I recommend you get yo' ass outside an' find out." Sadler grinned triumphantly. "An' while yo' at it, bring along yo' squad."

Snake laughed in spite of himself as he rounded up his men. Now how can you argue with logic like that?

Outside the tent there were uncertain rows of men he

no longer recognized. His own squad held a dozen people beside himself, eight of whom were nothing more than vague, uncharacteristic faces, unmarked flak jackets and helmets, unscuffed boots. Not one of 'em even has a name yet, he fretted.

He viewed the row that was primarily new dudes and each face reminded him of some other man who had flowed through the unfortunate conduit, who was trolled like bait along the Basin floor, and who now rested comfortably in anonymity as a reward for his effort. All the faces who had appeared and were real to this surreal world, a year of faces now, and who had disappeared on big green birds and were eventually replaced, as if the conduit itself were an organism capable of gorging itself on bodies and, especially, excreting the ones it had totally devoured.

He counted his people. Nine, ten, eleven, twelve. All here. And *tonight* I just *gotta* give 'em names.

The platoon strolled along the dirt road in three rough squads. Sadler walked casually at the side of the column of threes. Snake called to him. "Hey, Sarge. I asked and nobody knows. What the hell is going on?"

Sadler answered Snake as if he were calling cadence or leading a chant. His voice was deep, full. "Way-ull. First we goan' git everybody clean uniforms. That means new *everthang*. Flak jackets, hay-ulmet covers. *Everthang*."

Snake whistled. "Whooo-boy. Something heavy's coming down, I can tell already."

Cannonball agreed. He howled, jive-chattering. "Ohhh, man, *you* ain' lyin'! Ah tried to git a new flak jacket when *Ah* come back fum R & R an' that motherfuckin' Supply Gunny act like Ah was tryin' to take the gold right outa his teeth!"

Sadler strutted like a cock rooster. He still led the chant. "Now, I din' say nothin' about you all bein' able to *keep* this trash. I jis' said we goan' *git* it." The platoon cheered: now don't *that* figure? Sadler chided them. "Go on, now. What you all want with a clean flak jacket in the bush? You doan' need no clean flak jacket to fight."

Cannonball removed his flak jacket and held it out for Sadler's perusal. It was empty of protective plating, a veritable rag. "Ah doan' care if it ain't clean, but Ah wish Ah could get me some o' them thangs. This ol' rag ain' nothin' but *hot*, Sarge."

Sadler examined it quickly, not breaking stride, then chanted again. "Ain' nobody said nothin' about *that* kind o' shit. Doan' you worry 'bout a *thang*, Washington. You keep the one he give you. An' if he doan' like it he can try an' walk over *me*."

Murmurs in the platoon. Hey. Old Sadler's gonna be all right.

Snake called to him again. "So what's this all about, Sarge?"

"Way-ull. After we get you all lookin' cool, we goan' teach you how to *march* again." There were disbelieving hoots. "That's right. Then we goan' take you all down to the landin' strip tomorrow moanin' an' let the General give you a Meritorious Unit Citation. An' some medals."

Hodges sat on an old ammunition box and watched in amused awe as Sadler taught the platoon parade procedure. When the practice ended, the old-timers from Snake's squad ambled over to where he sat. He laughed to them. "No-o-oo shit. I'da never believed it could happen."

Snake lit a smoke. "Just like the Old Corps, huh, Lieutenant?"

"Hell, I wouldn't know!"

Bagger scowled to Hodges. "Hey, Lieutenant. What's this all about, anyway? I mean really. Why the hell is this General—it's a real Heavy, ain't it—from the World?" —Hodges nodded in affirmation. Visiting Royalty. In An Hoa, no less—"Why the hell is he coming all the way out here, just to give a couple of awards out like this? The way we heard it, he's just gonna jump off the chopper, give the awards, and then jump back on it again. Sounds *crazy*."

Hodges nodded, grinning sardonically. "That's what I hear, too. Hell, I don't know why. Maybe they're just covering their asses with ceremony."

"What do you mean?"

"Ah, they're giving the company a unit citation for something that happened before any of us were here. Those things take years, you know?" Then Hodges grimaced with some of the shrewdness he inherited from the departed staff Sergeant Gilliland. "But they're also giving the Sergeant Major a Commendation Medal."

Cannonball rolled his eyes. "Noo-o-o! Not *the* Sergeant Major?"

"Him-self."

Snake's eyes narrowed. "The one Gilliland said was gonna be investigated?"

"That's affirm."

Bagger squinted unbelievingly, holding the top of his head. "What the hell did *he* do?"

"Oh, I hear he did a lot. But they're giving him an award for what he's *about* to do." Hodges grinned. "He's leaving. They're giving him a meritorious Navy Commendation as an end-of-tour award."

"He ain't been here a whole tour. I was here when the bastard got here." Snake was adamant, but then assumed a knowing grin. "But I guess he's been here long enough." He shrugged, shaking his head. "So much for God, Corps, and Country, eh, Lieutenant?"

"It figures. It goddamn figures." Goodrich walked away, his face a brooding grimace.

"Well, this Green Suck. Here we are living like mud hogs and that bastard sells off our only comforts." Bagger pointed accusingly at Snake. "Is that why you're staying in, Snake-man? Huh? Be a lifer and get rich."

"You better lay off my Marine Corps! One turkey don't mean a goddamn thing."

"Snake's right, Bagger." Hodges pulled on his cigarette, a mediator. "Just about every Top and Sergeant Major I've seen are damn good people. Look at our Top. Look what he did for us just last night. All the food and booze. Who knows where he dug the stuff up?"

"Hah. Prob'ly had to buy it off the fucking Sergeant Major."

Hodges laughed, shaking his head at Bagger. "Well. I'll admit the man's a turkey. And he sure as hell deserves a court-martial, instead of a medal. Figure our company by itself. Never mind the others. About a hundred men in the field at any one time, maybe a little more. Beer and soda per man per day. That's two hundred cans. A day. At a dime apiece, that's twenty bucks. A day. No overhead.

Hell. Him and the resettlement ville chiefs should get along just fine."

Snake guffawed, unsurprised, then shook his head in disgust. "But what I can't handle is the medal. That General is coming all the way out here to wave good-bye to the bastard."

"Well. He *was* gonna give Baby Cakes the Navy Cross."

They suddenly fell silent. Cat Man got up and walked slowly away. Snake shook his head and stood up. "What a bummer."

Long rows of men stood rigidly inside the morning drizzle. The helicopter made a runway landing, touched down smoothly, and maintained an idle pop-pop-pop of rotors as the General descended. Before him was the awe-inspiring sight of combat troops who only days ago were bleeding in the unproductive sand and weeds of Go Noi. Today they stood disciplined and scrubbed, dressed out in newly issued gear.

The General's wrinkled face was stern and solemn. He marched to the company staff. His aide began to read the wording of the unit citation. There was a pole, and a flag with the company's letter on it. The General hung a streamer on the end of the pole, and addressed the company. "The Twenty-Fifth Marines is not a Regiment," said the General, proudly. "It's a State of Mind."

"Yeah," said Goodrich, *"Dinky-Dau."*

Bagger stared incredulously, slack-jawed. "A General. A goddamn three-star General."

Snake's eyes scanned the wet horizon beyond the airstrip. "We're lucky as hell it's raining, or we'd be getting mortared right now. No bullshit."

Bagger's eyes had not left the stern-faced officer. "They wouldn't *dare.*"

The General stood before the Sergeant Major, and his aide read the Commendation Medal citation. The General pinned the medal on the Sergeant Major's flak jacket, and shook his hand.

Goodrich spat disgustedly. "The bastard."

Cannonball shrugged. He was beginning to shiver in the rain. "Aw, come on, Senator. He done a lot of good things, too, man."

"Name one. Come on. Name one."

"Well." Cannonball's creamy face smiled softly. "He never bothered us when we was in the bush."

The General walked briskly back to his waiting helicopter, followed by a small convoy of aides. Bagger's eyes still followed him. He shook his head in raw admiration.

"Goddamn. What a thing to do. To come all the way out here just for us. Christ, I'd follow that man anywhere."

Goodrich grunted. "Yeah. Kind of makes you want to kill, doesn't it?"

"Hey, Senator." Snake still stared at the wet fields beyond the runway. "Come on over here and *kiss my ass*."

The helicopter departed, and Sadler faced the platoon once again. He grinned amusedly. "Awright, y'all. You got till noon to get over to Supply and turn those flak jackets and hay-ulmet covers back in. Anybody I see after that with green on better have a *reason*."

They received a letter from Waterbull, sent from the hospital in the World. Old Bull's a gutsy fucker, they all agreed. Hardly been a month and he's on his feet.

He had addressed it to "Third Herd, Snake's Squad." It was their mutual property and they possessively passed it around to each other, making sure that everyone in the squad had a chance to read it and contemplate Bull's vindication of their existence. "I really miss you guys. We had so many good times, lost so many good people. I really wish I was back there with you. No shit. I mean it. The World sucks. Hey—tell Baby Cakes he can have my Bangkok wife. He's such a horny bastard. Christ, I miss you assholes. Now you got my address. Write me, huh?"

The squad talked animatedly about Waterbull throughout the day. Snake and Cannonball wrote him cheery letters, not mentioning Baby Cakes' death. They both agreed unconvincingly that they would do that in the next letter. Some of the others cut him a cassette tape full of wise jokes and happy stories.

It all confused Goodrich. He thought he understood the momentum involved in Waterbull's feelings, the sense of loss caused by his serious wounds, the visceral grasping for the past, when he had been a whole man. He even thought he understood the apparent emotion that considered the past less harmful once it had been survived, and a future with a disability threatening enough to make the World seem to "suck."

But let's be realistic, Goodrich mused after he read the letter. You don't *really* want to be back here, Bull. Really? Can you label this part of your goddamn life *rewarding,* something that you miss? You hated it. I remember. Don't bullshit me. I listened to you bitch.

Why don't you write us about the hospital ward, Bull? Does it suck? There's your *reward.* And would you want to come back here and go through that again? And we'll write you about Baby Cakes. Then you can *really* miss Baby Cakes.

An open-bedded six-by truck pulled up near the company tents and honked twice, then waited, idling roughly. The working party sat against a sandbag bunker, inside its morning shade, and peered stodgily at the truck's impatient driver. Finally the driver jumped down from his cab and walked over to the six men.

"Come on. All right? Let's get this over with."

Bagger took a slow drag from his cigarette. "Fu-u-uck you. All you gotta do is drive the truck."

The driver cocked his head. "Look, man. The sooner we start, the sooner we get finished."

Bagger shook his head negatively. "Wrong. The sooner we start, the longer we gotta work. I played this silly game before. Hey. Take it easy, all right? What's a few sandbags one way or t'other? Have a seat, man." He gestured magnanimously next to him, at an unoccupied square of red dirt. The driver declined.

Lister, the troop handler, stood slowly and dusted off the seat of his trousers. "Well. We better get it on. Some lifer gonna see the truck and come over here and shit on me. Next thing I know I'll be back in the bush, humping mortar rounds."

The other five men rose slowly and climbed onto the bed of the truck. In a moment it lurched forward, churning clouds of red dust. Bagger lit a cigarette with one hand, holding to the side of the truck with the other. Suddenly he squinted, focusing as if he had been slapped. His eyes remained fixed on one tent. The truck turned a corner and Bagger jostled Cannonball, who sat low in the truck, catnapping.

"Cannonball. Hey, man. Why'd the Black Shack take their sign down?" Bagger had become used to assigning each morning's frustration to the presence of the sign, and the remembrance of his encounter with Rap Jones.

Cannonball shook his head, attempting to evade the question "*Ah* doan' know, man. Doan' ask *me*."

"Don't bullshit me, man. 'Course you know. C'mon. Level with me. Somebody did 'em a Job, huh? Busted their asses?" The three new men watched the encounter, interested. Lister ignored them, accustomed to Bagger and Cannonball's squabbles.

"Look. Doan' always ask me what Ah know, man. Ah doan' always *know*. Now, Ah *heard*—"

Bagger snorted. Gotcha, you mother. "All right. What did you *hear* about the Black Shack, Cannonball?"

Cannonball recited, mildly irritated. "Well. Ah *heard* that Sergeant Sadler an' Top Lee from over in Charlie Company cleaned 'em out. Ah *heard* there ain' any such thing as the Black Shack anymore. That's what Ah heard."

Bagger slapped his thigh, delighted. "WHOOOeee. Man! I'll bet Top Lee and old Sadler really made the list. I'll bet they're Number One Enemies of the People, all that shit. Oh, yeah. I think I'm gonna like old Sadler. Yes, sir. He don't take shit off *anybody*." He grinned to Cannonball, who was attempting to resume his catnap in the bouncing truck. "Well, what'd they do with Rap Jones. And—who else?"

"Knock it off, O.K., Bagger? Ah doan' know who else. Homicide's in the Da Nang brig. Rap Jones is back in the World."

"The *World*? How did he get back in the *World*?" Bagger mulled it. "He murdered somebody."

Cannonball remained silent. Bagger nudged him with a boot. "Huh?" Cannonball elbowed Bagger's leg away. Bagger repeated. "How, Cannonball? Huh?"

"He got a medical."

"A *medical*?" Bagger contemplated. "Psycho. Had to be."

Cannonball spoke slowly. "Hemorrhoids."

Bagger groaned. "*Hemorrhoids?* Oh, Cannonball. Say it isn't so." Cannonball ignored him. "Well, that goddamn does it. No shit. I *quit*. That's just another reason why. All you got to do to get outa this Green Motherfucker is lay down and *quit*. All right. I *quit*."

Cannonball sighed resignedly. He was thinking about his brother. "No you doan'. You ain' got the balls. Ah doan' either."

The truck stopped suddenly, throwing them forward. They were at the edge of An Hoa's outer perimeter. The truck had stopped outside an opening in the wire, next to a wide, shallow hole with loose earth in it. The driver poked his head through the opening in the rear of his cab that once held a window. "This is it, folks. Start loading sandbags. Let me know when you're ready to leave." He stretched out on the seat of his cab and prepared to take a nap.

Bagger walked to the front of the bed and peered inside the cab, his muscular arms resting on his hips. "You know something? You piss me the hell off. Who do you think you are? Rushing us out here so you can take your goddamn nap. You should be out there helping us fill sandbags, you know that?"

The driver ignored him, feigning sleep.

"Just because you drive a goddamn truck. Uh huh. Drive a truck, play around here in the rear, sleep in a rack, get a little stoned. We get our asses shot off every day for months, and they bring us back to the rear for a couple days, and we load goddamn *sandbags*, while you skate."

The driver continued to ignore him. Bagger reached in and shook him awake. "Well, I'll tell you what. You ain't getting much sleep. I mean it. Cause I'm waking you up every five minutes." Bagger exited off the side of the truck. The rest of the working party awaited him on the ground, amused.

They worked listlessly, filling sandbags and loading them into the bed of the truck. True to his word, Bagger kept the driver awake. He kicked the truck door every time he passed. He stuck his head inside the window and screamed to the driver. The driver lay on the seat, continuing to ignore the stocky bully.

Small groups of Vietnamese approached the working party, conversing with them, or merely calling to them as they passed by. A boy sold ten sticks of marijuana to one of the new men, who lit up immediately, grinning. The ever-present babysans converged, these from the resettlement village in Duc Duc, and very friendly. A few even helped load sandbags, in exchange for cigarettes and gum. Bagger and Cannonball were especially playful with the babysans, warming to them after the stolid, empty faces of Go Noi and Arizona.

On the other side of the crater there were low mounds of earth and thick clumps of high weeds. A girl sauntered through the weeds, as if she were emerging from a mist, and stood across the crater from them, smiling brightly. She was perhaps eighteen, short and mildly attractive, her beauty a coarse, natural type that would likely fade in a few years with the emergence of betel nut and children. She wore a long shirt, and a scarf around her neck, even in noon's oven heat.

Lister gave her a familiar nod, then turned to the working party. "Anybody want a little boom-boom? Five bucks, unless you got a case of C-rats with you."

Bagger and Cannonball studied her. She smiled back unabashedly. Bagger queried Lister. "She clean?"

Lister shrugged. "Shit, I don't know. I screw her every now and then and I never caught nothing from her."

"Yeah, but what you been giving her?" Cannonball howled at Bagger's jibe.

Lister shrugged. "Suit yourself. Couple days you'll be out in Arizona wishing you had a piece of anything. Well, she's anything. Better'n beating yourself to death."

"What's with the scarf? She think she's Queen of Sheba?"

"She's got some napalm burns up one side of her. Starts at her neck up there. But she's O.K. Like they say, you don't fuck the face." Lister chuckled at his own joke.

Cannonball strode quickly toward her. "Ah'll go." He took her hand and they disappeared inside the high weeds.

Bagger startled. "Hey!" He shook his head. "Hell. I was the one asking all the questions. What's he think I am, his agent?"

Lister jibed him comfortably. "Well, hell, Bagger. You're a married man. Cannonball just done you a favor, boy. He's—how'd my preacher used to say it—keepin' you from the snares of indolence and vice."

Bagger grunted, staring toward the weeds. "Screw around, screw around. Tomorrow I might be dead. My woman wouldn't grudge me one last little piece of nooky. Damn Cannonball."

"You can still go. He won't take long."

"Forget it."

In ten minutes Cannonball emerged, grinning widely. "She a nice ride, Bagger. Ain' no bu-u-u-u-ullshit." He nodded to Bagger. "Go on, man. She's O.K."

The girl had not yet emerged from the weeds. Bagger's loins ached mightily, and yet the uncomfortable, denigrating thought would not leave him. Sloppy seconds to a—Shee-it. If they ever found out about that back in Bowman, man I'd—

"Think I'll wait and see if you come down with the clap. Give you a couple days, man. See how hard it is for you to take a leak."

Cannonball still grinned without suspicion, his spacious face lit from recent pleasure. "Aw, they ain' goan' *be* no couple days, Bagger. We movin' out tomorrow or the nex' day."

Bagger noted the glow on his friend's face, and felt himself begin to harden at the thought of it. My man Cannonball is right. This is *it*. What's the difference if I poke it in a hole filled with him? It's that or nothing.

"You're right, man. Where's she at?"

In the weeds she lay on someone's discarded poncho, waiting for him. She held her pajama bottoms casually over her middle parts, as if in modesty. He stood above her, undoing his trousers, and she grinned encouragingly, brightly, as if he were offering her a toy. She laid her bottoms next to her and lifted her knees just a little bit and stroked the inside of her own thighs, still smiling to him.

He was hard, watching her stroke herself, and dropped his trousers to his ankles, kneeling between her legs. She reached for him and caressed him, smiling almost innocently. "Ohhh, nice," she murmured. "Numbah One."

He entered her and she was hot and tight, even after Cannonball. She still smiled happily, talking to him urgently as he stroked her. He reached to caress her breasts and she frowned just a bit, keeping his hands from the scarred side of her body. She still wore the shirt and scarf.

He grabbed her shoulders and thrust deeply and for those moments she was not herself and he was not amid the weeds of An Hoa, coursing on another man's effluent. He was riding on a starship, above all misery, and she was his propellant.

He exploded, throwing off the agony of the bitter, unproductive months, for a moment united with a pleasurable moaning creature, interlocked in life's most creative act. And then it was over, the starship descended to the dirty poncho like a burning meteor, and he stared, almost embarrassed, at the too-easily-smiling creature who had just driven him through her very own Milky Way. He pulled his trousers back up, then paid her. She took his money and spoke deep, amused words.

"Hey-y-y. You Numbah One boom-boom. Mebbe you come back, huh?"

He did not answer her. He could only manage a faintly embarrassed smile.

At the edge of the crater the truck driver awaited his turn. He grinned conspiratorially to Bagger. "Was it any good?"

Bagger grimaced threateningly. "Go back to your nap, pogue. You don't rate any piece of ass."

31.

Snake strolled between red tents along the pallet-box walkway, each square of wood rickety beneath his feet. Fetid odors enveloped him as he walked, first the heavy repulsive mix of excrement and oil from the Officers' shitter on the other side of a tent, along the dirt road, then the nasal irritant of the oil-barrel urinals just to his left. Underneath one tent a dead rat decayed.

Smart bastards, he thought. Give 'em rat poison and forget they'll crawl under the boards to die. May as well let 'em live. They bother you but they don't smell when they're alive. At least you can sleep when they're alive.

What the hell. His hands were deep into his pockets and he contemplated the seesaw motions of the pallet boxes as he walked them.

Finally he reached the company office tent. He hesitated once, peering through the open flap. Inside, a typewriter pecked languidly. What the hell. *I already made up my mind.* He walked briskly up two wooden steps and into the tent, standing in front of a wooden gate, emanating mild arrogance. That gate had a hand-lettered sign taped to it: *Entrance by permission only.*

A narrow face with startled eyes and a small, puckered mouth looked up from the typewriter and recognized him. "Snake-man! Hey! What's happening?"

"Me and trouble. You know it. Where's the Top?"

"He'll be right back. Come on in. Want a smoke?" Snake nodded his thanks and sat on the edge of the clerk's desk. The clerk, a nervous, deferential man whom Snake had nicknamed Bugs months before, lit the cigarette for him. "Listen, man. I was real shook up when I heard about Baby Cakes. Oh, Christ. He just used to sit in here and shoot the shit by the hour. Used to spend ten hours a day inside that mail cage over there. Hell. I typed up his Navy Cross recommendation. He sure had balls. Man. What a way to go. Top was screwed up, too. He sure liked Baby Cakes. We both got shit-faced the night we heard about it. You all must have taken it pretty bad, too. You and him was pretty tight, weren't you? Hey. I just got a Situation Report on Wild Man. Picked it up at the Adjutant's office just a little while ago. Came in from Japan. He's been in Japan for a couple weeks. He must have taken a hell of a shot, huh? 'Condition guarded, prognosis poor.' 'Prognosis poor' is O.K., that just means he won't be back. To the company I mean. Once his prognosis is better, they'll ship him back to the World. At least that's good news, ain't it? Shit, I'll bet Go Noi was the biggest bummer you ever saw, huh, Snake-man? I'll bet you're glad as hell you're getting short. You're almost finished, aren't you? How many days you got?"

"Forty-seven. And a wakeup."

"Forty-seven. Jesus Christ, you're so short you better not take a long piss or you'll miss your plane. You gonna get a Rear job?"

"Nope." Snake looked levelly at Bugs, reveling in the impact his words would have. "I'm gonna extend."

"*Extend?* What the hell for?" Bugs caught himself. "I mean, what *job?* MP's in Da Nang? That's a good racket. Maybe Embassy. Hell, you got a good enough record to get Embassy duty, you know that? You're the only grunt I ever heard of, at least in *this* company, who's got combat meritorious Lance Corporal *and* combat meritorious Corporal."

"Groovy. But I think I'll stay with the company."

"In the *bush?*" Bugs squinted unbelievingly. "Oh, wow. You mean it don't you, Snake-man?" He pondered it, careful not to insult this minor legend who had condescended to smoke one of his cigarettes. "Man. It's people like you who make me believe in what we're doing over here. I'd just *never*—"

Snake laughed, looking ironically at Bugs. "Come on, Bugs. This ain't any politician's fairy tale. Just give me the papers so I can have 'em ready when the Top gets back."

One hour later the deed was completely done. Snake left the tent, weighted with a ponderous emotion, and strolled along the powdered dirt roads until he found himself at the western edge of the combat base. He found an empty sandbag bunker (it would be occupied at dusk) and climbed onto its roof and sat heavily, moodily peering across the fields of concertina, like a king on a throne, surveying his wide domain.

Far to the west the mountains rose fierce and blue and ominous, above low layers of thick white fog. They seemed peaceful but he knew their secrets, understood their mysteries more completely than he had ever mastered anything before. He was a comprehending denizen, master of a violent world.

He watched the mountains, and the almost quaint repetitions of paddy and treeline that led to them, and acknowledged that he could do this forever. He sensed that, beyond the terror that was today, there was a fullness that no other thing in the remainder of his life would ever equal. That, beyond doubt, the rest of his life would be spent remembering those agonizing months, revering their fullness. That, yes, he was now twenty—

well, *almost* twenty—and what would always have been
the greatest, the most important experience of his life,
had almost passed. If he were to go back now—when he
did go back—there was nothing, not a thing, that would
parallel the sense of urgency and authority and—need. Of
being a part of something. And of being needed and being
good.

Extend? Hell, yeah. I'll extend until this goddamn thing
is over.

He sensed that it was all here, everything, and there
was none of it there. All of life's compelling throbs, con-
densed and honed each time a bullet flew: the pain, the
brother-love, the sacrifice. Nobility discovered by those
who'd never even contemplated sacrifice, never felt an
emotion worth their own blood on someone else's altar.
The heart-rending deaths. The successes. All here. None
there, back in the bowels of the World. Except for the
pain, and even that a numbed, daily pain, steady, like
blue funk, not the sharp pain of an agonizing moment,
capable of being purged, vindicated, replaced by a beautiful, lilting memory: Baby Cakes was a Number One dude,
you know? He'da died for me. And I killed 'em back for
him.

32.

Goodrich walked endless strips of dust roads, red dirt in
the wind like sleet. The resupply helicopters passed overhead, carrying netted external loads from the An Hoa landing strip to places like Arizona and the Phu Nhuans and
Go Noi. They reminded him of hawks clawing dead mice.
Another helicopter mission popped past him, coming from
the western mountains, dragging a long rectangular net
under it like a plane pulling a commercial streamer at a
resort beach. Eight men hung from the net, in full combat gear. Four clung to it, peering down as the helicopter
hovered over the pad. The other four were dead, strapped

to the net. Goodrich watched them and felt sick: another Recon team had bitten the dust. The gooks were everywhere. Something big was about to blow.

Still he walked. No direction. Jeeps and mechanical mules raced past, throwing curtains of red powder over him. The rows of tents and sagging bunkers blended into blurs, punctuated only by occasional fetid, slowly moving whirlpools of bad air, like someone else's breath.

He kicked the dust, sending little powder clouds into the air with every step. Damn it. How did I ever get into this? He lit a cigarette as he walked. And there's no backing out. For the first time in my life, I have to make a decision, do something affirmative instead of letting life kick me around.

Mark, his old roommate, had written him from Canada, and the letter had been the catalyst that set him walking. Mark had sent a clipping from *The New York Times,* an article by an investigative reporter about a possible massacre of civilians by an Army unit. Mark had been in rare form in his letter. "And you tell me there are no more pogroms," Mark had written. "And you tell me I shouldn't see Nazi uniforms every time I turn on the TV. What do you call this—winning the hearts and minds?"

Then there had been the kicker. "I can't understand how someone could stand by and watch this happen. Do they make you all automatons? Do they intimidate you to the point you lose your consciences, for God's sake?" And then, crushingly: "I feel better knowing there are people like you in some of the units over there, Will."

Goodrich kicked another cloud of dust into the air, covering himself with it. He had mulled it for hours, and could not find a way out of confronting the issue head-on. He had justified his unpopularity within the platoon by his willingness to retain his moral principles. And damn it, I'm right, he thought, reassuring himself. The others just don't seem to have the maturity, or the moral referent. Or something. They just can't understand the things they're doing. Or have done.

Then he attacked himself. I don't know. Maybe it's me. I sure don't seem to be very swift about all this—*bush* bullshit. He regretted the immaturity he himself had displayed when he had serenaded Snake and Hodges. I can certainly be a goddamned asshole, without much provocation.

But if I ignore this, how can I ever face myself, much less anyone else? The moral purist, who copped out of his one real crisis. I'd be saying, in effect, that two—murders —weren't worth the effort, weren't worth the confrontation. Will Goodrich, moral purist and gutless wonder. And it *was* wrong. He contemplated the killings. We can't play God. We can't administer street justice—what the hell: *bush* justice—to every Vietnamese who pisses us off.

He contemplated the emotions that were transparent in the others, the hot, wronged urge to avenge that rushed from places inside them where he himself had only felt repulsion. For a moment he doubted his right to judge their actions from his own moral referent, since he knew that for some reason he and they reacted as differently as five dobermans and a cocker spaniel. But *damn* it, he decided, there's no way to justify murder. The rules say kill, O.K. But when the rules say stop, you've got to stop. We're not God. We're not barbarians.

He returned to the battalion area and found himself standing before the Legal Officer's tent. He immediately grew queasy. Who's his clerk? What if this gets out? Who knows what they'd do to me? They can be such— Oh, God. No way.

He walked the road for a short space again, feeling trapped, powerless. Then it hit him like a shock. Of course. Regimental Legal. At least they investigated the Sergeant Major. And it won't get back to the company from regiment. Too far removed.

Regimental command area. He reached a small, square sandbag bunker with a red sign above the door. The sign read REGIMENTAL LEGAL OFFICER. Goodrich checked the dirt road for familiar faces, then bolted inside the door. A Corporal looked up at him, mildly shocked by his dashing entrance.

"What do you want?"

"I'd like to see the Legal Officer."

"Do you have an appointment?"

Goodrich stared exasperatedly at the Corporal. He was tempted to leave on that note, to justify his retreat on

those grounds. But not so easily for murder, he decided.
"I don't have time for that. We're pulling out tomorrow.
Arizona."

The Corporal was unmoved. "Have you been to Battalion Legal?"

"You're kidding. Listen. This is important."

"What's it about?"

"I can't tell you."

The Corporal surveyed Goodrich with mild arrogance.
"Look. If you can't tell me, how the hell can I figure out
if it's important enough to bother the Captain about?"

Goodrich leaned over the man's desk. "Take my word
for it—"

The Captain appeared from a private portion of the
bunker. He was tall and slim, very young, only recently
graduated from law school. He nodded to Goodrich, giving him a tentative, embracing smile. "You sure it's that
important?"

Goodrich immediately warmed to the man. "Yes, sir."

The Captain smiled, gesturing toward his cubicle. "Then
come on in."

The Captain indicated a chair, and Goodrich sat obediently. The Captain sat behind his small field desk and lit
a pipe after meticulously packing it from a leather pouch.
"What can I do for you, Marine? Need a divorce? Been
AWOL? Getting busted for pot?" He laughed comfortably.
"I've got a whole bag of tricks."

Goodrich found himself hesitating to talk about it. It
wasn't something a person could just start describing on
command. And yet, he felt drawn to the Captain. He
smiled tentatively. "Uh. How about a job?" The Captain
looked curiously at him, and he leaned forward, toward
the man. "I'm highly qualified—for a Lance Corporal,
that is. My old man's a lawyer, my brother's a lawyer,
and I have almost three years of college. Harvard, better
than a B average." He shrugged, remembering. "Not *much*
better than a B, but what the hell."

The Captain almost choked on his pipe. "Harvard?
Jesus Christ." He laughed self-consciously. "I won't even
tell you where I went. Not that you'd recognize it. Where
do you work now?"

"I'm a grunt." Goodrich shook his head at the Captain's amazement. "Oh, shit. Don't even ask. It's worse than it sounds."

"Hmmm. I'll bet." The Captain checked his watch. "Well, to tell you the truth, I don't need an assistant. You noticed Corporal Murphy out front? Well, Corporal Murphy has two years of law school." The Legal Officer chuckled. "He got drafted. But he does all a man could ask. Now"—he checked his watch again—"I was just getting ready to eat lunch. You didn't hold me up just to apply for a job, did you? You seemed pretty worked up a minute ago."

Goodrich studied the Captain, feeling nervous, desiring some assurance that, should he reveal the information, it would not merely cause him trouble. "Are you the one who investigated the Sergeant Major?"

The Captain shook his head ironically. "Yeah, but that's done, unfortunately. We don't need anything else on him. We had so much as it was, he should have hung."

"I take it you weren't particularly happy with the outcome, then?"

The Captain stared at Goodrich with a taut, assessing smile. "No. You might say I was a little disappointed." He stretched in his chair, still assessing Goodrich. "Sergeant Majors, I have learned, stand somewhere just beneath Jesus Christ, and just above the Colonel. They aren't very fry-able." He relit his pipe. "But I don't think there would be a similar problem with anyone else. The system's fair, on the whole. Very fair." He took a final look at his watch. "Now. Are you going to tell me what's on your mind, or do you want to forget it? You seemed to think it was pretty damned important a few minutes ago."

"It is. It's really important." Goodrich pondered it a moment. His hands were sweating, and had taken on a nervous tremor. "It just isn't easy to talk about. It's not something you can just start in and discuss. I have to figure out my obligations, where my loyalties lie—"

"Maybe you should visit the Chaplain, and see me later." There was a hint of sardonic impatience in the Captain's voice.

Goodrich lit a cigarette, gathering himself. "I'm sorry. I'm making an ass out of myself. That seems to be the general rule, lately. Listen, Captain. You know how things are in the bush. I'm sure you've heard. Everything's screwed up in the bush. There's no logic to it. At five-thirty if you shoot out a light in a hootch and someone dies, you're in trouble. At six o'clock you can do it and it's all right, because lights are used as signals. Shoot a prisoner from five feet away, it's a kill. Touch him and then shoot him, and you're a murderer. You know how it is. So how can any of it make any sense?"

The Captain puffed slowly on his pipe, contemplating Goodrich. "So what do you want me to do about it, Corporal? Make it all go away?"

"No. I mean, yes, but since you can't, no. What I want you to do, sir, is tell me I didn't see a murder. For my own conscience. Tell me I saw something that was gray enough that we should forget it. Could you do that?"

"What are you talking about?"

"It looked like a murder. It sounded like a murder. But maybe it wasn't."

"Well, tell me about it."

Goodrich described, in intimate detail, the killings of the man and woman on Go Noi. He talked about Baby Cakes and Ogre. The killer-team patrol. Finding the bodies. Cat Man's assault on the man. He emphasized his own resistance, and his removal from the scene as the killings took place.

He finished, and sat motionless in the chair, emotionally drained. *There. I've done it.*

The lawyer studied his notes for several minutes, sucking on a pipe that had gone out without his noticing it. Finally he spoke to Goodrich, reading from his legal pad.

"I want to get a few things straight. First, you did not participate in any of this."

"That's right."

"And you were not present at the scene when it all took place."

"That's right."

"In fact, from your own statement, you didn't even see the incident. You—and I quote, roughly—'sat on the porch looking out at the field, and heard the woman scream. Then there were shots.' "

Goodrich sighed. He was tired of talking about it. "That's right."

"And finally, from your own statement, you did not see the bodies after the alleged killings."

The "alleged" stuck in Goodrich's tired mind. "Well, I—"

"I read again from my notes." The Captain sucked on his unlit pipe. "I heard them spading and then they rejoined me at the hootch. We made stretchers for Baby Cakes and Ogre and returned to the perimeter.' "

"Well, I—I *know* they were killed, Captain."

"They probably were, Goodrich." The Captain's face was intense, lit. "You asked me to tell that you didn't see a murder. All right. I'm telling you. You didn't see a murder."

"But one—two—took place."

"Do we know that? Do we have bodies? Do we have witnesses who will swear that people were killed? Were they even civilians? Was there something that happened near the grave site that would have made the homicides —presuming for a moment that there were homicides— justifiable? Did mamasan have a knife? Did papasan reach for someone's weapon?"

Goodrich shook his head, grimacing with a mix of disgust and disbelief. "Did mamasan have a knife. Holy shit. That's weak, Captain."

"You say the Vietnamese Scout identified them both as VC?"

"Dan? Everybody's a VC to Dan."

The Captain laughed, tossing his head and shrugging. "Well, he should know. He's probably pretty close to being right, around *here*. Who killed them, Goodrich? Again presuming they were killed?"

"They were. I know that. And Snake was the man who gave the orders. I was there for that much."

"But who killed them? Did the Vietnamese Scout do it? Do you realize that we have no authority over him? If he did the actual shooting, there's no murder."

"There were a lot of shots, Captain. A lot of shots."

The Captain shook his head, exasperated. "Haven't I convinced you yet? Isn't all that enough to quell your goddamn conscience? I'll tell you how I feel. Best friends murdered like that. For God's sake, there's been enough tragedy without compounding it. If they did kill the people, they'll have to live with it. It was a mistake. They're kids. They're fucked up and confused. You said it yourself. Nothing makes sense out here."

Goodrich felt his eyes narrow. "Boys will be boys, eh, Captain?"

"You know that's not what I mean." The lawyer scrutinized Goodrich, tamping out his pipe and repacking it. He lit it again, still staring. "All right. What do you suggest I do?"

"I don't know." Goodrich held both hands over his head. "Jesus Christ. I came here to ask you and now you're asking me."

"It's not exactly your clear-cut case." The Captain smoked pensively. "Well. We'll have to do an Article. Thirty-two investigation. If it ever hit the press that this event occurred, and we let it go by without investigating it, the shit—would—hit—the—fan." He continued to eye Goodrich, as if he were attempting to solve a puzzle that sat fragmented in the middle of Goodrich's face. "We won't indict. We'd never convict. No, I won't say that. With this My Lai thing in the press, we're going to be catching hell. Anything's possible. But I doubt it."

"So what do you want me to do?"

"Write me a statement. Just as you told it to me. Do it right now."

Goodrich hesitated. "All right. But, Captain—I hope you realize what could happen to me if this got out."

"It won't get out." The lawyer shook his head again, totally confused. "What the hell do you want? You just pushed me into this, now you don't want to cooperate?"

"I didn't push you into it. I just asked a question."

"All right, all right." The Captain seemed somewhat irritated with Goodrich. "I'll get you out of the company. It won't be that hard. We do it for our CIDs all the time."

"Your CIDs?" The full impact was hitting Goodrich.

"Yeah. Criminal Investiga—"

"I know, I know. When can you do it?"

"A couple days. I'll get orders for you when Division approves the Article Thirty-two." The Captain sighed. "You may end up working for me, after all."

33.

Hodges met a classmate from his Basic School platoon in the mess hall when he went to eat his last hot meal before departing on the operation. It was lunch: B-ration freeze-dried hamburgers topped with brown gravy made from powder, a dirt-filled lettuce salad, and Kool-Aid. The classmate had only recently arrived in Vietnam, after finishing combat engineer's school. They had not been close in Basic School, yet Hodges greeted him as a long-lost friend, the man's enthusiastic awe a reminder of how it had begun for him five months before. Grasping the man's hand and staring into rested, curious eyes, Hodges sensed an innocence that was as far away as his own childhood. He thought of the advice of Major Otto, who had spoken so honestly to him the day he departed for the bush, and again lamented the fact that the Major was in Da Nang on the Division staff. His friend's face convinced him that he and Otto now shared a jealous ethos, gained in fear and dirt and blood and hassle, that would have made it possible to talk, really talk, for the first time. This was me, mused Hodges, listening to his friend's questions. But it isn't anymore.

The classmate had kept up with the doings of all the other Lieutenants who had graduated with them. He knew who had washed out of flight school. He knew who was up for medals. He knew who had died.

Hodges downed his meal without enthusiasm, listening absently while thinking of the operation he would embark on in only a few hours. There was a tickle in the back of his head that mildly resented this new arrival's knowledge. From the man's perch in engineer's school, in the calm of a Fort Belvoir building, he had kept score, as if it were a basketball game, while Hodges and the other grunts had slugged it out in isolation from each other.

But it was irrelevant, anyway, at least right then. Basic

341

School, with all its earnestness and idealism, was an unreachable part of his life, blocked off from him by combat's warp of terror. Flight school was for other people.
Medals were for heroes. Relevance was Snake and Cat
Man and Cannonball. Importance was keeping them alive
through another week.

Twenty dead, his friend was saying, giving the numbers
with the careless abandon of one who had never experienced the quick death of a friend, then commenting
in the same breath on the unbearable heat and dust of An
Hoa. Seventy grunt lieutenants in our Basic Class, and
twenty dead in five months.

The deaths reached Hodges, brought him from his
moody contemplation of the coming operation. The twenty dead would not pass through his mind like the other
chatter from his classmate. He chewed a piece of gritty
lettuce, considering it a luxury, and remembered Basic
School, only a half-year removed, yet like a dream from
innocent childhood. The platoon runs, the feisty chants, the
nights they would return to O'Bannon Hall after field problems and climb three flights of steps to the floor that held
their rooms, leaving thick mud trails from their boots and
camouflage smears along the handrails. Singing in loud
unison:

"Fuck, fuck fuck this TBS shit,
Three more weeks and we'll be home.
Then it's off to Vietnam, lose a leg or lose an arm,
And be pensioned by the Corps forever more!"

But not believing it.

Twenty dead. His friend continued, giving all the details
of how each man had died, seemingly more amazed that
so many were capable of dying in such a dirty little war
than with the fact that they had actually died. He knew
all the details, and was able to transfer each death neatly
into a lesson, a comment on the character of the man who
had died. The family man died on the day his son was
born. The super-hero assaulted a North Vietnamese bunker
and caught a grenade in the stomach (it had never happened to John Wayne). The best athlete willed his own
death after losing both legs to a mine. The salty ex-en-

listed wiseass refused to listen to the advice of a Kit Carson Scout and walked his platoon into an ambush. The class jokester's helicopter had caught vicious fire going into a hot landing zone, and had crashed, then blew up, the ammunition inside the helicopter detonating and killing every man (a most ironic way to go, the jokester would have agreed).

On and on, as if they were textbook deaths. The lessons irritated Hodges. His friend had no right to package them so neatly, to make them sensible.

And how would he characterize mine, Hodges wondered again and again as the man issued his examples. He knows I came from Okinawa by my own free will. Oh, God. I'd be the gungy one. Hodges shrugged. Ah. What the hell does he know, anyway. And who the fuck cares.

Hodges drained his last bit of Kool-Aid. It was time to round up his platoon. He stood and shook his classmate's hand, feeling he had little in common with the man anymore. "Remember how we all were afraid it would end before we got a chance to get a piece of it?"

The man clasped Hodges' hand. It was the eyes, Hodges finally decided. Too—enthusiastic. "We can still win it, I think. Don't you?"

Hodges heard himself issue a surprised chuckle. "I don't know anything about it anymore."

34.

They poured in trickles from the tents until, in minutes, the road became a teeming teenage wasteland. They were fully burdened. Packs bulged on each back as if every man carried a fat, hidden papoose. Men were strapped with three and four bandoleers of ammunition, and counterstrapped with thin cylinders of LAAWs. One in four carried a heavy square bag containing a claymore mine. Machine-gun teams sported boxes upon boxes of ammo

on long green straps. Mortarmen carried tubes and
base plates and packboards laced with ominous dull-
green mortar rounds, looking like small, fin-tailed
bombs.

They gathered on the dirt road as if at convention on
some hotel floor, chatting in small groups, filled with
mixed moods, suppressing the electric anticipation that
coursed through all of them. A few brooded alone at the
edges of the mob, miserable with fear.

Staff Sergeant Sadler strutted through the platoon troop
tent, fully burdened also. His helmet was low in front,
down over his eyes. He urged the remainder of the platoon out onto the road, "Come on! Come on! Git it on the
road! We got a war to fight!"

He jammed a letter into his flak jacket pocket as he
walked along the center row of the tent. So, he thought,
motioning to a man to go back and retrieve a C-ration
meal on his cot, she doan' like Philly. So Philly ain' good
enough for her. Shoulda left her in Noath Carolina, she
says. Folks treat her better in Noath Carolina. So kids get
used to white folks better in Noath Carolina, go to
school with more white folks in Noath Carolina.

He snorted, shaking his huge round head. Well, if Noath
Carolina so damn *good,* why the hell are there so many
niggers in *Philly?* Oh, I doan' know. You never can keep
'em happy. Shoulda left her in California. I *know* I
coulda found some place in California. But it's the same.
It's her. I keep tellin' her. When she goan' listen?

Rule Number One, thought Sadler, exiting the other
side of the troop tent. People ain't never goan' forget
you're a nigger. People ain't never goan' think niggers an'
honkies are the same. Only thing you can do is be so
goddamn *good* that it doan' matter. An' if you ain' any
good, you can cry all you want an' it won't make you
good. But if you good, you doan' need to cry.

Them mothafuckas an' their "Black Shack" he thought.
I work twelve years at bein' good even if I'm a nigger
an' they want everybody to say they ain' *bad,* no matter
what kind o' shit they put down, just because they're niggers. An' the only thing they do is make everybody hate
all o' us 'cause they think we need a damn crutch. Well,
the best damn NCOs in this here Marine Corps are *black*

—the Major made a point o' tellin' me that when I left Camp Lejeune—an' we doan' need no punk imitatin' Cleaver to do us in. I'da liked to kill them toads.

Now, where the hell is Snake-man?

"The Plan," the Colonel had advised the company's officers at a meeting in the Regimental Command Center the day before, "is to run a large-scale sweep-and-block to begin our operation. We know there is a full regiment, and another main-force battalion, operating in the central Arizona, getting ready to make a major assault, probably on An Hoa. We haven't been able to pin them down in a major battle yet" (bait dangling, alas, had failed), "so we're going after the whole kit-and-kaboodle in one shot. We have the Second Battalion of our own Twenty-Fifth Marines in the western Arizona, roughly here" (the pointer slapping expertly on the map) "and here. We're going to insert four more companies at night, into a block in the eastern Arizona. We're pulling two down from the Fourteenth Marines that will set up here" (the pointer slapping) "and here. Alpha of our First Battalion will move in here. Your company will move along the southeast edge of the Arizona, and set up in a block on the northern part of Football Island, completing the block. There's a wide paddy, a good half-mile across, that will be to your front. It should give you excellent fields of fire when the day's festivities begin" (Wry smile: a touch of humor always helps rapport).

"You'll take the afternoon convoy from An Hoa to Liberty Bridge. That will conceal your movement." The Colonel smiled winsomely. "And frankly, we don't have any helicopters available to move you, anyway. Then you'll cross from the Bridge into the Arizona sometime after midnight. We'll give you the word.

"Just before dawn, Second Battalion will sweep across the Phu Phong paddies, through the central Arizona treelines. We should roust something big out. It will probably run right into you and the other blocking companies. Be ready." He grinned one last, hopeful time. "You might not believe this, but I really wish I was going with you. Now, let's count some meat, all right?"

Hodges had grinned resignedly, remembering Bagger's

usual retort: Some days you count the meat. Some days the meat counts you.

The trucks were packed like crowded subway cars. Some men sat tightly on the two boards that ran the length of the truck bed. Others lay on the sandbagged bed itself, between the seats. The trucks followed one another closely, winding along the red earth.

Clouds began to form, first turning the sky entirely white in their distance, as if they had enveloped the earth and were now descending like a tightening grip, gradually graying, finally developing deep streaks but never pausing long enough to be cumulus or nimbus or cumulo-nimbus, merely racing toward the earth until at last they reached it in the form of steady, persistent, windless rain. A few pulled on ponchos when the rain began. Most accepted the wetness rather than expend the energy to undo packs and roll out ponchos and repack.

Hodges sat on one of the long boards, accepting the drenching rain, peering out at landmarks along the convoy road. They emerged as the truck ground toward the Bridge, allowed inspection, then disappeared behind him, as if becoming a part of his past. The old brick factory that the French had built an empire ago, lying fallow under blankets of red dust that were rapidly becoming an ooze of clay. The German hospital, sitting yellow and sedate, haven for hurt children, still missing three fräuleins that the VC had hauled off to the mountains several weeks before. The children from the hospital gathered along the road, even in the rain. There were the ambulatory ones who were still receiving treatment. There were the recently released, who had found new homes in the nearby Mau Chanhs rather than returning to Arizona or La Thap or Go Noi to die.

They made a haunting crowd. They were pocked, eyeless. They were burned, one-armed, one-legged. One hobbled painfully, his toes spaced from the end of his foot to the top of his ankle, five grotesque toy soldiers, melted by napalm into rigid attention. The children waved merrily to the convoy and received cigarettes and gum for their effort. The Marines in the convoy did not mangle them. Buddha merely turned his head. Some days it rains rain,

Hodges thought, thinking of Dan's acquiescent philosophy. Some days it rains other things.

The road opened up and Hodges watched the bald red circles of earth spaced on both sides, surrounded by C-ration cans and weeds, where small groups of men now huddled under makeshift hootches in an attempt to stay dry. Road outposts. He had stood them with his platoon. They, too, seemed a somehow tranquil part of his past.

The convoy passed through the Phu Nhuans. He peered through the gloomy rows of trees and ridges, remembering past patrols. Over there, somewhere, soaking with the rain into the earth, were a hundred pieces of Big Mac, and the bones of Phony's arm. And an invisible, rain-soaked bloodstain from himself. Far into one paddy a helicopter hovered in the rain, soaking a rice seedbed with aviation fuel that had been rigged to shower down in the rotorwash. In a few days the seedbed would be dead. The helicopter, remembered Hodges, as a part of Operation Rice Denial. If We Kill Off All The Rice, the logic ran, There Won't Be Any To Give To The Enemy. If The Enemy Doesn't Have Rice, It Will Have To Quit Fighting.

Hodges shook his head, watching the helicopter. Not a totally bad rationale. But, meanwhile, the villagers will starve. Ah, he remembered ironically. But they can always move to the resettlement villages if they really care. Ri-i-ght. Underneath the hovering monster a mamasan stood, squarely in the middle of her seedbed. She peered through the gasoline rain, reaching both hands toward the inanimate machine that soaked her and her life source. Hodges watched her chest heave. She was either crying or screaming. The helicopter did not hear her. Nor did it see.

Finally the convoy reached the Bridge Compound. It paused only long enough to excrete its cargo, dropping the company in clusters along the mud-soaked road where it passed through the wire. They stood, drenched already, splattered with red mud from the grinding, departing truck wheels.

Snake slung his rifle over his shoulder, upside down to keep the rain out of the barrel, and hunted down Hodges. Both wore soaked utility shirts underneath their flak jackets. Neither wore a poncho.

"Where to, Lieutenant?"

Hodges looked at his watch. Four-thirty. Eight hours to kill before the company would leave the compound. They still stood in huge knots along the road. The compound was so small, and so tightly structured, that there appeared to be no place for the company to pass the time. Hodges looked around for Captain Crazy, and could not see him. The platoon stared patiently, waiting in the mud.

There was a small clearing in front of the Battalion COC bunker, not quite the size of a basketball court. Hodges pointed to it. "Get with Sergeant Sadler and put 'em over there. I'll go check inside the COC and see where they want us."

Inside the bunker it was warm and dry and fluorescently bright. Hodges stood in the room, surrounded by maps and squawking radios, remembering the gruesome terror of the night the Bridge had been overrun, contemplating his and Snake's earlier confrontation with Kersey. Nothing in the bunker had changed. Old Kersey's probably praying every night the Bridge'll get overrun again, so he can cop another Silver Star, mused Hodges.

He looked around for his company commander, who still was not apparent. But speak of the devil, mused Hodges. A wide back leaning over a chart straightened, then turned to face him. He caught the jowls as the head turned. The narrow eyes inspected him haughtily. Kersey. Hodges feigned casualness.

"Hey. We got a company out in the rain, you know, just sitting there in front of your bunker. And we got eight hours to kill before we make our bird. Got any place we can hole up?"

Kersey grimaced at Hodges' greeting. "No, I don't. This isn't a hotel, it's a combat base." He folded his arms, his head tilted back. "What the hell you complaining about, anyway? If you were in the bush you'd be wet. You're gonna cross the river and get wet."

"Something called leadership, Kersey. Taking care of your people. You wouldn't know a thing about that. Ahh, forget it." Hodges turned to leave, but could not resist a dig after Kersey's arrogance.

"Hey. You and the Colonel get your Silver Stars yet?"

The radiomen in the bunker exchanged knowing smirks. Kersey stood erect. "Colonel rotated. I'd guess he got his. I got mine a few days ago."

"That General from the World."

"That's right."

"I figured that." Hodges smiled blandly. "He gave the Sergeant Major a Commendation just for having the good sense to leave before somebody did him a total job." Kersey stared threateningly at Hodges. Hodges was enjoying the amusement of the radiomen. "Oh. But I forgot. That's how you got your Purple Heart."

The bunker broke out into muffled guffaws. Hodges turned to leave. "Yeah. I hope your legs are O.K. You know, where those—*gooks* shot you?"

Kersey challenged him with a curse, but Hodges was already out the door.

It was a Pyrrhic victory. For eight hours the company sat packed in the dirt yard, under sheets of intermittent rain, huddled inside leaking ponchos. They sat mournfully in the black as the rain beat at them, nibbling from tins of C-rations, smoking wet cigarettes. The rain soaked their clothes and equipment. It crinkled their skin. It deadened every ember of what used to be their spirits.

35.

The river was high and swift, cool from recent rain. Goodrich slid clumsily through wet grass down the steep bank, squinting at the wavy line of figures that disappeared in mist and darkness halfway across the water, then stepped carefully into the current. The water filled his boots, coldly shriveled his groin, tickled his armpits. He held his weapon over his head. His cigarettes were in his mouth. Every other part of him and his equipment was soaked. In front of him New Mac stumbled, going underwater briefly, and lunged to catch his helmet as it began to float off his head. He succeeded, but his cigarettes bobbed quickly downstream in their waterproof container. New Mac swore after them.

On the far bank cobwebs of limbs and roots from shattered trees reached through the mist. Goodrich approached them, haunted by their shapes, by the craggy pocks of sand and earth below them, by the very silence that greeted his first step onto the Arizona shore. Where are they? The valley's filled with them, they know we're here. It will only be a moment and then they'll kill us all. None of us knows where the other is except for the ones just in front and behind. Why haven't they hit us? Maybe just beyond this curve, behind that mound.

But there was nothing. Only a forest of devastated trees, its floor so deeply rent that it seemed they walked through sand-dunes. For an hour they experienced the moon, following a winding trail. The column was continually halted. Men fell into craters that they did not see. They tripped over trees and lost the man in front of them. The point squad lost the trail once, and had to double back to find it.

Then the trail broke north. To the west, their front, was a ridge that dropped into a wide river of sand. The sand separated Football Island, to the south, from the rest of the Arizona Valley. They dropped down the ridge and walked in the sand, thankful to be out of treelines, away from near ambushes. The sand was loose, like walking on thick, wet sponges. They walked it for two hours, stopping periodically and resting in its openness, some of them now collapsing on it when the column stopped, mindless of the grainy irritants that stuck to all parts of them because they were still wet.

Abruptly, in the middle of the sand, as if by divine command, the column moved north. No landmarks guided it. They reached the ridge again, and climbed back into thicks and stumps and mounds and also hootches this time. They fought a thick treeline that was interlaced with trails and deep trenches, moving through it rather than along it, and finally reached its northern edge. There before them, like a seashore swallowed in its evening fog, was a wide, seemingly endless paddy, blanketed with mist. They took positions along it, making a thin, elliptical perimeter with the back side on a nearby trail, and awaited first light.

Hodges lay dozing in the mud of a bomb crater, supposedly on radio watch. The radio was an uncommunicative hiss against his ear. Mosquitoes hovered and swarmed
lazily around his face, whole flocks of them in motion
after the drenching rains. Ten yards away a group of rats
played on the porch of an abandoned hootch. Across
the crater, Sergeant Sadler snored, occasionally slapping a
mosquito or slumbering against the crater's mud. There
were slaps and mutterings in all directions, punctuated
by exhausted groans. Just through the trees was the black
and silver gloom of paddy.

Then the booms began. The crunch and whump of
artillery digging out some distant earth, round after
round, a dense bombardment, like rolls of thunder and
deep drum crescendos. Ten minutes. Fifteen. The ground
vibrated gently. Hodges was fully awake now. He crawled
from the crater and made his way to the edge of the treeline, watching. Two miles away flashes that resembled
storm clouds lit the mist.

As the prep fire continued the black lid of sky lifted,
allowing an eastern gush of blue. The awakening fields
now creaked and moaned. Tanks. Then, from where the
tanks creaked, there came other new sounds: machine
guns rattled doggedly, rhythmically, steadily.

The sweep was on.

The sky lit and the mist began to lift and the fields
were lush, rain-soaked, and green. Hodges peered along
the treeline and could see the other Marines of the company set in at its edge, watching also. They lay in the mist
and weeds, faceless in their distance, and it struck him
that he was watching a timeless vision: the taut stillness of
a hundred men frozen by their individual fears. This part
of it, at least, was eternal. They could have been anywhere—in a jungle clearing on Saipan, a quarter-century
before. In the sweet spring grass at Shiloh. No matter.
These were his people, passed down by time to fill a warrior's conduit, and this was where he belonged. He
dreaded what the rumbling tanks, the sputters of machine
guns would bring, but at the same time the very prospect
energized him with awe and determination.

Bred to it, like a bird dog.

In front of them another treeline bent, perhaps two
hundred yards away. Hodges peered through lingering

wisps of fog and felt his eyes enlarge. A rush that resembled passion crept from the insides of his guts and somehow drew the skin from every part of his body toward that center of his joy and fear, so tight that when he smiled it made his cheeks burn.

Gooks. Hundreds of them, trapped in the treeline, swarming with all the apparent order of a mob catching a subway.

We *got* you! You bastards, we got you! He felt like standing and screaming at them, slapping the others in his platoon on the back, declaring the war finally over. Artillery crumped in the treeline and the sweep from the west roared with tanks exploding 90-millimeter shells.

The enemy, a North Vietnamese Regiment, had left outposts to delay the sweep, and was searching for a point to consolidate and regroup. Later, in their best tradition, they would attempt to chew up the sweeping companies piecemeal, after the sweep expended itself. But now, they were indeed trapped.

A group of perhaps twenty soldiers bolted south out of the treeline, which was becoming saturated with artillery. They ran wildly toward Hodges and the others. Closer, closer they came, and Hodges felt a joy and anticipation so hard to contain that he found himself bobbing up and down inside the trench where he hid. Come on, you bastards. After all the months, all the bullshit. Come on! Ten more meters and you die.

The soldiers ran to within fifty meters of the company. Abruptly, the machine guns signaled the beginning of the ambush. The NVA were caught between two paddy dikes, and had no cover. Some fell immediately. Others ran or crawled back toward the paddy dike behind them. The company unleashed a fierce barrage of machine-gun and rifle fire, gunning down most of the soldiers before they could even return fire.

Above the roar of a hundred weapons, like a curdle in the blood that had been passed down to him from some other dust-filled field, Hodges could hear the Marines screaming. He joined them. It seemed appropriate, a century later and half a world away: a chorus of Rebel yells.

In five minutes it was over, and the company lay spent, watching other enemy groups pour out of the far treeline, moving east, across another open paddy. "Bron-

co" observation planes arrived and dove busily at the fleeing enemy, firing rockets and miniguns, then stayed on
station to direct artillery strikes, generous with air-bursting
antipersonnel rounds, into the open fields.

They remained in the treeline as the sun crawled over
them, watching the Broncos work out, in awe of the sheer
numbers of enemy soldiers who were still fleeing the
sweep. There were now literally hundreds of North Vietnamese soldiers crossing the paddies from west to east in
large droves. They did not flee toward the company
again. They had begun moving in a large circle, unbe-
knownst to the Marines. They moved south until they were
almost in range of the company. They moved east until
they were almost in range of the other blocking companies.
They moved north to the far fringe of the valley.
Then they moved back to the west, escaping through a
crease in the sweeping battalion's coverage caused by
thick foliage. Even in their fleeing there was order. Later,
with eight Marine companies converged haphazardly in
the eastern section of ,the valley, they would attack,
choosing their own targets. They had taken casualties de-
termining the location of the blocking companies. They
were taking continual casualties from artillery and air
strikes. But they had already broken out.

For two hours aircraft zoomed and dove, artillery made
continuous eruptions in the dirt and air, and the tanks
pressed east. Finally the targets were gone. The regimental
commander, somewhere back in An Hoa (sitting on top of
his command bunker in a lawn chair, sipping on a high-
ball, watching it all through field glasses, maintained Bagger) then ordered all companies to sweep northward immediately. Consolidate. We Swept East, the logic ran.
They Fled The Sweep. Somewhere Between The Sweep
And Block There's Got To Be A Regiment.

The company was the furthest unit south. They left the
treeline in a wide, sweeping line, moving cautiously across
the open paddy. They waded through waist-high, brushy
grass, then stepped into wet, green fields where fresh
hectares of rice had recently sprouted. The mud soaked
their boots. The low dikes tripped them. They were exhausted.

They reached the group that had fled toward their
blocking position. The dead soldiers lay in no particular

order on the glistening mud, some weighted with large packs, some carrying only weapons, some dressed in uniforms and some in villagers' clothes. They checked the bodies quickly, with little excitement now. The weapons were taken, unwillingly due to their weight. Some Marines souvenired packs from the dead North Vietnamese soldiers: NVA packs were the most comfortable of all varieties carried. Ornaments from uniforms were quickly pocketed, lest the men be required to surrender them to Battalion Intelligence for scrutiny—and unearned souvenirs.

Cannonball walked listlessly, weighted by his pack and by nearly a hundred blooper rounds that he carried strapped to his thigh in a large bag, at almost a pound apiece. Ah need me a target, he thought mournfully. Ah need to shoot off 'bout half these things. They give me all this ammo, we see all these damn gooks—never seen so many damn gooks in all my life, an' Ah only shoot about ten rounds all day. Ten damn rounds.

In front of him, behind a low dike, was a sprawled body, dressed in black. Cannonball squinted, awakening from his numbness. Hmmmph. Ah got this one. He's mine. Mebbe Ah'll get me a pack. Or one o' them SKS rifles. This one's mine.

He squinted again. The sprawling body's rifle pointed straight at him. He walked closer, to perhaps five meters away. The eyes behind the rifle were open, glaring hotly, feverishly, into his. Cannonball halted quickly, sucking a lungful of wind through clenched teeth.

The rifle erupted, its rounds so close that he was sure he felt them pass near his head. Automatically, without deciding, he braced himself and popped off a blooper round. Thunk. The round dug deeply into the dirt just next to the hotly staring figure. It was spin-armed, and had to travel several yards before it would go off. Cannonball was too close to his target.

The two men stared quietly at each other, separated by what seemed only inches, two strides and the distance of the paddy dike. The man in black watched Cannonball with animal intensity, like a cornered fox that faces certain death in the only manner his instincts will allow, prepared to fight all overwhelming comers because his senses inform him there is no other exit but to die clawing. Cannonball stared back, waiting for the next blast from the rifle that pointed toward his innards, aware that his own weapon was a single-shot type that had to be broken open in order to be reloaded, and realizing that his first move to break the weapon would summon the burst from the pointed rifle, knowing also that he would have to search his packed blooper bag for a buckshot round, the only type of ammunition he carried that would kill his adversary from that distance. Both men sensing they were doomed, and yet neither having the wherewithal to prevent his own destruction. Or, as it turned out, the means to bring about the other's death.

A blast rang out from Cannonball's right. The man in black slumped to his side, dead. Bagger jogged up to the body, pumped a half-dozen more bullets into it, then knelt next to it. He looked up to Cannonball, who was breathing rapidly now, shaken by the standoff.

"God *damn,* Cannonball. You scared the shit outa me."

"Outa *you?* Hey. That man had me cold. Why din' he pull the trigger?"

"Because he liked you. And besides, he was outa ammo." Bagger broke off the magazine from the AK-47 and showed Cannonball. "He was prob'ly too weak to change magazines. Or too gone to think about it."

Cannonball strode over the dike and knelt next to the body. The soldier lay in a huge bloodpool, having been shot through the lower waist several hours earlier. Cannonball shook his head. "Ha-a-ard core, what Ah mean."

They searched the body. The man was older, perhaps forty. Inside his pack there was a letter. Cannonball showed it to Snake, who brought it to Hodges. Hodges called Captain Crazy and asked for the interpreter, Sergeant Thuan. Thuan strode over to the platoon, and dutifully translated the letter in his nasal, academic English. He would read a paragraph, then look up to the cluster of Marines, smiling fraternally to all of them, seeking their approval.

"He is same-same Gunny." The men brightened. "He write letter to North Vietnam, to—how you say, same-same Congressman." Collective "no shits." "He say, he fight French, then he fight in South for four years now, he want to go home. He say, he been in Army since 1949, time to get out. Say he got five babysans, time to go home."

Sergeant Thuan beamed, nodding graciously, and returned to the company command group with the letter.

Bagger stared at the riddled body. "Well. We got ourselves a Gunny. A *lifer*. No shit."

Snake shrugged the dead soldier off. "Hey, man. They are *all* lifers."

They swept through open fields, intermittent villages and treelines, past hundreds of bodies littered randomly, as if sown across the valley floor like seeds by some Great Hand. Finally they reached the tank. It rested humbly in a paddy, between two lush treelines, a great dragon felled by a slingshot: a shoulder-fired B-40 rocket had blown one of the treads off. A platoon from Second Battalion departed immediately when the company arrived, anxious to catch up with its own company, which had swept northward. The company had been ordered to provide security for the tank until repair parts arrived.

The company set up in a hasty perimeter around the tank. Hodges joined the conference with the tank commander, who was talking with Captain Crazy. The tank commander was a Gunny. He was very thick, with rolls of fat around his bare midsection, faded tattoos on both arms, and folds of loose skin on his face and neck. He kicked the tank and looked fearfully at the treeline in front it.

"This ain't no goddamn place for a tank is all. I been driving tanks for eighteen years, I know where tanks should be. And this ain't no place for tanks." He turned to Captain Crazy. "I'll be honest with you, Captain. I'm surprised we made it this far. Yup. I'm damned surprised. You take these choppy little fields, all these damn hedgerows. No damn roads. And the treelines—hell, there's only certain places we can make it through those damn treelines. Shit, Captain, it was just a matter of time is all. They were waiting for us. Yessir, they were just sitting there waiting. We were lucky it was the tread." He eyed the Skipper tentatively. "Anyway, we'll be here all damn night, I guess. We can't get parts in till tomorrow. I called. They'll have the part out to Marble Mountain first thing. Yup." He surveyed the shadowed

treelines that loomed in all directions, near and far, like
bleak promises. "This ain't no place at all."

It was midafternoon. The sky descended again, as the
day before, turning white and then gray as the rain formed
spontaneously without the ceremony of threatening clouds.
The rain fell in shivering sheets, catching them hot and
sweating with its suddenness. A helicopter powered through
the wet air, moving lazily toward them. It descended inside their exhausted perimeter, pausing for one moment as
it discharged its cargo, then powered off, whipping them
with wet wind.

Hodges peered at its leavings. The battalion commander,
new to Vietnam, had jumped a portion of his command
post in from Liberty Bridge. He stood in the wet mud with
three radiomen, a Major who was his operations officer,
and a scowling, jowly First Lieutenant.

Kersey.

36.

"I don't give a damn what your Lieutenant said, I said
move your holes out! When battalion CP is in your perimeter, it controls it. Now, don't give me a bunch of your
wise-ass shit, Corporal. Move your holes out."

Snake stood on the traveled paddy dike that was the village's edge, looking out into the open field. He had set his
squad in behind the dike, where it would have a natural
abutment, impenetrable by even B-40 rockets. A position
in the paddy itself would be mercilessly exposed to the
treeline that ran in front of the lines. He remembered the
last time he had caved in to Kersey's demands, when
Speedy's team was destroyed at Liberty Bridge.

"There ain't no way, Lieutenant. That's stupid."

Kersey was enraged. "Listen, you little shit. This perimeter is so goddamned screwed up there's only one family hootch inside it—"

"We didn't ask to set up in a paddy around no goddamn
tank."

"—and the Colonel's gonna have that hootch!" Family hootches were highly prized by staffs. There were the bunkers when mortars fell. There was the thatch when it rained. The hootch was just down from Snake's hole, right on the edge of the lines. "And that means you're going to move your lines out to protect it."

Snake suppressed a grin as he stared back into Kersey's hating eyes. What are you gonna do if I say no, Lieutenant? Cut my hair off and send me to Vietnam? He remembered earlier battles with Kersey, ten and eleven months before, when Wild Man Number One had finally run out of patience and ended Kersey's bush tenure with a bullet in each of his legs. Before, every day, it was like this. The nonsensical battles, the jockeying for status inside the platoon and between Kersey and the other platoon commanders. This dude, mused Snake again, is a sick puppy.

"I ain't doing it unless my Lieutenant tells me to."

Kersey's lips went tight. "All right. Go get him."

Snake stared deep into Kersey's face. The rain poured down from his helmet, in front of it, like a veil. Snake pointed. "He's setting up a platoon CP, if you wanna talk with him. Sir."

"I gave you a direct order to go get him." Kersey paused, as if remembering. "But before you do, there's another thing. And this can't wait. The Major saw three gooks running down that treeline about five minutes ago. Get a team and go check it out. Now."

Snake peered into the treeline. It merged with the perimeter just down from his squad lines. The company had set up in the paddy, around the tank, with one small section of lines in the village. The treeline was the continuation of the village. It was a natural avenue of attack. Snake and Hodges had already decided to place a listening post inside it after dark. It was thick and gloomy, ominous under wet, shadowed skies. Kersey's right, Snake decided. We better check that out, put an OP in it.

"All right. Sir."

"And then go get your Lieutenant."

Snake nodded, heading toward Goodrich. Yeah. I'll go get my Lieutenant. And after I tell him what you got in mind he's gonna personally take a bite outa your ass. And if you want somebody in that *paddy*, you're gonna have to go out there yourself.

He reached Goodrich. "Senator." Goodrich was asleep, totally exhausted. His face was uncovered as he lay on his back, oblivious to the rain that washed it. "Hey, Senator. Wake up." Snake booted Goodrich in the chest.

"Get your team together. Hurry up."

Goodrich lay, his head back in wet weeds, trying to awaken. Rain pattered on his face but instead of a cold irritant it was a lullaby. He felt his dull mind drifting back toward sleep's warm escape and then was stunned by the sharp jolt of a hard, rough hand. He sat up quickly, suddenly chilled and angry.

"You didn't have to hit me!"

"I'm sorry. I forgot to set your snooze alarm. Now wake the fuck up. We got movement. Get your team. We need an OP out there in that treeline, right now."

"I thought you said we had the LP tonight."

"Change of plans. Take the OP, and I'll have Cat Man's team take the LP tonight. They're digging in. You can have their fighting holes. Now, get going. Take your team and check the treeline out, maybe a hundred meters down it. Be careful. We seen some gooners in there just a minute ago. Then drop back a little and set in. Let us know where you are, and Cat Man can relieve you just before dark."

Goodrich searched out his team, rubbing the parts of his skin that were becoming numb from the wetness. He measured it out, trying to concentrate through the dull fear that fogged his logic. An outpost was better than a listening post. After what had happened on the Bridge, and after his visit to Regimental Legal, he dreaded the thought of spending a night in front of his own lines. Too easy for accidents, he mused. It's bad enough when you have to worry about what's in front of you.

They stood in a weathered huddle at the edge of the treeline, peering into it, searching for chimeras. The rain had soaked them so thoroughly, was such a part of them and so inescapable, that they were no longer even conscious of it. They feared the shadowed caverns of the treeline, though, and were conscious of every menace, each clump or bend that threatened them.

Goodrich searched the gloom before them on the trail. He was so tired that his mind felt numb. He was nonetheless petrified of the treeline, especially following the morning's revelations, and the hump to the tank. They're *really* out there, he thought numbly. Hundreds and hundreds and *hundreds* of them, waiting to kill us. He looked at the uncomprehending faces of his fire team, made up entirely of new arrivals. How can they understand? It's still like TV to them. They don't know what can be in that treeline. Uh-uh.

The rain was now so loud on their helmets that Goodrich almost had to shout to be heard. "That's a bad-ass treeline. We could get hit from five feet away in there." The team stared naively at him, awaiting his logic.

Next to the treeline, a thin cemetery ran the length of the trees. The cemetery was in a field bordered on three sides by similar thicks of trees and hootches, the open end toward where they stood. Goodrich pointed toward the cemetery. "Let's move through the cemetery and check out the treeline from inside the mounds. We could see into the trees, and we'll have good cover. We won't get ambushed in there."

JoJo, tall and thin, wiped rain off his nose with a huge black hand. "Snake say put it in the treeline, man. He goan' get on yo' case if he knows we in the cemetery."

Goodrich was mildly rankled, no longer in awe of Snake. "You let me worry about that. We'll let 'em know where we are when we get set in. If they don't like it, they can come out here and change us."

They walked across high wet grass and moved inside the mounds, paralleling the treeline, peering into it from thirty yards away. Halfway through the cemetery Rodeo grabbed Goodrich, his eyes scrutinizing a clump of bushes inside the trees. "I saw movement in there! No bullshit! Something moved, man!"

They knelt behind the mounds, silently watching. Three minutes. No movement. They moved cautiously along the mounds now, watching the treeline carefully. Finally they reached the end of it. The treeline they were watching met another one that passed in front of the mounds until it joined yet another treeline that paralleled the other side, like a great, upside-down U at the end of the cemetery.

Goodrich was spooked. The whole sky hovered, gray

and ominous, weeping on them. The treelines loomed, thick with vegetation, each inch holding promise of some unseen danger. And they cowered insignificantly among the mounds, inches from the forever dead of the valley. Goodrich shuddered, then turned. "Let's get out of here. Let's move on back to the other end of the cemetery."

New Mac was frozen behind the end mound, watching carefully to his front. "Wait a minute! Something moved, man! Right out there!"

In a fraction of a second, a whole hour of events occurred. Goodrich spun around to see New Mac shoulder his weapon behind the mound, aiming in on a target. He peered across the wet grass and noticed that the target was a babysan, a little girl perhaps seven years old. The girl waved happily, smiling to New Mac's rifle.

The instinctive reaction, brought on by months of frustration, of fighting with himself and the others over just such predicaments, exerted itself before Goodrich could even comprehend his own movements. Lunging, seemingly so slowly, in that slow motion which adrenaline causes minds to assimilate lightning acts. Pushing New Mac's rifle down, even as Mac's finger slowly pulled the trigger with a jerk that would have seemed rapid to the uninvolved observer. Falling facedown next to the mound, beyond periphery, three feet outside the cemetery. Standing quickly, intent on New Mac, not the girl, New Mac leaning to help him, then aware that New Mac was watching the babysan with wide, horror-filled eyes, but not seeing the girl himself, seeing only Mac's eyes as they widened terribly at the sight of something they had only nightmared about. Then watching the center of Mac's face erupt gently with the entry of the bullet, even noticing the back of Mac's head fly apart, pieces of red and gray dripping from the back end of Mac's helmet before Goodrich finally realized that he had erred, that the babysan had dropped into a ditch, disappeared, that the roar he heard was not his own heart pumping blood madly in fear, but a cacophany of weapons aiming at him and the others from three sides, devouring them as they waited deep inside the U.

And even, not more than a second or two having passed, being able to observe with a sort of haunted, detached objectivity, his own frantic effort to retreat behind the mounds again, as if the two feet he had to run were a hundred-yard dash, a cross-country mile. And almost laughing at himself when he did not make it, when the tremendous explosion occurred in one leg, as if the inside of the leg itself was self-destructing from its effort to make the stride that it failed to accomplish. Then rolling in the wet grass in front of the mounds, thinking almost humorously that he would die like a duck on a shooting-gallery pond, squirming in front of the ambush only to give them a bit more challenge before they made mincemeat of his body.

But suddenly feeling the wondrous, welcome muck, the slant of slope, and literally swimming inside it. Bomb crater. Oh, you beautiful mudhole. He crawled inside the crater, lying at the bottom of it, inside a pool of water. The rounds passed fiercely over him, a relentless attack on Rodeo and JoJo, who did not yet fire back. He wondered numbly at his own luck, discounting the fact that he was still outside the cemetery, across an unreachable, two-foot plain of meadow. He looked up the mud slope of the crater and noticed slivers of red along the trail where he had slid down the bank. And in the grass where the mud groove began, lying motionless, was a dead part of Will Goodrich. The boot was blonded by months of misery, scuffs of dirt and wet stream crossings. The calf was mildly athletic, perfectly formed but for angry tears at its top, from the explosion.

He looked down at his left leg. Most of it was gone.

37.

They were still digging their fighting holes when the cemetery erupted. They lay down flat behind the traveled dike, thinking they were being hit. They peered tensely at each other, trying to find a target to shoot back at.

Snake listened attentively. Rounds were high, mostly. Hundred meters out, maybe more. He shouted. "They ain't hitting us! That's Senator's team!"

Down the dike, Cat Man nodded affirmatively, his ears antennas. "They ain't in the treeline, man! That's the cemetery. It comes from over here, too!"

Snake screamed again. "They're getting their asses kicked. We better get out there, man!"

He chided them. He mothered them. He helped them. He scolded them. In moments they were creeping under stray rounds, fierce even at that distance, toward the cemetery. They worked in two teams, using fire and movement to get across the waste of grass into the mounds. Cat Man's team laid down a base of fire, and Cannonball's team rushed into the mounds. Cannonball's team shot into both treelines and Cat Man's team bolted. They crept through the mounds toward the end of the cemetery, under merciless fire now, but protected by the chest-high hills from direct fire. They moved quickly, sucked along as if in a vacuum, aware that this was periphery, that for all the talk of dangling bait, they now were consciously setting the hook on themselves.

Halfway to the stranded team the cemetery bottle-necked, its thinness reduced to one mound. They groped, stared at the far side. Rodeo and JoJo were visible fifty meters to their front, cowering inside the mounds, occasionally lifting a rifle and firing an unaimed burst.

Bagger huddled behind a mound, staring at the single grave in front of them. No cover. He screamed to Snake, his voice filtered by rain and rifle fire. "We can't! They know we have to cross that! Let's wait here for the React! We can cover Senator's team from here."

Snake stared at the mound. "We can go over the top. One man at a time. Now. Put out rounds!" Cannonball fired blooper rounds steadily into both treelines, alternating his shots. They made flat booms in distant, wet earth. Termite and Cat Man put out LAAWs, standing quickly and shoulder-firing them. Snake ran at the mound and took a flying leap, sailing over it, bouncing just on the other side and rolling into the sanctum of more graves. He huddled against a mound and called to the squad.

"Come on! Let's go!"

The remainder of the squad stared at each other, waiting to see who would be next. Finally Cannonball shrugged, set up like a halfback, and ran for the mound. He made to leap and slipped in the wet earth, the weight of his blooper bag having caused him to slip. He fell belly-first onto the mound, his powerful legs still churning, moving him only inches at a time.

The firing increased. Bagger screamed incoherently and rushed for Cannonball, tryng to push him over the mound. The blooper bag erupted with tear gas, a bullet having pierced a gas-crystal projectile, exploding it. Bagger took the brunt of the explosion in his face, which was positioned near the blooper bag. Snake had reached for Cannonball from the other side. He also was covered with the crystals. The projectile, which was designed to saturate an area and make it unlivable for six months, covered the whole squad with the powder. Bagger persisted, however, and pulled Cannonball off the mound, back to the starting side. Then he collapsed in the grass, holding his face.

The squad vomited. It ceased its covering fire. Cannonball groaned inside the mounds, shot through the leg, tear gas scorching the inside of his wound. The men huddled against the mounds as the rounds became more intense, punctuated with B-40 rockets.

Snake was alone on the other side of the single mound. He vomited twice. He cried blearily, finally clearing his eyes. All parts of his skin burned. The crystals had melted into his clothing and now sought his pores. They raged along his crotch. They filled the inside of his nose and mouth.

He made his way to the end of the cemetery, crawling along the bottom of the mounds. Rodeo and JoJo were huddled together, terrified. He crawled to them, noticed New Mac's body lying on the foremost mound, and did not see Goodrich. He screamed to the two men.

"Where's Senator?"

Rodeo screamed back, pointing to the front. "Out there!"

"Is he dead?"

"He's in a crater. He was alive a minute ago. I was talking to him. I think he's hit. I couldn't understand him."

"Where's the crater?"

JoJo elbowed the mound he was against. "On the other side of this, man. I doan' know how far. Senator was standin' next to Mac." Mac lay dead on top of the mound.

Snake crawled to the mound. Rodeo sensed his intent and sought to change his mind. "React's on the way." He tapped the radio. "I just talked to 'em. Where's the rest of the squad? What happened?"

Snake was on top of the mound, snuggled next to Mac's body. From there he could see the far edge of the crater. It was just beyond the mound, no more than three feet away at its near edge.

"Put out rounds, man. *Boo-coo* rounds."

He climbed off the mound, moved to one side of it, and made a running dive in front of it. Bandoleers sailed, hanging in the air as his body fell. The treelines erupted more fiercely. He bounced once in the grass, just at the edge of the crater, then slid down its mud embankment, bumping into Goodrich. There was a pool of water at the bottom of the crater. The water was chalky brown with mud, and streaked deeply with large amounts of blood.

Snake examined Goodrich's leg, which Goodrich had managed to tie off with a belt in one of his more lucid moments. Snake pulled the belt tighter, cutting off most of the blood flow, lacking a stick or bayonet with which to make a proper tourniquet. He lay next to Goodrich and slapped him in the face.

Goodrich turned to Snake, smiling just a bit, coming out of shock again. He had drifted on the fringes of consciousness since tying himself off. Snake turned him around, placing his head at the bottom of the crater, near the pool of water, to lessen the bleeding and bring Goodrich out of shock.

Goodrich noticed the blood streak and the deep stains in the water. He smiled again to Snake, somewhat drowsily. A B-40 rocket exploded above them. Rodeo and JoJo fired back. "Blood and water mix. It doesn't matter."

Snake lit a cigarette, waiting for the React patrol. He huddled next to Goodrich. The cigarette was wet. Another B-40 ripped the earth above them. More small arms rounds to and from the cemetery.

"Want a smoke, Senator?"

"No. It's all the same."

Snake puffed on his cigarette, almost languidly. "Hold on, Senator. You're gonna be O.K., man. React's almost here."

Goodrich shook his head from side to side, his helmet gone, each wave of his head scraping off more mud in his hair like a mop. "No no no it's clear now. Blood and water mix it's all the same like paddies empty without rain and when it rains you think it's always wet but when the rain stops it's gone and you never even know. It's like blood. I know now. They mix."

Snake took another drag from his smoke. "You hit anywhere else? How'd that happen? Did you fuck something up, Senator? I'll bet you did."

"It doesn't matter." Goodrich came out of shock briefly, the blood having returned to his head as he lay upside down in the crater. "It isn't far. They could run out here and kill us." He rolled his head in the mud again. "We're going to die."

"Nah. They'd have to cross the paddy twice. React's coming, hear it? They won't do that. Besides. We're the bait, Senator. They want us here."

38.

Snake had told Hodges about the listening post, and they had discussed Kersey's attempt to move the squad positions away from the protection of the dike. Now Hodges was sitting against a wet dike in the middle of the paddy. He scraped out the bottom of a C-ration tin of Beef and Potatoes, moodily contemplating the impotence of the tank that had anchored them in such an indefensible perimeter. When the ambush had erupted he listened absently to its distance, wondering if one of the sweep companies to the west had been hit, then decided it was too close for them. Perhaps, he mused numbly, another platoon in the company had a patrol out. Then Warner, now his radioman, had run to him, his arms flailing, the spacious face in a panic.

"It's the OP, Lieutenant! They've been blown away!"

Then gathering the platoon, finding that Snake's squad had already bolted to the cemetery (not being surprised, and in fact having expected that), so pushing the remainder of the platoon and some volunteers from company headquarters across the perimeter to the dike where the squad's defensive positions had been. And finally past the hootch that held the battalion staff, moving toward the cemetery under relentless fire even from that distance.

As he passed the hootch, receiving an embittering shock, again not surprising or unexpected, but made acrid by the expression on Kersey's face. The staff hugged tightly to the dirt floor of the family hootch, dry under its thatch, and watched the platoon inch past them. And Kersey peered out to him, his face set in tight aloofness, but the message was more than aloofness. I got mine already, the scowl was saying. I already proved I'm a hero and that mess out there is *your* war.

Watching Kersey stare at him and remembering Sergeant Gilliland's cynicism and finally understanding it, realizing what he meant when he said that Vietnam had done something to us all, even to the Corps. That there was no great effort for anything anymore, only thousands, no, millions, of isolated, individual wars. That it broke down even here. If They Die It's Not My Problem. They're Yours.

They pressed hurriedly across open grass like moths toward a roaring flame, losing two new dudes whose names he did not remember at the edge of the mounds. The rest of Snake's squad lay paralyzed by the tear gas, littered like live carcasses inside the mounds.

He looked at them. Cannonball was in agony. Rabbit tended to him. Bagger appeared blind. He bled out of one eye, rubbed the other, then both, absently, as if the pressure on them would be enough to bring back sight.

Hodges had people throw smoke grenades on both sides of the single mound that had caused the bottleneck, creating a screen. Then he rushed the React through in groups of three and four, anxious to be away from the lingering tear gas. He left one fire team and his new corpsman with the casualties. The others reached the end of the cemetery and Hodges set the platoon in along the mounds in a half-circle.

Rodeo called to Hodges: "Snake and Senator are out there!"

Hodges crept to Rodeo. "Are they alive?"

"Yes, sir. I think. There's a crater out there."

Hodges called to Snake: "Snake. Are you all right?"

A voice filtered through the rain. "Senator's all fucked up."

"Do you need help?"

"Wait a minute."

Snake slapped Goodrich again. "Senator. Wake up, man. Come on. Listen to me. Can you lay on top of me? Can you get on your hands and knees?"

Goodrich rolled his head in the mud, half-conscious. "I wish I knew I wish I knew. It doesn't matter. All the same. Blood and water mix. I'm going to die. It makes sense."

Snake grabbed Goodrich by one arm and rolled him over on top of him, then tested the weight. No sweat. He called to Hodges. "Lieutenant! I'm coming round the mound on your left! When I yell at you, have somebody catch Senator! I got him on my back!"

There was a pause. Finally Hodges called back. "All right. We're ready."

The platoon put out a steady rate of covering fire. Snake dug his boots into the mud of the crater, tested the weight again, and rushed up the side. Goodrich was large, heavier. He draped Snake's form.

"Here I come!"

Snake crawled the mud bank, stepping over Goodrich's former leg, pallid in the weeds. The treeline erupted with concentrated fire. A machine gun had a bead. Mathis, from Pierson's squad, stepped out from the mound to receive Goodrich and was shot. He crumpled. Snake felt Goodrich being pulled forward at the shoulder as a round worked its way through his upper chest. Goodrich's body tugged at him. He tripped. Goodrich fell next to a mound. Snake moved to his elbows in a low crawl and was ripped by half-dozen machine-gun bullets. They split his middle parts, killing him.

Hodges stared in horror. Cat Man grabbed Goodrich, who still breathed shallowly, and pulled him behind the mound. Snake lay dead, touching Mathis. That close. He stared into wet grass with bored eyes, his face expressionless. Hodges examined the face, and noted the holes that filled the weather-beaten flak jacket, and for the first time his own death seemed logical.

The treeline saturated them with fire. It poured in from three sides, immobilizing their retreat. Behind them, the company perimeter was now being hit also. Two more casualties from Pierson's squad. Only one thing to do, decided Hodges.

He called to Sadler. "Sarge! Put 'em all low, inside the mounds. Make sure everybody has some kind of cover."

He called an artillery mission. Too close for even "Danger Close." He explained it to the forward observer, and called the mission on himself. The treeline was thirty yards away on both sides, perhaps fifty to the front. Finally the guns were up. The radio hissed. "Stand by for a Willie Peter. Shot Out."

He heard the puff, could not see it from behind the mounds. He lifted his head quickly to view it. It was not to his front. Where the fuck—

He saw it to the left, two hundred meters off, a breath of white cloud beyond the trees. At the same time his face erupted, driving him to the grass. Sadler ran over to him, his eyes unbelieving.

"Lieutenant! I never—"

"Right two hundred, Sarge. Fire for effect. Tell 'em." He could feel himself mumbling. No motion from jaw.

"You doan' understand!" Sadler yelled. *"Doc!"*

"Right two hundred, Sarge. Hurry up." The radio handset was calling him, five feet away.

"You got a golden ass, Lieutenant." Sadler was in awe.

"I feel like I got a broken jaw. Like somebody hit me with a baseball bat. Sarge." He gestured weakly to the radio. "Hurry. Right two hundred."

"You doan' understand, sir. You been shot right through your face!" Sadler grasped the handset and adjusted.

An eternity of eruptions, rain on face like washing, spitting blood that gathered like saliva in his mouth. Visions racing past, screaming to each other. Sadler calling more artillery. It screamed like quick, violent rockets, dug the earth around him. Numbly, lying almost pleasant after two hits of morphine, he felt a jag of metal rip into his side like hot knife slicing butter, cleanly through. Felt his new leak and attempted to call but morphine made him lazy and his jaw was shattered and his words rolled limply down his chin with the ooze of blood. More racing figures, even taut words of encouragement and he tried to talk but couldn't and no one could see the low deep wound that stole his blood and drained him.

A last faint vision, seeing helicopter settle toward mounds, almost feeling the rotorwash inside his numbness. But a sudden rush of fire that he did not comprehend and the helicopter settled abruptly next to the mounds, failing him in the moment he had earned the privilege of escaping on it. He did not see its crewmen rushing from it to join the already trapped.

Finally another helicopter. They came to load him on it and after one step noticed the limpness, the nerveless muscles of a dead man. They loaded him nonetheless, next to all the others, the Emergencies who could now escape from hell. He lay drained of life on the floor of the helicopter next to Bagger and Goodrich. Goodrich himself seemed almost dead, legless and shoulder-shot, pallid from loss of blood. Cannonball was just down from him, with three others.

Cat Man and a new dude who never knew him dropped him on the bird, finally accepting that he was indeed dead, and sprinted down the rear door, back into the cemetery. The helicopter escaped. Rounds sought it as it lifted off.

Cat Man was crying. His face held the confused pain of an abandoned child. He knelt in the wet grass, enemy bullets passing over his head toward the helicopter. A B-40 rocket impacted just behind him. He ignored it.

The new dude grabbed him by the back of his flak jacket and tried to push him toward the cemetery mounds, where the remnant of the platoon fought on under Sadler's guidance. The new dude screamed, terrified.

"Cat Man! For Christ sake, man. Do you want to die?"

Cat Man shuddered in the wet grass, holding his face, then bolted toward the mounds.

"No."

PART III

VESTIGES: VIRTUES REWARDED AND OTHER CRIMES

39.

DAN: Sometimes I think it will never end, this war.

LAOS, 1971.

OPERATION LAM SON 719   There was an urgent, unstoppable rumble and the ground trembled, vibrating angrily. The dust rose in a hazy blanket that covered the hill and coated lungs and stung eyes. Across the narrow valley was a stream of steady flashes and a black cloud that grew quickly behind the flashes, puffing up like exhaust fumes from a poorly tuned truck. Dan pressed his sweating face into the dust and clutched his rifle and wondered at the ground beneath him as it quivered. It was the arc light again. Perhaps that will stop them, he thought, knowing that nothing would stop them.

The arc light finished and a black cloud hung low over the thick green canopy of the ridges across the valley. There was a moment of hesitating silence. They will come now, he decided. The B-52s are gone and there is nothing to stop them. As if on cue the artillery crunched into the hill, saturating it and the valley in front of Dan with angry clouds, devastating crunches. 152s. They will kill us all, Dan decided. So strange to die in this country I do not know. But, he sighed, hugging the barren ground, that is the nature of things. I warned them. I told them but they would not listen. A Private is not listened to. And it was so logical. A Private knows intrinsically what a General must learn through experience. That is because a Private thinks with caution since he will be killed. A General can be daring when only the Private will die for his mistakes. But it is useless to think about it. Thoughts will not change it.

The night before the operation began they had sat in the

abandoned ruins of Khe Sanh and watched the jets as they saturated the Laos road with bombs and napalm. There had been much talk about Khe Sanh among the soldiers. This is where the Marines killed so many North Vietnamese, they had agreed in awe. A great battle for the Marines. Now it was abandoned and the airstrip was tatters of curled plating that used to be runway and the bunkers had dissolved into the earth. And the Marines were gone. But it was a great battle. Thousands of ghosts haunted the dark perimeter.

There had been a pep talk by the company commander. He had clasped his hands in front of his chest, intent. "Tomorrow will begin the greatest test for our Army," he had said. "Tomorrow we attack Laos."

Dan could not fully comprehend Laos. Nor did he understand why it was a test. To him it was absurd. So many problems right here, he thought. So many North Vietnamese soldiers in my valley. And no Government soldiers there, since the Marines left. And yet we are attacking this Laos.

Finally his reticence was overwhelmed by his common sense. "And what is this 'Laos' that it is so important," he had asked. "Why do we attack this 'Laos'?"

The *Dai Wei* had looked at him with contempt. "It is a country," he answered. "We attack it because enemy soldiers and supplies are there. Many soldiers. Much supplies. It will be a great victory."

Dan shrugged, meeting the company commander's eyes. "Enemy soldiers and supplies are everywhere. There are easier places. We do not know this 'Laos.'"

The officer had become angered. He walked over to Dan, standing over him. "Are you a General, then? Three years you spend doing nothing with the American Marines. Before that you are the enemy. And now you are a General. We attack Laos for the good of the country."

Dan was not afraid of the *Dai Wei*. The man could only beat him. "We do so many things for the good of the country," he answered. "We kill so many. We destroy so much. And what is a country? Is it a group of people who think alike and work together and want all other people to leave them alone? Then my valley is a country. Is it a piece of land that can be separated from other land? Then my valley is a country. Two rivers come together and a cliff joins them at their wide part. I do not do this for the people of my valley. And I do not know your country."

The officer slapped Dan hard on the face. "Your valley is VC. You are VC. I should kill you." The officer slapped him again. "You want me to put you in prison so you will not have to attack Laos with us. Peasant coward. *Que lam.*"

Dan stared tiredly at the officer. "I am not afraid," he said slowly. "I do not have to be afraid to think it is wrong."

The officer stomped off and Dan sat down and lit a cigarette. Across the border another air strike was dropping bombs along the road. The air strikes are like a magnet, Dan mused. They know what we are going to do. They will wait for the right time and mass on the road and destroy us. It is so stupid.

A group of soldiers crowded eagerly around Dan when the officer left. His willingness to stand his ground in the face of certain pain and ridicule gave him a strong charisma. There were many in Dan's squad who felt the way he had spoken. They did not resent his past. He had been with them for six months, and had always been reliable.

And there were the stories. Dan's melodious baritone sang out the pain of his past in a hard, unemotional ballad that they loved to listen to. They were eager to learn of the VC and were mildly assuaged when Dan spoke of them with disgust. The VC had taken his family and his land and thus his life, for the sake of discipline. He would never forgive them. It was the only passion he felt and it was a personal one. The other soldiers interpreted his passion as one against the VC movement. He did not attempt to distinguish the hate for them. It would not change anything for him.

And they were eager to learn of his years with the Marines. Dan spoke of the Marines with mild warmth. They were good years for him and the warm ember of their remembrance was the only pleasure he was able to speak of. So many great battles. So much respect. "I would have stayed with them until I died," Dan would tell his eager listeners. "It was the best life for me. But they left and there was no place to go. I could not return to my village because of the VC. I have not seen my valley since I was conscripted." Dan never questioned why the Marines left. It was the nature of things that they would leave. Always the foreigner leaves. This was not their home.

They spent an eerie, restless night amid the ghosts at Khe Sanh, and in the morning began following Route 9 into Laos. The fog was dense and heavy in the lungs and its isolating thickness created an air of unreality about the column's movements. Dan was surprised when Laos appeared no different than Vietnam. He had been sure that different countries would look different. But they are all the same, he had mused in awe. What is this that it is Laos and not Vietnam?

For two weeks they twisted along narrow trails, under thick canopy and bamboo trellises where canopy ended. There was almost no resistance. The *Dai Wei* ridiculed Dan occasionally. "So we do not know this 'Laos,' eh, General? So it is wrong?" Dan did not answer. The North Vietnamese will speak for me, he thought.

He was right. When the column was far enough into the trap that supply lines could be cut, the NVA massed with thousands of troops and hundreds of pieces of heavy equipment. Whole battalions were overrun and destroyed. Dan's battalion had been attacked the day before, and had moved onto a scarred, barren hill in order to defend.

The heavy artillery had shelled the hill for a full day. Dan's battalion now shared an unspoken but permeating conviction that they would be defeated soon. The men stayed in hastily dug fighting holes only because they were more afraid of running than of fighting. There was an undercurrent of panic in every unit.

A medevac helicopter made it through enemy guns and landed on the hill, and was immediately swamped with frightened men. Soldiers hung on to the outsides of the helicopter when the insides were too full. American crewmen cursed the panicking soldiers and kicked at them, knocking them off the helicopter railings so they could depart.

Dan crouched inside his fighting hole, not understanding the depth of the other soldiers' panic. Why would a man risk his life on a helicopter railing, wondered Dan. It is so stupid. When the helicopter lands he will only be taken by the officers and sent somewhere new to die.

The artillery fire became more intense. The hill was under a cloud of dust. Then there was a creaking rumble to the front, where the arc light had been, and the narrow valley filled with a dozen Russian tanks. The artillery shifted to behind the hill and the tanks charged out of the trees to the front of it, spitting huge explosions and churning curtains of dust behind them. The soldiers watched a Cobra gunship scream above the tanks, pumping rockets. The gunship disintegrated in the air. Someone on the ridge behind the tanks had blown it up with a Russian SAM missile. A second gunship screamed in and also exploded.

When the second gunship blew up there was a high, collective scream of terror and the battalion snapped. Masses of troops and officers fled the hill, running through the artillery barrage behind it. The tanks climbed the hill, taking it easily, and consolidated on the other side of it. Behind the tanks a battalion of NVA advanced in skirmishes, moving quickly up the hill. The Political Officer of the NVA battalion spoke melodiously into a loud speaker. *"Hoan ho Bac va Dang!* Surrender to us and you will not be harmed. We are fellow countrymen! Throw down your arms and join us in our struggle! Surrender and you will not be harmed!"

Dan had watched the tanks in amazement. There are so many, he had marveled. And they are so good. He knew it would be no use to run. They would kill the ones who ran. He lay curled inside his hole as the tanks passed over him. Then he heard the loudspeaker. He sensed with his natural, uncanny shrewdness that the message was a true one. They truly believe these things, he remarked inwardly. Countrymen. Struggle. They were the words he himself had urged upon villagers years before, when the VC took him into the villages at night.

Dan stood in the haze of dust and put both hands into the air, leaving his rifle in his hole. He joined a group of surrendering men, the men crawling out of similar hiding places, arms in the air. His face was the definition of endurance, cracked with a small, ironic smile. He was not afraid. If they killed him it did not matter. But they would not kill him. He was sure of that. He knew the words they desired to hear and his strong, melodious voice would carry the words into their senses and they would nod and accept his words as urgent truth.

The group of beaten, surrendering men was swallowed by the North Vietnamese. The NVA soldiers were flushed with their victory and eager to interrogate their prisoners.

Dan sighed. They seemed so naive. And it was such a game.

40.

SNAKE: Well, I'm gonna get me some of that. Bring me home a medal. No more mopping up other people's pee.

Outside, low gusts of wind rattled trash and made dirty eddies in the sidewalks, but never blew high enough or strong enough to move the amber haze that hugged the skyline. The streets were filled with garbage and spiraling trash. Fronts of buildings were piled with junk and stained by soot. Everywhere there was lifeless, controlling concrete. Wasteland. Home of the regurgitated and the lost.

It was late morning. Inside the creaking, fetid rowhouse the windows whined and rattled at the wind, leaking arctic currents through their looseness when the gusts beat at the panes. Snake's mother sat up in her bed, waking late and alone, and felt her feet grow icy as they moved from the bed to the floor.

Just can't keep it out, she mourned to herself. This damn place. Like living outside. No use caring 'bout it, either. Won't change it. She caught a glimpse of the picture on the dresser, then settled her gaze on it and smiled briefly. She felt a secret sweet elation, just a current of unadmitted elation.

He'da changed it. Yeah. I think he would have.

She stood beside the bed, feeling old and shivering in her underclothes. Feeling old was a recent misery that had crept up on her. She was not yet comfortable with it, or even able to accept it. But it was a real emotion on lone cold mornings. Old. She took a cotton robe from the bedpost and threw it around her shoulders, snuggling into it. She would wear the cotton robe all morning. Perhaps all day. So little to dress for. So little to care about. Then she picked the picture up and held it, remembering.

It was his Boot Camp picture. He was short-haired and uniformed. The elation came back again, mingled with just a tinge of relief. The picture stared back, eyes cool, invincible behind the glasses, chin forever tilted in arrogant bravado.

Crazy kid. Always fighting. She smiled sadly. Always in trouble. But you sure did a wonderful thing over there, Ronnie. You sure did. Wonder when that medal's gonna come?

She held the picture to her shrinking, hollow breasts and imagined the ceremony. What will I wear, she wondered for the latest innumerable time. I'll have to buy a suit. A good one. She touched the bleached hair, now lusterless and brown from being forty-five and not caring any more. And get my hair done right. And I'll stand there on the White House lawn and cry just a little—I know it's gonna make me cry, hearing 'bout the brave way he died —and I'll just say Thank You, Mister President. This'll never take his place, you know that, but I'm so proud of what he done. Died for his country. Died a hero, my little Ronnie did. Then after they give me the little shadow box—I seen 'em in the magazines, a handsome officer all fixed up in his Number Ones walks up and stands in front and hands it over, maybe touching my cheek to help wipe tears and all—then after that we'll go inside the White House and we'll all have a cocktail. I'll stand there chatting with the President, maybe even have lunch. Wonder when that medal's gonna come? Been over two years now. Sure takes a long time. But I guess they got a lot of paperwork.

She reached into the top dresser drawer and took out a stack of letters. On the bottom of the stack were the cryptic messages Snake had sent her from the bush. She flipped through them. Saved 'em so he could tell me the stories. Every one of them's a story. She shook her head, near tears. That little fart sure could tell a story.

On the top of the stack was the other letter. Two days after Snake was killed his company commander had written to her. He wrote of what a fine Marine her son had been. He wrote of the universal respect he had known, of the combat meritorious promotions he had received. Then he described the way her son had died, fighting tear gas and incredible odds and single-handedly saving the lives of at least two people.

She had marveled at the description of the things Snake had done. She had slowly waved her head from side to side, reading the Captain's letter. Like something in a movie, she thought wonderingly. To jump out in front of all those guns so many times, to save a wounded friend. And, the Captain had written, I want you to know I am recommending your son for the Medal of Honor. I am getting witnessing statements right now. I think he deserves it. I think he'll get it.

That had been more than two years before. She stood reading the letter in the arctic clutter of her bedroom, the pages stained and wrinkled from having been read at times like these. Such times came often now.

A wonderful thing. To jump out in front of all those guns like that. Wonder when that medal's gonna come?

She did not know it but the medal would never come. Three days after the Captain wrote the letter, the Regimental Legal Officer had visited the field. He was in the process of completing a formal investigation regarding an alleged atrocity that had occurred on a patrol some weeks earlier. It was alleged that six members of the company had participated, either as perpetrators or as aiders and abettors, in the murder of two Vietnamese civilians. One of the six had actively discouraged such heinous acts, and had willingly cooperated in the investigation. In fact, he had initiated it. The others, it seemed, had participated fully, according to the statement, and were to undergo an Article 32 investigation to determine whether charges would be filed against them. Snake, according to the statement, was the main perpetrator. Division has a special interest, the Legal Officer made a point of saying. The General himself. These things can cause serious political difficulties.

The company commander took the report from the Legal Officer and glanced at the names. Snake: dead. Bagger: blind. Cannonball: shot. Goodrich: amputee. Cat

Man: still here—squad leader now. Dan: not chargeable by American authorities.

"Well," said the Captain. "They're pretty well avenged already, wouldn't you say?"

Then he read Goodrich's sworn statement, and felt a hot ball of disgust roll through his abdomen. Unarmed. No direct provocation. Executed firing-squad style in front of their graves. Goodrich wrote well. The Captain was infuriated. Two civilians killed in cold blood. Snake had ordered it done. It was all in the statement.

"Tell Division the murderer is dead," the Captain said. "He died a week ago out in the My Hieps. Tell Division we regret the incident, and we'll cooperate fully with the investigation of all participants. Tell Division I'm relieving the squad leader, and canceling an award recommendation that I just started on the murderer. Tell them that, Captain."

The Legal Officer nodded, writing laborious notes in his notebook. The company commander lit a cigarette and thought of what the newspapers would say if they found out about the incident. Perhaps they would even use his name. It might ruin, and would certainly affect, his career. He shook his head. People like that, he mused. I'll just never understand what gets into them.

And in the icy bedroom Snake's deluded mother swayed, the letters a small warmth to her. Such a wonderful thing, Ronnie. To jump right out in front of all those guns and save a wounded friend. Well, you always had the guts to do that. You just never seemed to have that kind of friends. You finally found them. Must have been a hell of a friend, that you would die for him.

I'da liked to hear the story.

41.

ROBERT E. LEE HODGES, JR.: And will I, in the end, meet your fate, Father? I'm not afraid. You and the others taught me that.

I

They sent his mother a flag and a gold star and the medals he had earned and she put them into the footlocker he had prepared before going overseas. She could not bear to touch the locker again and whenever she allowed herself the miserable luxury of looking at it she would break down. After a few weeks of such disruptions her husband moved it into the dusty dankness of the back shed, placing it beside an older, similar footlocker that a few remembered but none would ever open.

II

OKINAWA, 1976 The small boy shuffled into the cluttered shop and looked up to her. He had a long, angular face and wavy brown hair that tufted in occasional piles of waves, and his skin was just a touch diluted from the gold. The rest of him was unmistakably Oriental. He was a beautiful child, a complementary mix of gold and white. He looked up to her and clenched little fists and softly broke down into confused, painful tears.

"My father is not dead and I am not Japanese."

She knelt to him, looking into his eyes. "Your father is dead." About the other she could not argue. It was the law. A child was the nationality of his father. Her son was an American. The law did not solve problems. It merely created new ones. The boy was becoming old enough to understand such things and his life was confusing, unanchored. Seven years, she thought. Has it been that long?

"My father is not dead. He ran away. He went to America and left us."

She sighed. The other children had been taunting him again. She took his shoulders and squeezed them and embraced him, feeling him shake with silent misery.

"Your father is dead, Hitoshi. He died before you were born."

"Then why do we never speak of him? And why do we never visit his family tomb?"

She sighed again, stroking the tiny back. It is time. He is old enough that he has become aware, and it can no longer be ignored. He must be told. It has been wrong not to talk to him about it before. But one cannot speak warmly of a former lover and continue to be welcome in another man's bed.

Kakuei had been understanding, and had forgiven her for her earlier errors. But he would not tolerate the flaunting of them, even to assuage the confusion of the product of the error. Hitoshi had spent his early years inside a shadow, knowing he was different, knowing his father was American, but knowing only that. Not understanding the origins of his difference. He had instinctively felt his stepfather's resentment, sensing in his child's way that he was a millstone to be carried by the older man in order to obtain the affections of his mother. And she had gently, steadily loved him, with a special tenderness, perhaps even more than the other children. He, the upshot of a month spent dreaming, the prize and punishment of her momentary unfettering.

It was so crazy, she thought, the memories surrounding her. He was so crazy. A gentle, crazy man. But it had been so easy to get caught up in his eager insanity. She continued to soothe the crying boy. And this is all that is left of him. This crying child who does not know who he is. Or what he is. It has been so long and now there is Kakuei and I cannot say I loved him. Perhaps I did. Perhaps beneath the excitement of him, beyond his urgency, there was love. But it does not really matter now. The boy is all that is left and he faces a resenting world that he did not ask for and does not comprehend. I must save the boy. I must, for his own sake. And, I suppose, for the remembrance of a man I might have loved.

The boy was finished crying now, still sniffing and catching his breath, but the tears stopped by his mother's warmth. She continued to hold him, thinking of the dead man who had created him. Half of this boy is him, she pondered. More than half—it is a boy. He somehow lives in the sniffling warmth I am caressing. Did I love him? I don't know. I love this part of him so deeply. I must have loved him.

She took his shoulders again and looked into his eyes, her oval face a warm smile. "Would you like to go for a taxi ride? Just you and me? There is something I would like to show you."

The boy smiled back, excited now, the hurt slowly evaporating into the air of his excitement. He nodded eagerly. She walked into the darkened, cluttered back room of the store and awakened her husband. I am lucky I found a man such as this, she thought as she shook him, memories of the earlier years now painfully in focus after her thoughts while consoling Hitoshi. So many did not understand. Perhaps it was because he was older. He did not forever turn his back because I slept with an American. So many turned their backs.

Kakuei rolled on the low board that he had been resting on, and then stretched lazily, looking at Mitsuko. "Why do you wake me?"

"I am taking Hitoshi to Kin. The children have been teasing him again and I must explain it to him. It must be done. Will you mind the shop and watch the other children?"

Kakuei sat up, rubbing his eyes slowly. He was a large, heavy man, more than ten years older than Mitsuko. He did not like to watch the children. Women watched children. It had always been that way. "I will watch the store. Take the children to your mother. And do not stay long." He looked meaningfully to her. "Kin is not a good place to spend long periods of time."

She nodded her silent agreement. Kin was the Gomorrah where she had lived her sinful past. "I will not be long." She picked up the baby and took the hand of the little girl, now three years old, and called to Hitoshi. Outside the store they walked down the narrow road past overflowing shops, turned onto the narrower strip of dirt, becoming lost inside a mass of stalls and bustling people and wispy, smoke-filled odors, and reached her parents' stall. Her father sat on the bench at the rear of the stall, smoking a cigarette and drinking green tea, watching television. He noticed her and nodded a short hello.

She walked to the rear of the stall and went behind the curtain there and found her mother cooking over a small stove. They spoke briefly, amiably, and she left the two younger children and walked out of the stall. As she reached the strip of dirt again her father looked up from his television and called to her.

"Where do you take Hitoshi?"

"To Kin. To show him."

Her father grunted. "You should have seen enough of Kin by now. You should never need to show him."

She smiled tightly, slightly irritated but unable to contradict him. It was the wages of her past not to contradict such assertions. Besides, she reasoned, he is old. He does not understand Hitoshi and he does not understand Kin. He only understands that he somehow won a major victory when the American who threatened his existence was killed. He will die with the taste of victory in his mouth. But he will never understand.

Mitsuko took Hitoshi's hand and they walked silently to the main street. Once outside the netherworld where people knew her the stares of the curious and the leering began, and she sank behind a practiced mask of unseeing indifference. Hitoshi's features were a magnet that drew stares from Okinawans as well as Americans. It is worse for him, she thought. When I am without him there are no such stares. But there are always stares for him. And unkind words. I must find pride for him. He is such a good boy.

They remained quiet during the taxi ride. Hitoshi stared out the window, contentedly watching beach and bustle. Taxis are a treat for little boys. Mistuko stared out, too, filled with thoughts of her rides along the same road with a fleeting lover, now long dead, who left her with a dream that disappeared and a legacy that now sat, at once both curse and blessing, where he had sat those years before. So crazy. But it had been so nice to dream.

The taxi pulled up to the gate and she paid the driver, remembering the first night at the same gate, when his refusal to leave the car became the driving force that made them lovers. She helped Hitoshi from the taxi, he staring with excitement at the spaciousness across the fence, and at the frothing green sea of men and equipment there.

She stared too, feeling a curious mingle of emotions that left her strangely aching. So much had changed. Nothing had changed. The military camps on Okinawa were a constant in her life. They had always been where farmland was to Mitsuko. She did not question that. But beyond their presence there were changes that were so great that she stared at the constant in front of her and could not recognize a part that might have known her once, those few years, those lifetimes ago.

It was a sameness on the surface: a military sea of trucks and jeeps and green-clad warriors, dotted with islands of Quonset huts and square, same buildings. But the currents of wild emotion caused by men being launched into a war zone were calm now. It somehow seemed a different sea. And her friends who worked there were all gone. Reversion to Japan and yen inflation had eliminated the jobs. Such a different sameness.

Green-clad warriors passed in trucks and jeeps, staring at the girl and her half-American son, commenting freely to themselves, reveling in inferences. She was beautiful and she stood gazing through the fence, dreaming of some moment years ago that made the green sea suddenly have meaning, and she felt the hungry stares of men gone vagabond from homeland separation. But she was immune to them, having grown up under thirsting glances. Only once did the immunity dissolve. Why, she wondered, staring at the green sea, her face an emotionless mask adrift in aching memories. Why did it dissolve? It would have been so simple if it had not.

Hitoshi hugged her legs then, awed at the military bustle. But I would not have him. Sweet nemesis. Reminder of the crazy days. Preserver of a dormant dream. I must find pride for you.

Her son looked up to her. "Why are we here?"

She knelt on the sidewalk, the mesh fence on one side and the busy road on the other, Kin beyond the busy road, and talked above the traffic noise. She was smiling a secret, hoping, smile. "I want to tell you about your father," she began. "And this—" she remembered urgent, laughing words, a particle of conversation from a moment long ago—"this is, like his family tomb. We can remember him here."

The boy was at once hushed and serious. He did not hear the traffic churning past him. He was lost inside his mother's eyes, waiting to at last learn of his father. "Is he buried here?"

"No." She tried to find the words. She felt a helplessness in trying to find descriptions that would be meaningful, and give her son strength. How to explain? She had not understood it totally when he had explained it to her those years ago. She had dwelt on it for weeks when she learned of his death, finally garnering the courage to ask the Assistant Club Manager to check on him after having received one letter and then nothing for a month. She was certain that she felt the emotion he had attempted to convey.

But it is so difficult to articulate this emotion, she fretted. "No. He spent the last days of his life here. He is buried in America."

The boy knew much of America. It was a place, far distant, where fathers ran away to. It was also his homeland, although he could not comprehend America. He was American. The law said that. "But he did not die here. Or in America."

Mitsuko felt an embryo of deep frustration in her chest. "No. He died in Vietnam. Far away."

"Why was he buried in America?"

"Because it was his home."

"Then why did he die in Vietnam?" Hitoshi did not know Vietnam.

"He was a warrior there. These men—these Americans you see. They are warriors. They fight in many places."

The boy looked puzzled. His mother had told him it was wrong to fight, even when the children taunted him. "Why? Why do they fight in many places? Are they angry?"

She had never considered why. She smiled, helplessly stripped by the innocent questioning. "I do not know why."

The boy persisted, sensing that he would not have another chance to so openly discuss this shadowed vision that somehow was his father. "If he did not die here and he is not buried here, then why is this his family tomb?"

She was sorry that she had used the analogy. She had believed that it would help him in his quest for pride by giving him something on Okinawa that was constant and involved his father. But the boy was too filled with questions after years of waiting, and the emotion was unexpressible.

She shrugged, stripped again by his questions. "All such places are his family tomb."

Hitoshi watched Marines pass in and out of the gate and marveled at them. Americans. I am an American, he thought. Am I like them? I do not feel that I am like them. But then, I do not know them. He turned to his mother, now lost in velvet remembering thoughts. "What was he like?"

She stared through the fence. Mercurial memories rolled through her, heavy with ache, like water-filled balloons that would burst if handled.

"Your father was—a very brave man," she sweetly told the boy, trying to remember something of him worthy of recounting to a little boy. So few days together. So little knowledge of each other. He forceful and sensitive and persistent, a ball of curious, foreign emotions that simply would not be denied; she swept up by his attractiveness and persistence, standing helplessly as the immunities wore down.

A beautiful man. But I did not know him, she thought sadly. Not really. How can I tell our son that? How can I tell him he was born of honest attraction and a frantic confusion that may have been love? The result of it has crushed part of him already. I cannot tell him that. I must help him be a strong man.

The boy cocked his head and stared curiously, deeply interested. "How was he brave?"

She held his face, still kneeling by the traffic, the bustle of Kin on one side of them and the military sea beyond the fence on the other. "He was a brave warrior. He was not afraid to fight in battle for his country. Once he was shot here, and here, and here, and here—" she touched her head and arms and back and legs, remembering—"yes!"

The boy was astounded and touched his own body in the same places, his eyebrows arched and his mouth agape. She smiled, sensing a spark inside her son. "Yes! In all those places! But he went into battle, even after that. And he was killed in battle."

The boy was sombered and slightly drained from the story. "Is it good to be so brave? To fight for your country like that? Was it a *good* thing that my father did?"

She squeezed his shoulders, anxious to fan this first spark of identity. "Yes! It was a *very* good thing your father did."

He smiled then, grateful to discover such a key, and spoke with hushed determination and a fierceness that surprised her.

"Then I too will be a warrior."

42.

GOODRICH: The only meaning was the thing it-self. And what does it get me to know that?

I

AUTUMN, 1969   "Suffering," he had told them, with a stonefaced attempt at nobility, "is inherently undignified when shared."

They had been sitting in an expectant circle in his parents' living room, his brother and sister and their families, five grade-school children between them, two high-school friends, and his parents. They had even collaborated on a bed-sheet poster, his mother coughing up an old sheet, and the gathering of uncomfortable misery mates venting their uneasiness with each other on great swirls of letters from old cans of house paint stored for years out in the garage. The sheet had hung limply over the outside door like a bleak, windless sail on a ship marooned in Nowhere. WELCOME HOME WILL! the sign announced in large letters painted garage-wall green and shutters-brown.

He had exited painfully from the car, backing out of

the door, babying the still unpredictable artificial leg, then groping into the back seat for his crutches, and had finally faced the sign, absorbing it through the pillwarmth that surrounded him, protected him from what he had become.

"Oh, God," he had mumbled. "Oh, no." He then turned to his father. "Do you really have people in there?"

His father had smiled faintly, hopefully, firmly believing that this was exactly what Will needed, lamenting, even daring to be angry at the fact that there were so few welcoming procedures for Vietnam casualties, and remembering the gala welcome-homes of World War II. This is the least we can do, his father had reasoned, upset. I won't have him walk into an empty house, as if no one cares what's happened to him.

His father had swung the seabag over his own shoulder and then smiled slightly again, patting Goodrich on the back. "Come on. Go on in!"

And he had worked his way on crutches underneath the welcoming entranceway, daintily mounting the one step from the sidewalk to the porch, and the other from the porch inside. He was unable to grasp the left crutch properly because of the nerve damage that had atrophied and numbed his left arm. And the artificial leg rode uncomfortably, threatening to leave him.

His mother had opened the door for him and embraced him warmly, a deep hug that lasted two full seconds longer than it rightfully should have, and then stepped back, revealing the living room filled with hushed, painfully smiling faces. For several seconds he merely stared at them, they coming in and out of focus like rocking, misty visions. He had attempted to examine his own emotions, but found that they were so blanketed by pillbuzz that his core was almost numb, that if he had wanted to cry he would not have had a difficult time, since his most easily achieved emotion of late had become a sort of pathos, but he dismissed the temptation. He still clung to the subconscious delusion that his state was temporary, that the proper penance, just the right amount of suffering, would purge his pain and misery and he would Win, Prevail, triumph over adversity and once again be whole.

So he had stood solemnly and delivered his little speech about suffering, fretting even as he spoke that he was being a bit melodramatic about it all, and rude as well. After all. He was even tempted to end it with a joke that would set them all at ease, but was unable to concentrate long enough or hard enough to come up with an appropriate abnegation. Finally, as they realized that he was indeed serious, and began to file uncomfortably out the door, each person mumbling some inane encouragement to him, as if he were the center figure in a receiving line following a ceremony, he managed a weak joke. He smiled mournfully and rubbed his face, catching his older brother as he opened the door.

"I'm sorry, Pete. If I'd known you were going to be here I would have figured out a way to lighten this up a little. Maybe I could have stolen a stick of morphine and let you all watch me shoot up, or something." He hated himself as soon as he uttered the comment.

Finally they were all gone and he dropped to the sofa, his crutches clacking to the floor, and lit a cigarette, shaking his head. He grinned gamely to his parents. "I feel like I've just had a glimpse of my own wake." The house was empty now, dreadfully silent except for the scratchings of his mother's parakeet, one room away. He smoked his cigarette pensively, leaning back on the sofa, and absently popped a Darvon and a Valium, long past needing water. Finally he shook his head again. He forced out another mournful smile and gazed at his parents, who sat silently across from him, still slightly shocked that he had ordered his welcome party out of the house.

"Look. I just need a couple weeks. O.K.? I really appreciate what you did. Really. It was—nice. But I just can't handle it yet."

His mother leaned forward, anxious and confused. "Would you like a glass of Cola?"

"No. Listen. I'm really screwed up." He eyed them almost facetiously, rubbing his left leg where the stump joined the prosthesis. "If I was a horse they'd shoot me."

"Are you sure?"

"Sure of what?"

"That you wouldn't like something to drink?"

"Oh, God." He remembered that the best way to calm her was to set her into reasonably productive motion. "Do you have tea?"

His mother contemplated it, her bagged face serious. "Well, let me see."

"Oh, never mind. I'll take a Coke."

"No. I have tea." She bit her lip, somewhat ashamed that she was nervous about having him home again. "I'll have to make it, though."

"I'll just take a Coke, Mom."

"No." She rose almost relievedly. "No, I can make tea. It's no bother. You just talk to your father, William. I'll be back in a moment."

She exited quickly toward the kitchen, and there were brief clangings, then all was quiet again. The parakeet scraped along the floor of his cage. Goodrich found himself grinning to his father, shaking his head in amusement at his mother's antics. He hummed a few bars from the George Burns and Gracie Allen theme song, their secret code for joking about his mother's tendency to become flighty under pressure. His father grinned back, nodding.

Goodrich relaxed, lighting another cigarette. "How's work?"

His father shook his head, which was wide and fleshy, an older model of Goodrich's own. "Oh, the same old stuff, Will. Old wine in new bottles." He grinned amusedly. "One thing about being a lawyer—you gain an appreciation of the ability of the average human to twist and turn the rules of society to his own advantage, in the most unique and remarkable ways."

He and Goodrich grinned identical grins. Under the numb of pillbuzz, Goodrich found himself deeply relaxed. His father's acerbic, humorous drone was like the stroking of a warm hand that comforted him. His father scrutinized him. "Well, I'm glad it's over for you, Son. It must have been terrible."

"It'll never be over, Dad. Most of it hasn't even happened yet." He noticed the pained reaction on his father's face. "I'm sorry. But coming back here, seeing the house and everything, it's like coming out of shock. Nothing hurts when you're in shock. You're just numb. But when you come out of it, every nerve-end aches."

His father rubbed stubby, wrinkled hands over his face and hair. "Well, if I thought it would do any good, I'd say I'll never understand why the hell you did it anyway. It was crazy." He suddenly looked much older than his sixty-odd years. "But we're beyond that now, aren't we?"

"I have some good memories." Goodrich smoked pensively. "I have some *bad* memories. But I do have some good ones, I even miss it, in a way. I can't explain that. But the hard part is now." He stared closely at his father, watching him come into focus and then drift back out. "I've got to get my head screwed back on. It's like I'm running loose inside it. No, really. I look at you and it's like I'm watching myself look at you, from deep inside somewhere." He shrugged absently. "It's the pills. It's like I'm standing in an empty room and looking out a window at myself, only every time I talk it echoes back inside the room. Hey, Dad. I'm *all* fucked up."

"You'll be all right. You will. You will," his father mumbled in a litany, as if the mere repetition would make it so. "You need to go back to school. Once you get back to school it'll work itself out. You'll be all right."

"Yeah. I suppose."

His mother returned with the tea and served it ceremoniously to him, dropping a napkin to his lap and then sitting the saucer and teacup on it. He sipped the tea quietly, draining the cup, then set it on the coffee table.

"I'd just like to sit around the house for a while. Maybe read a few books. Watch TV. Stuff like that. I don't want to see anybody. *Any*body. I need some time to sort things out, to get used to all this. Would you put out the word? I just need a few weeks, that's all."

His father nodded. "Take all the time you need, Son. School doesn't start for another two months."

Goodrich gained his crutches, wincing as he climbed to his feet. He stared for a long moment at them, his face sagging. "I just don't want to be weak about this."

He spent a strange, numb week inside the cloister of his bedroom. Outside the trees wept withered, spent leaves on the brown grass but he did not see them. The curtains were drawn, the lights were off. In the shadows and the lonely dark, surrounded often by dull artificial warmth from pills, he sought to find his head.

Or, perhaps, merely to avoid himself. He searched all the laughs and rages of his past, playing old songs on his stereo, reading and rereading old school annuals, savoring spent moments. Surprisingly, he found himself most often inside the pages of his Vietnam scrap book. He had put it together in the hospital, spending whole dull days sorting out the stacks of Instamatic photos, placing them in their proper chronology, identifying grinning, youthful faces and writing names underneath the photos. There, captured in the wonderglow, sterilized and motionless, were all the things that had ravaged him and finally left him lame. The pocked, rent earth. Hootches blown to bits. Shaved-headed babysans, mixed with grins and frowns. And the friends. Yes, friends.

And on every page he saw himself. Or what he used to be. Or maybe never was. Page after page of foolish grins or stubborn frowns, the unathletic body shrinking and acquiring gook sores, thinner with every page. The eyes growing bright from fear and lack of sleep. The body finally browned and scarred.

And them. He would gaze at the pictures of them, noting all the penned-in names of dead men, lamenting their loss and so lamenting himself. Senator. Yeah. It was a kick, all right. Sharing cigarettes and dreams, fighting holes and ammo. They gave me a hard time, but that was all a part of it. And now the dreams are dead. And he would sigh and pop another Darvon.

Another empty night. He dozed, absently watching a re-run on the television his father had moved into his bedroom, and his window rattled with urgent knocks. He stared at the drawn curtains, curious, and the knocks came again, quick and bunched, as if in urgency. He searched out his crutches, leaving the artificial leg on the floor beside his bed, and made his way to the window, opening the curtains hesitantly. Below his window, a frantically waving figure.

Mark. No. It can't be. Mark's in Canada, for the rest of his life. But yeah. Mark. Goodrich grinned hugely and began to open the window and Mark placed his finger in front of his mouth, indicating that Goodrich should be silent. Goodrich laughed, wondering at his own sudden good humor. Then he opened the window six inches and called to Mark in a loud hoarse whisper.

"Go to the kitchen door!"

He made his way quickly down the hall and through the kitchen, chuckling privately to himself. He opened the back door and then Mark was inside, his red hair wild and thick, like a flaming bush, smelling of the frost and faintly of a recent bowl of pipe tobacco. They were both laughing and he found himself leaning forward on his crutches, slapping Mark on the shoulders of his thick parka, then grasping him and shaking him.

They stared fondly at each other, remembering simpler days of unclouded idealism. Goodrich shook his head. "Solomon, you son of a bitch! What are you *doing* here?"

Mark smiled exasperatedly, almost defensively. "I've been lonely for my family. Then I heard you were back. That did it. I came down. Don't ask me how. I can't tell you." The secrecy seemed to make Mark uncomfortable. "I just spent a night with my parents at a motel near the campus. It was a good place. There were a lot of students and I didn't stick out. And I know they're watching my home."

"Who?"

Mark darkened. "The pigs."

There were brushings on the living room carpet, faint clacks on the kitchen floor, and Goodrich's mother appeared. She peered at Mark as if he were a visiting ghoul from some earlier life. "My word!"

Mark grinned feebly, taking off his glasses and wiping them on his scarf.

"Hello, Mrs. Goodrich."

"Mark?"

"How are you?"

"Oh." She looked to Goodrich, confused, and grasped the kitchen counter. She pondered it a moment, gray and somewhat matronly, apparently as embarrassed at being seen in her robe as at viewing Mark. "Can I get you something?"

Mark rubbed his hands together. "I could use something hot."

She brightened a bit. "I could make some tea."

"Good, Mom. Why don't you make us a pot. We'll be in my bedroom."

Mark followed Goodrich into the bedroom and Goodrich reached the bed and flopped on it, his left trouser leg dangling empty over the side. Mark shook his head bitterly.

"I look at you and feel so old, Will. It's been a hundred years of misery, all this. I feel ancient."

Goodrich sought to brighten him, falling back on their old pattern of challenge and retort as naturally as if it were two years before. "You *are* ancient, Mark. The suffering Jew." He laughed, chiding his old roommate. "Duty-bound to suffer over wrongs. Perceived or otherwise."

Mark shook his head, looking at Goodrich. "Is it painful for you?"

Goodrich held up a bag of brightly colored pain pills. "Inside this bag is the god of Numb. I worship him with great regularity." He tossed down a Darvon, demonstrating, and smiled. "Care for one? They're quite good."

Mark declined, obviously upset. Goodrich shrugged, putting the pills back into his pocket. "Are you still waiting tables?"

"The best waiter in Toronto. Can you imagine it? Seven-seventies on my College Boards and I'm a waiter." Mark allowed himself a smile. "It's been good for me, in a way. I always had this—arrogance—toward waiters until I became one. I see it in others, too. The ones I wait on. Everyone feels superior to a waiter, until they've been one."

Mrs. Goodrich knocked and entered carrying a tray with a teapot, two cups, sugar and cream. She looked nervously at both of them, her eyes flitting over Mark as if a close stare would burn out the retinas.

Mark was gracious. "Thank you very much, Mrs. Goodrich. You're so kind."

She still avoided his eyes. "Why, you're welcome. Now—" She looked at her son and then down to his artificial leg, which lay brazenly between him and Mark— "let me know if you want more tea." She exited quickly.

Mark had shed his coat. Goodrich poked his midsection with a crutch. "You've put on weight."

"I work in a restaurant. What do you expect?"

"Do you miss it?"

"What?"

"Everything. School, friends, family. You must miss it."

"You know what makes me the maddest?" Mark seemed confused and somewhat sullen. He took out his pipe and began to pack it from a leather pouch. "That I have to act like a criminal. Like a MURDERER, for God's sake! I have to sneak around and hide and always fear I'll be discovered, every time I cross the magic boundary line between sanctity and rabidity. I have to act like a MURDERER just because I refused to participate in MURDER. You tell me the sense in that!" He lit his pipe. It seemed to calm him. "But, yes. I do get lonely. I miss my family. I'd like to be able to come over to your house like this and visit you every day, without having to sneak back and bang on your window."

"You should surrender, Mark." Goodrich said it absently, without rancor or evangelism. "If you'd just gone to jail before, you'd be out right now. You'd be free to do those things. It would be over for you." He shrugged. "No one would resent you if you did that."

Mark had obviously contemplated it and rejected it. He was livid. "And why should I go to jail? Am I a criminal? Have I hurt anyone? Am I *bad?*" He puffed angrily on his pipe. "Why does the law create such absurdities?" He snorted. "The law. The law is an ass. Someone famous said that, once. Dickens, I think." He looked up to Goodrich. "And it is. It doesn't respond anymore. It's a straitjacket. What kind of coercion is it when your alternatives are to kill or to go to jail?"

Faint memories of arguments with Snake crept steadily through Goodrich's blanket of numbness and he found himself smiling ironically, as if he had just discovered a deep secret. He listened to his voice as it spoke, an echo from another room. "You might not believe this, Mark, but you sound a lot like some of the Marines I served with. On the opposite ends, but on the same wavelength. They used to ask, what kind of law is it that allows a person who doesn't understand your motivations to say you're right or wrong? They never said it that way, but it was the same. And they came out the same. When the rules didn't fit, they ignored them. Only they were pissed off because the law harnessed them, while you're complaining it coerces you."

Mark puffed his pipe, studying Goodrich. "What about you, Will? Has it affected you?" He nodded toward the empty trouser leg. "Other than physically? I guess that's a dumb question, really. But you were always such a give-a-shit."

Goodrich smiled resignedly. "I don't know, Mark. I don't know who I am anymore. I don't know how it's affected me." He eyed Mark mischievously. "I guess it's made me a more *dedicated* give-a-shit." He leaned back on his bed. "But I suppose I can say that because I've already lost. I don't know. It can't coerce me any more, and I never had the kind of animal in me that needed to be held back. I guess it's all just become irrelevant."

"Big Brother is never irrelevant."

"You've gone paranoid, Mark."

"That which you call paranoia should be the natural state of man."

Goodrich sat back up and eyed Mark seriously. "Is there anything I can ever do to make you believe again?"

Mark ran a hand through wild red locks and contemplated Goodrich's artificial leg. "After what it's done to you, how can you still believe? For what did you give your leg eight thousand miles away? Because if you didn't let them line you up like a duck in a shooting gallery they would throw you into jail? What kind of belief is that?"

For the first time, Goodrich felt the itches of unreasoned anger. "Now what the *hell* do you know about it? What standing do you have to tell me how or why I lost a leg? How many—"

Goodrich's father entered the bedroom without knocking. He stood solemnly, slightly disheveled after his habit of absently massaging his scalp when in deep or troubled thought, and nodded to Mark. "Hello, Mark. How are you?" His voice had the low warblings of an aging man, the troubled flatness of an unsure judge.

Mark rose, mildly startled, and extended his delicate hand toward him.

"Mister Goodrich. How are you, sir?"

"I'm fine, Mark." Mr. Goodrich gestured toward the door. "I want to talk with you. Would you come with me into the living room?"

Mark glared at Goodrich, then back to his father. "Sure, Mister Goodrich. Sure."

Goodrich peered curiously at his father. "Come on in, Dad. Have a seat. Talk as long as you like."

"No." His father avoided his eyes. "I have something to say to Mark that can't be said in front of you, Will. Now." Mr. Goodrich gestured to the door. "Would you come to the living room with me, Mark?"

"The living room. All right, Mister Goodrich." As Mark left the room he raised his eyebrows and shrugged to Goodrich.

Goodrich lit a cigarette, lying across his bed. He sensed that his father wanted to berate Mark for evading the draft, and to question his right to come into their home so blatantly when he was a fugitive. His father, he mused, was like that: the last of the old-time moral-purist lawyers. But it irritated him that his father thought he should confront Mark in private. What the hell does he think I've become—a hunk of Jell-O that can't take part in a debate like that? Who the hell got burnt in Vietnam? That's my debate.

There were no voices from the living room that would indicate a debate. A few low-toned exchanges had reached the isolation of his bedroom, but that was all. Goodrich became impatient, and climbed onto his crutches.

I'm not going to sit back here like a schoolboy.

Outside, a car door slammed. Its engine started, racing angrily, then faded with the car's departure. The noise of the car, just in front of their house, caused Goodrich's blood to pulse in anticipation. Something was happening.

In the living room Goodrich's father sat in a large chair across from the sofa, motionless. He appeared very tired. His mother stood nervously behind the chair, obviously dreading his entrance into the room. She had clothed herself, even at near-midnight, and brushed her platinum hair.

"Where's Mark?"

His father eyed him tiredly. "He's gone."

His mother kneaded the fabric of the chair in both her hands. "Oh, you have to tell him, Peter. You can't just say that."

"All right." His father stared straight ahead for another long moment, precisely into nothing with his opaque, aged eyes. "The police took him away."

"The *police?*" Goodrich leaned forward on his crutches. "In *here?*" He remembered the car that had raced off a moment before. "They came inside to get him?" His father nodded. "I didn't hear a thing. Not even a shout."

"He didn't fight it. What could he do?" His father's voice took on just the slightest acerbic edge. "He isn't a fighter anyway. He's a runner."

Goodrich eyed his parents with growing awareness. "How did the police find him?"

"I called them."

They peered into each other's faces for a long, mute moment, Goodrich pondering absently that he was looking into a mirror that reflected how he himself would appear in another forty years, if he somehow managed to survive the insanity that Vietnam had brought him and live that long.

His father continued. "He should have known I would do it. In a way, I think he did know. He acted almost as if he expected it when he saw them. The only thing he said was—"

"What *did* he say?"

His father smiled faintly, almost daring to be amused. "He said, 'So it's time to come and lock the savage up.' How about that? 'The savage.'"

"How could you do something like that, Dad?" Goodrich dropped heavily to the sofa, his crutches crashing to the floor. "He came here trusting me. And you, too!"

"I'm not sure he did. Maybe so. He looked awful relieved when he left here. And he knows me. He must have known I would do it. Maybe he didn't expect it. I don't know. But it doesn't matter, anyway. He asked for it and he got it."

"You're not that much of a martinet, Dad! You've never been that way."

His father peered solemnly at him. "It doesn't take a martinet. You act like the boy did nothing more than steal a stick of bubble gum from some department store. To my mind, he committed the ultimate crime, Son. He re-rejected the society that nourished him." He softened a bit, eyeing his son. "It wasn't an easy thing for me to do, Will. I like Mark. But I can't forget what he's done and I can't ignore it. He did it willingly, with his eyes open, and he has flaunted the law by coming here from Canada."

"I can't believe this." Goodrich was nearing tears. "He hasn't harmed anyone, Dad. He was only following his conscience. You have to respect him for that. It isn't easy."

"Then respect me, too. I'm only following mine. And you're wrong about the harm, Son. He's harming a whole nation. Those people have no sense of country. They don't look beyond themselves. That's as far as their obligation goes. Well, so be it. But if they're willing to accept the benefits of this society—like a Harvard education—they should also accept the burdens." His father looked up at him. "I'm not happy you went into the Marines, Will. But I accepted it. I wouldn't have been very happy if you'd refused the draft and gone to jail, but I could have accepted *that*. But I'd have buried my face in mortal shame if you'd done what Mark did. He ignored the law. He turned his back on the whole structure that binds our society."

Goodrich held his buzzing head in both hands. The world had just succeeded in finding the final little nudge that sent it topsy-turvy. "He didn't do anything really *wrong*, Dad. I think I have the standing to say that."

"You were arguing with him when I came in—"

"I don't want him to tell *me* about Vietnam. But he isn't wrong."

"You know what we've lost, William? We've lost a sense of responsibility, at least on the individual level. We have too many people like Mark who believe that the government owes them total, undisciplined freedom. If everyone thought that way, there would be no society. We're so big, so strong now, that people seem to have forgotten that a part of our strength comes from each person surrendering a portion of his individual urges to the common good. And the common good is defined by who wins at the polls, and the policies they make. Like it or lump it."

"For a lawyer you're being pretty idealistic, Dad. And—"

"The legal end of this can only work in Mark's favor. He may very well get off on a technicality."

"What about the duty to protest? What Mark was doing is as old as Thoreau. Civil disobedience is as American as —killing Indians!"

His father smiled, just the smallest curving of his mouth. "That answers itself, Son. Thoreau went to jail, not to Canada. That's civil disobedience. The other is self-interest, cloaked with morality."

He held his head again. It was going to explode, blow

him mindless. "How can I face Mark after this?"

His father pointed to his leg. "How can he face you after that?"

"That's not important. I did it to myself. He didn't do it to me."

"That's called accepting responsibility for your acts, Son. If Mark does the same, you'll have no trouble continuing your friendship. He did it to *him*self, too. At least in the larger sense."

"It's not that simple."

"Self-discipline is never simple."

Goodrich rose, with great effort, and inched his way back toward his room. "I need to go to bed. I need to get some sleep. I need to take a pill."

II

The buildings were the same. Trees still sprawled thick and old. The students were only mildly different: hair a bit longer, clothing more casual, the ardent issues war and ecology rather than civil rights and Red China. But in the core they were the same: idealistic, inexperienced, waiting to be molded by some event, to react gallantly to cleanse the social order of its dark spots.

It was all the same, and yet he could no longer identify with it. He had grown beyond it, or perhaps merely away from it. His intimate rubbings in the dirt and bake of Vietnam, his exposure to minds unfogged by academic posturings, his months of near-total dependence on the strengths and skills of persons who would have been no more than laughable pariahs, or a moment of chic elbow-rub, to the students who now surrounded him, joined to make him question all his earlier premises.

It took the school experience to make him realize how much he had changed. He became something of an instant curiosity on campus, a Real Live Wounded Vet, as rare at Harvard as a miner at a tea party. He remained silent in his classes, and was alternately cynical and sardonic when called on to recite. Between classes he was recognizable on the long stone walks, a solitary, limping figure whose head was often down, who worked his artificial leg with effort and seldom looked or spoke to the ones he passed.

He would play a game with himself, walking through the hallways and the crowded cafeterias. Conversations would drift toward him from the groups of people nearby —all the subtleties and nuances of Veitnam: Moral Obligation Dominoes Containment Nuremberg Geneva Intervention Hearts and Minds . . .

And he would wonder if any of them saw him limp. He tried to walk correctly, exerted much effort in his attempts. But it doesn't matter, he would muse sarcastically. I'm invisible. I'm on the ground. They can't see me, I'm too fucking *real*.

But it cut him deeply. He would often return to his small apartment rather than attend class, and sit in the dark for hours, under the wail of acid rock that belched from his stereo. He would pop a full quota of pills (the body no longer needing them but the mind craving them desperately) and once again, for the millionth time, explore the reaches of his nerve ends, searching out emotions that might help him face the empty words, and the stares that followed his limp. The stares were the worst part. And their insinuations.

> No one knows what it's like to be the Bad Man
> To be the Sad Man
> Behind blue eyes.
> No one knows what it's like to be hated
> To be fated
> To telling only lies.
> But my dreams they aren't as empty
> As my conscience seems to be
> I have hours, only lonely
> My love is vengeance that's never free.

I try, he would mourn. I really do. Not as hard as I could, I guess, but I'm not one-way about this. And I can't try any harder. I've lost respect for these people. They're so—ethereal. In fact, they're downright spacy.

He continued to contrast them with the members of his squad in Vietnam, and slowly he came to realize that his deep exposure to each group had spoiled him, detached him from the other. It had not been in him to accept the primitive viciousness that came naturally to Snake and some of the others. He was equally uncomfortable with the fog-headed intellectualisms of his schoolmates. His classmates and professors reminded him of Tocqueville's descriptions of the stratified, vaporous intellectuals who brought about the French Revolution in the name of unattainable ideals. Someone needs to clue them in, he would muse, about what's really happening down there where the spears fly.

Then one day the thought knifed through his pillbuzz that he was the only one who could do it. If he could ever gain the energy to confront the stares.

Unexpectedly, they came to him.

Cambodia. He had seen the President's address on television, and remembered all the silly, irritating restrictions of Vietnam combat, and actually felt pleased about the announcement, in a detached sort of way. It was all irrelevant anymore, none of it mattered, but if it had to continue, at least it should be rational. And Cambodia seemed rational.

He was asleep when the door buzzer rang. It blasted flatly through his slumber, again and again. He found his trousers and crutches and made his way through the apartment to the door. He opened it and faced two men he had never seen before. One was short and stocky, with dull blond hair and a wide, placid face. He wore a Pendleton shirt and frayed Levis. The other was frail and hooknosed, with lit, angry eyes and an impatient posture. He wore a jeans jacket, with a clenched fist and a Viet Cong flag on the back. Both had shoulder-length hair.

The short man spoke. His voice was deep and modulated, almost sad. "Are you Will Goodrich?" He nodded toward the empty trouser leg. "I assume you are."

Goodrich leaned forward on his crutches, wiping his face in an attempt to shake the drowsiness. "Yeah. What do you need?"

"Can we speak with you for a moment?"

Goodrich checked his watch. It was past midnight. The short man caught his gesture. "I'm sorry about the time. We've been working steadily for a couple hours now, and we have to be ready to go tomorrow first thing. So it had to be now. We'll be up all night."

"Doing what?" Goodrich gestured for them to come

inside, and made his way to the couch. They followed, the short man still talking.

"Getting ready. It's going to be big tomorrow. It will be the biggest one we've had. I'm sorry. You probably don't know us."

The frail, impatient companion finally spoke. "But you saw Tricky Dick's speech tonight, didn't you? The fucking fascist. The bastard's sick, man."

The short man continued, obviously tolerating his companion's outbursts with some discomfort. "I'm Paul Kerrigan. This is Sid Braverman. We're part of the Student Coalition To End The War. You probably aren't aware of what's going on at the campus. People are pretty upset about this Cambodia thing."

Goodrich was mildly surprised. "Really?"

Braverman nodded quickly, inspecting Goodrich's stereo. "That's right. They're tearing that place apart, man."

Kerrigan corrected him. "Well, not really. Not *yet*, anyway. But it's pretty active. And tomorrow we're having a full-fledged rally. We're setting up a platform, down where they used to hold the football rallies. You know the place."

Goodrich smiled vaguely through a lingering drowsiness. "Oh, yeah. I used to be in the band. We were at all the rallies."

Kerrigan and Braverman exchanged tentative glances. Kerrigan spoke. "Well, we're lining up speakers for tomorrow. And as near as I can determine, you're the only person who's really been *in* it, you know what I mean?" Goodrich nodded. Kerrigan continued, encouraged by the nod. "We think you could really give the rally some credibility if you would speak at it."

Braverman joined in. "Yeah, man. You could really lay it on everybody about how bad the Nam stinks. You know, like what did you see that was worth giving a leg for—" Kerrigan cut him off and he shrugged as if preoccupied.

They both seemed slightly embarrassed, as if they had unwittingly tipped their hands. Goodrich absently rubbed his stump and managed to smile to them. "Look. You don't have to try and buffalo me. I know why you want me to speak, and it doesn't have a hell of a lot to do with what my opinion might be." Goodrich mimicked the announcer at the rally, gesturing like a circus master of ceremonies. "Here, folks, on our very stage, is graphic evidence of experiment gone afoul. Specimen reports unfavorable reactions to terror and misery. Examine left trouser leg, which now is empty. Specimen is entirely credible to make observations on experiment. Now specimen will say, in his very own words, that it was shitty. Take it awayyyyy, Goodrich."

Goodrich lit a cigarette. "Does that embarrass you? It shouldn't. But let's start with honest premises, all right? Now. If I did this—and to be honest, I'm not terribly worked up about it—what would you expect me to say?"

Kerrigan folded his arms, studying Goodrich. "Well, within reason, you could say whatever you wish. I mean, we don't expect you to come out and ask for more troops to the war zone, or anything like that."

"No. That's not what I had in mind."

"And what we *really* need is somebody who is able to talk about how shitty it was in the Nam. How senseless the killings were. How it felt to see your buddies get wasted. The whole immorality bit. You know, the desecrations, the tortures, the atrocities. I'll bet in the Marines you saw a lot of that."

"That's all a bunch of shit."

"What?" Both stared incredulously at Goodrich.

"It's all a bunch of shit. I have more standing to say that than any person in this school. And I say it's a bunch of shit."

Braverman peered at Goodrich with unmuted hostility. "With My Lai in the paper every day you tell me it's a bunch of shit?"

"I didn't say things don't happen. And I don't know anything about My Lai. But it's a bunch of shit to say it's regular or even condoned. Look, man. I fought with myself about this for *months*. I even turned a guy in for murder. I thought it was my duty. But I just *don't know anymore*. What you guys are missing is the confrontation. It loses its simplicity when you have to deal with it."

Braverman and Kerrigan appeared confused and hostile. Goodrich continued. "Look at the people. Are they murderers? You don't know. You haven't dealt with them, and you haven't been through what they've been through.

It's easy to sit here and say that. But you haven't had it eat away at you. It gets you. It gets everybody, man. It took five months, but it got me, even, and good Christ if it got me it gets everybody. You drop someone in hell and give him a gun and tell him to kill for some goddamned amorphous reason he can't even articulate. Then suddenly he feels an emotion that makes utter sense and he has a gun in his hand and he's seen dead people for months and the reasons are irrelevant anyway, so *pow*. And it's utterly logical, because the emotion was right. That isn't murder. It isn't even atrocious. It's just a sad fact of life."

He pondered the two. "You know why I'm all fucked up?" He waved his stump, forcing them to look at it. "Because of a little girl. That's right. A little babysan sucked me right out into the open so the NVA could start an ambush." They did not seem particularly surprised: The People's War Against Imperialism. Right in the books, Will. He continued. "I was a team leader. I had a kid who was going to shoot her. I knocked his rifle down. Just in time to see him shot in the face." Still no reaction from them. Also in the books: The Goo That Was Your Best Friend's Face. Already been done once. Sorry, Will. Be original, will you?

"Do you know how it feels to know you caused that? I'll see his face staring at that babysan for the rest of my life. And I'll tell you what. If I hadn't had the shit blown out of me, it would have given me great pleasure to hunt that little girl down and blow her away."

He eyed them with a shrewd grin. "And I'll bet a month's pay that you two would have been the first to join me in the hunt. It's like role-playing. Activists will always be activists, and you'd be the first to get uptight."

Braverman seethed with anger. "I've had enough. Take your artificial leg and shove it." He rose from his chair and began to walk to the door.

Kerrigan still pondered Goodrich. "I'm sorry you feel that way." He folded his arms again. "You said something about your own statement. Do you have a statement you'd like to make?"

"I don't know. Like I said, the idea doesn't exactly move me. But they—you—should know what you're doing to a lot of people. It isn't this simple, man. You're hurting a lot of people."

"Do you want it to end?"

"The war? Sure I want it to end."

"Can you start your speech with that? That you want it to end? As long as you make that clear, you'll serve our purposes." Kerrigan shrugged. "You said you appreciated honesty. We need your statement. After that, I'll give you a couple minutes." He smiled, then turned to leave. "But I'd appreciate it if you'd hold back on your theories."

He drove to the wide, flat field, scene of so many innocent events in years gone by, pep rallies and rock concerts. There was a good crowd on it, scattered here, close together there, some sitting on its outskirts in little groups as if it were indeed a picnic. There was an air of merriment among the gathered students. They were camouflaged in jeans and khaki, masked with unkemptness, almost as if they were secretly ashamed of the largeness of their own futures, or felt constrained to deny the certainties of their own lives.

Kerrigan and Braverman had arranged for him to park near the speaker's platform, along the road. He stopped the car and undid his artificial leg, as they had asked, leaving it in the car. Then he made his way up the platform, on his crutches.

The crowd had begun to chant. "HO. HO. HO CHI MINH. THE N.L.F. IS GONNA WIN."

He stood uneasily on the platform, agonizingly self-conscious of his legless state. Just below him a girl in cut-off jeans sat comfortably on someone's shoulders. Her arms were outstretched, fists clenched, moving up and down in rhythm to the chants. Her face smiled excitedly. Her shirt was tied in a knot above the belly button, and unbuttoned except for the bottom two buttons. Her breasts were huge. They also bounced with the rhythm. Goodrich watched the breasts bounce merrily and tried to remember if he had ever experienced such lovelies. He hadn't.

Across the field the flag came down. A new one rose. It was red and blue, with a bright gold star in its center. Goodrich's insides churned mightily. He told himself that he was able to intellectualize such frivolity, that although it would have enraged those like Snake and Bagger, he himself understood it. But soon he stopped pretending:

He was shaking with a deep rage. If he had been stronger, he would have crossed the field and lowered the flag himself. Or so he consoled himself as he peered at waiting eyes, isolated on the stage.

"HO! HO! HO CHI MINH!"

And a thousand corpses rotted in Arizona.

"THE N.L.F. IS GONNA WIN!"

And a hundred ghosts increased his haunted agony.

Snake, Baby Cakes, and Hodges, all the others peered down from uneasy, wasted rest and called upon the Senator to Set The Bastards Straight. And those others, Bagger, Cannonball, and Cat Man, now wronged by a culture gap that overrode any hint of generational divide. Goodrich took the microphone and cleared his throat. Well, here goes. He thought of them again, wishing some of them were in the crowd.

"IT'S TIME THE KILLING ENDED." He was surprised at the echoes of his voice that careened across the field. The crowd cheered. It shocked and emboldened him at the same time. Kerrigan and Braverman were watching him closely. He nodded to them and they nodded back. Braverman was squinting. "I'D LIKE TO SEE THE WAR END. SOON." More cheers. He gave the two men a small smile. There. I said it. Dues are paid.

He eyed the crowd. His blood was rushing. His head pounded from the rapid pulsing of the blood through his temples. "ISN'T THAT WHY YOU CAME HERE? TO TRY AND END IT?" More cheers. Yeah. Groovy. End the war. "THEN WHY ARE YOU PLAYING THESE GODDAMN *GAMES?* LOOK AT YOURSELVES. AND THE FLAG. JESUS CHRIST, HO CHI MINH IS GONNA WIN. HOW MANY OF YOU ARE GOING TO GET HURT IN VIETNAM? I DIDN'T SEE ANY OF YOU IN VIETNAM. I SAW DUDES, MAN. DUDES. AND TRUCK DRIVERS AND COAL MINERS AND FARMERS. I DIDN'T SEE YOU. WHERE WERE YOU? FLUNKING YOUR DRAFT PHYSICALS? WHAT DO YOU CARE IF IT ENDS? YOU WON'T GET HURT."

He stood dumbly, staring at querulous, irritated faces, trying to think of something else to say. Something patriotic, he mused feebly, trying to remember the things he had contemplated while driving to the rally. Or maybe piss them off some more. Another putdown, like some day they'll pay. Pay what? It doesn't cost them. Never will cost them. Like some goddamn party.

He gripped the mike, staring at them. "LOOK. WHAT DO ANY OF YOU EVEN KNOW ABOUT IT, FOR CHRIST SAKE? HO CHI FUCKING MINH. AND WHAT THE HELL HAS IT COST—"

Kerrigan stripped the mike from his nerve-damaged hand without effort, then peered calmly through the center of his face, not even bothering to look him in the eye. "You fucking asshole. Get out of here."

Goodrich worked his way down the platform, engulfed by confused and hostile stares. Many in the crowd were hissing at him. He chuckled to himself. Snake would have loved it, would have grooved on the whole thing. Senator, he would have said, you finally grew some balls.

He noticed the car then. There were swastikas painted in bright red on both doors. On the hood, someone had written "FASCIST PIG." Across the narrow street a group of perhaps twenty people watched him, all grinning conspiratorially. Braverman stood at their head, holding a can of spray paint.

The paint was still wet. Goodrich smeared it around with his hand, then took his shirt off and rubbed it. The markings would not come off. Finally he stopped his futile effort and stared at the leering Braverman. He thought of flying into a rage, of jumping into his car and running over all of them, but he found that he was incapable of great emotion. It would never make any sense, and there was no use in fighting that. He swung his head from side to side, surprising everyone, including himself, by making a series of sounds that resembled a deep guffaw. Finally he raised his head.

"Fascist, huh? Hey, Braverman." He pointed a crutch. "Pow."

Then he drove away.

GLOSSARY

ACTUAL: The Unit Commander. Used to distinguish the commander from the radioman when the call sign was used.

AK-47: Standard infantry piece of the North Vietnamese and Viet Cong soldier.

AMTRAC, AMPHTRAC: An amphibious tractor, mounted with a machine gun and capable of traversing water barriers.

AO DAI: Traditional Vietnamese woman's dress. A flowing, colorful garment seldom, if ever, seen in the countryside.

ARVN: Army of the Republic of Vietnam. A South Vietnamese soldier.

B-40: A shoulder-fired, rocket-propelled grenade launcher, similar to the American 3.5-inch rocket launcher; carried by Viet Cong and North Vietnamese soldiers, used for antitank and antipersonnel targets.

BAC BAC (perversion of Vietnamese *ban ban*): To shoot, to engage in battle.

BAC SE (Vietnamese for "doctor"): A medical corpsman.

BASKETBALL: An illumination-dropping aircraft mission, capable of lighting approximately a square mile of terrain.

BIRD: Any aircraft, but usually a helicopter.

BLOOPER: Nickname for the M-79 grenade launcher, a 40-millimeter, shotgunlike weapon that shoots spin-armed "balls," or small grenades.

BOO-COO (perversion of the French *beaucoup,* passed down to Americans by Vietnamese, who learned it from the French): Many.

BRONCO: A twin-engine observation aircraft equipped with rockets and miniguns.

BROTHER: A fellow black Marine. Sometimes used as slang for all black males.

BROWN BAR: A second lieutenant.

BUMMER: A bad occurrence.

BUCKLE: To fight. BUCKLE FOR YOUR DUST: To fight furiously.

BUSH: The outer field areas where only infantry units operated, in nonpermanent positions.

C-4: Plastic explosive, carried in one-pound bars. Often used for cooking as well as detonating.

CAN CUOC (Vietnamese): An identification card.

CHIEU HOI (Vietnamese for "open arms"): A program whereby enemy soldiers could surrender without penalty; an enemy soldier who so surrendered.

CHOP-CHOP: Vietnamese slang for food.

CHOPPER: Helicopter.

CHUCK: A term applied by black marines to identify white individuals. Often used derogatorily.

COE: (Vietnamese *co*): A girl or young woman.

CP: Command post. Units platoon-sized and larger established command posts in order to coordinate the activities of the unit from a central point.

C-RATS: C-rations; also Cs, etc.: The standard meals eaten in the bush. Provided in cartons containing twelve different meals, complete with such extras as instant coffee and cigarettes. The cardboard which wrapped the cartons had many uses.

DIDI: Vietnamese for "to run." *DIDI MAU LEN:* To run quickly.

DINKY DAU (Vietnamese *dien cai dau*): To be crazy, or, literally, "off the wall."

DUNG LAI!: Vietnamese for "Stop!"

E-TOOL: An entrenching tool. Small, folding shovel carried by infantrymen.

FLAKY: To be in a state of mental disarray, characterized by spaciness and various forms of unreasoning fear.

FLESHETTE: Anti-personnel rounds which burst after travelling a certain distance, saturating the immediate area with dart-shaped nails.

FRAG: A grenade. TO FRAG: To wound or kill someone using a grenade.

GET SOME: A common exhortation to kill the enemy.

GOOK: Korean slang for "person," passed down by Korean war veterans and others who had served in Korea.

Generic term for Oriental person, especially an enemy. Also, GOONER.

HE: High-Explosive, usually with reference to artillery and mortar shells.

HEART: A Purple Heart; a wound. THREE HEART RULE: Any Marine who was wounded three times during one combat tour was immediately removed from the combat zone.

HEI: Japanese for "yes."

HONCHO: Vietnamese slang for a unit leader.

HOOTCH: Any dwelling, whether temporary, as in a Marine poncho hootch, or reasonably permanent, as in a Vietnamese villager's home.

ICHI BAN: Japanese for "Number One," the very best.

ILLUM: An illumination flare, usually fired by a mortar or artillery weapon.

INCREMENTS: Removable charges attached to mortar fins. If they became wet, the mortar round would misfire and fall short.

KHONG BIET: Vietnamese for "I don't know."

KIA: Killed in action. A man killed in action.

KIT CARSON SCOUT: Former enemy soldier who defected and actively aided American Marines.

LAAW: A shoulder-fired, 66-millimeter rocket, similar in effect to a 3.5-inch rocket, except that the launcher is made of Fiberglas, and is disposable after one shot.

LAI DAY!: Vietnamese for "Come here!"

LAY CHILLY: To freeze, to stop all motion.

LIFER: A career person. Often used derogatorily.

LP: Listening Post, where a fire team went outside the perimeter in order to give advance warning of any probe or attack.

M-16: Standard rifle carried by American soldiers.

MEDEVAC: To medically evacuate a wounded or ill person. *Emergency* medevacs were those near death. *Priority* evacs were those seriously wounded and unable to ambulate. *Routines* were ambulatory or dead. All Vietnamese casualties were routine.

MOST RICKY-TICK: Immediately, if not sooner.

MULE: A small, motorized platform originally designed to carry a 106-millimeter recoilless rifle, but most often used for transporting supplies and personnel.

NUMBER ONE: The very best.

NUMBER TEN: The very worst.

NVA: North Vietnamese Army. A North Vietnamese soldier.

O DAU?: Vietnamese for "Where?"

OPEN SHEAF: A term used in calling artillery, whereby the artillery rounds were spread along an axis rather than concentrated on a single point (as when it was desired to cover a treeline).

OP: An outpost, manned during daylight hours to watch for enemy movement.

PAPA SIERRA: Slang for Platoon Sergeant.

POGUE: A Marine assigned to rear-area duties.

POS: Slang for position, usually meaning a friendly location.

QUE LAM: Vietnamese for "backward person"; a peasant. Used derogatorily.

R & R: Rest and relaxation leave. A one-week vacation to an exotic place, allowed once during a thirteen-month tour.

THE REACT: A unit assigned to aid another unit which had become incapacitated.

THE "SIX": Any Unit Commander, from the Company Commander up.

SKATE: A task of accomplishment that required little effort or pain.

SKY OUT: To flee, or to leave suddenly.

SPLIB: A term originated by black Marines to identify other blacks. Supposedly meant to imply superior qualities.

SPOOKY: A C-47 cargo plane mounted with Gatling guns.

STROBE: A hand-held strobe light for marking landing zones at night.

TAIL-END CHARLIE: The last unit in a long column on the move.

TEE-TEE (Vietnamese *ti-ti*): Very small.

T.O.T.: Time on Target. A prearranged mortar or artillery barrage, set to occur at a specific time in order to coordinate with an infantry assault.

VILLE: Any collection of hootches (slang for village).

WILLIE PETER: A white phosphorus artillery or mortar round, used for adjusting onto targets, for marking

targets, for incendiary effects, and for smoke screens.
The WORLD: The United States, where, supposedly,
   sanity reigned.
ZULU: A casualty report.

ABOUT THE AUTHOR

JAMES WEBB is an Annapolis graduate who served nine months in the field in Vietnam as a platoon and company commander. He was wounded twice, and was one of the Marine Corps' most highly decorated Marines, receiving the Navy Cross, Silver Star, two Bronze Stars, plus unit and campaign awards. After he returned from Vietnam, he was meritoriously promoted to captain, and served on the Secretary of the Navy's staff. He was awarded a Navy Achievement Medal for his service there. Separated from the Marine Corps because of his wounds, he attended law school and is now an attorney. He currently is a counsel to the Veterans Affairs Committee in the House of Representatives, and is otherwise active in matters relating to veterans. Webb is married and lives in the Washington, D.C., area with his wife and daughter. He is now planning a second novel.

RELAX!
SIT DOWN
and Catch Up On Your Reading!

BOOKS BEHIND THE LINES:

The side of war you will never read about in history books

☐	12976	**THE HOUSE ON GARIBALDI STREET** Isser Harel	$2.50
☐	13084	**THE WAR AGAINST THE JEWS** Lucy S. Dawidowicz 1933-1945	$3.50
☐	12754	**THE UPSTAIRS ROOM** Johanna Reiss	$1.75
☐	12527	**THE HIDING PLACE** Corrie ten Boom	$2.25
☐	12460	**THE PAINTED BIRD** Jerzy Kosinski	$2.25
☐	12537	**FAREWELL TO MANZANAR** Jeanne Wakatsuki Houston and James D. Houston	$1.75
☐	12347	**SUMMER OF MY GERMAN SOLDIER** Bette Greene	$1.75
☐	12510	**THE LAST OF THE JUST** Andre Schwarz-Bart	$2.95
☐	10482	**90 MINUTES AT ENTEBBE** Dan Stevenson	$1.95
☐	13078	**HIROSHIMA** John Hersey	$1.75
☐	11877	**HOLOCAUST** Gerald Green	$2.25
☐	12313	**FIELDS OF FIRE** James Webb	$2.50

Buy them at your local bookstore or use this handy coupon for ordering:

Bantam Book Catalog

Here's your up-to-the-minute listing of over 1,400 titles by your favorite authors.

This illustrated, large format catalog gives a description of each title. For your convenience, it is divided into categories in fiction and non-fiction—gothics, science fiction, westerns, mysteries, cookbooks, mysticism and occult, biographies, history, family living, health, psychology, art.

So don't delay—take advantage of this special opportunity to increase your reading pleasure.

Just send us your name and address and 50¢ (to help defray postage and handling costs).